BLACK HEART OF THE DRAGON GOD

CRAIG MARTELLE

JEAN RABE

Published by Craig Martelle, Inc
PO Box 10235, Fairbanks, AK 99710
United States of America
First US edition, January 2021

CONNECT WITH THE AUTHORS

Craig Martelle Social
Website & Newsletter: https://craigmartelle.com
Facebook: https://www.
facebook.com/AuthorCraigMartelle/

Jean Rabe Social
Website & Newsletter: https://jeanrabe.com/
Facebook: https://www.facebook.com/jeanrabeauthor/

Black Heart of the Dragon God
Thanks to our Beta Readers
Micky Cocker, James Caplan, Kelly O'Donnell, and John
Ashmore

We can't write without those who support us
On the home front, we thank you for being there for us

We wouldn't be able to do this for a living if it weren't for our
readers
We thank you for reading our books

THE MAP

THE MAP

FROZEN WASTE

ICE LAKE ABRIGON

NORTHERN SEA

THE RIFT

GLACIER

GROENAR

PUSTIN YAR

KUIPER DESERT

BEREGAR

TSENTAR

GABIGAR

KUSTAR

OZER LAKE

MOHIRIYA

BOREZHYA

OKUTA

HAWK ISLANDS

BARBERTOWN

MUGUNTA RIVER

SELOMONGA

EASTERN SEA

SOUTHERN SEA

MIGORO
IN THE TIME OF
GORANTH THE MIGHTY

CHAPTER ONE

Bend your back and row
Feel the power and know
Black sails in the sunset
Blood flows up the inlet
All the way to Barbertown
Sails go up. Ale goes down.
"Sonnet of the Black Sail Brotherhood"

"Strike its head!" Goranth bellowed, wrestling with the dragonette's wing. A young beast, it still towered above the tall man.

A dark-skinned warrior wearing a hardened leather cuirass swung his club, but easily because he didn't want to unduly harm the beast. His soft blow only served to make the creature angry.

From snout to tail tip, it was as long as three men. Its scales glistened rocky-gray, marking it as out of place in the forest of eastern Okuta. It screamed in anger at the trivial beings trying to bring it under control. A powerful wing stroke threw Goranth into the air.

"Be wary!" Rif, the club-wielding warrior, called, too late. "There was a day, barbarian, when you would not have let go." Rif the Barber lunged to wrap his arms around the dragonette's neck. Being close meant safety from the breath as hot as hellfire that came from the depths of the beast's dark soul.

A man and a woman circled beyond the clawed wings and stout legs, staying clear of the wide head that loomed like a cobra's. Goranth hit, rolled, and ran back into the fight.

Jumping high with a single push from its powerful legs, the dragonette dodged the Northman and nearly made the treetops, but the massive Rif's weight was more than the young beast could carry and kept it from winging away.

It dropped to the ground, where Goranth waited. He vaulted to its back, avoiding the spines, intent on hammering its skull with the pommel of his sword until it surrendered consciousness or bowed to its human masters.

"Adro be damned!" Rif exclaimed as he was wont to do; he often assailed the god of the subcontinent. She laughed at his insolence because he provided her with fresh blood, flooding forth from wounds carved with a razor's precision. But not today. He had a different mission: capture the beast whose neck he fiercely squeezed. Goranth held Rif's arm to keep from falling off the raging dragon while he hammered at it, trying to force it to bend to his will.

"Damn your eyes!" Goranth shouted, almost losing his sword as the beast flapped its wings, seeking to violently unseat its undesired riders. The Northman could do nothing but grip a neck ridge and the arm of the leader of this ill-conceived venture.

The group had made a five-day journey inland from Barbertown located at the end of the navigable waters of the Mugunta River. Esh're and Varlten're had plied the seas with Rif, and for a while with Goranth. The couple had retired to Barbertown to be respectable and start a family.

Esh're, master of rope and knot, fashioned a net for the creature's head while circling, looking for an opening. He twisted and adjusted, looped and tightened, building a basket to lasso the great snout and cinch it closed. It would give the humans leverage and a lead to drag the beast back to Barbertown where Rif had designs on raising dragons. This would be the first prize. He expected the second would be easier to catch.

Rif's plan: become an exotic rancher. Goranth, Esh're, and Varlten're followed because it was Rif who had asked. Madness! The dragons of the Mohiriyan Mountains would refuse to be tamed; Goranth was certain of it.

What would it take to domesticate a dragon? Rif said he would figure it out. He had been convincing in his arguments. He seemed less convincing now.

"Squeeze the life from him or let go," Goranth demanded while Rif swung from the beast. The Barber obliged. He unclasped his hands and fell free from the neck. The creature reared, stamping to crush the life out of its attacker, but he was already gone, leaving only a sweat trail in the dirt where he had crawled away. The dragon lifted its maw to the sky and screeched a terrible cry.

"Time to go!" Goranth threw himself off the broad back, hit the ground, and rolled away.

Esh're tossed his rope trap with unerring precision. It slipped over the head the instant the jaws closed. He yanked it tight, and Varlten're wrapped the remaining rope around a tree at the edge of the clearing. The beast yanked its head back, came up short, and jerked toward the stout tree, the rope unwilling to yield to its strength. It flailed, claws digging deep rents in the dirt while its wings hammered helplessly at the air.

The young dragon was going nowhere. Esh're crossed his arms and leaned against a gnarled trunk. Varlten're took the long way to get to her partner, having no wish to get between the dragon and that tree.

"A fool's quest!" Goranth wiped the sweat from his brow. "Kill it, Rif, and let's be done with today. No good will come from this. Mark my words, you heathen swine!"

"Ha! Goranth. More heathen than I, my friend. We will wait until the beast tires, and then it will be ours. We will ply it with food and drink. It will learn to follow orders if it wishes to eat, to survive. Aye. It will hate us. So did our mates on the *Lady's Prow*, but they followed orders and were rewarded for it. That is how we will grow the herd."

"You are mad. But here we are, with the first dragon to be captured." The beast continued to thrash with unrivaled intensity, then stopped for a moment, looking for other options. Humans. Nearby. It tried to breathe out heat, but its mouth remained clamped shut. The more it struggled, the tighter the rope became.

Barely the time to cook a meal passed before the dragonette's fury subsided. Its nostrils flared with each strangled breath. It backed itself into the forest, beyond the tree to which it was bound. It settled into a nest, wedged within a too-small gap between soaring pines. Branches sheered away. Needles and dirt stuck to the sap splattered across the gray scales.

A casual observer might have missed the dragon since it blended into the forest proper but for its eyes, pure iridescent malevolence.

"These creatures were not meant for us."

Rif shook his head violently. "The world is changing,

Goranth. The world is evolving. Think of what we could learn from these creatures while also pocketing more coin than we can carry. Knowledge *and* power, my heathen friend."

"I doubt Adro agrees. Let it go, Rif. Look at it." The Northman gripped the Barber by the shoulder to hold his gaze and show the sincerity of his words. "I was a fool to even try this with you."

Rif's rough features softened. Together they turned toward the creature. It glared at them with the intensity of the mid-day sun, its eyes fiery enough to dry a man to a husk. But worse. The darkness within. A shiver ran through Goranth, chilling him to the core of his soul.

"You could be right, but it doesn't matter. I fear it is too late to release it. The beast hates us but does not yet respect us. Turning it loose now will only magnify that hatred. It would find its fellows and return, and we would not be able to stand before the onslaught. No, Goranth. We must teach it to venerate us. There is no going back."

It took one long exhale for Goranth to cycle through his options and make his choice. "Varl, toss me that shield."

The woman turned sideways, showing a familiar bulge. "You are with child," Goranth said aloud, skirting the clearing to join the couple. He had noticed on their journey to find a dragon but had not yet delivered his congratulations or concerns.

"I am. So what?"

"Why are you out here? There is danger and you, you're..."

"Pregnant. You can say it, Goranth. You can also say that men do not own all that's dangerous. We fight together." She nudged Esh're. "That's how it has been. That's how it will be."

Esh're shrugged.

Goranth nodded, terse and quick. "It is on you, then." He hadn't worried until the fight with the dragon showed this would be neither quick nor easy.

"As it always is, Goranth."

She handed him the shield. He slid it over his arm and hugged the couple to him. "Then congratulations are in order! A hearty cask of ale for my friends when we return. There will be song and meat off the bone. All we need do is drag this poor creature through the wood and rolling fields of eastern Okuta. No task too great if we know full mugs and plates piled high wait for our triumphant return!"

Goranth took one step into the clearing before thinking better of it. He threw his sword at Rif, sticking it point-first in the ground at the big man's side. "Throw me your club, Barber."

Rif tossed the club, spinning it to watch the Northman's catlike reflexes as he snatched it from mid-air.

Goranth stalked through the open area, the dragonette watching him closely. He neared with shield raised and club held high. The creature's eyes whirled and danced, belying the abject hatred beneath. It waited while the human inched closer.

With a slash as quick as lightning, the wing claw crashed into the Northman's shield. Goranth's swing equally captivated. His counterstrike slammed into the small wrist attached to the front of the wing joint. Fire flared within the dragon's eyes at the sharp pain delivered. It eased out from between the trees, raking at the human more cautiously, refusing to get too close.

Goranth dodged inside its reach, swinging with all his immense strength to hit the dragon at the base of its neck, then danced backward, his arm stinging from the blow. "Like striking the side of a mountain! By the Ice Dogs' lair, you shall submit!"

The dragonette sensed the challenge and roared a muffled reply. It stepped lightly to the right, the rope holding its head as tightly as an anchor trapped in the rocks during a blow and locking its jaw closed. Goranth eased closer, enticing the claw to seek his entrails. The dragon jumped and raked with its two front legs, slicing through the air with six-inch claws, as heavy as iron, edged hard as diamond.

The Northman ducked, swung from his knees, and hit a thick ankle. He reared back for another club blow, but the dragonette dropped back to the ground, nearly falling over as it tried to balance on one leg. It stumbled back. Injured from Goranth's attack, and sought shelter from the man.

When it tossed its great head, the rope snaked through the clearing and caught Goranth unwary. The rope slapped the Northman's body, threatening to coil around his legs like an angry python.

He looked down for a moment to clear the rope. The shadow was his only warning. He pushed with as much strength as he could muster to dive away from imminent death. The dragon came down with both front legs, its eight claws tearing deep into the soft earth. Then it stepped back, not limping from the blow Goranth had delivered earlier.

"A ruse, eh?" he told the dragon. "I shall not underestimate you again. Come now, fight me or bow your head and submit."

Goranth waded back into the fray. He swung his club high and low in a continuous whirl of blinding speed. The club flowed like fast water over rounded rock, becoming a blur. He stepped slowly forward, one foot after the other.

The dragon rammed its head into the tree branches and ripped backward, furiously dragging at the ropes. One knot gave, then another. The basket came free.

The head whirled toward the Northman, maw open to send a hurricane of breath into the clearing. As Goranth sprinted away, the heat scorched his armor, leaving the skin on his legs bright red. He staggered from the pain and found refuge behind a tree as the dragon surged into the clearing, free of restraint. It snapped at the one who had tied its head. Varlten're, an expert with her weapon, reversed her well-used staff and jabbed the rounded end into the creature's eye.

The dragon screeched in agony, drawing back to loom over the couple. Goranth came at the side to draw the beast away. He hammered a mighty blow into a wing, snapping the forearm leading to the wing tip. The dragon whirled, sweeping the good wing around to strike the one who had attacked from its blindside.

The wing caught Esh're, foreclaws spearing him thrice in the chest and tossing his body into Varlten're. They both crumpled to the ground.

Goranth wasn't finished. He flowed in from the blindside and drove a second blow into the wounded wing. The dragon slammed its remaining wing into the tree whose shelter Goranth had fled. A third blow, and a fourth.

The beast dropped, both wings damaged, eyes twirling red with pain. Goranth jumped and clubbed an earthshaking blow between the dragon's eyes.

Rif ran from the woods and vaulted onto the creature's back. He stood on the beast's broad shoulders to wrap an arm around the narrower neck close to the cobra-shaped head. He flexed and pulled, choking the dragon until it started to waver.

It was done. The fight was over.

"By the Ice Dogs, I've never fought such a titan, and this is but a youngling! Larger than the great birds of the Hawk Islands."

"I'll secure it. You check on Esh and Varl." Rif's voice was grim and strained from his efforts.

Goranth threw the club to the side. Esh're moaned while Varlten're pressed cloths to his wounds.

"I thought you were gone. By all that's not frozen, you live!" Goranth exclaimed.

Varlten're pressed down heavily on her partner's chest to stop the bleeding.

"What can I do?" Goranth offered.

"Our packs. Healing salve and bandages."

Goranth raced to where they had stashed their travel gear in the trees. When he returned, he lugged all four packs. He dropped three and kept Varl's. They traded places while she removed what she needed and prepared it, using her saliva to create a paste.

She threaded a needle, checked twice that she had enough to do the job, and delivered the order. "Let go." Goranth leaned back, and she slapped paste into the rents in Esh're's flesh before pulling the loose skin together. She plunged the needle through again and again, then bit through the string after tying it off before starting on the next wound. Three claws had sunk into his chest, and three wounds were dressed.

Had the dragon struck with its leg claws and not its smaller wing claws, they would have been digging a hole to bury their companion.

Rif retied the basket and secured the dragon's head. When the creature came to, it didn't fight. "And that is how you do it, Goranth the Mighty!"

"Save your cheers. We've an injured man who needs carried." Goranth knelt near Esh're's head, watching his labored breathing. "Broken ribs, but no blood on his lips. His breath is strong. He shall recover."

"I'll do it," Varlten're stated. She stared Goranth down

before he could object. "You two are needed to haul that *thing* back to the pen outside Barbertown." She propped Esh're against the tree, trickled water into his mouth, and set off with her knife to build a stretcher that she could drag behind her.

Goranth and Rif used extra rope in their packs to tie a second and third lead to the beast. Goranth disappeared after Varl to help her build the stretcher. As soon as it was ready, they would leave.

The dragon watched them, a curl of steam spiraling up from its raised lip.

CHAPTER TWO

Listen one, listen all
The rise before the fall
Bring me their captain
I'll send him to his men
Without his head
Cold and dead.
"Sonnet of the Black Sail Brotherhood"

"Two more nights," Goranth estimated. He leaned close to the fire and studied a crude map painted on a flap of boar hide. Stabbing a calloused finger at roughly where they'd set up camp, he traced a path to Barbertown.

"Less," Rif said. "It would be less, *should* be less, but for that litter. It slows us, Northman."

Goranth caught Varlten're glaring. Rif was oblivious. Goranth watched him closely. Too much greed led good men astray far too often, delivering them to their doom.

"It's the beast," Goranth corrected. "Tugging that

dragon with us, stopping to beat it into submission; *that* is slowing us."

Rif grunted and poked the fire. Embers drifted up, some landing on his arm and turning to ash. He reached for the spit that held a small tapir and turned it. "Whatever the reason, we are not making a good pace. And this pig is cooking too damn slow. My belly burns with hunger, Northman."

"All of us are hungry," Varlten're put in softly.

"Patience has always eluded you." Goranth stood, worked a kink out of his thick neck and padded toward Varlten're. She'd been Varlten, or Varl, in the years on the ship, the " 're" added when she'd formally joined with Esh in some ceremony in Barbertown that he hadn't attended.

Goranth and Varlten had been lovers once; he remembered those few months happily. He'd been drawn more to her spirit than her beauty in those days, and he noticed that she'd not lost either of those traits. Goranth had never stayed with any woman long, but he regretted parting so quickly from her. The light and heat of the fire painted her face with a faint sheen as she sat cross-legged next to the stretcher where Esh're slept.

The forest was as dark as ink around them, the trees close and the canopy tight. Goranth knew the dragon was indeed responsible for the slow pace since they had to cut a serpentine course through the dense trees. Rif had elected not to take a nearby game trail. It would have been easier, but the trail would have given the dragon more space to maneuver, and with only two of them to manage the creature, they hadn't wanted to take the chance. Also, Rif worried that some of the forest tribes used the trail, and he didn't want anyone else to know about his endeavor.

The density of the dark woods was both constraining

and concealing. Goranth thought himself a fool for coming here.

The clearing they'd picked was so small that only a chimney-sized hole in the close-knit branches above it gave a glimpse of the night sky. Three stars, Goranth counted. Only three stars could be seen, and everything else was black.

Black like the sails they used to fly. He thought he should be missing the sea, the open air, and the smell of salt on the breeze that drove them onward.

There were noises in the darkness: the dragon's measured breathing that sounded like a muted bellows, the occasional chitter of spider monkeys and the annoying screech of a howler monkey that must be close, the shush of something that passed through the groundcover, and the cry of a nightbird. Goranth had his moments differentiating the prattle of birds. He suspected this had been a parrot.

"Why did you come, Goranth?" Varlten're asked after he moved next to her.

He shrugged and pointed at Rif, who was still turning the tapir on the spit. "Him," he said finally, taking a breath and pulling the scent of the roasting meat deep into his lungs. "He'd sent word, and the message caught up to me in the Hawk Isles. Said he had a way to become wealthy without piracy. Said he needed my keen wit to make it true."

"Are you sure he didn't say he needed your sword?" She chuckled at his quip. "He didn't mention dragons." She gave a half-smile. When they'd sailed together, her skin was tanned from the sun and sea but smooth like water at rest. Her long, silky hair, the shade of summer-dry grass. Her skin was lighter now and bore faint scars, including a long, fresh-forming one from the bout with the young dragon. Her hair was cropped short and looked as if she combed it with her fingers when she bothered to comb it, and her ears were adorned with several silver and gold hoops. Only her eyes had remained unchanged, large and amber and childlike.

"No, he didn't mention dragons."

"If he had, would you have stayed away?"

A silence settled between them, and in it, Goranth listened for the spider monkeys, which had gone quiet. A subtle breeze teased the leaves of the upper canopy, but he couldn't feel the stir on the forest floor. The fire crackled as fat from the tapir dripped into it.

"Ten years ago," Goranth began, "maybe it was eleven or twelve. Time's passing doesn't matter much to me. Rif and I were mates on the *Hellfish*, and we—"

"Before the *Lady's Prow*."

Goranth nodded. "Before that. Before you and Esh. Before a lot of things." He noticed Rif was watching, clearly interested. "*Hellfish* was a ketch, a two-masted beauty rigged fore and aft, with a long foremast engraved with the names of every man who'd ever sailed on her. She was fast and had a good crew, seasoned veterans. Pirates. We clung to the coast and sometimes came into the coves and crept into the wide rivers, our draft shallow enough. Raided sloops mostly, some small caravels along merchant routes. Successfully. The gains were steady and kept us happy. Then one crisp night, just as the sun was kissing the horizon, we went after another sloop—the *Dreaming Sea-Spirit*, her prow read. And we took her. It was almost too easy. Left all the men alive and disabled the masts so they couldn't chase us. We only killed when we had to in those days, when our targets foolishly put up a fight. Most never fought us. *Hellfish* was known and feared, our conquests usually bloodless."

"Except for that sunset," Rif said.

"Yes, except for that damned awful sunset."

Varlten're leaned close and nudged his knee. "On with it."

Goranth took another deep breath of tapir. "There was a second ship following the *Sea-Spirit*, staying 'round the point, unseen to us in the cove. She swept around after we'd axed the *Sea-Spirit's* masts and were loading the poor showing of treasure onto *Hellfish*. We'd grown too complacent in our raiding. We hadn't thought to keep a scout posted."

"It was full, square-rigged," Rif grumbled. "A warship. *Sea-Spirit* was the bait, and we had swallowed the hook."

"Never caught the name of the warship," Goranth said.

"*The Silver Cairn*," Rif cut in. "I'll never forget her." He spat on the ground. "In the fires of the world beyond this, I'll always remember that name."

"We saw her, sails full, and headed out. The wind billowed our canvas, pushing us away from the trap. Smaller, sleeker, we thought we'd outrace the devil that was twice our size. We were well clear of the coast, reaching deep water. We thought we were free."

"But you didn't outrace her."

"No, Varl. The Ice Dogs curse us, we didn't. The frigate was running lean, probably nothing in her hold. A pirate-hunter, certainly. She wasn't flying a flag that marked a homeland. She was fast, faster than she should have been."

"Rammed us." Rif was turning the spit again. "Cracked our hull like it was a gull's shell."

"Didn't take any of us prisoner, didn't loot our hold. Turned and gave us distance."

Rif's haunted laugh gave her goosebumps. "Turned and watched us go under."

"The sun was a sliver on the horizon by the time we

listed so far to starboard there was no saving us. A streak of orange dancing on the water, the color looking like coins floating on the chop. The wind had picked up, and we were going down fast, the pirate-hunter still receding. I lost sight of her as we kept taking on water impossibly fast. We were far from shore, and the lucky among us found sections of the hull to cling to." Goranth paused. "For a while, the lucky ones did."

"It was dark that night," Rif said. "The stars had just started to show when the screams began."

Goranth saw Varlten're shiver. "Tell me the rest of it," she said.

"The beast was sixty feet long if it was an inch," Goranth said. "A monster squid with eyes as large as a ship's wheel and black as the pit. Those eyes, they pulled any hint of light left in the world into them, then the tentacles started wrapping around our men and pulling them under."

"The screams went on," Rif added. "Grown men wailing in pain and fear and calling out to gods who didn't bother to answer that night."

"Mates I'd sailed with, drank with, I saw them disappearing all around me."

The howler monkey let out a piercing cry, and birds hidden by the darkness shot from the trees. They returned, and the woods quieted again.

"I felt a tentacle wrap around my leg, and I knew I was next. I'd lost my sword and belaying pin, and I was going to lose my life." Goranth paused. "But Rif had kept his sword, and he sliced me free of the demon-squid, risking his own life to save mine."

"I didn't want to be the lone survivor," Rif explained.

"We swam toward the shore. So dark, we couldn't see it."

"Wasn't even sure we were going in the proper direction."

"But it was away from the squid," Goranth said. "A few of the others were swimming too, all of us churning away with as much speed as we could manage. There were still screams. I'd kicked off my boots, dropped my empty sword belt. Dropped anything that would slow me."

Rif stopped turning the tapir. "We made it."

"Somehow."

"Me and Goranth collapsing in the sand. Come dawn, we dragged our beaten asses away from the surf."

Goranth stood. "I don't know if anyone else from *Hellfish* survived. I wouldn't have, save for Rif."

"Which is why you're here," Varlten're said, "in the midst of a forest minding a youngling dragon that would like to have us for dinner."

"Is the pig ready?" Goranth asked.

Rif nodded and pulled a knife from his belt, sliced off a piece of meat, and leaned back from the fire to take a bite. "Good pig."

"Bring me some, Goranth." Varlten're waggled her fingers at the fire. "And some for Esh. I'll wake him and—"

The dragonette chose that moment to again test the ropes that secured it to the trees. Monkeys screeched, birds erupted into the sky, and the ground trembled from the beast's efforts. Goranth was closest and he charged the dragon low and tight, then whipped his arms around the snout and cursed. He heard Rif behind him.

This close, Goranth saw that its teeth were flat, typical of a grazer, just what Rif had said they wanted. He'd told Goranth that a grazing dragon was not as clever, a simple beast, able to be dominated, not like the flesh-renders that were brighter in color, smarter, and to be avoided.

This young dragon was clever enough, Goranth

thought. It had waited until they'd relaxed around the fire, tired from the trek. It had been working on the ropes while they'd talked, and the one lashing its wings to its sides had broken.

"This is no simple beast," Goranth growled. "Your club. You need to—"

"Don't tell me," Rif snarled. "I know what to do." He swung his club at the dragon's side, catching a scalloped wing.

It inhaled sharply, and Goranth felt its jaw work like it was gathering saliva to turn into steam to scald them with. He doubled his efforts to keep the maw closed and felt his arms burn. He gagged on the scent of the beast, redolent of the earth after a rain. It was a concentrated odor because the breeze did not reach down here, and it settled on Goranth's tongue and left a sour taste.

The dragon's front legs were slender and shorter than the rear ones, making its back arch. Parts of the hide were covered with interlocking bony plates, effectively armoring the beast. Goranth dug his heels into the earth as it shook, trying to dislodge him. He heard the tail thump against the trees and set his breath in time with it. He heard Rif beating its side with the club, not holding back to keep from hurting it, cursing even louder. Perhaps Rif had tired of trying to subdue the thing, or perhaps he'd realized this was a fool's plan and they should kill the dragon and be gone from here.

The dragon twisted, more agile than Goranth thought it could be given the box of trees into which it was wedged. In the light from the fire, he could see that the rough strands of rope around its muzzle were fraying. The heat against his arms and chest intensified, and he likened himself to the tapir on the spit.

"A smaller one, Rif. You could have found a smaller

one!" Goranth was yanked off the ground and slammed into a trunk. Still, he refused to let go. If the beast got its mouth open, it could boil them alive with its furnace-breath.

He heard Rif cry out but couldn't see what had happened.

Goranth was slammed against the tree again. A sharp pain raced through his back. The air was forced from his lungs. He felt the world spin, and white spots like stars flashed in his eyes. His fingers went numb and refused to cooperate. Another jolt against the trunk and he felt boneless, a limp limbless thing. Breath became a memory, and he swore he could see in the firelight his face reflected in the dragon's remaining eye.

The eye of the squid; it had been a mirror, too.

Rif shouted something, but the words were lost in the dragon's thrashing and the howls of monkeys—so much chatter. The brawl must have drawn all the woods' creatures to watch the show.

Goranth had known fear that night on the water, real fear of the sort that made his heart leap into his throat and hold there. He'd not allowed himself to feel like that since, and he wouldn't let this damnable young dragon send him quaking.

Varlten're had moved close. Maybe she'd been against the beast all along and he'd not noticed. She started singing and shouldering ropes, then she wrapped a length around the dragon's snout and danced out of the way of its front claws. She pulled herself up the beast's neck. Goranth tried yelling at her, but no sound came out. The motes of white were coming faster now, and it was all he could manage to stay locked onto its jaws.

"Do not let go!" Varlten're called to him. "Do not release its mouth!"

Rif was shouting, too, the words buzzing like insects.

Varl wrapped another length of rope around the snout and pulled back and gathered up the rest of the rope and made a loop before catching the wingtip and disappearing from Goranth's sight. Her song was sounds, not words, and the pitch rose and fell. He remembered her singing on the ship, the cadence in time with the waves, her way of mastering worry.

More rope was twisted around the dragon, and Rif continued to hammer away until the beast quieted and mewled in pain. It seemed like forever had passed, yet Goranth knew it had only been minutes. He stepped away from the dragon and close to the fire, seeing blisters on his arms where the beast's heat had boiled him.

Rif stumbled around from the back of the thing.

"That's the last of my ropes," Varlten're pronounced. "If that dragon breaks those, we're—"

"Eat," Rif said. "All of us eat. We're leaving at first light. No rest. No stopping. We walk straight through to Barbertown. We'll take the trail."

"Then what will you do with the dragon? In Barbertown, what will you do?" Goranth looked past the fire and saw that Esh're still slept; the cacophony had not disturbed him. "It is not subdued. It does not respect you. Two days gone and nothing has changed." *And you cannot let it free.*

Rif was right; it would seek vengeance and no doubt in numbers. If they freed it, they would die.

"It will be subdued," Rif insisted. "It will respect me. We've more men and more ropes in Barbertown. We will win."

"He does not give up easily," Varlten're said. She glared at the dragon, then at Goranth and Rif. Turning to the fire, she sliced off a large piece of meat and carried it to Esh're. "In fact, I've never known him to give up."

Goranth remembered the feel of the squid tentacle around his leg. "No, never."

Rif slapped him on the back. "We'll be rich, Northman. This will work, taming dragons. We'll be richer than we can imagine."

Right now, Goranth thought he'd rather imagine ale sliding down his throat. Lots of ale, a soft bed, and a few hours of oblivion.

CHAPTER THREE

Come one, come all
Answer the sea's call
Unfurl the sails
Man the bails
From dawn to night's fall
"Sonnet of the Black Sail Brotherhood"

"The beast thrashes less when we watch," Goranth noted. "I'll take the first watch." Goranth ignored the pain in his arms from the burns and lamented a quest that grew more dangerous with each step. He brooded darkly while pacing quietly.

The dragon's single eye opened and stared at the Northman. "You know, don't you?" Goranth asked softly. "You know this doesn't suit any of us. If you could guarantee our peace, we could go our own ways, but that's not something you'd care to consider, is it? Catching you set us down a path that we must see to the end. We will suffer as you have. In the end, we won't be rich, and you won't be alive. Mark my words, beast."

Rif stirred and stood. He stretched before finding the Northman. "Were you saying something?"

"Nothing," Goranth replied. "Give me two hours, and then I'll relieve you. No sense bothering Varl. She sleeps for two."

"Aye, she does. But you'll tickle her ire by treating her differently. She'll make you wish you had given her a fair share of this business."

"She's earned her fair share already. I'll wake her before dawn. She can have the last watch, and neither of us will be on the wrong end of the lady's sharp tongue."

They had both earned their share of rebukes over time. Rif's low, rumbling mirth was all the reply Goranth needed. The Northman crept close to the small fire and curled up to fall asleep almost instantly but never fully. His hand gripped the pommel of his sword as he slept, making it dangerous for anyone to startle him.

When Goranth woke after dreams filled with the dark eyes of demons seeking his life, he found it was already near dawn. "Rif!" he growled, but the Barber slept fitfully nearby. At the edge of darkness, Varl leaned against a tree and watched him.

"Rif had nothing to do with it," Varl said barely above a whisper. "I carry my own weight, Northman. You know that. But methinks you conveniently forgot. I should have kicked you in the face to remind you."

The youngling dragon snorted as if agreeing with the staff master.

Goranth drank deeply from a full flask before stalking into the woods to refill it. *Don't thrust and parry with her.*

You can't win, he told himself, stepping soundlessly, eyes seeking the darkest shadows, looking for what shouldn't be there. He stopped, crouched, and strained to hear what the woods offered.

After many heartbeats, he rose and approached the trickling stream. The water ran clear. He topped off the flask while watching the woods, then drank of the cool flow before him, dipping his hand and bringing the water to his face. Danger lurked; he could sense it. Close or no? He backed slowly into the darkness, sword held high.

He was surprised he returned to their small clearing unmolested. "By the Ice Dogs, this venture has put me on edge, seeing faces where there are none."

"It's quiet as a temple during the harvest," Varl added. "I think it's you, Goranth. The sun shall drive away your barbaric fear of the dark."

"Bah! The dark offers an advantage to those whose senses aren't dulled by city living."

"Then why do you look shaken after getting water?" Varlten're wondered.

"It's that damn eye! Stories of the squid's one eye and this beast. We should kill it and be done with it."

Varl stood and strode to the beast.

"Take care!" Goranth shouted, bouncing on the balls of his feet, sword ready for the grim task of ending the dragon to save his friend. "Keep your distance."

She walked under the looming head and leaned against its neck. It dipped its head to nuzzle her.

"What have you to say now, Northman, about irrational fear and a failure to understand the creatures around us? You and Rif both, beating LeReon into submission. A softer touch was called for."

"You've given it a name?" Goranth growled.

"Maybe LeReon told me his name?"

"It's a he?"

"Kind of. They all lay eggs. You'll catch more dragons with a honeyed tongue and a peaceful soul, neither of which you possess, Northman, or you, Barber." Rif stirred, scratched, and rolled over, doing his best to ignore his companions.

"You have observed the truth, but maybe my kind heart can win the beast's favors," Goranth tried.

"LeReon is not a beast to be tamed, not a beast at all." She stroked the dragon's neck.

Goranth kept his eyes on the creature's single orb as he backed up until he could nudge Rif with his toe. "Get up, you lazy bastard. We need to find maidens to soothe the savage beasts."

Varl harrumphed and turned to the dragon. Their heads nearly touched as they communed privately. Goranth couldn't tell if the dragon was setting her up as a means to disarm the targets of its pain and fury, Goranth and Rif.

"It tolerates you, but it'll turn on you. Mark my words, Varl."

"Varl?" Esh're groaned, struggling to sit up before collapsing back onto the stretcher.

Goranth cast a wary eye at the beast as he knelt beside Esh're. "Easy, my friend. Trust Varl. She wishes no harm to any of us, least of all herself or the baby. By the Ice Dogs, if she can make peace with it, we may yet return to Barbertown with our limbs and wits intact."

"There can be no peace, only a frail truce waiting to be broken," Esh're croaked. Goranth held the flask for the injured man to drink. The Northman wrinkled his nose at the stench. "It's time we all washed. The dawn brings light to calm the beasts of the night before the chaos of daytime brings the damn monkeys and vultures."

Goranth straddled Esh're and lifted him, turning to drape the man's arm over his broad shoulders.

"We'll be back." Goranth made the mistake of looking upward at the eye and the pit of darkness behind it.

Rif caught him staring. "That way lies madness, Northman. Steer clear of it. Let Varl handle it, and aye, we will rally the maidens to our cause. Who among them wouldn't love a dragon friend? We may never share another wench's bed if their foul beasts carry the disdain of this one."

"Such brutish words, Barber. You share no bed because of you alone. The only beast standing in your way is you," Esh're retorted. Goranth roared his mirth at Rif's discomfort when the jibe struck too close to home.

Rif started to follow.

"Ho, there! Who watches Varl?"

"She can take care of herself, Northman," Rif countered.

"No," Esh're stated weakly, gasping from the pain of trying to turn and face Rif. "For me. Stay and watch her."

Rif threw his hands up, sighed, and returned to the clearing to find Varl conversing with the beast as if she could hear its replies.

Goranth continued to the stream. The two men stepped into the cold water with a soft splash and a catch of Esh're's breath. He started to cough. Goranth held up his hand for silence. The birds had stopped, and not a single monkey chittered overhead. The underbrush failed to stir. Not even the leaves moved with the light breeze. Goranth looked for his sword, but it was back in the clearing, lying beside the stretcher.

"One dragon and you lose the last of your mind," he grumbled.

"What's that?" Esh're wondered. "Did the dragon scramble your good sense?"

Goranth shook off the joke at his expense. "In you go. Let the water cure your ills."

Esh're dropped his loose clothes. "Cure? No. Varl cures what ails me." Esh're eased himself down, leaning heavily on the Northman until he was sitting waist-deep in the water. He let it flow around him.

"Pull those bandages off and clean those wounds. It will heal quicker. You'll be better for it." Goranth stabbed a finger at the wounds to reinforce his point. "And take care you don't rip those stitches. We don't have enough twine to stitch you up a second time."

"I'd rather Varl help me bathe."

"Who wouldn't? You're clearly no fool. Now wash." Goranth stepped away from the stream to give the man some privacy, but a movement from the brush on the far side stilled him mid-step. Grass bent on a heading toward the stream—a small animal of some sort.

Esh started to whistle as he carefully rubbed the stream bottom's sand over the uninjured parts of his body, saving the wounds for last.

The grass parted to expose a snake. It stopped and looked at the man in the middle of its stream. Its forked tongue darted in and out as it tasted the air. The triangle-shaped head with ridges behind the eyes suggested it was venomous—a viper.

It slipped into the water and fought the current on its way to Esh're. Goranth crouched, coiling the muscles in his legs to unleash them when the time was right. The snake disappeared under the water. Goranth froze. It surfaced, and he jumped.

When a shadow blocked the early sky, the snake turned, seeking freedom. Faster than the viper, Goranth's hand lashed out, catching it behind its head. The Northman went face-first into the water, bounced off the shallow bottom, and sputtered to the surface, still holding the snake. He twisted the neck between two fingers, crushing the viper's life from it. It hung limp from his hand, its tail barely reaching his elbow.

"Looks kind of small for all that splashing," Esh're joked.

Goranth tossed the body downstream without an explanation. He dripped into the stream, following his dunking. He resigned himself to his fate, dipping back into the water and washing his clothes while wearing them.

"Thank you, my large friend." Esh're spoke softly, the gravity of their situation weighing heavily on him. "We will get back to Barbertown. You and Varl will make sure of it."

"Aye, we will." Goranth ripped sweetgrass from the bank and rubbed it over himself, covering his man's scent with nature to become one with the forest, if only for a short time. He stood, and the water drained from his leather jerkin and cloth breeches. He stepped onto the shore to empty his boots.

Esh're stood without assistance. He needed help to get ashore and leaned on Goranth to get dressed. With an arm over the Northman's shoulder, they trundled back to the clearing to find Varl straddling the dragon's back while Rif stood ready to crack a whip.

"What goes here?" Goranth demanded.

"Break a bull. Break a dragon. 'Tis all the same." Rif snapped the whip to the side of the beast's neck above the wing. The second crack was closer and the third closer still. The beast bowed and dipped to the ground.

Varlten're pulled on the rope leading from the basket around the creature's head. It turned one way and then the other.

"Treat what you've done to LeReon's wing," Varl

commanded from atop the beast. She stroked its neck and cooed to it.

Rif and Goranth contemplated each other without moving within striking distance.

"Well?"

"Well, what? Rush to our deaths? What bargain have you struck with the creature, Varl?" Goranth asked. He hefted his sword and stood as if ready to join a battle. Rif carried his club, equally wary.

The staff master turned the dragon's head away from the men and gestured impatiently. Goranth tucked his sword through his belt to keep it handy while Rif stalked forward, ducking to get close. The broken wing bones were starting to heal, but not straight. They needed to be aligned.

"If you get us killed…" Goranth growled. "Hold there, Rif." Goranth pointed to the wing root. "I'll pull to straighten the bone, and we'll see if either of us survive the day."

Rif carefully gripped the wing where it met the dragon's body. He braced himself and nodded. Goranth took hold, squeezing until he had a good grip. Varl started to sing while hugging the beast's neck. She glanced at the Northman.

His muscles corded across his chest and bulged in his arms. With one powerful heave, he let the break align itself before the tendons brought it back together.

The dragon raised its head to the sky and tried to bugle its pain, but only gurgles and coughs escaped its closed mouth. Steam and snot sprayed from its nostrils.

It dropped its head, sighing and trembling, not looking to attack those who had harmed it and were now trying to heal it.

"I'd splint it, but there's nowhere to tie it to." Goranth

shook his head. The two men moved to the other wing. "Thank the gods, this one is healing properly. And fast." The Northman ran his hand along the forearms and wing bones, looking for cracks. "Get me the salve."

Rif dodged out from beneath the dragon and ran to the pack. He returned with the greatest care, not trusting the dragon despite Varl's assurances.

Goranth poured the mix of herbs and minerals into his hand and spat into it to form a paste. He rubbed that into the wounds he and Rif had left on the wing when beating the creature into submission. "By the Ice Dogs, this is the damnedest thing!" He finished ministering to the beast.

All the while, Varl sang. LeReon calmed and tenderly flexed its wings before tucking them against its body.

"He's hungry," Varl proclaimed.

"And?" Rif said, but he suspected what she had in mind.

"You'll be the death of us, woman!" Goranth shouted.

"Unbind him!" Varl left no doubt that she would do it herself if they didn't. Rif and Goranth grumbled their dismay.

"I thought *you'd* be the one to get me killed," Goranth told Rif.

"Bring the ropes once you have them," Esh're called from across the clearing.

Goranth shook his head, his mane of long black hair dancing back and forth across his broad shoulders as he worked beneath the dragon to undo the knots he had taken great pride in tightening.

Rif tasked himself with forelegs, and soon the ropes came free. Both men dodged out from beneath the creature to avoid getting trampled.

But Varl... She continued to soothe the dragon.

"She's broken it, damn you!" Rif declared and smacked

Goranth on the back with a blow that would have staggered a lesser man. "It's broken!"

"Be not so sure, Barber." Goranth stepped to Esh're's side to deliver the ropes. The injured man worked to tie a different headpiece for the dragon—a halter for the rider, not a cage for its maw. Goranth caught it watching him with its single eye. "I'll not walk in front of it, not without my sword at the ready."

Once the ropes were tied, Rif took them and tossed them to Varl. She talked to the beast while fighting with the basket. She finally pulled her fighting dirk and sliced the ropes. LeReon worked its jaws, then stepped forward and ducked its head. Goranth threw himself over Esh're, prepared to burn alive to save the man.

The dragon snapped up the remains of the tapir, cracking the bones of the carcass as easily as a child chewed a sweet treat. In two bites, the tapir was gone.

"So, not just a grazer after all. Gather our packs and let's go. We can take the trail to town. No one will bother us. LeReon will make sure of it." Varl laughed from her place astride the dragon. She guided it through the clearing without waiting for the others.

Goranth and Rif looked at each other. The Northman picked up the packs and nodded at Esh're, who settled on the litter.

"Fine. This is a great day, my friends! A great day." Rif picked up one end of the litter and hurried after the dragon on the trail it cleared.

Goranth brought up the rear with the remaining rope in his hands, worrying it unconsciously as he walked. He never took his eyes off the creature.

What would have taken two days without the dragon's cooperation took a fraction of that since its long strides carried it farther and faster across the rolling hills between the forest and Barbertown. Varl guided the beast toward the river, which was a slightly longer route, but it needed to drink.

When they reached the headwaters of the Mugunta, Varl stayed astride the creature as it wallowed into the river, little more than a wide stream this far beyond the town. It ducked its head beneath the surface and spread its wings to flop weakly in the water.

"What does it do?" Rif wondered.

"Maybe they are more bird than we know. It gives itself a bath. The gods know the thing smells of death and shattered souls."

"It smells like gold and platinum to me," Rif suggested, setting Esh're down and rolling his shoulders. Goranth dropped the packs, accepting the well-earned break.

LeReon beat its wings dry before tucking them along its body. It shook its head before fixing the Northman with its malevolent glare before it ran upstream.

"Hold!" Varl shouted, yanking on the harness. "Hold!"

She tried to hang on as the dragon twisted and bucked. She flew off its back, tucking and flipping to land feet-first in the water.

Goranth bolted at the first sign and pounded along the shore, matching the dragon's speed. It neared the bank after dislodging Varl and Goranth leapt, arms outstretched. His body slammed into the dragon's neck. He caught it and hung on, straining to choke the creature with a burly arm while seeking the rope halter with the other.

His fingers closed on the rough hemp and he jerked downward, then wrapped the slack around his arm and yanked again. The dragon's head dipped each time, pulled lower and lower until it could only stagger. It stumbled ashore and collapsed. The Northman kept his arm wrapped around its neck.

"Don't hurt him!" Varl shouted. She arrived, dripping and out of breath, to slap the arm around the dragon's neck. Goranth let go and slid to the ground.

"This fool's quest is going to get us all killed." He stalked away, fists clenched and eyes narrowed beneath his troubled brow.

CHAPTER FOUR

The fat pigs wallow
Holds filled. Heave ho!
Plunder riches untold
Bodies bought and sold
Bending back and knee
The sailor's life for me
"Sonnet of the Black Sail Brotherhood"

Barbertown was built in the shape of a wagon wheel, its streets spokes feeding into a large central marketplace. It was perched on the Mugunta River up from the coast of the Southern Sea. The river was wide and deep enough to accommodate most merchant ships and just far enough inland to discourage pirate raids. It was sheltered on the east by mountains that helped provide an agreeable climate and kept away winter snow. The buildings at the outer edge were of more recent construction, made of wood and thatch, and some of the nicer ones were of uniform bricks that had been formed and baked in a factory kiln—the homeowners displaying their affluence. The older buildings toward the town's center were mostly stone, which Goranth knew had been quarried from the crest, levered down the slope, and barged across the river.

Varl perched on the dragon's neck between spiked ridges, maneuvering the beast like one would use reins on an ox. In the lead, Rif directed it, the rope dangling from the beast's harness wrapped around his left arm. His right hand held his club. Goranth figured the posture was so Rif could bash the dragon into submission if need be and at the same time serve as a threat to anyone in the crowd who might come too close to the prize.

Rif strutted like a scantily clad Borezhyan harlot.

Goranth followed at a fair distance, watching the almost gentle sweep of the dragon's tail and pulling Esh're's litter...and ignoring Esh're's claims that he could well walk under his own power. Rif had made it clear this expedition had been his endeavor, and leading the beast into Barbertown would be his task and gain him great esteem.

"The champion returns home," Goranth said softly. "But not to cheering masses."

Indeed, the inquisitive residents were mostly silent.

They'd come out of their homes and shops and in from the fields to gape at the spectacle—children, adults, and the seemingly ancient with stooped shoulders and wrinkles as deep as weathered tree bark. All races, all walks of life, from those barefoot in threadbare tunics to meticulously groomed folk in clean, colorful dresses and trews and wearing polished leather boots and shoes. He recognized seamen in their midst since sailors had a certain look about them. A few faces tugged at his memory, perhaps men he'd sailed with or stolen from in his pirate days. Many pointed at the dragon, and a plump woman with a baby on her hip shoved her fist in her mouth to keep quiet. A street entertainer imitated Rif's strutting. Eyes were wide with fear, wonder, respect, curiosity; Goranth could read a dozen emotions sweeping through the crowd.

What Goranth had thought the sound of a breeze coming in from the river, he realized were whispers, a susurrus that washed along the street they traveled. The people not silent after all. It took on the subtle hint of a funeral dirge played on the harp strings of a blazing pyre.

Rif, what are you going to do with this damnable dragon? Goranth mused. *Put it on display? Charge the people good coin to ride it? How will that net you—us—a fortune? Or will you charge them to keep the dragon from eating their families? You mentioned treating it as livestock, and dragons are not that.*

Again, he thought himself a fool for answering Rif's call.

Scents displaced the pong of tight-pressed people the deeper they went toward the marketplace—roasting meats, strong spices, heady ale from a tavern they passed, and manure from a stable. It was too far from the shore for the air to be salt-tinged here. They passed a tanner, and the stench overwhelmed the other odors. Goranth noted that the dragon's hindquarters quivered as if the tannery disturbed it. Would the beast rebel like it had a few times in the woods? Would they finally be forced to slay it and give the skin to the tanner to fashion into breastplates and shields?

Red and white pennants fluttered from cords strung between buildings, flowers filled window boxes, and flags flew from rooftops. It was as if Barbertown had dressed up for this special occasion...Rif delivering a dragon. Music drifted from the marketplace: flutes, horns, and drums that grew louder the closer they paraded.

The people finally raised their voices. Some cheered and clapped, others shouted at Rif.

"You bring doom to us!"

"A demon!"

"Rif is no longer the Barber. Rif the Game Warden leads death to Barbertown!"

"A hero!" someone countered shrilly. "Rif tamed a dragon!"

A small dragon, Goranth thought. *Rif, but mostly Varl, had seemingly tamed a small dragon. For the moment, at least, it was subdued.*

"Hail, Rif!"

"All hail Rif the Warden!"

Goranth kept his eyes on the dragon's haunches, watching for its muscles to tense. If it broke free here, dozens would die, first of all Varl and Rif for their crime of deigning to think they were masters of the beast.

"A fool to do this with you," Goranth grumbled. "Always a fool, me. A dragon is not livestock." Perhaps there'd be a merchantman down at the docks looking to take on crew. He could sail to another city, far from Rif and his crazed schemes. He'd not have to witness whatever foul thing would happen to the people of Barbertown because a dragon was led down their streets. Goranth could leave with his conscious clear. He'd come in answer to Rif's summons and helped him catch the beast. His obligation was fulfilled.

The marketplace assaulted the senses with a blur of colors and sounds. It was packed with vendors displaying wares Goranth could not take in because he was focused on the dragon, fearing it would try to bolt amid the cacophony.

"Madness, Rif," he cursed. "Madness to parade this

beast. All of this is madness." He should have brought it in at the height of darkness when most folk were in bed.

Rif was shouting, but Goranth couldn't make out the words for the competing racket. He watched Varl lean forward and grip the ropes, tugging, heard Esh say something. He couldn't hear that either, probably again claiming he wanted to walk. Goranth's head pounded from the racket.

Then Rif made a sweep of the round central road that ringed the market and chose a spoke at a right angle to the one they'd taken here. More people pressed forward.

"Hail, Rif!"

"Rif the Warden!"

"Rif the warrior!"

"Rif the victorious!"

Rif the mad, Goranth thought.

Rif-Rif-Rif became a mantra that rose like a wave and did not recede until they reached the eastern edge of Barbertown that butted up to the river. Twin barges had been lashed together at the docks, and Rif coaxed the dragon onto them while Varl sang a wordless song and caressed the creature's neck. Goranth stayed on the shore with Esh're and watched the barges shove off, cross the Mugunta, and reach the other side, where a palisade of thick wooden stakes and iron rails stood, shadowed by the ridge. There were guards atop it, and they opened a massive gate.

Rif led the dragon inside, Varl riding with her head held high. Goranth was curious, but his charge was the wounded Esh're. He'd take care of the man and come later to the palisade to sate his curiosity and at the same time inquire at the one merchant ship he saw. Some of the townsfolk had wandered to the riverbank, pointing across and jabbering about how awesome was Rif the Warden, and that Barbertown would now thrive.

Goranth thought it was thriving just fine the way it was and that a scaled, unhappy beast would not improve it much.

"A healer," he said to a doughy-faced woman an arm's length away. "Can you direct me to one?"

She looked him up and down, then cast her gaze on the litter and Esh're as if she'd not noticed them before. Goranth figured she probably hadn't, having been captivated by the dragon parade.

"A healer," he repeated sternly.

She wiped her thick fingers on her skirt, then turned and pointed down the street. That was the extent of her directions.

Goranth left the assembly behind, almost grateful to be away from curious townsfolk. Perhaps Barbertown had several healers and Rif was partial to one. However, the man was more preoccupied with the dragon than his wounded old friend and probably hadn't noticed that Goranth and Esh're had not followed them to the palisade.

"I could have walked," Esh're said as Goranth pulled him down the street.

"Maybe," Goranth replied. "You were not so steady on your legs in the woods. Your injury is infected. Be glad Varl did not see that. Otherwise, Rif would not have had her to ride that beast—"

"LeReon. She named it 'LeReon.'"

"Varl would be with you and not the dragon, and I'm not sure Rif could have managed the beast without her."

"Varl named it LeReon."

"Aye, LeReon," Goranth growled. He lowered his voice: "Farmers don't name their livestock."

He spotted small offering bowls in front of some of the

residences and businesses. Incense burned in a few, though he couldn't find the scents; his nose was overwhelmed by everything else. All this for Rif's return? The pennants and flowers, too. It seemed excessive.

The healer's shop he'd been directed to was narrow, roughly eight feet across, and it was nestled between a cobbler's and a tavern called the Honorable Skull, which Goranth planned to visit next. He helped Esh're off the litter and propped it against the building's front. He went to put an arm around Esh're's waist but got waved off.

Esh're hobbled through the beaded curtain ahead of Goranth. A close look at it revealed a mix of carved and painted wooden beads, shells, and small charred bones.

"You came on the heels of the dragon," the shopkeeper said.

"My friend was injured capturing the beast."

"LeReon," Esh're replied. "The dragon is called LeReon."

The shopkeeper pointed at the back, and Goranth and Esh're headed there. The building was three times as long as it was wide, and the rear of it was thick with shadows and the bite of a strong, fusty smell. Goranth hoped this man was a reputable healer and that Esh would not end up worse for the visit. Esh're stretched out on a cot. The healer ministered to a large lantern, cursing until it blazed to life. He grumbled for a moment, then ran his gaze over his new patient.

"Infected," he pronounced. "Badly." He was an old man but was far from infirm. His hair was only a suggestion, a few white strands like spider silk that circled an otherwise bald head. Thin but not gaunt, wrinkled but no age spots. His eyes were a rheumy blue and intense. "The infection could take him if it is not worked out of his body."

"And you can do that?" Goranth asked.

"Certainly, I can. Tell me about capturing the dragon. It will pass the time while I do the mending."

Esh're elaborated on Rif's dragon-hunt while Goranth padded up and down the shop, looking at the plethora of bottles and jars that contained various powders, unguents, and crumbled leaves. Muscle-sore from wrestling the beast, he made some selections—chicory, carob, ginger, valerian root, and motherwort—and placed them on the counter before returning to the cot.

Once the healer's stinking salve had been applied to Esh're's wounds and a compress to his forehead, Esh're's breathing was steady and slow. He appeared to be sleeping.

"Your friend needs to stay here. I have more to do in a while. The infection is deep."

Goranth thought it was indeed fortunate Varl had been unaware of the severity. Without her, the dragon—LeReon—could well be rampaging through Barbertown. It might end up doing so anyway. He would find her later and let her know where her mate rested.

"Tomorrow, then. I will come back tomorrow and—"

"There is the matter of pay," the healer said. "My services and my tinctures are not free. Even for dragon hunters." He stepped away from the cot and glided to the counter, eyeing Goranth's selections. "These are for you?"

"Aye. Can you grind them? Brew a strong tea?" He placed his empty waterskin on the counter. "Fill this with it."

"It takes coin."

Goranth thrust a hand into the pocket of his trousers and brought out a small leather bag. He nearly spilled it on the counter to let the healer take what he required, but he thought better of it. The man might want it all, and Goranth had yet to see any return on his part in the dragon hunt. He pulled out five gold coins and set them out.

"That will cover your friend. Two more for the brew."

Goranth grumbled. "One." The Northman's tone suggested a further attempt to bargain would not be well received. The healer's lip curled into a snarl, but in the end, he nodded. The exchange left Goranth with a dozen.

"Come back in a little while and I'll have your tea."

Goranth intended to spend that "little while" in the tavern next door, soothing his throat and fogging his mind with a few tankards of spiced ale.

The place was not busy at this time of day. Likely, people who would otherwise be drinking were out on the street with their tongues wagging. He chose a table in the middle and sat watching the door.

The surroundings were comfortable, the wood dark, and just the right amount of light spilled through the front window. The floor creaked with a subtle sound, and the table was clean and smooth save for a few spots where initials had been carved into it. There was no music or boisterous conversation from the few patrons; they talked in soft tones and spent their time eating and drinking. He wondered how the place got its name: the Honorable Skull. Perhaps he'd ask the barkeep before he left.

The ale was tasty and strong and went well with the turkey stew and bread. He had not expected to see Rif stride into the tavern as the barkeep poured his third mug.

"Hail New Rif the Warden," Goranth said as the Barber settled into the chair across from him and waggled his fingers at the barkeep. "All hail Rif the dragon-tamer."

"You're drunk."

"Not yet. But I plan to get there."

Rif scowled. "I looked for you. And Esh're. Varlten're is worried unto sick over where you two went."

"And where is she?" Goranth drained the third mug and waggled his fingers, too.

"In the palisade with the dragon."

"You mean, LeReon. The dragon is named LeReon, remember?"

Rif's scowl deepened.

"Esh're needed a healer," Goranth said, his tone suddenly serious. "And he's at one. Right next door. If the healer is to be believed, Esh's wound is badly infected." He paused. "I believe the healer. The wound does not smell good."

Rif's features softened. "I will let her know. Right now, I need her to keep the dragon settled. I've plenty of men and hundreds of yards of rope. The palisade is high and thick, and—"

"If you have plenty of men, why did you need me to help capture a dragon?" Goranth leaned back in the chair and had to steady himself since he nearly toppled it. "Plenty of men would have—"

"—made a lot of noise in the woods. There's a difference, Northman, between soldiers and warriors. Not one of them...not several of them together...could match your strength and definitely not your stealth of foot."

Goranth figured Rif was trying to soothe him with flattery. He pointed at his tankard when the barkeep came over with a pitcher.

"Leave it," Rif said, stabbing a dirty finger at the pitcher.

"Good of Barbertown to welcome its returning hero," Goranth observed. "How did they know when we would arrive? The flags, flowers, the incense and offering bowls. You truly—"

Rif shook his head. "I did enjoy the crowd, old friend, but the decorations are not for me. This is a holy week for Vujo. All of this is to honor the demi-god."

"Ah. I rarely pay attention to religious festivals." Goranth figured the gods likely found such celebrations insipid and a waste of time. He knew of Vujo, a minor deity in the scheme of the world tied to combat, luck, and plagues. "The party is to appease him, eh? To keep diseases at bay."

"Aye." Rif took a deep pull of the ale and let out a long, loud belch. "Fortunate that our delivery of the dragon accorded with the holy week. The people were all out to see the magnificent creature. Great timing, eh?"

Goranth suspected Rif had planned it that way.

"There will be a grand ceremony tomorrow for Vujo, and you must attend. The high priestess Kalida—I'll introduce her to you—is revered here."

Goranth mumbled and refilled his tankard from the pitcher.

"She will bless the dragon, too. You'll take a look at the palisade, see just how large it is and that it will hold more young dragons. That it is secure, safe, and—"

"Rif, between us men, what do you intend to do with them?"

"I told you. Livestock. Special livestock that will—"

"—make us all rich. How? Honestly, how?"

Rif lowered his head so his chin rested on the lip of his tankard and spoke in a conspiratorial whisper. "Our farms, we're expanding them. They'll stretch to the edge of the forest and into the forest. Barbertown is expanding, too; more people coming on ships and staying, sinking their roots. The dragons, we'll tame them like one masters a surly ox. We'll plow the fields with them, cut down trees, and they'll haul the wood. Strongest animal there is. The dragon will pull stones from the mountains and the ruins in the woods, and we'll use them for buildings. The dragon —dragons when we get a few more—will provide labor for our growing city. Perhaps we'll catch some to sell to other cities or to wealthy barons or some such."

Goranth saw Rif's eyes gleam. His old friend had turned into a businessman—a citified leader, far removed from the pirate he had once known.

"Their labor will help us build a stronger and higher wall around Barbertown, fortify us. And the byproducts! We'll use shed skin for clothes and armor and roofing material. Broken claws will be made into weapons, dung into bricks. Nothing will be wasted. It is a perfect and marvelous plan."

It is idiocy. He kept those words inside.

"Young dragons working for the betterment of us and Barbertown will—"

"What will you do when the dragons get bigger? Dragons do that. Your palisade cannot withstand a great one."

Rif squared his shoulders and thrummed his fingers on the table. "Dragons live a very long time, Northman. Hundreds of years, maybe a thousand. It takes a long, long while for such a creature to grow to some size no longer manageable."

"So, you don't expect them to outgrow your palisade in your lifetime," Goranth mused. That part of the grand plan would not be Rif's problem, just the here and now where he could soak up the glory and not have to worry about future generations. "Or do you plan to slay your livestock when they start to get too big? When a beast has outgrown its usefulness and presents trouble, you'll—"

"That's nothing to consider today, Northman. I must visit Esh're," Rif announced. He pushed back from the table and stood, ending the argument. He tossed enough coins on the table to cover their drinks and Goranth's meal.

"The healer's been paid, Rif."

"Thank you."

"*I* have not been paid," Goranth continued.

"You *will* be rich," Rif said. "Have some patience."

"I will have another tankard of ale," Goranth replied. Just one more; he needed to be able to walk next door and claim his tea, then climb the stairs to his rented room and the waiting tub of water. He did not care for his sweaty stink.

"Tomorrow, my friend," Rif said, smiling like a hawker of wares as he strode to the door.

Perhaps that two-masted merchantman will still be at the docks tomorrow, Goranth thought. And perhaps he'd find himself on its deck, putting Barbertown in its and his wake.

CHAPTER FIVE

Bow before the Sea Wench
Pay homage to the Merman's Hall
Run! Duck the hangman's bench
Time to dance! Time to fall...
"Sonnet of the Black Sail Brotherhood"

The night passed quickly for the Northman. He slumbered deep from the effects of too much ale and the healer's powerful herbal draught. "Tea," aye. He'd called it tea.

It was a witch's brew, for the morning came and Goranth was a new man, pain-free, bruise-free, and ready to sail. He dressed and made to leave, opening his door to find an embedded dagger pinning a note to it. The hallway was devoid of life or any sign that anyone had recently passed. He yanked the dagger out of the wood, caught the note, and stabbed the weapon back into the door. The cold hilt told him it had not been placed in the past few moments.

How long had the note been there, and how addled had he been to miss the dagger's plunge into the wood? He went inside to read the message.

Kalida requests the honor of your presence for a tour of the city and enlightening of your soul.

"By the Ice Dogs, I won't be lectured to by some ill-begotten demon's cleric!" Goranth declared to the empty room. "I'll be on my way now, and the Barber can owe me. I'll not bandy about getting my ear bent with temple rumors and expressions of faith. I see with my eyes and I trust what I see!"

Goranth stormed back and forth between the bed and the door until his blood had cooled enough for him to leave without killing someone for looking at him sideways. His mood soured as his patience fled from the trials of the past week.

He dropped the note on the bed before striding into the hallway and kept going, down the stairs and outside, eyes scanning and searching, looking for any man who might be watching him. Goranth had made enemies—men who were afraid of him, men he had bested in one contest or another. Men who had lost their women to the Northman's rugged features.

In the street, he found a two-wheeled chariot waiting.

"You are Goranth the Mighty? I am to take you to the Lady Kalida."

A few passersby stopped to watch the exchange.

"I've no use for your priests or conjurers." Goranth turned away, but the driver's laugh caught him off-guard.

"I assure you, she is neither of those things. You may find your time with her to be rather exhilarating."

"Exhilarating like combat or like men and women can be when alone?"

"Exhilarating like an awareness that you never knew

existed. She won't lecture you. If you find her company to be less than pleasant, you can leave. No one will stop you, Goranth."

"Which way is she?"

"Toward the river."

"Then you'll save me a walk. I'll give her a few breaths of my time before I have to go. I have a ship to catch." Goranth climbed aboard and gripped the chariot's front rail with one hand.

"We were led to believe..." The driver let his words drift off. "No matter. I shall convey you to Kalida."

With an easy slap of the whip, the single horse pulled. It found traction once the chariot started rolling and increased its speed.

This will save me a hearty walk, Goranth thought.

The chariot stopped in front of a humble building beyond the inland end of the docks. Goranth thanked the man, who promptly drove off, leaving the Northman on guard. He held the pommel of his sword as he looked about, feeling a peaceful aura tug at him.

"By the Ice Dogs," he growled, fighting the pressure on his soul.

The door opened. He whipped his head around to fix Kalida with his harshest glare. An instant later, he was blinking in disbelief.

Golden cornsilk hair cascaded over soft shoulders in a gentle curl toward ample breasts that were half-exposed beneath a low-cut tunic that left her firm midriff bare. A short tan skirt of deer hide exposed long and shapely legs, unblemished as desert sand after a heavy wind.

"Would you care to join me on a tour of our community, of Barbertown?" asked a voice like the tinkling bells of snow angels.

"I am smitten!" Goranth claimed, taking a reluctant step forward. "What devilry is this?"

"There are no spells beyond the desire in one's heart," she replied.

Goranth looked away from the striking figure to study his feet. They still responded to his commands, but he had to see if she was real. He lifted his eyes, and again he drank in her beauty. This time, his feet remained planted in the ground.

"Let us walk, Kalida, but I intend to be on the ship that sails with the tide."

"Pity, but you are your own man. No one will hold you against your will." She walked past the Northman, touching his arm with a single digit and sending tingles through his body. She smelled of newly opened flowers.

His lip twitched as he fought her hold on him. He felt the stirring and tamped it down. Now was not the time. She wasn't his to tame, but wouldn't he enjoy trying! Borezhye, where the dancing girls were plentiful—that was the place for him. He shrugged and took his place by her side, walking at her pace as she talked.

"Barbertown is an agricultural center because man cannot live on meat alone. The land here is fertile, but the growth is angry. I help the farmers bridge the gap between what they want and what must be."

"You speak in riddles with a silken tongue and the cheer of gold. Tell me, Kalida, what does tomorrow hold for Barbertown?"

"The celebrations for Vujo will continue. Vujo smiles on Barbertown."

"Vujo! There are too many gods and not enough worshippers, by the Ice Dogs!" Goranth quipped. She laughed, and Goranth joined her in her mirth.

"To wit, Goranth. You have a sharp humor and a dark

view of our wonderful world. Without the gods and their demi-god minions, we would suffer greatly from the demons that haunt the dark corners."

"Like that abomination in the stockade across the Mugunta?"

"The dragons have their own god, and they are not happy with the strain under which that beast is burdened. You feel it, too, don't you, Goranth?"

"That I do, lass. It was a terrible thing we did. I regret my part in it and refuse to see it through to the bitter end. I have counseled Rif as much as he'll listen, which is not at all. I'll have no further role in this tragedy."

"Come with me from the city to the fields. Let us speak with the land."

"Talking to dirt. Just when I was lulled to sleep that you were firmly rooted in the real world."

"You shall see for yourself, Northman. Don't be quick to judge. Migoro is a place of push and pull, lift and drop, give and take. Let the land speak to you, and you will be amazed at what you hear."

"I let my sword speak for me," Goranth replied.

"And the land appreciates the sacrifices and blood tolls that you've paid to it."

Goranth refused to continue the verbal sparring. She had a wondrous look about her, but he thought she had not a brain in her beautiful head. The Northman sighed. She was not for him. He'd hold out for Borezhye.

Visible above the waterfront's buildings, the merchantman's furled sails remained at the dock. He had time to humor Kalida. Maybe he could grab a fresh tomato for his breakfast.

She walked fast for one who seemed not to be in a hurry, and they left the city in short order. Not ten paces beyond the last hovel, the fields began. The hard dirt played host to rows of green, while brown grass straggled around the field's borders. Beyond the fields, the earth seemed barren.

"How do these grow in such a place? Have you dug a trench to the river?"

"With your feet on the ground and your heart open, listen and I will explain, but not with words." Kalida closed her eyes and held her hands together before her chest. Her lips moved in a whispered prayer.

Goranth scoffed until he heard her voice inside his head—the crystalline pipes of a snow angel singing.

Goranth, I can speak to you like this as long as we are both firmly on the ground. The earth relays my thoughts, not at my command, but because she is a benevolent keeper of life. The earth is not dead rock and soil but the body of a living being! She carries water through her veins like blood. She feeds and breathes as she must. Her will keeps us alive. If she wished it, the world would turn barren, and human and beast alike, no matter where they lived, would perish. This is her power. This is her hold over us, yet she demands nothing except that we live in peace with her.

"By the Ice Dogs, I don't like this, woman! Stay out of my head, and I'll be on my way. Your beauty is one thing, but filling my mind with your thoughts is something different."

Relax and feel her strength, came Kalida's siren call.

Goranth felt himself being pulled through the ground and outside Barbertown, well beyond. The roots of plants and small rocks played against his skin as if he burrowed with the insects. He swore he could taste and smell the earth.

You can see the world, Northman, without taking a step. Thank you, Vujo, and thank you, Dragon God, for being at peace with us, even if only for the moment. The moment is all we ever have. Right here and right now.

Goranth's hand sought the tender skin of Kalida's shoulder. He let his fingers enjoy the softness of her bare skin, smooth and tender. She leaned into his hand.

He could feel the earth cocooning him, and he sensed that she was pleased.

Kalida extended the view to him. Far beyond Barbertown and its people, he saw them: men on horses coming toward the Mugunta. Mabayan Raiders from the southeast, the Selemongan steppe.

"Is that real or a vision?" Goranth demanded, shaking Kalida by her shoulders.

She opened her eyes and looked at his hands until he let go. "It is all too real. That war party is on its way here."

"Because of the dragon?"

"I think not, no. I cannot see into their hearts, but I think they come just to raid, to take what Barbertown has."

"Barbertown has a dragon."

"I do not need to see into their hearts to know that once they learn of the dragon, they will leave no palisade standing until it is free. They will unleash the wrath of the Dragon God."

"Then we have to stop them. Rif has warriors. We must tell him."

Goranth held out his hand and she took it. They ran toward the center of Barbertown before heading toward the healer where Esh're was. Rif would be nearby or somewhere between there and the stockade across the river.

They burst through the healer's door.

"Barbarians!" the old man shouted before returning to his ministrations.

Varl stood. "Goranth. I thank you for covering Esh're. I

53

shall repay you once Rif pays his debts." She spat on the floor.

"Hey!" the healer called, his straggly hair waving with his wild gyrations.

"Where is Rif?" Goranth asked, not bothering to ask about Esh's health since he sat up with full-color in his face and gave the Northman a crooked smile.

"At the stockade where he torments LeReon with his presence. I need to get back there." Varl glared at Kalida. "Who is this strumpet?"

Goranth shook his head slowly at Varl's fearless judgment.

"I am Kalida, mistress of the earth."

Varl grunted. "Stay with Esh, Goranth. I must go."

Goranth shook his head, sending his mane of black hair waving. "We need to find Rif. Now! We have information for his ears only." Goranth inched toward the door, foot tapping, impatient to be done with the healer, the dragon, and Barbertown.

"I'll be fine," Esh're said. "I'll join you across the river as soon as I can." He touched Varl's leg since that was the only part of her body he could reach. She crouched, and they held hands.

The partners kissed, and Varl stared Kalida down as she passed. Goranth and Kalida followed her out. Once again, Goranth and Kalida held hands as they ran. They raced onto the barge and helped the ferrymen pull it across the river.

On the other side, Varl led them up a ladder to a platform overlooking the stockade and the dragon within. Rif stood tall, drinking something bitter-smelling while staring at the beast.

"Mabayan Raiders are on their way here. They won't take kindly to finding a son of their dragon god a prisoner within these walls," Goranth explained. "We've at best an hour, maybe two, before they storm into Barbertown and discover your prize."

Rif didn't flinch at the news or ask for its source. "The dragon remains, so what would you have me do?"

"Make sure they never learn of the beast's capture."

"Ride out and kill them? Dead men reveal no secrets, Goranth. How many are coming?"

"I counted no less than a hundred."

Rif winced. He looked over the stockade at the men patrolling the balustrade and outside the timber walls, where more men camped. "A hundred I can muster, but no more. Will you come with us, Goranth? Put an end to this threat?"

"I suppose I won't be paid until this new threat is dealt with," Goranth growled.

Kalida held his arm, looking like a favored concubine. She started to sway, and her knees buckled.

"The earth," Rif said. "She's not connected to it up on this wall. She needs to touch the earth."

Goranth caught her as she passed out.

"Will you come with us, Northman?" Rif persisted.

Goranth looked at Kalida as if he carried a child. She stared up at him, eyes narrowed. "I shall join you, Rif, but you owe me, and I *will* collect."

CHAPTER SIX

The firestorm of battle
Plunging tide and creaking sail
A cutlass stroke and a death rattle
Enemies tossed over the rail
"Sonnet of the Black Sail Brotherhood"

Goranth grabbed the raider's leg and pulled hard, ducking her sword before unseating her. The horse raced on as the Northman slammed the woman into the ground, planted a knee on her stomach, and thrust a dagger into her heart. Around him, the fight raged.

The Mabayans were shirtless, even the women warriors, wearing only trews and loincloths. They had strings of beads draped around their necks, and their gold jewelry glinted. Their skin was the color of polished walnut, and their oiled muscles fairly glowed in the sun. Some had tattoos and painful-looking brands Goranth knew symbolized victories and honors their villages bestowed. He'd sailed with three Mabayan brothers on *Hellfish* and was friendly with them, though he would not call them friends. He saw them killed that night by the massive squid.

A raider jumped off his wounded horse and rushed Goranth, slender spiked club in one hand and short curved blade in the other. The Northman met his rush, crouching below the swing of both weapons, then pivoting and coming up behind the man and bringing his blade down hard on the man's neck. A second swing decapitated the Mabayan. Before the corpse could hit the ground, Goranth spun away to fight another mounted raider.

Most of Goranth's memories of the Mabayans were foul. Years past, before settling on the eastern coast of Migoro, the tribesmen were known to be seafarers only, with no claimed land to call home. They traveled on ketches and stolen sloops, connecting the boats into floating islands at night and between raids, and they harried merchants on the fringes of the major trade routes, occasionally striking at small coastal towns. They competed with ships Goranth, Rif, and other pirates sailed on, and their assaults were so vicious that countries put fleets out to hunt the Mabayans...making life difficult for more civilized brigands. Goranth heard they left no one alive on the ships they plundered, unlike the crew on his own ship, which avoided killing unless it was necessary. The Mabayan-hunting fleets were responsible for the raiders eventually abandoning the sea and settling on land.

The Mabayans seemed to hold little regard for life. *Human* life. He knew they revered sea creatures and land animals, and they honored the stock and game they butchered for food. *Had they learned Rif had gained a dragon?* The thought hung at the back of Goranth's mind like an annoying biting fly. Were the Mabayans raiding, as Kalida suggested, merely to take Barbertown's bounty, or were they after the dragon?

The charging female rider was young and lithe, with the broad shoulders of a swimmer. She carried a spear and thrust it at Goranth as she passed, then speared one of Rif's soldiers who wasn't as deft at sidestepping her. Her horse stopped on her command, and she struggled to tug the spear free of her victim. Those few moments were her undoing. Goranth ran at her, sword high, and brought it down on her leg. She screamed, tugged the spear free, and leveled it at him, but too late. He swung again, cleaving through her wrist. Her hand and the spear dropped, and Goranth swung once more to end her anguish. All three strokes occurred within a single heartbeat.

Nearby, Rif sparred with a particularly large mounted Mabayan who seemed familiar. The rider took a swipe at him and charged away. Rif had his club in one hand and a short thin-bladed knife in the other. He had acquired the name Barber when they sailed on the *Hellfish*. Rif, though reluctant to take a life in those days, did so in fights by moving in close and slashing a shaving razor across his opponents' throats. Goranth had noted symbols of razors carved into some of the shops' signs in Barbertown.

Rif had marshaled his soldiers immediately after the Northman's warning and led them all southeast across the Mugunta, staying just inside the edge of the forest, scurrying on foot as if a swarm of maddened hornets chased them. He had said it was not worth the time to collect and saddle Barbertown's horses, and the pounding hooves would alert the raiders. Better they run like their lives depended on it, he'd said, and strike without warning from cover to gain an advantage.

With stealth and the woods on their side, Rif's force had sprung on the raiders and caught them in the open well before the river's banks. He'd led the skirmish with a volley of arrows that took down at least two dozen raiders before the rest could react.

Goranth thought well-placed Mabayan scouts could have alerted the raiders to the presence of Rif and his men, but it didn't appear the force had used any. Indeed it seemed, they had not expected to be noticed prior to reaching the river. *Fools, they. Overconfident in their numbers.* His estimate of one hundred raiders had been light. Closer to one hundred and fifty, he thought. Perhaps all the Mabayan warriors from the Selomongan coast had been heading toward Barbertown.

But why? And why now?

"Have they raided Barbertown before?" Goranth had asked Rif as they ran through the woods.

Rif had not answered, instead busying himself with directing his men, keeping them under his loose control.

One of the soldiers had replied, a youth Goranth thought too young for a skirmish.

"Never," the youth had said. "Merchant caravans, yes, coming from and going to the city, but never have they come directly against us."

So, why? Goranth again wondered. *Had the storehouses in their villages become depleted? Had Rif done something else to attract their ire?* The Northman had no love of the Mabayans, but he wanted to know the reason why he was forced to slay so many of them.

Horses screamed, steel rang, and warriors shouted curses. Rif's club swung so hard Goranth imagined that it whistled as it thumped into the side of a large black warhorse, bringing the animal down. The Barber followed through and struck the falling rider's head, smashing it like a ripening melon. Then Rif disappeared in a sea of men and horses.

Goranth rolled right as two mounted riders bore down on him. Clear of the hooves, he bounded up behind them and hurled his dagger at the back of one rider, where it struck square between the shoulder blades. The man pitched forward and fell from his saddle, the stirrups not strong enough to hold his lifeless body. His companion reined his sorrel around but lost precious seconds. Goranth had drawn his sword in those breaths, and in his left hand, he'd scooped up a dead man's *makhaira*, the slightly curved short sword favored by the Mabayans.

His leg muscles bunched, and he leapt at the charging raider. Twisting in the air and slashing with both blades, he cut into his foe's center and gravely wounded him. They hadn't been kill-strokes, though Goranth had intended them as such. Still, they'd taken the man out of combat; it was all he could do to maintain his saddle by wrapping his now-weaponless hands in the horse's mane as his blood spilled down its side.

Goranth sprinted toward another rider, then vaulted up and swung wildly with his longsword while stabbing with the *makhaira*. The stolen weapon was sharp; its edge glinted like liquid silver in the sun, and the pommel was carved from some dark wood and inlaid with brass and mother-of-pearl. It had belonged to someone of stature, and Goranth knew it was valuable. Perhaps it and other weapons he might acquire from this field would make this reckless gamble worth his time. Initially, he'd intended to tell Rif no, that he would not accompany his soldiers to meet the raiders. That he'd done enough for his old friend by assisting in the capture of the damnable dragonette.

But a venomous glance from Kalida had changed his mind. Her look had said, "How dare you turn your back on us?" As weak as she was, Kalida had offered to head out with them, but Rif had stopped her, saying her job was to keep a lookout through her earth-vision and to post sentries in the event some raiders made it through. Goranth realized Rif didn't want her involved because worrying about his precious priestess might distract him. Someone with her abilities was too valuable to risk.

However, Goranth wished Varlten're had come. Varl was twice the warrior of any of Barbertown's soldiers. He watched as a nearby soldier parried the attack of one rider while he ineffectually stabbed at another darting by. Varl was quick and agile, and these soldiers could learn a lot from her; she'd have taken both riders down in half the time. He grumbled that they could learn a lot from him, too, as it appeared that he was the most competent swordsman on this plain.

His bravado was stifled by an arrow piercing his right leg. More arrows landed around him, and he took a snakelike path to avoid another strike. He'd not noticed the archers among the Mabayans when he and Rif surprised the raiders minutes ago. How many of the raiders were thus armed? It had added an element of terror to the field, not able to see where the enemy arrows were coming from. The Barber had left some of his archers inside the tree line, and they continued to send volleys at the mounted raiders.

Goranth watched a trio of Rif's soldiers fall to Mabayan arrows; another two managed to dodge the volley, only to fall to the raiders' blades. What had started as a battle in Barbertown's favor was turning for the Mabayans. Rif had been wrong; he should have sent his men out here on whatever horses Barbertown had. The Barber had been an expert strategist at sea, but apparently he lacked land-fighting tactics.

Perched higher, the Mabayans were both protected and had the ability to strike from above. Goranth spotted a familiar figure to the south. The massive man was using his right hand to hurl javelins at the soldiers, while his left swung a cutlass. *Who was that Mabayan?* Goranth forced the question out of his head and cut down another opponent in a single swing.

"The horses!" he heard Rif bellow. "Gut their horses! Take them down!"

Goranth cringed at the tactic. It was sound, he knew, and would even the field, but he hated the notion of destroying beautiful and valuable animals to get at their riders. The horses were no one's enemies. The soldiers complied, turning their attention from harrying the riders to slashing and stabbing the horses' chests and bellies. The cries of the animals became deafening, melding with the angry shouts of the Mabayans and the victorious whoops of the Barbertown men.

Goranth tugged at the arrow in his thigh, then stopped. He could tell it was barbed and would cause more damage coming out than going in. Instead, he snapped the haft off and tried to ignore the pain. He chose another target, a thickset rider who'd raised a sling and was twirling it over his shaven head.

Not much more than a boy, Goranth thought as he stepped in and shoved his sword blade up through the Mabayan's ribs. The young rider looked frightened and surprised and opened his mouth, but nothing came out that could be heard over the cacophony of this contest.

"Not enough years for you," Goranth pronounced sadly as the youth fell from the horse, twitching. Goranth put the makhaira's blade between his teeth, kept the sword in his right hand, and grabbed the reins of the dying youth's horse with his left. He sprang into the saddle and clamped his knees tight. From his higher vantage point, he could better see the bloody battle and noted that some of Rif's men had also gained mounts.

The Barber's tactic of taking down the horses was turning the skirmish back to Barbertown's advantage. Goranth noted that some of the Mabayans were retreating or trying to, wheeling their mounts around and attempting to leave the field.

"No survivors!" one of the soldiers hollered, and the shout became a wave that swelled like a growing wind. "No survivors! None!"

Rif's archers cut most of those fleeing down. The horses continuing their mad dash to safety, but a few Mabayans were able to ride out of sight.

A stench rose around Goranth: blood, excrement, and fear. He continued to swing at and parry the attacks of the Mabayans still in the fight but made no attempt to go after those in retreat.

"No survivors!" continued the wave. "None!"

"Kill them all!" This came from Rif, who Goranth caught out of the corner of his eye.

Goranth didn't support that notion, but he understood it. Leaving enemies alive might mean they'd return and try again. It wouldn't be like it had been out at sea, where he and his fellow pirates had left crews alive to sail again. In those days, they'd wanted the shipping to continue so they could keep plundering the same ships. The opposing sailors and their ships were not enemies; they were simply targets.

His thigh throbbed from the embedded arrow, and he felt blood running down his leg. The persistent ache helped him concentrate and spurred him to act even faster. He directed the horse into the thick of the fight, slashing and stabbing until his arms burned from the effort. He wasn't worried about Rif; somehow Goranth knew the Barber would emerge from the skirmish.

Indeed, Rif was but a dozen feet away, balancing on the hindquarters of a fallen horse and swinging his club at the familiar Mabayan.

"Narlun," Goranth realized. The massive Mabayan was Narlun, who'd they fought more than once while sailing on the *Hellfish*. They had all been younger then, and he and Rif had left the raider alive, much to their current dismay. Goranth maneuvered his horse closer to better hear the heated exchange.

"The dragon!" Narlun hissed. "Surrender him, Rif. You've no right to such a beast!"

It was *about the dragon! How could the Mabayan have discovered Rif had one?* Following the beast's capture, most of their trek back to Barbertown had been through the woods. Only the final stretch had been on a trade road, and they'd seen no sign of anyone until they reached the city. Had there been Mabayan scouts in the woods? Goranth knew the Mabayans respected animal life. *Was this raid to free the dragon or to capture it for their own use?* Goranth wondered. Rif had not exaggerated the value of the creature, and the Northman knew the Barber would not give it up.

Especially since Rif and his soldiers had turned the tide of battle, having bested the raiders at a high cost.

The plains were red with the blood of men and horses, and the air buzzed with the cries of the dead and dying, mixed with the exultations of Rif's men. Everything was painfully loud. Goranth had difficulty hearing Narlun and Rif, but he caught a few words.

Dragon
Black heart
Return

Death

Vengeance

Then Rif was down and Narlun turned his horse and galloped away, motioning for what remained of his force to join him. Arrows from the tree line caught some of the fleeing Mabayans, but Narlun was not among them. He had survived to fight another day.

Goranth slew another three raiders before he reached Rif, who was struggling to stand, his feet caught in the spilled intestines of a horse. The Barber was covered with mud and blood, so it was impossible for Goranth to see the severity of the man's wounds.

Rif's face was etched with rage, and he shouted for his men to "Kill all the raiders!"

They obeyed as best they could.

When there were no more standing, Goranth slipped from the horse's back and hobbled on his wounded leg to reach the Barber's side.

"This blood is not mine," Rif said, sluicing it off his skin with his bare hands. "Blood of my enemies. I should be pleased to bathe in it."

"They rode for the dragon," Goranth said.

"Aye," Rif admitted. "But only Vujo knows how they found out about it."

The conversation ended. Rif and his men—and Goranth, too—busied themselves walking the field to learn who was dead and who was wounded. Injured Mabayans were swiftly finished. A dozen or more injured of Barbertown's forces, who were likely to survive, were draped across captured horses. Rif quietly killed those among his men who were suffering and beyond help.

"Thirty dead of ours," he pronounced. "Nearly a third of our force."

Yours, Goranth nearly corrected. *Your men, not ours. Your force.*

The Barber ordered some of the soldiers to take the wounded back to town. Others were free to loot the fallen.

Goranth found no other weapons as fine as the makhaira he'd acquired and now carried in his belt, but he did divest some of the Mabayan corpses of their jewelry. He thrust the assortment of gold and silver armbands, earrings, and torques into a saddlebag and tossed it across the rump of the horse he'd claimed. The dead didn't need the wealth, and Goranth wanted something in exchange for his pain and grief.

"Barbertown will celebrate us," Rif said. "We have victory and thirty-four fine steeds to add to the stables."

"Kalida, your priestess, deserves the accolades, not us," Goranth said, his voice flat and carrying above the scattered conversations of the men still pilfering the bodies. "She looked through the earth and saw the raiders coming. Without her, the Mabayans would have stormed your growing city."

"Not enough of them to best us," Rif snarled.

"But enough to cause great damage and death." Goranth sucked in a deep breath, pulling the battlefield stench to the bottom of his lungs.

"Your leg needs tending," Rif observed as they left the remains for the carrion and rode toward Barbertown.

"I will see Esh're at the healer's," Goranth replied. "I will keep him company for a while and drink some of the old man's 'tea.'"

"And then—"

And when he was mended, Goranth intended to find a ship and leave this madness.

CHAPTER SEVEN

Earth abides the subtle stream
Or raging river, whitewater froth
Or ocean calm and horrors abeam
To the crushing deep's burial cloth
"Sonnet of the Black Sail Brotherhood"

Goranth's return to Barbertown was made tolerable by the fleet Mabayan pony, spoils of a sour battle. Too many animals had been killed and too many men slain in a fight that splashed life's blood on mother earth's soil, feeding her. All because of a dragon, an evil creature pent up in a stockade across the Mugunta. A fight that would not have happened had Rif not talked him into helping capture the beast.

The Northman growled and glared from beneath his matted black hair and heavy brows.

"What bothers you?" Rif asked from his own captured mount. The heavily muscled warriors looked comical on their diminutive rides, but their grim faces and the signs of battle forestalled any mirth from those able to walk. The ponies soldiered on, carrying the men to a place only one called home.

"They came to release the dragon." Goranth fixed Rif with a glare. "They'll be back."

"The Mabayans are too weak now. We have taken the heart out of them, my friend."

"Guard your tongue, Barber, lest you think we hold the upper hand. We need to stretch eyes and ears across this plain. Next time they come, we won't be so lucky."

"Aye, Northman, we do need to keep a weather eye out, but the enchantress can do that for us, and Kalida has taken a shine to you. The rewards there could be beyond avarice. Every man succumbs to her charms, but no man reaps the reward. No man but perhaps you."

"I've reaped no rewards but the blood and guts of this foul day." Goranth scowled at the plains before him and the first structures of Barbertown. "I have an arrow in my leg for my troubles. You owe me, Barber! I'll peel it from your hide if you don't pay."

Rif's twisted half-smile gave Goranth no confidence that he would ever receive the promised treasure. "Tomorrow. After you've visited your healer friend, see me at my home, a compound not far from Kalida's."

"I'll crawl there on one leg if I must."

"You have a fine Mabayan pony, Goranth! You shall ride throughout Barbertown on the spoils of war. We didn't start the war. They were coming for us, but aye, did we finish it!" Rif declared.

"They were coming for *you*," Goranth corrected. His hand sought the comfort of the makhaira's hilt. The weapon was new to him, but it felt better in his hand than his longsword's worn and trusty grip. "More than just a horse."

Rif looked sideways at the Northman. "I have caused you grief, and for that, I apologize. A bold adventure; only the bravest and most worthy could capture a dragon! Esh're came out none the worse for it all, and we did it, Goranth! We captured a dragon and bent it to our will."

"Varl bent it to hers. We would have had to beat it to death to bring it from the wood, and you know it."

"I do," Rif conceded. "But it worked out. We took the right team to the brink and came away with the demon."

"And riled mother earth and the dragon god. For what, Rif? You've lost more than thirty men. How will this fill my pouch with gold?"

"Breeding domesticated dragons. Imagine a town protected by one. Who wouldn't want that? They would pay all they had and promise more for such a thing as a dragon that follows their commands."

Goranth shook his head and parsed his next words carefully. "We are an ocean separate from having a dragon and selling its domesticated offspring. Such a thing will take many strong men's lifetimes. I'll thank you for your time and take my share now. Elsewise, I won't live long enough to see the glint of gold from this scheme."

"Have it your way, Goranth. You have been a good friend and done far more for me than I deserve. Meet me tomorrow, and I'll make it right by you." Rif guided his mount toward his men and rode among them to cheer them into a victory cry. Despite their pain, even the wounded joined the celebration. Rif wove through them, waving his arm in the air. Those walking jogged to catch up, shouting their support for the win against a superior enemy. The archers finally left the sanctity of the woods and ran to meet the others.

Riders slowed their ponies so Rif and his men could reenter the town as one. The ale would flow this evening; of that, there was no doubt. Refrains stolen from the Black Brotherhood would be sung heartily by the men and women of Barbertown.

Goranth approved. No matter the fight, one must always sing its victory.

"Sit still, you uncouth barbarian!" the healer shouted.

"Mind your tongue, old man. I pay for your healing skill, not your insults."

"Maybe you need to pay a jester to keep you out of trouble," the healer countered.

Goranth tried to stare the man down, but the healer focused on the manipulation of the barbed arrowhead using a narrow probe to help guide it out without cutting more skin. Goranth clenched his teeth and tried to slow his breathing.

"Do you have any ale?" Goranth demanded.

"Of course not! I'm a healer. Why would I poison my patients with that swill?"

"Because I like it." It made sense to the Northman. "And it would take the edge off your less-than-tender ministrations."

The healer pushed the probe in the direction of the barb while pulling. The probe stretched the skin without ripping it and the arrow's point came free. The healer studied it before tossing it into his trash bucket.

"Nasty business, that," he mumbled to himself. He kept pressure on the freshly leaking wound while digging through the shelf beside him, then pulled the cork from a bottle using his teeth and tipped the foul-smelling liquid over the wound. He pulled his hand away, and precious drops fell into the hole.

Goranth grunted as if a new arrow had plunged deep into his leg.

The healer pulled a needle from a pincushion, checked the thread, and started singing to himself. Goranth grumbled at the ease with which the man inflicted pain, but soon enough, the wound was closed and no longer bleeding. The pain had disappeared, and only numbness remained.

He tapped the Northman's leg after he finished, then moved to the counter, where he finished the final steps for brewing the healing tea.

"I've been waiting for that," Goranth mused.

"Most of my return patients do. This is my secret elixir. Even the powerful wizards of Tsentar have nothing to rival it. What they wouldn't give to know my formula!"

"You know what you're doing," Goranth grudgingly admitted. "You are always welcome in my camp."

"Seeing the wounds inflicted on your mighty thews, I'm not sure I want to be anywhere near your camp. Your lady friend already paid me. She knew you would end up in my chair."

"Kalida?" Goranth wondered, the thought tickling his inner man.

"Varlten're, Esh're's mate."

"She did, did she? I shall thank her for her foresight and kindness." Goranth breathed deeply of the healing draught before throwing it back, taking care not to spill a single drop. It felt like magic, but the healer wasn't a wizard or a worker of the mystical arts. No, he was only well-schooled in his craft. "You should take in apprentices, teach them. More blood will be shed in Barbertown because of that dragon. Much more blood.

You won't have enough hands to deal with the pain the people will suffer."

"I've heard. I'm still a young man. Maybe later, when I get old."

"A sense of humor, healer? Maybe I shall carry *you* with me when I ride out of here as my jester—to keep me out of trouble, of course." Goranth flexed his leg as he took a few measured steps. "Good. In a day's time, I'll be ready to fight. In a week's time, I'll be as good as new."

The healer held out his hand, and the Northman reached beyond and grabbed his wrist. The healer's fingers wrapped only halfway around Goranth's forearm.

"I respect you, healer. Don't take that lightly."

"I see from the scars on your body that it is probably best to be on your good side. Cuts and blows that would have killed lesser men and you walked away, the victor in terrible battles too numerous to count."

Goranth nodded and looked deep into the healer's eyes for a moment before striding out of the shop with barely a hint of a limp. He stopped by the pub next door for a tankard of ale, inhaled it in a single drink, slammed the cup on the bar, and walked out.

He had no place to stay, but he had a pony. He was surprised to find it waiting for him outside the healer's, still hitched to the post.

"Come, you old nag. Take me to Kalida's." He loosed the reins and took his place in the saddle. The pony trotted down the road to the central hub of the town and then took the road that paralleled the river. He stopped at the hovel of the earth priestess. She was on the porch waiting for him.

"You look ridiculous on that poor animal," she said with her arms crossed and a twinkle in her eye. When his feet hit the ground, his mind filled with her angelic voice. *Come inside and rest, Goranth the Mighty.*

"I've more than rest in mind." He wrapped the pony's reins around the post before Kalida's home and walked up to her, wrapping an arm around her narrow waist and pulling her to him.

"I know you do, Northman, but rest is what you need and what you'll have. I am not willing to be with you this night."

"And?" Goranth's lip twitched because she had been in his mind and knew the truth of his character.

"You take no woman against her will. You are a rare creature." She bowed her head. He let his hand drift across her backside before she slapped it away. "Maybe in time, but not today. There is work to do, and you must be ready."

"Kalida knows more of my life than I do. Counsel me, woman. What must I be ready for?"

"Another dragon hunt. More pain. More challenges to your life."

"Another dragon? How daft *is* the Barber!"

"He saved me years past, along with others. He brought me here and set me up because of my arcane gift for communing with the earth. I will always be loyal to Rif."

"Aye, he is my friend, too, despite his fool's quest. I will meet him tomorrow to be paid my share. After that, who knows? I was thinking of sailing away, but I may stay around if there's a reason…" He looked at her in a way he knew she was used to being looked at. This time, she appeared to welcome it, but it changed nothing.

"Rest. I'll put on a crock of a thick stew."

"No meat, I suspect."

"None, but it is good all the same." She winked at him. He chuckled and took a weak step, and his leg almost

CRAIG MARTELLE & JEAN RABE

collapsed beneath him. Kalida draped his arm over her shoulder.

"Never have I had a better crutch."

She guided him inside. "You smell of cheap ale."

Goranth bounced away on one leg, wincing with each impact as the foot of the injured leg tapped the floor. "It's like we're already married!"

It was Kalida's turn to laugh. "Sit. I'll bring you a bowl and ladle for that endless vortex of a maw you call a mouth."

Goranth relaxed on a couch covered in woven fabric as soft as Mohiriyan sheep's hair. He grumbled. "You are right, damnable woman. There will be more pain. It is the foundation on which my life is built."

Kalida returned carrying a normal-sized bowl with a normal-sized spoon. "Who were you talking to?"

"No one but me, lass. I needed an expert's counsel."

She sat across from him as he took the bowl and sniffed. It was heavy with herbs and thick with vegetables and a brown broth he swore was gravy. He took a careful bite, eating like a cultured city dweller.

Her eyes continued to twinkle as she watched despite the dimness of her hovel. "You intrigue me, Northman. You are one with the earth while eschewing its rewards."

"I've plenty of rewards."

"You have nothing but your sword and now a new sword and the pony outside. Both of which you'll probably lose before the week's end. Rif will pay you tomorrow? How long will you keep that?"

"Week's end?" Goranth was in no mood to discuss how quickly he lost his hard-earned treasure.

"Probably so, but your real treasure is something that no one can take from you." She didn't elaborate. Goranth continued to eat, and once finished, he smacked his lips and sighed.

"As much as I hate to say it, you were right. Your stew was damnably good."

"Why would you hate to say it?"

"I hate being wrong. In my life, being wrong will get me killed."

"But not being wrong with me, Goranth. Relax and open your mind."

His eyelids fluttered as he fought the sleep that sought to take him away from the pleasant moment. She took the bowl from his fingers before he dropped it. Fury rose within him, but the calmness without soothed him. Kalida sat next to him. Through the earth, she whispered to him, *Sleep, my champion. Tomorrow you shall see what is below and I will show you what is above. Your path is charted, whether you choose to follow or not. Your agreement is unnecessary. You will do as has been destined. Sleep, my champion, and dream of me.*

Kalida walked with Goranth to Rif's compound, not far from her hovel. Unlike her home, his was massive, with stone walls surrounding it and men patrolling the perimeter. Goranth pulled Kalida to him. "I feel like a new man," he admitted. "That healer's draught is a sorcerer's brew, to be sure."

"Go and get your due, Northman." She held her finger to his lips to keep him from trying to kiss her. He chuckled and kissed her fingers instead.

"You gave my pony away."

"It seemed the right thing to do, but if you need it back, I think you'll be able to borrow it."

He patted her backside before she walked away. "You

make me want to swear off Borezhyan dancing girls, woman."

"And make an honest man of you? I'm not sure that's possible," she replied over her shoulder, waving indiscriminately.

The guards had opened the gates and were waiting. A diminutive man met him when he strode through. "I shall take you to the prefect."

"The prefect? The Barber has a title. I should have figured."

The aide said nothing more as he conducted Goranth through the outer halls to the inner chambers, where they found Rif pacing.

When the aide closed the door behind him, Rif faced the Northman. "The dark days are behind us, my friend," the Barber said mysteriously. He gestured with his head for Goranth to follow, and they went through a door hidden behind a tapestry. The room beyond looked to have no other exits. Coals glowed in a brazier on a stone dais, and torches burned in sconces on the walls.

"What dark magic are you playing with, Barber?"

"None." Rif shrugged innocently. He braced himself and pushed on the dais. His muscles bulged and the stone began to move, but it didn't scrape like stone on stone. Cleverly hidden rollers, well-oiled, made it nearly effortless once the stone was moving. Beneath, well-used stone steps led downward.

"More games? I'll not take a step down before I know what you're up to."

"It's where my wealth is located. Don't make this a fight between us because I know I would lose. I will show you my secret for your share, your silence, and your *loyalty*."

He took one of the torches and Goranth took the other. Rif led the way. The Northman followed, torch held in front of him while he kept his fingers wrapped around the hilt of his precious makhaira. Skulls were set into the wall every five steps, some human, some monstrous, all of them with bits of flesh. They descended through easily a hundred paces a rough-hewn passage before they hit the bottom, where cool air sought escape up the steps and into Rif's home.

"What is this place?" Goranth asked.

"From a time long before we walked mother earth. Two mates and I found the entrance while digging the foundation for my home. I covered it back then with a stone and built the house around it." He pointed down a side corridor. "These passages go for as long as a torch will burn and then some."

"You built your house on ruins, didn't you?"

"You know me well, Northman. I did. Out with the old and in with the new. Little did I know the secret hidden below. We would not have found it had we not used stone from the ruins for my palace."

"Prefect?"

"Just something to keep the homeless away. A title gives the appearance of power. The real power is in the loyalty of my men and in what lies down here."

"I smell death," Goranth stated matter-of-factly. He removed his new sword from his belt and held it before him. He couldn't be sure, but he thought the blade glowed.

"It is where we bury our dead. Yesterday, while you were tending your wounds and receiving Kalida's kindness, we buried the thirty souls we lost in our fight with the Mabayans. We do it because some of my men believe there is magic down here and the dead shall rise again."

"They won't." Goranth wasn't sure what to think.

"No." Rif smiled and nodded. "There's no magic down here, just a history we will never know."

"Your mates?"

"Alas, they have not survived. They are buried here as well. There is a shaft down which we send the bodies after a few kind words of prayer to Vujo or the dragon god or whoever the dead prayed to."

Goranth's eyes darted back and forth with the torches' flickers, seeking the horrors he knew dwelled in the shadows. The tomblike feeling made his hair stand on end, but he wouldn't flinch. Rif was leading him somewhere. Maybe into a trap. Maybe worse.

Rift hadn't gone far when he turned into a side chamber. "Your reward is in here, Goranth."

"My loyalty only goes so far, Rif. This smells like a trap. It looks like a trap. It *feels* like a trap."

Rif stepped back into the corridor. He tossed the torch into the room before lacing the fingers of both hands together and putting them on top of his head. "Put your sword to my throat and we shall go in together."

"Don't take this the wrong way, but I *am* going to put my dagger to your throat. Don't do anything that will make me draw its keen edge through your flesh."

"I have no intention of dying today. And you won't either. There is no one down here but us."

Goranth tucked the makhaira into his belt and drew his dagger. He thrust it between the gap in Rif's arm and his head before angling it across his throat.

"I'm walking forward now. Please keep up and watch your step. I'll not be on the wrong end of your clumsiness."

Inside the chamber, Rif's burning torch lay on the floor, revealing piles of gold, silver, and gemstones. A king's ransom stared back at the Northman. He pulled Rif to the side to keep his back to the wall.

"With this treasure, why have you not paid your debts?"

"It's not you, Goranth. We are here because I owe you and mean to pay. The other debts? Well, too often, aggressive men die. Better the gold stay here than getting spread among murderers and thieves."

"Like us?" Goranth removed his blade from Rif's throat. The Barber slowly lowered his arms and stooped to pick up his torch. He dug into the treasure pile, looking at a handful of gold coins.

"Take what you need for now, and when you decide to leave Barbertown, you can take as much as you can carry. My word to you, Goranth, as a friend and business partner."

Goranth stepped close. His dark eyes bored deep into Rif's soul. "You are hiding something. Tell me."

"Has Kalida told you she found another dragon? We leave tomorrow to fetch it."

"She has, and you say 'fetch it' like it is a loose dog. It's a dragonette, hopefully smaller than LeReon, the creature with a name. I hope Varl is coming. I've no patience to learn the dragon's tongue, but it seems she is already schooled in its language. Let her talk the thing into coming with us before it shreds and burns our flesh."

"So, you *are* joining me again." Rif gave a half-smile.

Goranth leaned sideways to fill his pouches with whatever he wrapped his fingers around—gold, silver, gems, and jewelry. He held a necklace toward Rif and kept one eye on the Barber while examining it.

"Kalida is not one to be swayed with baubles."

"But I am, and this would look fine adorning the tender skin of her graceful neck and plunging into the space between those perfect breasts. Maybe this is for me to look at on her."

"My barbarian friend is smitten by one who communes

with the earth! She'll be with us, too, in mind but not body. This time, it shall be different. Come now, let us drink to our victories and our lives. On the morrow, we'll be headed for the wilds, the forest, to pluck a friend for LeReon."

CHAPTER EIGHT

Wistful throes under bonnet black
Terrible foes storming attack
Winsome ladies and worthy spoils
Fail not, raise the fire, water boils
"Sonnet of the Black Sail Brotherhood"

It must have rained here recently, Goranth thought, since the ground was springy and the smell of loam and bright lichen heady. There were wildflowers thick amid the ferns, their scent reminding him of Kalida. He wondered if the promise of Rif's gold had lured him on this second dragon-hunt, or if the notion of spending time with the priestess when they returned to Barbertown was responsible for drawing him deeper into Rif's scheme. It had been years since he'd dwelled on a woman.

At the deep river docks, a two-master named *Mermaid's Tears* had been set to sail to the Hawk Islands, which Goranth had never wholly explored during his time with the Black Sail Brotherhood. He thought a stop there might be intriguing and less dangerous than pursuing another dragon, and yet he was here instead of standing on the forecastle. The image of the priestess hung in the back of his mind. Maybe Kalida was dangerous, too.

Goranth took the rear and held his makhaira in his right hand. The pommel was warm and fit his grip so perfectly, it was as if the weapon had been crafted for him. This section of the forest was dense. He couldn't see Rif cutting the trail, but his keen ears heard the Barber, who was making no attempt at stealth. Varlten're directly followed, then a musclebound youth named Jaeg who struggled to carry a great pack filled with long coils of rope. Goranth had a length of rope, too; Varl had toted it, but he had taken it from her about a league into the journey, and she hadn't objected.

Kalida had divined the dragonette's location by sending her sight through the earth. "To the northeast," she'd said. "In the shadow of the mountains beneath the formation of the Three Sisters. The dragonette lives there and feasts on unfortunate goats in the foothills." She'd drawn a map and circled the area with a long, delicate finger. Goranth pictured her manicured nails and smooth skin and recalled the musical lilt in her voice.

He remembered asking her why she would help them find another dragon when she seemed none too fond of the first mewling its displeasure in Rif's stockade.

The earth mother is not pleased with the dragon god and her creatures for coming down from the mountains. We are but instruments of retribution. That is why I help, Goranth, but I help you. Rif benefits from your link to me.

"Madness," he whispered too softly for the others to hear. Being besotted with a *woman*—an enchantress, no less—was true madness and could lead to nothing good.

Had she cast some spell on him? Or was this infatuation of his own making?

Madness. Yet he was here and not sailing to the Hawk Islands.

He felt her inside his head, a presence hovering like a waking dream. She was connected to all of them through the ground, a tether to check their progress and guide them. How deep inside was she? Could she pick through his thoughts, see his deepest secrets? Goranth growled at the invasion. Did she know he thought of her?

He fixated on the sounds of the woods, forcing his focus back to the mission. The breeze was strong this morning, and when it gusted, it made the thin branches higher up *shush* and clack. Water droplets struck his broad shoulders and dimpled on his arms, the wind freeing the remnants of the earlier rain that had collected in the leaves. Birdsong was plentiful. He picked out the cry of a hawk and the twitter of small things, red and yellow parrots that fluttered amid a world bathed in green. Goranth almost allowed himself to enjoy the day and the setting. *Almost.* There was a young dragon to consider, and catching it would likely bring pain.

Jaeg was talking to Varlten're. Goranth had missed some of it, caught up in the birds and his brooding.

"When will your baby come?" the youth asked.

"When it is ready," came a terse reply.

Goranth faintly heard Rif chuckle.

"Do you worry about trying to catch a dragon in your condition?" the youth persisted.

Rif chuckled louder, and Varl did not answer.

"She's tough," Goranth offered. "Her babe will come out ready to fight."

"But isn't she worried that—"

"Varl worries about little. But you, Jaeg, you should worry about insulting her," Goranth warned.

The youth quieted, and they continued their march through the woods. Goranth still sensed the presence of Kalida, and he stepped on the stump of a fallen tree to test a theory, then reached up and grabbed a thick branch, tugging himself up despite the weight of the rope he carried. He climbed higher. Perched above the earth, he watched Varl and Jaeg verbally sparring as they walked, catching a few words and finding their conversation amusing but uninteresting. Then they were beyond his hearing.

He balanced there as his companions moved farther away, the birdsong continuing, the breeze rattling the thin branches and sending more captured rain down. He felt Kalida's presence dissipate. The earth enchantress needed the connection of the ground, he suspected, to work her art and insinuate herself into his mind. A dozen feet above the soil in this tree, the tendrils of her thoughts could not weave into his. Goranth would sleep in a tree tonight if he had to for privacy. She did not need to know he was obsessed with her.

After dropping down, he hurried to catch up with his companions, noticing that the birds had stopped singing. He doubted he'd spooked them.

But something had.

The hairs quivered on the back of his neck. Was the dragon close? They were two days from the spot Kalida had indicated on the map. Perhaps a different predator was nearby. He'd not looked for tracks or spoor along this trail, and he suspected Rif hadn't either. A wolf maybe, or a big cat, or a large monkey that vexed the parrots.

Ahead, Jaeg stumbled under the heavy pack but managed to right himself. *A cart or a mule would have been more useful than the youth,* Goranth thought. If this were to become a frequent endeavor, hunting dragons, he'd demand Rif bring pack animals to tote the supplies. They could double as dragon bait.

Varlten're had stopped and was facing Jaeg, hands on her hips, eyes narrowed. Goranth drew to within a few yards, expecting her to berate the youth for some affront.

"The silence," she said, looking past Jaeg at the Northman. She kept her voice low and leaned on her staff.

"I hear the wind." This from Jaeg, who clearly did not understand her concern. "It's not that quiet. The branches—"

"Aye," Goranth replied to Varl. "Something stalks us."

"*Follows,* not stalks." She stuck out her lower lip. "I can sense the difference. You and Rif fought the Mabayans yesterday, and he said some fled. Narlun might have sentries in these woods. Maybe some Mabayans are spying upon us. Rif said they wanted the dragon."

It didn't have that feel to Goranth, so he shook his head. "No, Varl. Not spies. I think—"

She cut him off. "You don't think often enough, Northman, and when you do think, it's about gold or ale or women. Kalida. You think about her, I can tell. You think about simple things. You think—"

"I think something is stalking us."

Jaeg opened his mouth to interject his nonsense but thought better of it and started after Rif, hoisting the oversized pack to his other shoulder.

"Rif is up there," Varl gestured behind her, "somewhere. He's not stopping. Catch up to him, Goranth, like Jaeg is doing. Catch up and tell him. I'll lag behind. I'll lose myself in the bushes and see if there are spies. See how many Mabayans ghost us." A pause. "Or see if it is your noisome tread responsible for spooking the birds and the monkeys."

He knew she was faster and stealthier than him and could close the distance when she'd settled her curiosity, but she'd be vulnerable alone. In the end, Goranth decided not to argue, a useless waste of breath; he never could win a disagreement with her.

"Suit yourself, Varl, but be wary of man *or* beast."

She shook her staff defiantly and stepped off the narrow game trail they'd been following. In a heartbeat, she disappeared into the undergrowth with not a wisp of movement to mark her passage.

"Women," he muttered. Goranth barely saw Jaeg's pack since the foliage was even thicker ahead and spilled over the path. He felt for Kalida's presence but did not detect it. He'd apparently lost the connection when he went into that tree. "Women." Goranth liked women; he just didn't understand them very well.

The silence of the birds still festered, and he'd heard no monkeys chittering, no movement of anything passing through the underbrush. He doubted there were Mabayan spies since Rif's force had reduced their numbers severely. If anything, the Mabayans were licking their wounds and plotting to regroup. But a dragon? A dragon could hush the forest. Maybe Kalida was wrong and the dragon was closer, not beneath the Three Sisters. Wouldn't she sense it, though, and alert Rif?

Perhaps he shouldn't have severed the connection with the enchantress.

Perhaps he was on this damnable dragon hunt because of her and he needed to think about something else.

Goranth thought about the treasure again, the piles of gold, silver, and gems in the cavern Rif had led him to and promised him a share of—more wealth than the Northman had ever seen in one place. Likely it was the treasure that had lured him after a dragon.

Regardless of the motivation, at the bottom was lunacy.

"Madness," he repeated.

"Cat!" came the shrill cry from behind. "Rope!"

Goranth whirled and dropped his length of rope, then raced back down the path, leading with the makhaira and drawing his sword with his left hand. He heard a heavy thud behind him and feet pounding, then Rif shouted, "Catch it! Don't kill it!"

Goranth charged around a curve, ducked a low-hanging kapok branch, and skidded to a stop. Roughly twenty feet ahead, Varlten're stood on the path, her staff leveled in front of her, dancing with a massive jaguar in the foliage. Goranth took a step forward as he heard Jaeg stop behind him, panting. More heavy footfalls signaled Rif's arrival.

"Careful, Varl," Goranth cautioned.

"This is *my* prize," she said, stabbing forward as the creature led with a paw the size of a rock melon.

It snarled and hissed, and through the ferns, Goranth saw its head, lips curling back displaying ivory teeth smeared with blood. The beautiful creature had an unusual black coat spotted in places with white, giving the appearance that it had stepped through cobwebs. It was well over six feet from nose to the base of its tail, muscles quivering, ribs showing like it hadn't eaten well lately. It probably intended for Varl to fill its belly.

Goranth took another step and then another, gripping his weapons' pommels tighter as Rif pounded up behind him.

"Don't kill it, Varl. We can—"

"I damn well don't intend to kill it," she spat. "Look at the coat. It's remarkable."

"Someone would pay well for a beast like that," Rif continued.

"Fools," Goranth said. "Chase it off and—"

"Bring a rope," Varlten're ordered. "Now!"

"I dropped it," Jaeg said. "Back there. My bag of ropes."

Out of the corner of his eye, Goranth saw Jaeg tug a mace from his belt loop.

"Goranth, my rope!" Varl shouted. She stepped back when the cat lunged and poked at it to bat away a paw. Goranth spotted blood streaming down her leg; the cat had wounded her.

"Enough!" The Northman stomped forward, leading with his sword, drawing the makhaira back as if to swing. "Heyah! Heyah!" Jaguars didn't typically hunt people; none of the big cats did to the Northman's thinking. A lone traveler like Varl it might pursue, but not men in a group. "Heyah! Follow me, Jaeg, Rif!" Time to scare it away and tend to Varl's injury. "Heyah! Heyah!"

"No! It's mine! A rope!" Varl cried.

"Don't kill it," Rif urged.

Goranth nudged Varl aside, then swung at the jaguar and sliced the air a hair's breadth above the great cat's wide head. "Heyah! Scat!"

"A rope!" Varl argued. "Don't hurt it!"

"Don't kill it," Rif demanded. Goranth saw that the Barber had a rope and was working it into a loop.

"I dropped your rope," Goranth said as he struck a paw away. "Move, Varl. Don't crowd me. Get gone! I'll—"

"Do nothing," Rif finished. The Barber's newly fashioned lasso swirled while he widened the loop even as Goranth ignored him and swung again, connecting with the jaguar and slicing into its foreleg. The cat screamed.

"No!" Rif howled.

The jaguar snarled and showed no inclination of fleeing, swiping with its injured leg, rising on its hindquarters, and clawing at Goranth, who barely dodged its wicked-looking talons. The great cat leapt as Rif tried to lasso it and Goranth swung once more, cleaving into its shoulder as it cleared the ferns and pounced on the Northman, driving him down. The back of Goranth's head slammed into the earth. In that instant, he felt Kalida again.

The jaguar's maw opened, and foamy spittle fell on Goranth's chest. Its breath was hot and smelled of fetid things. The Northman brought the makhaira up and sliced its neck, the blade easily parting the thick flesh. Rif managed to drop the loop around its head and pulled, creating a leash and yanking the injured jaguar off Goranth.

The Northman vaulted up, edged Varl aside again, and crouched, blades in both hands, watching the great cat gyrate wildly in an effort to break free. It thrashed on the side of the path, snapping at the rope and breaking the strands.

Jaeg darted in and thumped the jaguar in the side, which only made it angrier. It was a blur of black and white amid the greenery, flashing eyes wide and unblinking and teeth bared, foam flecking its tongue and lips and bubbling like soap lather.

"It's skinny," Jaeg said as he thumped it again and jumped back. "Hungry."

It looked like Rif was putting all his effort into holding onto the rope. Goranth saw the Barber's muscles bunch and recalled how he'd looked when they sailed. Rif was still a formidable figure and reasonably strong, but he'd lost some muscle in his city years, the Northman realized. The life of a businessman had softened his old friend.

"You've damaged the pelt," Rif growled. "It'll heal, but—"

"You can't mean to catch this like you did the dragon,"

Goranth shot back. A glance at Varl showed the outside of her right leg had ribbons of blood flowing down it.

"I can!"

"The Barber's menagerie, eh? Come see the dangerous animals!"

"It is worth—"

"Nothing!" Goranth spat. "It's worth nothing." *And you do not need more wealth, Barber.* The mounds of gold and silver coins and piles of gems twinkled in the Northman's memory. "I'll kill it!"

"No!" Rif and Varl shouted in one voice.

The jaguar forced the issue when its jaws snapped the rope and it sprang at Rif, talons raking the air and not finding skin because Goranth pushed his friend away and drove his makhaira down, severing its neck.

The jaguar fell, twitching as if it didn't realize it was dead. Finally it stilled, and Jaeg and Rif prodded it with their booted feet. Varl stood back and glared at Goranth.

"I shouldn't have called for you," she hissed. "I could've managed the cat. I just needed rope. I'd given you my damn rope." She dug her foot into the ground and made a twisting motion. "By Vujo's fist, I could've caught it, sold it, and—"

She would have sold it to gain coin because she didn't know about the treasure beneath Rif's abode, Goranth thought. If she knew, she'd be wearing some of the baubles and might not be part of this hunt.

"We're after a dragon," Goranth said. "Not a starving cat."

Rif knelt next to it and ran a hand over its sleek fur. "Kalida tells me she did not sense this animal. She was focused on the path ahead of us, and the cat came up too quick."

"Had to be starving to go after Varl," Goranth

pronounced. He wiped the makhaira's blade off in the ferns, sheathed it, and turned to Varlten're. "You're hurt, and we need to dress your leg."

"I can tend it myself."

"No," Rif said, rising. He reached into his pack, where he carried a second shirt. "We're fixing you and moving on after the dragon." He paused. "Moving on after we skin what we can of the cat and feast on its meat. There is no sense in wasting it."

She continued to glower at them but sat on the fallen log Rif indicated.

"Jaeg? Some water."

The youth produced his skin and handed it over, and Goranth watched Rif almost tenderly minister to the woman warrior.

"Maybe we should go back to Barbertown," Rif said, his voice not hiding his disappointment. "Get you to the healer's, pick up another man or two."

"It would take three to replace her," Goranth whispered.

"I can walk. I can fight." She reached down, pulled up a clump of moss, and rubbed it on her wound. The gouges looked deep. Rif poured more water over it. "Just get it to stop bleeding. I'm not going home. I'm after the dragon with you."

Rif tore his shirt and wrapped it around her leg, tying off a strip and adding two more. "Have it your way," he said. "But if it bothers you—"

"It won't."

"—tell us and we'll come this way another day. Kalida says the dragonette lives in the foothills. It will be there when we return and—"

Varlten're stood and grabbed up her staff. "If you're going to skin the thing, do it quick, Rif. We've a friend to find for LeReon."

There was a small clearing north along the path, and they stopped there a few hours later. They stretched the hide across rib bones Jaeg had harvested and set it between the trunks of two strangler figs. "We'll come back for it on our return trip," Jaeg said. "Then take it to the tanner's."

If we come back this way, Goranth thought. "So, no Mabayan spies," he said to Varl. "The cat stalked us."

She raised her lip and moved close to the fire they'd built. A haunch of the cat turned on a crude spit, the meat charring. "When will that be ready?"

"A while," Rif said. He held the jaguar's head between his hands, staring into its eyes. "I wonder if I can do something with this. Give it to the tanner, see if he can fashion a trophy to hang on the wall."

Goranth looked away, finding the moss-coated trunk of a cedar more interesting. The trees were tall here as if they'd raced from the ground to the sky, greedily trying to be the first one to capture the most sunshine and rain. How old were these woods? Ancient, likely. And how many dragons lived in them and the mountains that were the continent's spine? Kalida had said dragons were scarce creatures, rare and precious. Again he wondered if he should be on his way to the Hawk Islands. Leave the dragons be.

"Pull out its teeth," Varl suggested to Rif. "Have them strung into a necklace. Leave the head for the carrion."

"Aye, now that's an idea," Rif returned.

Goranth thought of the necklaces in Rif's treasure horde and pictured the one with beautiful stones he'd selected for Kalida. He'd not yet given it to her; it was in a pouch at his side, nestled amid a handful of gold coins. He imagined what it would look like draped around her shapely neck, the glittering fob hanging down where his gaze would rest.

"Madness," he whispered, pacing in front of the stretched skin and batting away the flies that had gathered. Gnats coated his skin, and he brushed them away. "I'm going for a walk," he said. "Just down the trail."

"The cat will be ready soon," Jaeg said. "If you leave—"

"I'm not hungry," Goranth lied.

"Well, I'm starving," Varlten're said. "Give me a slab of that now." He watched her rub the bandage on her leg and noted the pink where blood had seeped through.

Rif leaned forward with his knife and started to slice the charred flesh. "Be back before the sun sets," he told Goranth. "We don't need to be searching for you in the dark, what with—"

"Aye," the Northman replied. "I'll be back before the sun thinks about kissing the horizon."

He left the fire and felt Kalida floating in his head, her flashing eyes superimposing themselves on the wide eyes of the cat he'd slain. He pulled the scents of the forest to the bottom of his lungs, picking through lichen and loam and rotting wood to find the wildflowers that had reminded him of the enchantress. He knew she "talked" to Rif through the earth, but she'd made no attempt to do that with him. Maybe she knew he valued privacy. Maybe she had nothing to say.

When Goranth returned to their camp, he saw Rif and Jaeg sitting cross-legged by the fire, hands on their bellies, chins on their chests. Varlten're was farther away on her hands and knees, retching.

What remained of the cat's haunch was in the flames, burning.

"The meat is bad," Rif said.

Goranth's stomach rumbled and he reached for his pack, then sat back from them and pulling out a hunk of smoked cheese he'd purchased before leaving town. He bit into it, chewing slowly and meeting Rif's pained stare.

"I'll take first watch," Goranth said. "Try to get some sleep."

Varl retched again. Her eyes aimed daggers at him.

"Or perhaps I'll sleep first," Goranth corrected. "You three look too miserable to nod off. Try to be quiet, eh? We've a long way to travel tomorrow, and I don't want my dreams interrupted." He suspected Kalida would figure into them.

CHAPTER NINE

The main masts crack and sway
The seas churn and froth
Lightning turns night to day
Terror, the sea witches wroth
"Sonnet of the Black Sail Brotherhood"

Goranth woke at the poke of the irascible Varl's staff. "Get up and take the watch. I have savaged the beast within and will find my rest now." She crawled beneath a bush, tossing a thin blanket over her as she curled up.

The Northman rose and listened before anything else. The forest whispered in hushed tones, punctuated by the light buzz of an insect or the woosh of a night wing. The slow breathing of his comrades filled the remaining space, bringing calm to the dark of night.

He stepped lightly into the trees, waiting and watching, then moving anew, changing his position to foil unseen watchers and presenting himself a fresh view with each new post. He pressed his back against the trees to blend in. Goranth's eyes became one with the shadows. Colors failed him, but the shapes and the trees were clear. Through the canopy, random stars blessed the black above.

Goranth... A voice tickled his mind, the one who had occupied too many of his recent thoughts but not enough of his dreams. Kalida hadn't come to him there, only the fury of the dragon and the oppression of an unbridled night.

The sultry voice taunted him again. *Goranth. The dragon awaits.*

"Woman!" he hissed. "The dragon knows we're coming? Is it a trap we walk into?"

No. The way ahead is clear. The dragonette has just fed. It will be slow if you hurry.

Goranth held a finger to his head and tried to reply without speaking aloud. *Did you see the jaguar? It caught us unaware and injured Varl.*

No. As you discovered, the earth hides creatures who travel through the trees. Even if I had been looking behind you, I would not have known. I will look around you in all ways from now on since I wish you to return. I rather enjoy your company. Worry not about the jaguar.

Aye, he grumbled in his mind. *And me. The jaguar's pelt is a thing of beauty. It shall grace the wall of a rich man's house. I took no joy in killing the beast, but it was half-starved and set on Varl as its next meal.*

A soft touch found Goranth's shoulder. He thought it was in his mind, Kalida's gentle hand pulling him to her, but no. A glance told him a tree lizard sought purchase. He pursed his lips and blew on it until it returned to the safety of the rugged bark of the forest's stately elder. Goranth moved on.

Worry not, Kalida pressed. *Mother earth accepts the sacrifice. Prey or predator. It is the circle of life in which you live.*

Goranth shared his concern. *Varl appears to have gained a fever and nasty disposition from the beast's scratch and bite.*

A nasty disposition, my large friend? She is with child. Have patience. A fever? That isn't how it should be. Watch for muscle weakness or if she lingers, confused. If she complains about tingling, you'll need to bring her back to Barbertown as soon as possible.

Easier said than done. That one is stubborn. But I'll watch and do what I can. Goranth moved to the next tree as silently as ice formed on the scrub of his homeland.

Continue east. The dragonette is there. There was a pause. *I miss your company, Goranth.*

Don't tease me, woman. I've enough of you in my mind as it is. If we're to survive this fool's quest, I need to keep my wits about me.

I'll make it worth your while to come back to Barbertown, with or without a dragonette in tow. I care not about Rif's fanciful zoo since it will surely fail. He will never bend dragons to his will. They have millennia of freedom competing with easy meals and the chains within a stockade.

Kalida! I'll crawl through the crushed shells of the Hawk Islands' outer banks to get back to Barbertown. I have a gift for you, the treasure of queens. Goranth pictured the jeweled necklace in his pouch and found his back against another massive hardwood. He listened to the forest quiet. He smelled the wildflowers Kalida used to adorn her hair. He reached into the darkness to touch her.

How easily you part with your treasure, Goranth. You value relationships above all else. That is where you find your greatest wealth. Hold those dear, my lover, and come home to me. There is a creature in the treetops I cannot see, but through the eyes of a forest runner, I know it is there. It waits for you to the east. Be ready.

Goranth tried to come up with the right words, but Kalida had stepped back from his mind. She was still there but no longer talking or listening.

The Northman circled the camp and headed east on the trail they would travel at first light. He stepped and observed, looking for movements, his sword held high in his left hand and the makhaira in his right. It would be best to deal with any threat now rather than be surprised later.

Varl's foul humor and quickness to argue along with Jaeg's youth and Rif's disdain for stealth would leave them vulnerable, no matter how hard Goranth pressed his comrades to be wary.

After a hundred paces from the camp, Goranth found refuge under a sparse bush. Through it, he could see into the treetops all around. He waited and watched.

And kept waiting until the first vestiges of the new day brought deep coolness. He was none the wiser about Kalida's warning, and it left him in a foul mood. He was not looking forward to nudging Varlten're awake to be on the receiving end of her addled glare and sharp tongue.

Under the cover of the coming day, he stalked back to the camp, casting furtive glances into the canopy.

Soft snores and slow breathing greeted him.

He made himself comfortable, chewing on a blade of sweetgrass while he waited for the sun's rays to shine from beneath the horizon to dim the stars. The sky transitioned from pitch-black to dark blue, and the stars winked out one by one.

Goranth nudged one after another with his toe until the other three were awake. They went about the business of rolling their blankets and repacking their gear.

"Slept like a baby," Rif said softly. "I never stood watch. Did you skip me?"

"Varl woke me and I had slept my fill, so I stayed up. I had a good conversation with Kalida. Something new has found us and is waiting in the treetops as we head east."

"Treetops? How could she see that?" Rif wondered while he removed a piece of hardtack and dark sausage from his pack. He offered Goranth a small piece. The Northman accepted it readily.

"She saw through the eyes of a runner. Stay sharp, Rif!"

"I'll keep my eyes keen. You can guarantee that. We don't need any miscreants to tell the world of our presence."

Goranth slapped Rif on the back. "You'll do enough of that for all of us with your lumbering and ripping trees out by their roots."

"Ha!" Rif chuckled. "I'm blazing the trail to make it easier on my fellow travelers so you can conserve your strength. Ripping trees out by their roots! Your jest is welcome this early morn, but I'm still not over the loss of that jaguar. I shall forgive you in time for killing it, Northman, but not yet."

"Keep that bilge to yourself, Rif. We had nothing to feed the starving beast. It would have been us or the jaguar in the end. Better it not injure anyone else." Goranth glanced at Varl. She winced as she tightened her pack's strap, favoring her injured leg. She raised her pack to her knees before it fell from numb fingers. She caught Goranth watching and snarled at him before redoubling her efforts and slinging it over her shoulder.

Goranth shook his head. "We should go back, Rif. Now."

"I worry about Varl, too. But the dragon is close, Goranth. One more day."

"Rif—" Goranth gestured with his head toward Varlten're. Rif shrugged.

"I saw that," she barked. "I'm taking point." She started to walk off, but Goranth was faster and grasped her arm tightly. She glared to the point of fury.

"Kalida says something is watching us from the trees. Take care." He let go, knowing her mind was made up. She nodded brusquely and forced her way through the nearest bushes. Once the lightest foot of them all, she lumbered ahead no more quietly than Rif.

"You need not worry about me. It is none of your concern. I'll take care of it from here," she called over her shoulder.

"Aye, Varl. You lead the charge." Goranth's words were laced with acid. He cared for the woman, who was a friend, and the unborn child, the fruit of her marriage to another friend. His feeling of helplessness grated on his soul. He tried to get behind her, but Rif jumped in the way.

"I'll watch. She's got an itch with you, Northman, that you dare not let her scratch."

Goranth pushed Jaeg into line behind Rif.

"Is there something ahead? Let me fight it. I'm ready."

Goranth snorted. "You will have plenty to fight soon enough. Save your strength and keep up."

The young man grumbled but hurried his pace to close with the Barber.

Goranth stayed back and watched for movement in the canopy as the group passed beneath. Varl powered forward far faster than Goranth expected with her limp and the weakness Kalida had warned him might come from the bite.

Varl maintained her grueling pace. Jaeg had his head down, huffing and puffing for air, but he kept up, forcing his way through the underbrush. *A mule would have been better,* Goranth repeated his thought. Jaeg would be in no shape to fight if they found themselves on the wrong end of a bitter enemy.

Or the dragon, for what it was worth. They needed Varl whole. Maybe she wasn't sick with what Kalida feared. With the sun high in the sky, Rif called for a halt, drawing Varl's ire, but he was having none of it. "I said we break."

She took two more steps forward before turning woodenly and struggling to sit on a stump next to the Barber.

Goranth dug into his pack for more of the cheese, hardtack, and a dried fruit loaf Kalida had given him. He'd wanted to save it for longer, but the effort to move silently through the woods threatened to sap his strength. Goranth took small bites to better enjoy the flavor and think kind thoughts of the one who waited for him, but his eyes never left the breaks in the canopy overhead.

A shadow crossed. Goranth stuffed the remainder of his meal into his mouth and stood. He held a finger to his lips before blending into the underbrush, stalking the creature to confirm his suspicions.

A praevo-pavor, a flying terror. It hunted alone but lived in a pack. If they killed it, the pack might hunt them down. *We must make it fear us,* Goranth thought.

As he stalked, he cut a sapling and shaved it with the keen edge of the makhaira to form a spear. A second sapling became another. He tucked the makhaira into his belt and gauged the heft and balance of his new weapons. With a spear in each hand, he continued away from the lunch camp.

The shadow returned. It was circling. He stooped and crouch-ran to the tallest tree and started to climb. He slowed when exposed to the sky and hurried his pace when hidden by the leaves of thick branches.

He made it into the canopy with a clear view of the sky, bound himself firmly to the trunk, and waited. The circling tightened.

"Die, beast!" Goranth shouted as he launched the first spear. It wobbled as it flew and quickly lost speed, but the second spear had a knot toward the sharpened end, giving it better balance. He launched it before the first spear passed the back-winging creature. The second spear raced true, poking a clean hole through a wing's membrane. The terror opened its long-fanged mouth and screamed a horrible cry. Eyes glowed red before it turned and flew north, away from Goranth and the others.

Away from where Kalida said the dragon lived.

He waited until he could no longer see it before climbing down. Rif and the others were waiting for him.

"Is that what I think it was?" Rif asked.

Goranth smiled. "Barber, if I knew what you were thinking, I'd probably find myself running from here as fast as these sandaled feet would carry me." Rif nodded. "A praevo-pavor, a flying terror. It has gone and won't be back if it wishes to live."

Varl grunted and brushed past them to continue her relentless push to the mountains. Goranth noted that her skin had taken on a gray tinge since the morning. She was not well.

"Not far now," Goranth told her. Rif fell in behind, then Jaeg. Goranth allowed his dark mood to cover him like a warm blanket. Varl paused, and Goranth took over. He grabbed Rif to get his attention. "Help her."

"I just need a moment. I'll stay on point!" she snarled.

"You know the rules. No one person can stay on point all the time. Their senses dull. Let your eyes and ears rest, by all that's holy, and curb your sharp tongue. No one is calling you less of a warrior because you're not on point.

Next will be Rif. Points stay fresh and sharp to keep the rest of us alive."

He growled at her as he worked his way around, taking in the forest to choose the best path forward. He picked the biggest tree in the distance to serve as a guidepost. Once he reached that, he'd choose another. Step by careful step, he sought not to disturb the undergrowth. The group slowed with Goranth on point and kept a pace kinder to the injured Varl.

Despite her vitriol and protests.

In a clearing ahead, he found the first sign that they were on the right track. A kill had been made, a mountain sheep. It confirmed two things. They were closing on the mountains, the home of the dragon. And after it had gorged, it had stayed on the ground, leaving a clear path ahead.

Like hounds on the scent, Goranth strode like the predator he was, ready to battle the great beast. The trees started to thin as the dragon's spoor led them toward its home.

A change in the breeze caught Goranth unaware. He froze.

He sniffed the air rushing from behind. Dark clouds rolled from the plains toward the mountains, and they were coming fast. He wished he could see more or had been more aware earlier when he was up the tree.

Goranth cursed himself and headed up, climbing with the fearless confidence of a jungle ape. By the time he reached the uppermost branches, which were barely thick enough to support his weight, the wind whipped, threatening to toss him out of the tree's clutches.

"Ho!" he shouted and threw himself downward, reckless in his descent. Rif and Varl were waiting on the ground by the trunk.

Jaeg was stumbling in his failing efforts to keep pace.

"We must take cover! That storm will devour us if it catches us in the open. The mountains are near. We have to find shelter there and now!"

They turned to look at the coming danger, and the sight drove Goranth's truth home. Even Varl refused to argue the point.

"Run!" Rif shouted and took off, leaving Goranth to give the reluctant Varl a hand. Necessity dictated she needed the help that she was ill-suited to accept.

Jaeg tried to run, but he was mostly spent, the heavy pack having worn him down. Goranth left him to fend for himself. A tree cracked behind them, succumbing to an angry gust. Rain pelted them, its massive drops the size and feel of gravel.

From up ahead, clear of the tree line, Rif waved for them to follow. He waited, but only long enough for Goranth to see where he went. With an arm up to protect his head, the Barber raced for a rocky outcropping up a slight rise and past the trunk of a fallen tree. He threw himself forward and crawled out of sight.

Goranth was nearly carrying the recalcitrant Varl, but when they reached the rocks, she hit the ground with a care for the growing baby within. She laid flat like pancake batter in a pan, exhausted and unable to follow Rif over the downed tree and into a hollowed-out area beneath a boulder. Goranth lifted her over and pushed her before him until she reached out for Rif to pull her in.

A pack slammed into Goranth's legs. "By the Ice Dogs, watch out!" he growled at Jaeg. The young man cried out in anguish as the rain pounded his exposed flesh. Rif pulled Varl farther back into the crevice, a slash in the stone that extended a few body-lengths into darkness. Goranth slithered behind her, and Jaeg abandoned the pack to get himself under cover.

The Northman crawled back to the entrance, eyes closed against the ferocity of nature, to recover the pack with the ropes they would need to control the dragon. Once it was in his hand, he retreated into the depression, then hurried out again, pulling at the downed tree and managing to tug in a large branch.

"We might want a fire," Goranth said. "And this might dry out enough."

They waited, barely able to sit upright, as day turned into night and the storm ripped the forest asunder. Thunder dominated, and the storm sought to break the back of the forest beyond. The gray sheet of rain became a curtain before the entrance to the four's hiding place. Water ran in and started forming a pool in the far end. Goranth gauged how long it would take to fill the space.

They had time, but not much. The wind needed to shift.

Kalida, the world has not taken kindly to our quest and endeavors to kill us.

I won't let that happen, the angelic voice replied in Goranth's mind. A tremor shook dust from the great stone over their heads. Jaeg screamed.

A crack appeared in the ground, and the pool drained into it. The earth stopped shaking. The rain ran in, forging a small channel in the dirt on its way to the crack in the darkest recess where it disappeared.

"Was that Kalida?" Rif asked.

"I believe so. She may have saved us. By the Ice Dogs, this storm must be the work of demons. Never have I seen its equal."

"Nor I, Northman."

The storm raged and the day passed in darkness that turned into night as the sun abandoned them, leaving a greater rage for the unleashed deluge. Lightning sparked the blackness and thunder shattered the incessant din of the rain.

A more terrible storm had never been. Goranth's faith in the Ice Dogs and the earth mother was shaken.

CHAPTER TEN

Red sky in morning
Sailors take warning
Women who mourn
Sailors forlorn
"Sonnet of the Black Sail Brotherhood"

"The sun should be up soon," Varl said.

"You've a fever." Goranth leaned over Varlten're and held the back of his hand against her forehead.

"No, I don't." She pushed him away and scratched at the bandage on her leg. "It's warm near the flames. I like the warm. It's not a fever." She sat cross-legged against the stone wall, her bare skin glistening in the firelight. Goranth had managed to break the big branch into pieces and coax a small fire into life. She continued to scratch and stared at the embers.

Goranth eased down about an arm's length away and studied her. Near the lip of the overhang, Jaeg and Rif talked about reaching the area where their quarry lived and feasted on goats and sheep.

"Today, we'll find the spot," Rif said, his voice muted by the crackling fire and the rain that pattered down beyond their refuge. "If this rain ever stops."

"It has to stop," Jaeg mumbled. "Or it will drown the dragon we seek."

"Kalida will help us. I want enough light to work by, else we'll have to wait for the next dawn." Rif huffed, and a rumble deep within his chest sounded close to a growl.

Goranth reached over and touched Varl's arm. "You're sweating."

"I like the warm," she repeated, again batting his hand away.

"*I'm* not sweating, Varl."

"Good for you, Northman. Good for all of us because when you sweat, you stink like the dung of a striped weasel."

He set his back to the stone, closed his eyes, and listened to the rain, Jaeg's speculation about the dragon, and the sound Varl made scratching at her leg. He'd sensed Kalida earlier, or thought he did, but there was no trace of the priestess now. Maybe she slept. Everyone had to sleep sometime. He heard Rif yawn, and he yawned, too. It would be easy to drift off again, but he stopped himself from stretching out and instead opened his eyes to study Varl.

"You should get some more rest," Goranth told her. "Been through a lot, and we're not heading out until the rain's done. The big cat, the storm..." He looked at her belly but didn't mention the strain of the child growing within. "I'll keep watch for everyone. You should—"

"You should mind your own affairs," she shot back. Her words had a sharper edge than normal. "I am not tired.

Sleep wouldn't come last night. I haven't closed my eyes since we crawled in here, and we brought no healer's tea to nod me off."

"I'm concerned is all," he said softly.

She snorted and blew out a long breath that fluttered the strands of hair hanging down her forehead. "Concern yourself with the bears or whatever it is that walks past the opening. See, there's one now."

Immediately, Goranth, Rif, and Jaeg looked out into the rain, each man's hand dropping to his weapon. Jaeg rose to his knees, his head grazing the rock above. The Northman didn't see anything except the wall of water and the pre-dawn gray beyond.

"Just the rain," Jaeg said.

"No, I see it. Are you blind? Big. It is big," Varlten're insisted. "Not a bear? Maybe a very young dragon. It could be that. See the long tail? It *is* a dragon."

Her tone was serious; Goranth knew she was not jesting. He prided himself on his keen senses. There were breaks in the gray outside, showing when the fire flickered higher after catching a new piece of wood. There was little kindling left.

Varlten're made a hissing sound and scratched her leg faster. She'd opened the scabs and set her wound to bleeding. Goranth grabbed her wrist to make her stop. Indeed, she was feverish. Varl struggled with him, but he tightened his grip, and she gave up. Her shoulders slumped, and she blew another breath that teased her hair.

"So damn thirsty," she muttered.

Goranth released her and she dropped her hands to her knees, then started rocking forward and back, agitated. He passed her his waterskin but she didn't take it, just kept rocking. He uncorked it and held it to her mouth, and she gulped it down but had trouble swallowing. She coughed and shuddered and drank some more.

"It was the cat," Rif suggested, crawling closer to Varl and Goranth on his hands and knees. "We should not have eaten it. The thing behaved oddly, not spooking from our numbers and not fleeing when we wounded it. The cursed meat made my stomach jump."

"Its eyes were wild," Jaeg said. "And my gut twisted after I ate."

"Aye," Goranth added. "There was something wrong with the big cat."

"You didn't eat it," Varl hissed.

"No." Goranth hooked the empty waterskin to his belt; she'd drained it. "There will be other hunts. You can miss this one. You could stay here, wait for us. We'll come back to get you when—"

"No. I need *this* hunt. I need a full share of the bounty." She shook her head. "The babe in my belly is growing bigger. It has to be *this* hunt because soon I'll be a waddling pumpkin. I'll be no good at catching dragons. I need to do this *now*. While there's gold to be had."

Goranth dipped his fingers into the pouch at his side and fumbled past the coins to find the necklace he'd intended to give to Kalida in a quiet moment. He took it out and handed it to Varlten're. "I gained this on one of my grand adventures—pirate loot. Consider it my gift to your babe. It will buy—"

"—a lot," she interrupted. Her twitching fingers grabbed the chain and held it up to the firelight. The gems fairly glowed and the gold shimmered. "By the Ice Dogs, Goranth, this is a prize! It's worth—"

"—a great deal," he finished, picturing the gems and jewels in Rif's treasure horde and figuring he would find something else there for Kalida—a necklace with even larger gems with a fob that would sit prettily between her breasts. "Wear it, Varl. Or sell it when you get to Barbertown and use the coins for your family. Get some rest. At least try. We're not leaving until the storm is done."

The rain had stopped sometime during midmorning, and Goranth emerged from the overhang to look down the short slope into the trees beyond. The sky, which was the color of cool ashes, was covered by one perpetual cloud, and everything smelled wet and clean. He smelled clean, too, yesterday's deluge having pummeled the old scents off him.

"I could eat something," Jaeg said, stepping up behind him. "Do you have any of that cheese left?"

Goranth had a small chunk remaining. "No." He was not going to share with the youth. "How old are you?"

Jaeg replied: "I've seen fourteen summers."

"You're too young for this."

Rif edged past them and started down the rise. "Not too young, Goranth. We were on a ship at that age."

Goranth had signed on to his first pirate ship when he was twelve.

"We need to take Varl back to Barbertown," Goranth said. "She's feverish and not good for going after a dragon, no matter how much we might need her. And I don't think she could make it back on her own."

Rif stopped and turned to the Northman. "Aye, she is unwell. I spoke with Kalida a little while ago, while it was still raining. The priestess is sending four soldiers. Three to replace Varl—since she is as tough as any three men—and one to take her home. Truth, Varl needs to go back to Barbertown. I am concerned for her. But we need to go forward to find the dragonette. Varl can wait here for her escort."

"I'm not waiting anywhere." Varlten're strode past Goranth. He noted that she wore the necklace and her skin still gleamed with sweat. She looked pale and her hair was plastered to the sides of her head, but she held herself straight and gripped her staff. "I'm going with you. I don't need an escort home. The soldiers can catch up or not, but we will not need them. More men will only make more noise and destroy our chance of sneaking up on our quarry." She paused. "Damn, but I'm thirsty."

Goranth narrowed his eyes at her.

Rif gestured for her to walk behind him. Jaeg followed, struggling to manage the heavy rope pack as he stepped on the rain-slick stones. The mud in the gaps between the rocks was shiny, and water lay on the surface.

"This rain," Rif said as he continued in the lead, "has made everything more difficult. We'll have to rely on Kalida and our eyesight to find the Three Sisters."

Goranth searched but did not sense any trace of the enchantress in his head. That both bothered and pleased him. He wondered why Kalida had communicated with Rif this morning and not him.

"We'll continue north this way, on the rocks and out of the trees. Faster going, I think," Rif said. "Easier to notice the Three Sisters. Kalida tells me we are making good time. I want us to climb a little higher on this rise. Follow me."

The sun chased the gray away by midday, turning the sky bright blue. Jaeg had been looking up, studying the mountainous ridge, and had mis-stepped in a patch of slick mud. The youth fell, feet and arms flailing, pack slamming against the rocks. He grunted and tried to right himself, looking like a turtle that had flipped on its back.

Varlten're turned to help him, but Goranth leapt forward and pulled the boy up.

"By the Ice Dogs' hairy nostrils," the youth grumbled. "Ouch." He nearly fell again, off-balance with the pack.

"I'll carry it for a while," Varl said. She reached for it. Ahead, he saw Rif double back.

"You're not carrying anything, Varlten're," Rif ordered. "Jaeg is strong and—"

"I'll take a turn," Goranth said.

He swung the pack over his back, and the harness settled on his shoulder blades. It was uncomfortable and unwieldy, and that Jaeg had managed it this far made him respect the youth. It also made the Northman decide he would indeed demand pack animals or a cart on the next venture.

He felt Kalida settle into the back of his head, not communicating, just making her presence known. Had she been there all along?

"Let's go. Move!" Rif commanded. "I want to reach the Three Sisters while we have daylight. We're going higher."

Varlten're fell in step behind him, and Goranth noticed that she leaned heavily on her staff. *Damn stubborn woman should have stayed in the cave, waiting for her escort. Damn foolish Rif for not escorting her back himself right now.* He doubted she would be of any use hunting a dragon, other than singing her odd song at it.

He followed her, leaving three yards between them, and Jaeg took up the rear this time.

"Thanks," the youth said, "for carrying the ropes." He toted the lone length Goranth had previously carried. "I could've managed, but—"

"Just stay alert," Goranth advised. "Make sure nothing comes up behind us."

"Gods, but I don't want another one of those big cats."

Goranth couldn't contain his laugh. "You worry about a jaguar. Child, a jaguar is nothing next to a dragon, even a young dragon."

They trudged on in silence, Goranth watching Varlten're and cringing when she nearly slipped more than once. The marks of yesterday's rain had not yet worn off, and the mud was still slick. Birdsong was plentiful, sweeping up from the trees to their left. There were a few trees among the rocks, small cedars that had taken root in the little patches of earth between the stones. They would never grow to the size of the giants below, but they afforded perches for the small parrots that preferred the rocks to the forest.

"The Three Sisters." Jaeg interrupted the quiet. "Why is it called that? I mean, I've seen it on maps like the one we have, but why is it—"

Goranth let out a low breath. "It's an old tale. I'd wager most across Migoro know it."

"I'd never heard—"

"There were villages of goatherds in the mountains a long while past—a few hundred years, the story runs. The elders tried to stop the dragons from eating their goats and sheep. There have never been many dragons in this part of the world, but even one or two could decimate a village's livestock, so they cobbled upon the notion to offer sacrifices to the dragon."

"Why would that stop a dragon from eating goats?" Jaeg seemed seriously interested.

"It didn't. The village elders were witless. They beseeched families to give up their children in an effort to appease the dragon, and supposedly one goatherd who'd lost his wife and had difficulty raising his three daughters alone handed the girls over."

"That's horrid."

"Indeed," Goranth agreed. "They staked the girls on a peak where they could be seen easily and the villagers hid in the rocks, waiting for the dragon." The Northman paused and made to rush forward since it looked like Varlten're was going to stumble, but she kept her feet and leaned on the staff.

"And—"

"And one of the girls managed to free herself, then freed her sisters. They saw a dragon coming, and rather than risk dying to its claws, they leapt off the side of the mountain. Some say the earth mother noted their sacrifice by fashioning part of the mountain into three spires to mark the sisters' unnecessary deaths."

Jaeg noisily sucked in a breath. "What happened with the dragon?"

"It continued to eat the goats," Goranth finished. "As does the youngling we've set out to capture."

"Except this time, the dragonette feasts on wild mountain goats, not ones belonging to people."

"Aye, Jaeg. The villages are long gone."

The sun had started dropping to the horizon, and the air was warm enough now to bring a few drops of sweat to Goranth's forehead. A hawk followed their course; the Northman thought the bird was hoping Rif would scare up something tasty for it to eat, a rodent or a rabbit.

"No!" Varlten're tripped on something. Goranth had been watching the hawk and had taken his eyes off the warrior woman for mere moments.

She dropped and slid, and he jumped forward to catch her, but the big pack on his back threw him off-balance and his fingers closed on air. Goranth saw Rif spin and race down the mountainside after her, scree spitting up in his wake. The Northman fumbled to drop his pack, and Jaeg stepped up and helped pull it off Goranth's shoulders.

Then the Northman was racing after her, too.

Varlten're's staff flew out of her hands. She tried to grab stones to stop her tumble, but there was only scree, and the little bits of rock were no help.

"Rif!" she hollered. "Help!"

Goranth had never heard her call for help before. Despite starting behind Rif, he passed the Barber on a mad dash after Varl, half-running, half-sliding, hands and arms sliced by sharp edges of the small stones.

It wasn't that far a fall, Goranth thought as he saw Varlten're carom off an outcropping and fly over the side, but it was perilous. His muscles bunched, he pulled the mountain air to the bottom of his lungs and leapt after her, clearing the outcropping and dropping two heights of a man to the base of the slope. He landed in a crouch, his thick legs absorbing the impact.

Varlten're lay at an odd angle on her stomach. He hurried to her, knelt, and saw a pool of blood forming under her head.

Rif rounded the outcropping and scrambled down the rest of the way.

"Varl!" the Barber shouted.

"Dead," Goranth said, though he carefully prodded her to be sure. She wasn't breathing, and when he gingerly turned her over, he saw that half her face had been smashed in by the impact with a large rock. Her skin was still hot from the fever. He touched her gently rounded belly. "Varl is dead."

Rif raised his head to the sky and howled. The sound became wild and strangled. He slammed his fist into his open palm.

"Take me for a fool," Rif moaned. "This is on me!"

Goranth did not correct him. They had argued with Varlten're since the first foray to find a dragon. She wasn't one to be talked out of anything once she set her mind to it.

"Senseless," Rif continued, face still tipped up as if he didn't want to look at Varl's broken body. "Senseless, wasted."

"It was an accident." Jaeg had joined them, and Goranth saw the youth's legs were sliced up from his blind dash down the slope. "She tripped. I saw her, Rif, and—"

The hawk that had been following dipped low and cried, then flew off into the forest.

"Wasted," Rif repeated. "Two deaths. Hers and the child inside."

"An accident," Jaeg repeated.

"No grand death catching a dragon or doing something heroic for the city," Rif continued to rage.

Goranth stared at the necklace glimmering in the sun. Varl had looked beautiful wearing it.

"I shouldn't have pushed her," Rif continued. "I should have made her stay home with Esh're. I never should have let her join us, and when the cat got her, I should have taken her home. Esh're will—"

"Esh," Goranth corrected flatly. The 're was gone now since the pairing had ended with Varl's death. "This was not going to turn out any other way unless we tied her up and hauled her out like so much baggage, creating an enemy for life even if it did save hers."

Rif looked at her body and knelt. "My dear friend." He touched her wrist. Goranth saw that her arms and legs were broken, her body shattered from the impact. "My dear friend and dragon-hunter." Rif swallowed a sob.

"We brought nothing to wrap her in," Goranth observed. "A blanket must suffice. I'll carry her back to Barbertown. We'll bury her in your catacombs, Rif, with honor and—"

"No." Rif stood and pointed at Jaeg, then pointed at the rocky slope. "Up there with you. Get the pack of ropes and drag it down. We'll go forward in the forest until we've found the spot beneath the Three Sisters. No more walking on the rocks."

Jaeg hesitated and looked between Goranth and Rif, then glanced down at the body before turning away.

"Now, Jaeg!" Rif barked. "Up you go! Get the ropes."

The youth took a few deep breaths and started up carefully, using his hands and feet like a monkey would, sending scree cascading down but managing to keep his purchase.

"No?" Goranth scrutinized Rif. "No to her burial?"

"The catacombs is not a resting place for...it's not a public gravesite," Rif admitted. "It is only for the bodies of men and women I've had to eliminate. It is not for the likes of sweet Varl."

The Northman stared at the Barber, searching for a trace of the man who had saved him that night from the giant squid. He swore he stared at a stranger.

"Then we'll take her back to the city and—"

"We'll bury her over there." Rif indicated a grassy area at the base of a giant cedar. "Between the roots, near where she fell."

So deep the creatures of the woods cannot reach her. The words were Kalida's and cut through Goranth's thoughts. *And I will tell Esh of his loss.*

The Northman bent and removed Varl's necklace; the stones were smeared with blood.

"You'll have to clean that before giving it to Kalida," Rif observed.

"I gave it to Varl," the Northman cut back. "And I will give it to Esh so he can buy a small boat to sail away from this damnable place."

"It will be harder to catch a dragon, the three of us, though not impossible with your strength," Rif continued. "First, we'll rest here a while, after we bury Varl, offer our respects. Then we'll move on. Kalida sent soldiers. We can use the soldiers' help to muscle the beast back. Look, Jaeg's got the ropes."

Goranth didn't look. Instead, he pictured the treasure chamber beneath Rif's home. He was due a good share of it for the trouble and the loss. Signing onto Rif's scheme had become brutally costly.

CHAPTER ELEVEN

Ride the stallions wild and free
The rider's dynasty
From steppe to glistening sea
Leather, steel, and fury
"Tales of the Mabayan Raiders"

"This is a foul business, Rif." Goranth glared at his old friend.

"We must see it through." Rif gripped the Northman's arm. "For Varl."

Goranth threw off the offending hand. "Varl was in it for the treasure, to build her future life with Esh and their child. But that doesn't matter now."

"He'll have that necklace. It's worth a fortune."

Goranth balled his fists and lunged toward the Barber. "That came from me, but I'll replace it, by the Ice Dogs, and then some. And you'll pay her share to Esh as soon as we get back."

"Take it easy. I will. I will, my friend. No one feels worse about her death than me."

Goranth shook his black mane and continued to glare. He growled, deep and dangerous. "My turn, Jaeg. I'll finish the hole."

The young man stepped aside, handing the crudely carved wooden shovel to the Northman. He bent his back with newfound vigor, using his sword to hack roots clear before continuing to dig.

Deep enough so the animals couldn't get to her.

In short order, the deed was done. With a helping hand from Rif, Goranth climbed out of the grave. He washed his blade and hands in a nearby puddle, a remnant from the storm, then splashed water over his face before heading toward the hillside and a recent rockfall.

Rif and Jaeg waited in silence. The body, wrapped in a thin blanket, was ready for final interment. Goranth picked up a flat stone nearly the size of a man, and he walked slowly step by step under a burden greater than two men could bear.

"Hurry," Rif said. He took Varl's shoulders and the youth her legs. They slid her to the bottom and shoveled to fill the hole. Both worked with hands, feet, and tools. By the time Goranth arrived, the grave was full. He angled the rock and dropped it in place as a seal on Varl's tomb. He knelt on top of it and took out his longsword but thought better of it.

"Your dagger, Rif." The Northman held out his hand.

The Barber hesitated for a heartbeat. He looked down as he took out his dagger, flipped it, and handed it over.

Goranth started at the top left, using the blade to chip a line to the bottom center. He worked his way back up to the right. His handiwork was crude, but he'd never fancied himself an artisan. That wasn't his gift. He cleaned up the rough spots, leaving a stone with a V notched into it if facing the forest.

He handed the knife back to Rif. "I'll be on the rise. I'll be back in my own time."

"We'll be here, Goranth." Rif looked at the chipped and twisted tip of his favorite dagger, now useless for combat. He turned it point-down and stabbed it into the ground at the foot of the gravestone in the freshly repacked dirt. He dug a hole that reached to the hilt, then jammed Varl's staff into the hole, using his body's weight to drive it deep. Once in, he buried the blade to its hilt at the base of the staff. "For you."

He put a hand to his spare, smaller dagger in solemn remembrance of the group's loss.

The Northman turned his back on his two companions and climbed the small hill leading to rocks still slick from the rain. To the rocks and upward, he traversed the stone face as one born to it.

In his homeland he could climb rocks covered in ice, deep in snow. This stone was only wet. The clearing sky showed him the crevices to use for handholds and the small ledges on which to step. He vaulted onto a plateau to find a great flatland beyond, a refuge for grazing beasts.

And more.

Goranth pressed himself flat against a small boulder teetering on the edge of the drop beyond to watch a full-grown dragon eat. But that beast wasn't the one that had caught Kalida's ire. He checked his mind, but no, she was nowhere to be found.

He watched the great creature, having never seen a full-grown dragon before. The dragonette they had captured was a third the size. LeReon had more height and weight to gain, but it would most assuredly outgrow the stockade. When, though—that was the question.

It wasn't for Goranth to answer; he would be long gone before that day. The question that nagged him was if Kalida would be with him. *Damn that woman and her wiles! My but she is fine, an enchantress who can hold her own—a worthy partner.*

Goranth shook her from his mind, but the movement caught the eye of the great one feeding on a full-sized buffalo. He froze as the dragon looked his way. The two stared at each other across the broad plateau. A drop of sweat trailed down Goranth's forehead and into his eye. He fought the salty sting, refusing to move a single muscle.

The dragon threw its head back and roared its dismay before returning to its meal. Goranth blinked, but remained still, watching the creature rip and devour until nothing remained but the stain of blood. It ran toward the Three Sisters to pick up enough speed, then it was airborne with a single downstroke of fibrous wings that were the size of a great ship's sail.

With easy flaps, it flew toward the higher peaks. Goranth stepped away from the boulder and walked toward the kill site. On his way, he found smaller tracks, neither from a buffalo nor an adult dragon. A smaller dragon, then, one that might work for Rif's purposes.

He looked closer before glancing around. The tracks turned all of a sudden and headed for the ledge, away from the kill. Goranth followed them to the cliff. Below, only rock and foothills leading to the forest looked back at him. He returned to where the buffalo had been killed. The tracks were four times the size of the small ones.

"Do adults chase their young away?" he asked the emptiness.

The buffalo herd grazed at the far end of the plateau, well out of earshot. They took no notice of the stranger intruding on their remote land. He watched the mountains while he again walked to the cliff's edge.

"If memory of the last tracks serves me right, this one is smaller than LeReon. We are out here for a dragon, and by the Ice Dogs, we'll capture one, or Varl's sacrifice would have been in vain."

He looked for a way down that didn't involve death-defying jumps, then tracked to the north where an escarpment led from the cliff face. He stepped lightly over the edge, taking care with his tread to avoid dislodging loose stone, and started down. The going was slow, but his footing was sure. He roved across the rockface, looking for signs that a dragon had passed, but it would have flown this way and not walked.

There were no signs of its passing, yet he was certain it had come this way.

Goranth stopped to cast his gaze over the world below. Beyond the hills to his left, Rif and Jaeg waited. Ahead, the escarpment raced to meet the woods, leaving little land between. The area to his right was blocked by boulders and the cliff face.

To the right he went, scrambling across the rocks like a mountain goat. He increased his pace. It felt like he was racing for his freedom. He breathed deep, the forest scent fresh from the recent deluge. Sweat beaded on his body. He sniffed.

Varl wasn't wrong. He did smell like the dung of a striped weasel, but it helped him blend in with his surroundings. He moved among the vermin and creatures of the land as if he were one with them. There were times when he preferred the company of the wildlands to that of so-called civilization.

Times like now. The freedom of the open hills, his wits and skill against cliffs that would have sent a lesser man away without even attempting a climb, legs turned to mud at the thought of the dizzying height.

A sound caught his ear. Unnatural. Not the forest. Not a stream. Not the wind. The crunch of bone.

He focused the clarity of his senses on the source. It came from up ahead, near the bottom of the escarpment, beyond the last of the rockfall. He eased toward it, slipping the makhaira from his belt. It sang to him softly in his hand, not with words but with a calm before the violence he would do with it—the violence they would do together. He relaxed his grip in a way that made it one with his arm, flowing with his body.

He moved slowly, nothing to draw a wary eye.

The dragonette beyond the rocks fed happily on a light-furred simian that was smaller than a man but enough of a meal for the young dragon. Goranth could end it right there, he had no doubt. Its scales were barely formed and no harder than soft wood. As it matured, they would take on the strength of iron and be impenetrable to the weapons of man.

These were the creatures Rif sought to tame.

Madness! Anger rose within him. The fire of vengeance burned behind his eyes. There was no time to get Rif and Jaeg. He had to decide. Could he secure the creature by himself?

Not without the ropes in Jaeg's pack. Goranth waited for the beast to finish. It licked its face with a long tongue before stepping away from the kill and laying down, curling up like a cat, and wrapping its tail over its head.

That was all Goranth needed. He drifted away from his boulder, keeping it between him and the small dragon, then hurried down to the ground. He hit the last few steps running. Today, they would satisfy their quest and start the return journey to Barbertown and Kalida.

You are coming home to me, a voice said in his mind.

Not now, woman. I'm busy doing your bidding.

Now is always the right time, Northman, she countered.

What would you have me do?

Be exactly as you are, Goranth. No man stands alone. The help of your fellows will keep you all safe.

You see the future? Goranth wondered.

No. I see the here and now through the eyes of the earth. It is a better battle tactic to surround your enemy, is it not?

Goranth slid but caught himself and kept running. He hadn't thought he'd gone far or been gone long, but he had. It was already midafternoon. The heady scent of clean air and following his instincts had led him to the dragon.

To complete their quest.

He would demand his treasure and be on his way from these cursed lands before they took his soul, and yes, he would beg Kalida to come with him.

I will, she replied simply.

Damnable woman! Goranth growled in his mind, but the stirring within his body warmed him with a heat that shouldn't be. *Stay out of my head. I'm busy.*

He tried to shut her out but couldn't be sure he'd succeeded. She had rushed to the front of his thoughts and was still there. Her half-smile was frozen in his mind's eye, questioning him in a good way. The curve of her neck. The smooth skin leading down her chest. Soon, he'd feel her…

Rif and Jaeg came up behind him, shocking him back to the moment.

Did you call them? Goranth wondered.

One man, no matter how formidable, is not enough to take even the youngest of dragons.

"Grab your gear," Goranth told them. "The dragonette is just over that hill and little more than half the size of the one already secured in your stockade."

Rif smiled grimly. Vengeance fired behind his eyes as it had within Goranth. Jaeg hoisted the pack of ropes and threw it over his back.

Rif took the coil Varl had carried.

Goranth dug into Jaeg's pack to pull out the especially tied head basket and waved for them to follow. He didn't retrace his steps but stayed to the land side beyond the escarpment. He doubted the others could climb and cross it quietly, and he had no intention of arriving to find an alert dragonette waiting to ambush them.

They ran without words. This was the hunt, and their blood was up. The others were breathing hard, Rif from being out of shape and Jaeg from his burden.

Goranth held up his fist for them to stop. Jaeg ran into him and would have fallen had it not been for Goranth's lightning-quick reflexes allowing him to catch his arm. He made to speak, but Goranth silenced him with a finger to his lips. He looked at Rif and pointed up a rocky incline. After a short respite to let the others gather their breath and wits, they followed him up toward the boulder he had recently hidden behind.

Taking care with their steps.

Watching for movement beyond the rocks where the dragonette had last been seen sleeping off its small meal.

Goranth signaled for the others to stop. With a tread as light as a leaf kissing the ground, he covered the final distance and peeked around the boulder. The dragonette's slow breathing suggested it was sound asleep. The Northman gestured for the others to drop their packs and join him. The time of the capture drew nigh.

They placed their gear on the stone and walked carefully to Goranth. He didn't wait but headed around the boulder, not to the place the dragonette had made the kill, but to the place the dragonette had brought its kill. Goranth stalked into the lair of the beast.

He approached, and as the dragon's breathing changed, he leapt, wrapping the head with the rope basket and attempting to cinch it tight. Rif ran into the fray as the dragon came awake in confusion and pain. Before the basket could close, the beast keened an ear-piercing cry toward the sky. Goranth wrestled with the beast's head.

In an attempt to prove himself Jaeg raced in and drove his fist into the beast's snout, which was nearly as hard as the stone face. The youngster's fist caught in the rope, accidentally pulling it free. He yanked the basket off the creature's head to get his hand back and cradled his self-inflicted injury. Goranth snarled at the loss of control.

Goranth wrapped his arms around the beast's head, twisting and gripping to keep the jaws closed. His biceps bulged with the effort, sinews straining at the young dragon's strength.

Rif hammered its shoulder with his club, but as before, he was trying not to hurt it. And he wasn't. His efforts only served to make it more animated in its gyrations to throw Goranth off.

A thunderous cry sounded from above.

The great dragon Goranth had spotted earlier hadn't cast off its young. No doubt it had been teaching the youngling to be self-sufficient, and it had not abandoned the dragonette. In its time of need, the youngling had called its mother.

She came, bringing with her the full fury of her black soul.

"RUN!" Goranth dove away from the dragonette, hit the ground, rolled, and came to his feet in a full sprint toward the forest. Rif bolted after him, yanking the stunned Jaeg to his feet as he passed.

"For your life, boy!" Rif shouted in his face and let go.

The two bigger men flew like the wind. Without his pack and with a flying predator on his trail, Jaeg found his footing and soon caught Rif. By the time they reached the woods, he had passed the Northman, too.

CHAPTER TWELVE

A soul is a small price to pay for victory.
Mantra of the Mabayan Raiders

Snap!

Like a mast broken by a hurricane, a great tree fell, then another and another. The death of the forest giants was unbearably loud; their impact with the ground boomed like thunder and made the earth shudder in fear. Goranth felt the vibrations rise through the soles of his sandals and chase shivers up and down his muscular frame. The furious mother dragon tore at the tree line to reach them.

The forest erupted with cries—birds, monkeys, great cats, and more, all voicing their terror.

Snap.

Snap.

Snap.

"This is on you!" Rif screamed at Jaeg.

"It is on all of us!" Goranth countered. "And we'll be joining Varl in the realm beyond if we don't run!"

But how could they outrun something that could bring down the ancient trees?

"Running!" Jaeg called. "Running!"

In a gap between massive trunks, Goranth whirled and watched the dragon land, its huge ebon eyes mirroring him. Something flickered in that blackness, and she opened her jaws. The Northman stood transfixed by awe and terror, his feet seemingly rooted to the soil. Teeth as long as a man was tall glistened like wet pearls, and a tongue as red as fresh blood lolled out. The maw filled with a churning molten mass that swirled with the colors of a raging fire. Though she was the length of two galleons away, Goranth felt the heat rhythmically pulse from her.

Run, he told himself. *Run, you bastard!* But he couldn't move.

The dragon inhaled, and at that moment, it was as if all the sound in the world had been sucked inside her. No screams from monkeys, no shrill cries from parrots, no snapping branches or pounding footsteps from Rif and Jaeg. The silence was complete.

Then she exhaled.

The air shimmered like he'd seen it do once in a desert above scorching-hot sand, rippling as if it were alive. An intense wave of heat rolled down her tongue and raced toward him.

Run!

"Run!" This came from Rif; he sounded far away.

The hot wave crashed over him, and Goranth swore he'd been dropped into a vat of boiling oil. His skin blistered and cracked, and his world became torment. The intense agony broke whatever hold the dragon had on him.

Goranth spun, his feet churning over the forest floor, every step painful.

Snap.

Snap.

Snap.

The trees around him blackened like a fire had raced through, all moisture sucked from them. The underbrush and wildflowers melted, and the air Goranth gulped down tasted charred and bitter.

The dragon roared her anger and the ground shook again. He heard more trees snap and fall and felt the vibrations rising through his feet, but he didn't risk a look back. He ran faster and gritted his teeth so he wouldn't cry out from the pain.

Run! This was Kalida in his head. *I can't stop her. Run! Run for everything!*

The way ahead was not easy, the forest old and filled with ancient trees as big around as an elephant and small growth saplings trying to find a patch of sunlight to claim. There was no clear path; he had to slip one way and then another. Twice he stumbled over knobby roots and managed to right himself before falling. To fall would be to die.

Snap.

Snap.

Utter silence again, followed by another blast of heated breath that slew more trees and blistered his back. The pain was all-consuming, and for an instant, Goranth considered turning around and letting the dragon take him to end the suffering. Kalida kept urging him forward.

"Here!" Goranth didn't see Rif, but he recognized the voice. "Northman! Over here!"

Goranth ran in that direction faster, leaping over a tangle of ferns and then dropping down a slope to land on his back next to Rif and Jaeg. The ground shuddered, but not from the dragon this time. A piece of the forest floor rose up and over, burying them. Kalida's doing.

Quiet! Kalida urged. *Stay still and live.*

As if it came from leagues away, Goranth heard snaps and booms and felt the earth tremble from the dragon's ire. There was no part of him that wasn't aching. It hurt to breathe. It felt like hours passed, but he knew that wasn't possible.

She looks for you, Kalida said. *I'll not let her find you.*

No one would find them, Goranth reasoned, if they stayed buried for much longer. Hungry animals, perhaps, he mused. They weren't as deep as they'd entombed Varl. A bear could dig them up and feast on their corpses. Would he see Varl again in death? Was there truly a land beyond, or was there nothing? He suspected he would discover that as soon as the little pocket of air he'd found was exhausted and he inhaled dirt.

He felt someone struggling next to him—Rif or Jaeg, he couldn't tell. Their gyrations became more pronounced and painfully jostled him in the process. He felt hands grab his arm and pull. He came up and swallowed air that still felt hot and tasted burnt.

Rif climbed out of the hole first, then Jaeg, and when they bent to offer help, Goranth growled and climbed free on his own.

"You look—" Jaeg stopped himself. "You—"

Goranth saw that the skin on his arms and legs was red and blistered like he'd been lashed to a spit and turned over a cook fire. Places looked wet, but he knew they weren't. If he managed to heal from this, he'd be a mass of scars like one of the damaged souls who begged for coins and food at the edges of the marketplace.

"Does it hurt?" Jaeg risked.

Goranth glared at him.

Run! It was Kalida again. *She's not given up. She's come back! Run!*

Goranth realized she'd spoken to all of them when Rif and Jaeg sprinted to the east, where the foothills and mountains stretched. As painful as each step was, he managed to outrace them.

"This is on you!" he heard Rif holler again to Jaeg. "Fool child!"

Goranth cleared the tree line, and his feet hammered across the thin strip of grass shortened from all the animals that had grazed there. His feet pounded the ground, and he fixed his eyes on the ridge ahead.

Something blotted out the sun and set a shadow over his way forward. Goranth risked a glance up. The dragon was overhead, wings spread wide, clawed feet dangling beneath her. The belly plates were ridged and looked like armor segments, having a metallic sheen; they were rimmed by scales glimmering like newly-minted coins. Under different circumstances, Goranth might have appreciated her power and beauty. Now, he felt his heart seize with the thought that she could swallow them whole.

Run! Kalida cried. *Run for everything!*

Goranth's muscles bunched and he vaulted up the rise, blistered fingers grabbing holds and scrambling up, not caring where he was going other than away from the dragon. Faintly, he heard Rif and Jaeg before the dragon inhaled again, then he went faster still.

There was a slash in the rocks overhead. It might be nothing, a shadow cast by an outcropping, or it might be more. He made for it, and a heartbeat later, he squeezed inside. The crevice was tight but deep enough, and he edged back farther as Rif and then Jaeg made it inside, panting, chests heaving. The stone shimmied, then quieted, and the mountain trembled again. Goranth sucked in a breath that was filled with stone dust and dead air. But it didn't smell scorched, making for a glorious lungful. He breathed deeply again and again and tuned out the nervous chatter of his companions.

Goranth explored the crevice, which went deeper into the hillside before it ended in a wall of rubble. It was pitch-black this far back, and he returned to Rif and Jaeg by feeling his way along a wall. They were wedged into the crevice far enough from the opening that shadows covered them. Jaeg was standing and shifting back and forth on the balls of his feet. Goranth noted that the youth had blisters on the right side of his body; he'd not escaped the dragon's furnace breath. Rif sat cross-legged, elbows on his knees, back curved, like he'd folded in on himself.

"I was only trying to help you subdue that little dragon," Jaeg said. "I didn't think—"

"That's it exactly," Rif returned. "You didn't think."

Neither said anything for a few minutes, and Goranth edged past them and glanced through the crevice's opening. He saw the dragon flying in slow circles above a section of the woods as she searched.

She was a huge and magnificent beast.

"I should not have brought you," Rif said after a while. "Too young. Too inexperienced. And you lost our ropes. All of our ropes are out there in the woods. No ropes, no dragonette. I thought I was doing your father a favor. And you a favor." He laughed. "I'll do no one favors again."

"I'm sorry," Jaeg offered. "I'll make it up to you. I'll find the ropes. After the dragon leaves, I'll climb down and—"

Rif snorted and looked to Goranth. "Northman?"

Goranth stepped closer. "She's still out there."

"That looks painful," Rif observed.

"It is painful."

"You need a healer."

"I'm on this side of the dirt," Goranth said. "What I need is to know that dragon is done with us. Has given up. And she's not there yet." He eased himself down two arms' lengths from the crevice's opening. The dragon's head was too big to reach inside, though he supposed she could bring part of the mountain down on them if she wanted or merely breathe her heat and roast them.

"Is it possible," Jaeg prompted, "that the dragon doesn't know we're in here, that she didn't see us?"

"I don't think she knows we are here. I hope we are hidden." Goranth shrugged, the gesture setting a new ache birthing. "She saw us leave the forest. Might not have seen us on the rocks. We're ants to her. Maybe she thinks we ran back into the trees."

"I felt like an ant," Jaeg admitted, "trying not to get stepped on."

She's lost you, the dragon, Kalida offered. *But she is searching.* Goranth didn't know if she spoke to all of them or just him. *She's angry that you tried to take her offspring. Pity, you almost had the little dragon. Next time—*

"I haven't decided if there's to be a next time," Goranth growled. "I hurt too much to think about a next time."

Kalida slipped out of his thoughts and he brooded and stared, watching the dragon circle as the afternoon gave way to twilight. He was thirsty, and he'd drained his water skin an hour ago. Rif might have some or Jaeg, but he wasn't about to ask. He'd replenish his skin at a forest stream when it was safe to leave.

The air was close in the crevice. Not enough fresh air seeped in to suit him, and the space was too tight to spread out. Goranth wanted to venture outside, stretch his arms and legs, and let the breeze wrap around him and cool his blisters, but he knew that might be a costly pleasure. They needed this refuge until they were reasonably certain the dragon was done hunting them. How damn long could she fly without stopping? Didn't her wings get tired? Was she indefatigable?

He swallowed a laugh. They were the hunted when they'd come out here to do the hunting. Jaeg's youthful impetuousness had brought this on. Rif had been wrong to bring someone that young with them. They should have brought someone seasoned. Rif could have found someone better suited among his soldiers. The youth was muscular, but his bulk came at the expense of his wits. Why had Rif picked him? The Barber had ulterior motives for most of his operations. He'd mentioned doing a favor for the boy's father.

Rif slapped the palm of his hand against his leg and snarled.

"I am done talking," the Barber growled. "I want some sleep. Get out of my head, woman. Get —"

"Kalida talks to you," Goranth observed.

"Aye, but about you, Northman. Kalida talks to me about you." Rif managed to maneuver so he lay on his side, his pack serving as a pillow. "Out of my head, woman. I want to sleep."

Some time passed before Kalida again intruded on Goranth's thoughts.

So you talk about me, Goranth said. He noted the dragon was still out there, widening her search but still staying above the trees. The moon was coming up, and it caught her in its light. Did the beast never need rest?

I asked about you, Kalida corrected. *I asked Rif to tell me about the pirate days. I wanted to look at you through his eyes, gain a different perspective.*

Because your eyes— Goranth replied.

See what I want to see.

"And do you like what you see?" Goranth muttered aloud.

She didn't answer. *You should rest, Goranth. Sleep.*

"I hurt too much to sleep."

Goranth stared out the rift. The trees looked like charcoal smudges far below and past a small line of foothills. The moon full and bright, interrupted by thin strips of periwinkle clouds. The priestess intrigued him, and he wondered how powerful she was. Not as powerful as the large dragon; he could think of no single force more powerful than that. Were her enchantments limited only to scrying through the earth?

And the stone, she said, interrupting his thoughts. *I see through the earth and stone, send my senses through them. I can touch things connected to the land with my mind.*

"The dragon? The big one? Can you see it now? Above the trees?"

I cannot see what does not touch the earth, she said. *But the creatures that scamper on the ground see the dragon. They feel fear, and I can sense that. I will try to find the young dragon you nearly had.*

"It would be good if the damn big thing was far away. We could—"

Do not leave your safe spot yet, Northman.

Goranth remembered Varl singing to LeReon, calming it. Maybe Varl had possessed some magic of her own. He wished the woman hadn't been so stubborn; she and her babe would still be above ground if she'd listened to reason.

Search with me, Goranth, for the small dragon and for other interesting things. Come with me.

"I thought you said not to leave this place."

Your body does not need to go anywhere.

Goranth felt her wrap around him, comforting like a

blanket on a chilly night, holding him like a mother might a child. Then he was falling as if he'd stepped outside the crevice and dropped off the edge of the mountain. His throat tightened, and he tried to breathe; he was certain he was suffocating as he plunged. The moon's brightness disappeared, and thick fog of a gray hue replaced it.

The gray separated into shades, curling bands interspersed with stripes of cream and white and dotted by sparkling black motes.

We're inside stone, aren't we? Goranth asked. He didn't hear his voice, though he knew he'd asked the question.

We're inside the mountain, down and along it. The range is like a man's spine, don't you think? Ridges and curves, but mostly straight. Made of granite and chert and feldspar and more.

You have names for the stone.

Yes, Northman. Stone has many names.

Gemstones, he returned. *I know those names.*

You like things that sparkle.

There is value to gemstones. Goranth thought about Rif's treasure and that he would claim an exquisite piece of jewelry for Kalida.

It is difficult to surprise me, Goranth.

But not impossible, he wagered. He liked a challenge.

How do you feel?

The question caught him off-guard and he thought for a moment. *Better,* he said. *But I know it is a false feeling. I know my body is wracked with pain, burned, blistered, and—*

I am not a healer, Kalida said. *But the earth is. Some stones have healing properties. What you consider worth coins has a far greater value. I cannot call it magic; it is just nature. Open your mind to the possibility.*

Do I have a choice?

She wrapped him tighter and took him farther, finally

coming up through a ridge and laying their minds in a mountain stream. The Northman knew he wasn't drinking since his body was back in the crevice, but he felt refreshed, and he pretended to take in as much of the water as he could. The moon shone on them, making the stream shimmer white and silver, the whorls where it curved around rocks looking like a woman's pale tresses.

Down they slipped again, passing through stripes of glimmering rock. Goranth thought he should not be able to see colors inside a mountain, but he noted purples.

Amethyst, she said. *In jewelry it is worth coin, but here, uncut, it pulses with calmness and pleasant dreams.*

Deeper, they came to a band of iridescent yellow-orange rock shot through with motes of sparkling crystal.

Goldstone, sunstone. It has other names, Kalida explained. *It is a healing stone, soothing the soul, radiating warmth.*

Goranth felt the warmth of the rock or thought he did. It was not a painful heat like the dragon delivered.

We'll stay here a while, she said.

Eventually, they moved on, passing through small caverns, some littered with the bones of animals.

The remnants of goats, Kalida said, *likely fed to hatchling dragons. The babes are long gone from these places.*

Are there many dragons?

I've never counted them and never thought to find out, but few, I think. Creatures so big cannot be numerous.

But rare in the forest, Goranth said. *Else we would have found one days ago and would not have found the dragonette and its mother today.*

Beautiful creatures, Kalida admitted. *But they do not belong here. We'll go in search of the youngling now. I'll take us down the cliff and into the forest, and we'll—*

Not look for the dragonette tonight, Goranth said. *Finally, I think, sleep might claim me.*

You are tired.

Aye, I am that.

When he woke in the morning, sunlight streamed through the crevice opening. Had he dreamt about traveling with Kalida? Delirious from pain, had he drifted off and—

He glanced at his arms and legs. They were still blistered, the skin red, but the damage was not nearly as severe as it had been yesterday. The tortured skin looked like it might heal on its own, and the ache had descended to a muted, manageable throb. He flexed his fingers, pictured the sunstone crystals, and looked out over the forest. The sunshine revealed sections that had been melted by the dragon's furnace breath.

But there was no sign of the dragon.

CHAPTER THIRTEEN

Terrors of the mind climb and crawl
Until your head screams and you fall
Friend or foe
Stay or go
Flee for your life!
Save your soul.
A Minstrel's Tale

Goranth edged out of their crevice, taking the greatest care in how far he leaned into the open. He sucked in fresh air as his eyes scanned the entirety of the world before him, looking for a shadow, a movement—anything to reveal a dragon on a relentless search for them.

"Her fury is spent, methinks," Goranth called over his shoulder. He craned his neck to see the mountains behind him to be sure the dragon wasn't perched above them, waiting for a meal to step outside. But nothing was there.

He ventured to the ledge and downward, then roamed

left and right. The morning sun allowed for few shadows. A blue sky offered hope for a better day. Goranth returned to the ledge.

"Wake up. It's time to go." The Northman's lip twisted into a snarl. "We have a dragonette to find."

"You're still on board?" Rif wondered. "I was convinced you'd be first to head back to Barbertown to seek the warm embrace of your wench."

Goranth lunged past Jaeg to wrap his fingers around Rif's throat. "Your fool quests are going to be the end of us all. Most people get smarter with age, but not you. Your schemes grow more reckless. What happened to the Rif who built a city, a good city where people can live as they wish?"

Rif smiled under the Northman's light pressure on his throat. The chill of steel reached through Goranth's fury, and he looked down to find the Barber's blade at his throat. Goranth let go and pushed Rif's arm away.

"What happened is that Barbertown has needs and we're no longer growing. We do what we must, my friend, for those we take care of. That is all. The dragons are a scheme, I'll grant you, but it will pan out." Rif put his blade away and ran his fingers through his hair. "I know Kalida is not a wench, but it was illuminating to see how you responded to such a taunt. No matter. I am pleased that we continue our search. A second dragon will bring greater treasure to Esh to help him through Varl's loss."

"That's the only reason I'm still here," Goranth admitted. "We best split up. That dragon could be anywhere."

"Northman," Rif said in a low voice, "what magic has healed the worst of your wounds? Were you visited by Kalida and held in her tender embrace?"

"Aye, and you're jealous. I hear it in your voice. We

explored under the mountain where gems and jewels abound, bringing their power to those who are unwell. Even when my body wasn't down there," he pointed at the stone beneath his feet, "the gems still worked their magic on me."

"Save some for Jaeg, Northman. He took a nasty burn back there."

"It's not mine to give or save. Only Kalida can show you the way to the healing stones."

"Put in a good word, Goranth?" Jaeg pleaded, holding his injured arm.

"If she'll have anything more to do with me."

Rif laughed and stabbed a thick finger at Goranth. "Only a barbarian could understand that logic. She heals you so you can come back to her and she can revel in your arms. Bah! You aren't good enough for her." He capped his claim with a rude gesture, two fingers of one hand bouncing on the finger of another.

"'Everything Men Know about Women,' a poem with no words by Rif the Barber." Goranth offered his hand and pulled Rif to his feet.

"I should write that and put it in stone. The key to success with women. Succumb or don't start. There is no in-between." Rif continued to laugh. He checked his body to find that he hadn't been injured in their flight from the dragon.

Jaeg raised his hand. Rif stared at him until he'd said his piece. "I'll find our ropes and bring them back here."

"We need those ropes. That is a good task for you, but no. This isn't the place to rally." Goranth looked at the expanse of forest below and pointed. "There. See it on the edge of where the dragon tormented the trees? The large black oak that stands taller than the rest, defiant of the dragon, refusing to be damaged by the foul beast's hot breath. We'll meet there at nightfall."

Without waiting, Goranth started his downward climb, appreciating the frantic scramble up the slope less than a day before. He headed to the right. Jaeg would need to go to the left to find where they had encountered the dragonette and recover the ropes if they hadn't been burned. Rif could roam the forest to his heart's content.

Goranth cared not what the others did. He'd be free of them, if only for a short while. He jogged down the hill until he reached the short grass. Hunger suggested he'd need to hunt for tubers or berries or even small game. He hefted his makhaira, knowing he could throw it if needed to down a creature like a rabbit or even a sheep. His stomach growled its appreciation of his attention to its needs.

He eased across the narrow grassland separating the foothills from the forest. Once under the cover of the trees, Goranth relaxed but quickly found himself wallowing in anger.

"A fool's quest," he told the old growth. "Varl dead from the madness of this ill-conceived venture. Dragons to save the city? There is no chance of that. Mark my words, dragons will be the downfall of Barbertown."

No one argued with him, neither the leaves nor the wisps of wind lightly tossing the treetops.

He held his tongue as he padded through the woods, listening for the trickle of water and looking for something to eat. Ahead he saw a bush he recognized. Goranth knelt next to it and dug deeply into the dirt with his bare hand until he found the root and followed it until he could wrap his hands around a tuber. He dug for a second and a third. He rubbed the mud from them before putting two inside his tunic. He carried the other toward a puddle, where he washed it clean.

Goranth ate it, skin and all. It sat like a rock in his gut, but he knew it would sate him for the moment. He returned to his search, scouring the world around him for any sign of a dragon, large or small.

The Northman started to jog, putting more distance between him and the others. He saw a sheep and froze in his tracks.

Opportunity was a frequent visitor in his life. He often seized it when it appeared. This opportunity he would not pass up. A sheep—more than he could eat.

Unlike the dragon hunt, he had no stomach for a quest to capture the beasts, but his grudging respect for the man who'd helped him survive the squid had demanded that he come.

He remained as still as the trunk of the tree against which he leaned.

You shall have mutton for your lunch and dinner, an angelic voice whispered into his mind. He wanted to argue, but his stomach demanded a meal far more substantial than a raw tuber.

Goranth waited with the makhaira in his hand, held comfortably in a loose but powerful grip. The sheep wandered toward him, head down as if looking for something. It moved within arm's reach and Goranth struck a mighty blow, shearing the head from the befuddled creature. The makhaira's blade was that keen.

"While you're here, Kalida, tell me, is there a dragonette anywhere near?" Goranth wiped his blade on the soft wool of the carcass, then removed his knife and started skinning it. He worked quickly.

Yes, Goranth, and no. Not in the lowlands of the forest. You'll have to return to the plateau, where you'll be in the open. Your reward will be there.

"Once I'm done smoking this, I'll drop it off where the others can find it, then I'll climb."

You should cut off what you can cook later and go now.

"I will not." Goranth had the bright red meat of a fresh sheep. He needed to cook it.

The four soldiers dispatched from Barbertown are close. I tried leading them away once their intentions became clear and I realized they were not loyal to Rif, but they were able to break my hold on them. The leader's mind is more disciplined than the others, nearly as strong as yours.

What is their intention that you are protecting me from?

They mean to kill you all and take the dragonette from you. Then they plan to hold sway over Barbertown.

We don't have a dragon, Goranth countered.

They don't know that.

Tell me where they are and be quick about it. I need to finish them before the meat goes bad. Goranth hung the carcass from a low branch, then climbed up to lift it one higher, taking it out of the reach of most vermin.

What if they kill you? Kalida asked, a sharp edge to her words.

Then I won't care what happens to my lunch.

Taking them lightly will not serve you well, my Northman.

As much as I don't want it, you are in my mind. Do you think I'm taking this lightly? I will kill them, and it'll be easier if you tell me the route they travel. Then I'll cook this sheep since I still must eat. I don't lose my mind over something like a fight. I've walked away from every single battle I've ever been part of. I will walk away from this one, too. Now, tell me, and I'll take care of them.

Kalida surrendered to Goranth's reasoning and approach to life. The Northman knew she had seen into

147

the minds of the four men, who had also walked away from every fight they'd been a part of.

Due west. Not even a league separates you. They walk with one on point, two behind and to the sides, and the biggest one, the leader, bringing up the rear.

A league gave Goranth a few minutes to work. He gathered deadfall from before the storm, finding the driest to start a fire. It smoked extensively, something he had counted on to prepare the sheep, but now it was a lure to bring the soldiers directly to him. Once the fire was burning and the smoke spiraling skyward, he drifted into the brush and headed south before turning west.

He moved within the shadows, stepping lightly but quickly. He rolled into heavy growth and waited.

But not for long.

The crack of a branch signaled a nearby tread. Through the foliage, he saw the soldier, pike held before him as he stalked ahead, focused too much on what was in front of him and not enough on what was beside him.

Goranth came out of the brush like a leaping tiger. He caught the man's head and rode him to the ground, where he deftly opened the man's throat with the sharp makhaira. Then he ducked, looking for movement and listening for signs that his attack had been discovered, but no. He crawled into what would be the middle of the soldiers' diamond and waited, blade behind him, muscles in his arm coiled to deliver a killing stroke.

The soldier filling the role of rearguard walked easily, head swiveling as his eyes roamed the forest, looking for things that were out of place even though his fellows had just passed. That was what Goranth would have done. When it came to his life, he put little trust in others.

Two steps away, the soldier stared at the place where Goranth crouched. He lunged forward, and the Northman jumped straight up and over the steel death of the man's pike. Goranth swung but the soldier twisted away, letting go of his two-handed weapon and smoothly drawing his sword, a shorter cavalry blade about the same length as the makhaira.

Goranth slid his broadsword out of its scabbard and faced off against the soldier, two swords against one.

"Ho! He is here. To me! To me!" the man shouted.

Soon it would be three swords to two unless Goranth could even the odds. He approached without caution, his blades blurs as he slashed figure eights through the air before him. He darted left, then right, then farther right as he sought to overpower the soldier.

He backed away, and Goranth pressed forward. The hairs on the back of the Northman's neck stood as he felt the others rushing to the aid of their leader. The blades sang and clanged thrice before Goranth held his swords still to study his opponent for a moment. He surrendered ground, but not the battle.

His reinforcements were on their way.

Goranth heard them running through the brush and dipped to the side to back the soldier against a pair of hearty trunks growing close together. When the man reached them to find his way blocked, he charged, screaming a horrible war cry as his blade slashed back and forth.

The Northman's broadsword caught the hilt guard and stopped the soldier's blade. Goranth drove the makhaira deep into the guts of his enemy. With a vicious twist, the battle was ended. The soldier lost his smile in the terror of the realization of his own death.

Goranth pulled the blade free and placed his back to the twin trunks just in time to deflect the pike thrust of the first of the final two to arrive. Since the soldier had been overzealous in his attack after the sharpened point had been deflected, the pike continued into the tree. The soldier let go and jumped back, barely avoiding the whistling blade meant to disembowel him.

Goranth surged forward.

Before the blade could sing free of its scabbard, the second soldier arrived. Goranth lunged and sank the point of his broadsword into the chest of his opponent. The Northman was moving again before the soldier realized he was dead.

The last soldier knew he was overmatched but remained in spite of his fear.

Goranth kept his guard up but gave the man a chance. "I see courage in you, the courage to walk away before you die needlessly. I know you weren't the leader of this ill-conceived parade. Take what you've learned here and go."

"You know I can't do that, barbarian," the man replied. "We came here for one purpose. Returning alone and without your heads for prizes would brand me a coward."

So, there were others back in Barbertown, Goranth realized, who were not loyal to Rif and were part of this.

The man threw his pike at Goranth and pulled his sword, then dodged sideways, keeping a tree between them. Goranth backed away, taking the track back to the sheep he'd hung in the tree. The soldier waited as Goranth kept going. "This fight is over."

The soldier disagreed. He picked up the fallen sword of his comrade, and with one blade in each hand, he charged the Northman. He was clumsy with the two weapons and Goranth dispatched him quickly, shaking his head at the waste of life while acknowledging the man's bravery. The Northman used the soldier's tunic to clean his blades before returning them to his belt.

Goranth took the time to check the dead and relieve

them of purses holding more gold than a common soldier should have had, but these four were anything but common. The leader had an impressive bronze cuff inlaid with onyx, and he took that, too. The Northman added their treasure to his and returned to his kill, where the fire smoldered and smoked. He built it up, prepared a spit, and set the sheep to cooking.

"The dragonette is on the plateau, huh?" Goranth pondered. "I suspect there will be more pain. Maybe another trip to the stones under the earth to implore them to do what they do so well? My hide is well-tanned and could use the tender touch of the amethyst and the golden glow."

As you wish, Goranth, Kalida replied. *While your sheep cooks.*

"Why do you stay in Barbertown?" he asked when his senses had returned to the surface, and nearly all trace of his scalding injuries were gone.

Rif saved me and I owe him, even though I know he uses me to scry. But I only tell him what I wish him to know.

"But you tell me everything," Goranth taunted. He hoped she did.

If that feeling makes you comfortable, then yes, I tell you everything.

"Rif won't part with his treasure, will he? When this is over, I'll take my share anyway and go, but only if I don't have to fight him."

I don't know the answer to that, but you are the only man he's ever let see his treasure. Others who have gone into the underground have never returned.

"I should count myself lucky? I don't feel lucky. I feel like Rif has called in one too many favors. He let me fill my purse from his hoard to forestall his own death. Do I need to put him in fear of his life to get what I'm owed?"

Rif treats you differently. Accept that. Embrace it, and use it to take what's yours and no more.

"Does that go for everything of mine in Barbertown?" Goranth turned the sheep and added more wood to the fire.

You have more in Barbertown than you realize, but less of what matters. A pony waits for you...

"You speak in riddles, woman. You twist me about inside my own head. Give me peace for a while. I need to think."

You need to brood, Northman. It's your least attractive quality, Kalida replied.

Goranth didn't answer aloud. She was right, but she'd seen inside his mind. He didn't even have to speak for her to know. Anyone watching would have thought him mad for arguing aloud with himself...and losing.

He chewed on a blade of grass as he let the meat finish roasting and smoking. The sun had passed its zenith by the time he sliced off the outer char and began his personal feast.

"I should never have come, even with owing Rif. Friends don't throw friends' lives away. He broke our bond with this fool's quest. He broke faith with me." The Northman stabbed the coals with a pike he'd relieved a corpse of. "I'll finish this and that's it. One more dragon, Rif, then I'm gone."

CHAPTER FOURTEEN

Come, my brother
Once more for one another
We will fight and win
Rest and fight again
Until the treasure haul
Is enough for all.
"Sonnet of the Black Sail Brotherhood"

Goranth had time to squander before sharing with Rif that the dragonette was on the plateau. He could spend that time going to the plateau to confirm the small dragon's presence but thought it unnecessary. If Kalida said it was there, it was. But had she given the same information to Rif?

Sated and uncomfortable from consuming too much mutton, he decided to walk off his feast. Kalida had left him a short while ago, and he could think without worrying about a mental eavesdropper. Brood. Kalida had called his introspections "brooding."

If it is brooding, I brood well, he thought. Goranth had a lot to consider.

He'd agreed to pursue this dragonette for Rif, but the point would be moot if Jaeg had not managed to recover the ropes. There would be no tackling even the smallest of dragons without something to secure it. Goranth didn't want to return to Barbertown for more rope, only to turn around and come back out here. Risky enough that they'd run afoul of the mother dragon on this expedition. He prayed they'd seen the last of her since he doubted they'd be lucky enough to survive a second encounter.

He could go back to Barbertown right now, find Kalida, and sail away to distant shores. Maybe the Hawk Islands. Maybe find a schooner that would skirt the coast and go north. It had been years since he'd visited his homeland. Either destination appealed to him, yet he'd made a promise to Rif. Kalida had said she'd leave with him. Had that been a promise, too? Her allure faded with each intrusion into his mind, but damn, she fascinated him!

No matter where they ended up, Goranth wanted to leave with satchels full of treasure—more than enough to set him and Kalida up in a place of their choosing. The gems and coins under Rif's home glimmered in the back of his mind, his share of it burning bright. How had Rif managed to accumulate so much? He couldn't get that question out of his head. And how had he kept it hidden? Not any longer, since Rif had shown it to him, so Kalida also knew. A dark thought sent a shiver down his spine. Goranth had seen the full extent of the man's wealth. Would Rif try to kill him to keep it a secret?

He tamped down that notion. As brothers of the sea, Rif would not cross him.

A wide game trail led north, and he followed it. The tracks that cut across it were small: deer, rabbits, and more sheep. He wasn't interested in pursuing any of them since he was more than full, but it was good to know nothing bigger appeared to use this area. It was an old section of woods, the giants thick and tall and the exposed roots looking like great snakes slinking away and digging into the earth. The wildflowers were small but fragrant and competed with ferns and other greenery for space. He took in lungsful of the nature surrounding him in a bold embrace of the essence of life.

Goranth rolled his shoulders and flexed the muscles in his arms. Neither action hurt since the nature magic in the gems deep below the ground had chased away his pain. It had not, however, mended his trousers. The heat blast from the mother dragon had left his clothes in tatters. He briefly considered stripping the lead soldier he'd slain and wearing the uniform since it was cleaner, sturdier, and a good option, but there was something chilling about wearing a dead man's garments. The bronze cuff? That was another matter; valuables were fine to loot. Goranth would find something suitable to wear when he returned to Barbertown—something new and tailored to fit him. He hoped his tatters did not fall off and leave him naked before then.

Goranth stopped when he spotted a new track bisecting the trail, then squatted and ran his fingertips across the print. It looked human but so small it was likely a child. *Children.* There were at least four distinct sets, all barefoot. There were tribes in some sections of the forest, but not around the area they'd been searching for the young dragons, or none that he'd heard of in any event. This was far too dangerous a place for children to be on their own. He thought of the great cat that had been Varl's undoing. Such a cat would make a quick meal of an untended child.

Intrigued and wary, he drew the makhaira and padded forward slowly. The tracks were fresh, no more than a few hours old.

The soft backdrop of birdsong kept him company and suggested nothing dangerous prowled the area. The breeze, which had increased steadily as the day aged, rustled both leaves and small branches. A little of the wind dipped through gaps in the canopy, and the play of the air across his healed skin soothed him like the soft touch of a raven-haired beauty. He almost wished Kalida was physically here with him to share the setting. He found that he craved her company too often, which was unsettling because Goranth had believed he'd always tread the earth alone.

A short while later, the tracks became more numerous and fresher still, and the wind brought the scent of something cooking. Goranth's senses were keen but not accurate enough to identify what was being prepared. He edged forward with great care, noting a clearing east of the game trail and a fire burning merrily. Many small figures were crouched around it. What were the children cooking?

The birdsong persisted, and a monkey chittered. *The animals perceive no danger,* he thought.

Still, Goranth nearly turned around and crept back the way he'd come. No reason to risk an encounter without a threat, even though the figures were small and odd and his curiosity simmered. *By the Ice Dogs!* He gripped the makhaira tighter, his palm slick with sweat, and he purposely brushed a branch to alert the camp.

As one, the figures—a full dozen—shot to their feet, chattering as they looked at him through gaps in the foliage. Only one drew a weapon—the smallest and stoutest of the lot, who stepped forward and started talking in an odd tongue punctuated by clicks. The blade was similar to a makhaira but more slender.

The Northman didn't understand a single word, but he realized they were not children. He moved closer for a better look, his hands held in front of him to show he meant them no harm.

They ranged in height from three to four feet, and their skin was pale gray and hairless. Otherwise, they appeared human. The men—they all looked male to Goranth's eyes —were dressed in simple tunics that draped to just above their knees, the ecru fabric rough and of a coarse weave like potato-sack material. There was color among them; a few had belts of red and blue, and one had a sash draped from a shoulder to his waist. It was deep yellow with a checked pattern, decorated with buttons of various sizes. The shortest, the one with the weapon, wore an embossed black leather belt around his hips and the sword's sheath hung from it, along with a string of bronze beads. He appeared to be the only one with a blade.

The gray man continued to talk to Goranth and the Northman concentrated, hoping to pick out something familiar. He'd sailed with men and women from several different countries and had learned a smattering of foreign words, but nothing matched anything he'd heard before.

Until the gray man spoke Mabayan.

"You are a stranger to us," the gray man finally said. He had seemingly tried a few languages before settling on Mabayan and drawing a look of comprehension from the Northman.

"Goranth. My name is Goranth."

The group conversed softly, sounding like a swarm of insects in their unusual clicking tongue. Goranth noticed that two of them were wrinkled like tree bark and their eyes had a rheumy cast, suggesting they were old. He was transfixed by them, never having seen their like in all his travels. They had bulky packs sitting next to them, and there were a few folded nets. Maybe that was how they had caught the game they cooked. He searched for Kalida, hoping her mind danced at the edge of his, but found himself alone.

He didn't know whether to feel relieved or not at her absence. He had no time to ruminate on it.

"Goranth," the gray man said. He nodded to the makhaira, and Goranth sheathed it. The gray man did the same. "Rudran."

"Rudran," Goranth said, not quite matching the gray man's pronunciation.

"My name is Rudran, and I lead this band." Rudran gestured at the fire. Three large rabbits cooked over it.

"Join you?" Goranth asked in his own tongue. "I've eaten far too much already this day." He accepted the invitation since he sensed no malice in the small men and his curiosity had gotten the best of him. He sat cross-legged an arm's length from the flames and tried to recall enough Mabayan to carry on a simple conversation. That these people, or at least one of them, spoke that language further intrigued him.

"Who are you?" Goranth asked in Mabayan, indicating all of them. They'd resumed their positions around the fire, still chattering politely in their own language and cutting glances at him, a few pointing.

The reply from the apparent leader was long, and Goranth couldn't mentally translate all of it. He did make out "Undmen" and "woods."

"Undmen?"

Vigorous nods all around.

He let out a great breath, wishing he could

communicate better with these odd people. He doubted Rif was aware of them or had dealt with them before. Such a group would have rated a mention at some point during their five-day journey to the foothills of the Three Sisters.

"Where are you from, large man?" This came from a wizened one who spoke Goranth's language. "Where are you from that you wear ruined clothes and smell of rank things?"

The Northman blinked in surprise. Why hadn't this fellow talked to him earlier? And yes, he realized there was a stink about him that bothered even his senses. He'd been blistered by a dragon, hidden under dirt to save himself, and sweated in a tight-crevice. He definitely smelled of rank things.

That man had stayed silent until now because he was suspicious of you, Kalida answered. She'd returned to his thoughts. How long had she been there, hidden?

Apparently, Goranth, he has decided you are not a danger to them. More of an intrigue. I think he wanted to make sure you were friendly. These people are new to me—Undmen—though my memory tickles with half-glimpsed things from my earth travels. Dancing shadows that might have been these people. Pity I did not stop to investigate. Good that one speaks to you so that I can understand. Stay, Northman. I want to learn more about these Undmen. Rif and Jaeg can wait.

"I do not always smell so foul," he answered. "I've been too long without a bath and too long hiding from a dragon in close places."

"Dragon!" The wizened one rose to his feet and shook a fist. "Fear the dragons. Hate the dragons. There is a big one here. Somewhere. Nearby, maybe. Even far away, the beast is too close. Big as a mountain peak, she is. As dangerous as an earth tremor." He settled back down. "Chirl," he said. "I am called Chirl. My name is much longer, but that is a piece of it I will give you."

Goranth wanted to know more about these people, too, and so he engaged the wizened one with questions as the rabbits were passed around the circle.

"We live under the forest, in warm, happy warrens where we are safe from the hunting creatures of the woods and try to stay safe from the dragons." Chirl sighed, then translated what he'd said to his fellows. "We are not always safe from the dragons. Sometimes the very small ones tunnel into the earth."

"And sometimes they eat us." This came from the other older Undman.

Goranth waited while they talked and clicked in their own language, their gestures indicating the subject was dragons. When there was a brief cessation, he jumped in.

"How is it some of you speak my language when—"

"—we live under the ground? Chirl and I have seen more years," the wizened man began. "In our youth, we traded with some of the villages in these woods and the mountains. We had to learn their words to barter. Those places are gone now. There are other villages farther away, but we stay close to our warrens and will not go there unless it is necessary. And we will not go to the south. We believe evil simmers in the big city on the coast."

Barbertown, Goranth thought.

"The language still serves us when we find travelers like yourself."

"Sometimes," Chirl interrupted, "we trade with merchants who travel the wide trails. We've learned your language so we can better deal with them."

"What do you trade?" Goranth asked.

"Stones for everything," Chirl replied. "Stones with value."

He means gems, Kalida supplied.

I know he means gems, Goranth shot back.

"We trade for bolts of cloth, tools, toys for the little ones, and—"

"All manner of things," the wizened one said. "We enjoy trading when we can."

"Worked metal," Chirl continued. "Brass and silver, and steel blades."

"Bronze?" Goranth took off the cuff he'd acquired from the dead soldier.

"Oooooh, that is nice," Chirl said, coming close and reaching out.

Goranth gave it to him. This close to an Undman, the Northman picked up a faint odor. The small man smelled like rich earth, and his hands were thin-fingered and heavily calloused.

"What do you want in trade for this?" Chirl asked, turning the cuff over in his fingers and studying it, then rubbing his thumbs over the inlaid onyx. "Marvelous piece of worked metal. What do you want?"

"Information," Goranth quickly returned. It felt like Kalida was going to say something. The connection to her was deep enough that he could sense her questioning mind, but she stayed silent. "Information is valuable, Chirl, Rudran. Tell me more about yourselves." He paused. "And tell me how one of you also speaks Mabayan. Are there Mabayans in these woods? That you trade with?" Goranth had thought the Mabayans only lived along the east coast on the other side of the mountains.

Chirl spat and rubbed the ball of his foot over the spot as if he were stamping something out. "Fear the dragons. Fear the slavers. The...Mabayans, we fear them just as much. I did not know they were called that. We call them slavers. Yes, there are slavers in the woods, roaming bands.

They are worse than dragons. The dragons will only eat you. Slavers drag out your death by stealing your freedom for all your years."

"Tell me," Goranth said, settling back and relaxing his shoulders. "Tell me about all of it." He accepted a piece of rabbit and chewed it thoughtfully. The smoked lamb had been better. He noticed two more Undmen sitting farther from the circle, eyes scanning the area. Scouts. There might be more that he couldn't see.

"We learn languages from listening," Chirl explained. "And we listened to the slavers from hiding, watching them take some of us and not able to do anything. We listened when they camped over our warrens. Languages come easy to some of us."

"The slavers are too many. Too big. And they have monsters with them," Rudran added. "Horrid monsters."

Goranth leaned forward, waiting. They started passing around a skin, taking deep drinks. He was thirsty and took his turn, discovering it some sort of fermented beverage.

Chirl continued, "In your languages, the monsters are called praevo-pavors, or flying terrors."

The Northman instantly thought about his recent encounter with one.

"The slavers have bent the beasts to their will and use them as scouts and to aid in the capture of slaves. Mainly the slavers hunt far north of here, where villages sprawl in the clearings, or in the foothills and on the other side near the sea, taking travelers and explorers."

To the east, Goranth thought, where he knew they lived.

Rudran took a turn. "They come through here sometimes, this far down into the great woods, and so we rarely come above anymore. But we had arranged a meeting with a merchant, and that took us out of the warrens. The meet was to be yesterday. We think something ill befell the man." He pointed at the packs. "We were trading gemstones we'd mined for cloth and tools. Now we will return to the warrens without our prizes."

"But we will eat rabbits first," Chirl said. "And talk more with you, stinky man."

Kalida loomed and nudged Goranth with more questions.

"About you—" the Northman prompted.

"Our ancestors were the same," Chirl said, touching his thumb to his chest, then pointed at Goranth. "A long time ago. But our fathers, as the tales claim, grew tired of fighting and politics and the petty concerns of most people. They sought a different path and went below the earth into the belly of the mother, where they found peace."

"Yes," said another Undman. "For a long time, our people stayed in the belly and became like the earth, our skin colored like stone, our forms shorter to better navigate the tunnels, and our eyes keen to see in the darkness. It took a long time for the change, for us to become Undmen."

"Under-men," Goranth said, noting for the first time that their eyes were large like a child's within their heads and the pupils were oversized.

"Yes. And we have stayed too long above on this outing and should return home," Chirl said. "After we finish the rabbit. And finish talking with you."

Kalida said, *I will find them on my next foray into the earth. I will search until I find them and see where they live and what they are about. I will slip into Chirl's mind, and we will talk at length. How could I have missed them on all my travels?*

"How could I have missed knowing there are Mabayans with pet praevo-pavors?" Goranth mused. No wonder they wanted Rif's dragon. If the Mabayans mastered the flying terrors, imagine what destruction they could sow with dragons. "It is getting late, and I must return to my companions."

Goranth stood and reached for one of the coin pouches he'd liberated from a soldier. He tossed it on the ground at Chirl's feet. "For a future merchant exchange," he said. "Buy some tools and cloth." He added a second pouch; there was far more wealth waiting for him under Rif's home.

You are more generous than I expected, Goranth. Kalida's voice in his head sounded like crystal wind chimes brushed by a breeze. *Are you becoming soft-hearted?*

He grunted and looked through a gap in the canopy. The color was fading, and it would be dark by the time he reached the blackened tree. Would Rif and Jaeg be waiting there? And could he avoid any dragons, praevo-pavors, and Mabayans along the way? The seas were not as dangerous as this forest.

Rif and Jaeg. They'll wait, Kalida said.

"They'll have to," Goranth replied. "I'm not in any hurry."

CHAPTER FIFTEEN

Dig until your fingers crack
Fold the earth back
Look through her curtained window
Then leave her be, let her go.
An Undmen Chant

Goranth mused about his chance meeting. Traders had avoided sharing tales of the Undmen, keeping secret the existence of those who provided cheap gems. Picks and daggers for rubies and emeralds! No wonder they didn't share.

The Undmen feared the dragon, but not as much as they feared the Mabayans, who were south of where he walked, but also north. More information he hadn't known. Mabayans were more than steppe raiders. They were slavers!

An animal's snarl twisted his lips. He tightened his grip

on the favored makhaira, knowing that out here, it gave him peace and warmed his soul far greater than the comfort of a soft-skinned beauty.

More errant thoughts of the woman Kalida flickered.

They had much to discuss when next they sat under the same roof, but he knew he would get angry if she pressed him to talk about his feelings. Those weren't for anyone else to know.

Darkness came as the sun slowly descended below the trees. The filtered light cast long shadows around the Northman. He strode easily, glancing at the trees for predators and into the sky for the greatest hunter of all, but the threats left him alone this eve, like the Undmen on their trip above ground. The small gray people had failed to meet the traders but had found success in bringing three rabbits to their fire. They had respect for the world above but their lives were spent below, a place they hurried to return to.

Goranth saw no draw in such a life, but it wasn't his. He bowed his head to the Undmen for knowing what they wanted and embracing it. They had a choice of where to live, more so than the Northman, who felt trapped while he walked alone through the vast spaces of eastern Okuta.

Kalida. Rif. Varl. The names and faces rolled through his mind. Once again, as if it knew he needed its comfort, he found the makhaira gripped firmly in his hand.

An hour after nightfall, he smelled the smoke of a campfire. Soon after, he saw the flames and followed them to the black tree, where Jaeg and Rif sat, sated by the mutton Goranth had left for them.

"I see you ate your fill, Northman, but the rest served us well and will for many days to come. I compliment you on your hunting prowess." Rif stood and bowed.

Jaeg gestured with his chin toward the recovered pack.

"Well done, youngster. You'll carry them as part of your penance for nearly getting us killed. Next time, you'll not be so hasty. Follow the plan."

"I know, Goranth. I now know better than anyone how quickly the world unravels when one person doesn't pull their weight. I won't fail you again."

Goranth grunted his approval. That was all he could ask from the young man. Do better next time. Don't make the same mistake twice.

And by the Ice Dogs, live and learn.

Goranth made himself comfortable by the fire. It had been a long day, with a healthy fight and enough ground covered to make a hearty traveler jealous. He was ready for sleep, but he had information Rif needed to hear.

"Any dragon sign, Barber?" he asked.

"None. Next, we explore south, in the foothills."

That answered the question of whether Kalida had talked to Rif about the plateau. "Kalida says the dragonette is on the plateau. We must climb. East, not south."

Rif chewed on a blade of grass as he contemplated what to do.

"Don't be a fool. She has not been wrong," Goranth added.

"I have no intention of going anywhere other than the plateau. What puts you on edge, my friend?"

"Wiles and half-truths, a dragon who would love nothing more than to devour us whole, and a race of people living under the mountain."

"People living where?" Jaeg interjected himself into the conversation. He stammered an apology, but Rif gestured for Goranth to answer.

"What do you know of a race called the Undmen?"

Rif shook his head. "Never heard of them. Have you met them near here?"

"The Mabayans take their people as slaves when they can find them, but the Undmen stay underground now. Some traders come here, I suspect from Barbertown. The Undmen trade gemstones for metalwork. It is fair to them, but a steal for the traders. That's why you've never heard of them. They are intelligent people but small; the tops of their heads came to the bottom of my rib cage, no higher. Barefoot. I thought I was tracking lost children."

"Why would you track lost children in the woods?" Jaeg wondered.

Rif waved the question away. "Gems for metal, huh?"

"And here we are hunting dragons for less than what those precious stones would buy."

"Those gems will pale in comparison to the riches we will draw from the dragons of Barbertown!" Rif clenched his fists in denial and triumph.

Goranth wondered about him and the quest that would destroy him. Every warrior's soul went on a journey from which they would not return. Rif had his dragons.

"There's also Mabayan Raiders with tame flying terrors who travel through this area."

"Tame flying terrors? Twice today, you have told me tales I can barely believe, but from you, I must. This changes things, but on the plateau, we'll escape the raiders traveling below. First thing in the morning, we climb. From there, we search."

Goranth yawned. He'd said his piece and shared the information that needed to be shared. Almost all of it.

"I put my sword through the four soldiers who were coming to help. They were intent on killing us, so I killed them first. I'd be worried about my grip on Barbertown if I were you, Rif."

"How did you know they were coming to kill us?"

Goranth looked down his nose at Rif but didn't answer.

"I see. *Kalida*."

"I tried to let the last one go, but he insisted if he returned to Barbertown without our heads, he was a dead man. You have people wanting to usurp what throne there is. Watch your back, Rif, or your dragon venture will be stillborn without you at the helm."

"More information! You are a wealth of it this night." Rif scowled and started to sulk. "Aye, Northman. All of us need to watch our backs. With the loss of the soldiers to the Mabayans, my loyal followers are not many, not nearly enough. The usurpers could very well outnumber my guards. The flotsam-laden tide is coming in. We must buttress our shores against it."

"'We?'" Goranth asked.

"If you'll stay, aye, the right answer is *we*. I could never do this alone. I need you, Goranth." He looked suspiciously at Jaeg and held his tongue before reminding Goranth of the treasure below his home by tapping his purse.

"As to that, Barber, I won't leave without it, and I won't have it held back to make me stay. Kalida and I will go soon after we return. No, Rif. I won't stay, but I'll help you drag another bedamnt dragon to Barbertown. For Varl. For Esh. For you, who saved my life. But with this, my debt will be paid, and I'll move on. I'll stop by next time I'm through Barbertown, whenever that may be, if some king in training hasn't separated your head from your neck!" Goranth ended with a hearty laugh.

Rif rubbed his throat at the thought. "We'll have to see that doesn't happen, Northman." He joined Goranth in his mirth while Jaeg watched. The youth was obviously confused about what the two large men thought funny. It looked like he wanted to laugh, too, but couldn't manage it; he wanted to be one of them but wasn't. He sat at the same fire and ate the same food, but he remained on the outside looking in.

———

Morning came before dawn. Jaeg stepped on a branch. It cracked, and he cried out. The two warriors came up, ready to fight the unseen foe.

"Nothing but my clumsiness," Jaeg admitted.

"Think nothing of it, youngster. It's time to get up anyway. We need to tackle that climb at first light. With the Ice Dogs smiling on us, we may walk the plateau by midday," Goranth said as if he were already wide awake. He got up and rekindled the fire.

Rif grumbled a string of unpleasant invectives before rolling over.

The fire sparked to life, casting a red glow with dancing shadows across Goranth's face. He locked eyes with Jaeg. "Rif loves mornings."

The young man realized the Northman was joking with him, welcoming him to the tribe. Jaeg beamed.

"Pack up the rest of the sheep, youngster. That is our food for the next few days."

"Already done, Goranth."

The Northman lost his smile. "When you are on watch, you watch. You don't do other things to distract yourself from keeping your sleeping fellows safe!"

The boy grew flustered and stammered, "It was done before I took the watch, Goranth. I assure you, I watched and listened and nothing more."

Goranth rolled his head and glared at the oversized form under Rif's blanket.

"It was me." Rif threw off his covers and sat, scratching himself as if fleas infested every crack and seam of his skin.

"How did I know you stared at me, judging my ability to work and watch? I couldn't see letting the flies infest the meat and ruin it. Aye, Northman! It was me!" Rif bellowed.

"You have the wits of a toddler, Barber." Goranth snuffed out the fire. "Besides your siren's call, we don't need a beacon to draw the night hunters to us. We'll eat while we walk. We must get from this place, be ready to climb at first light."

"What's your hurry?" Rif asked in a far quieter tone.

Goranth stepped close until he was nose to nose with Rif. The old sailor put a hand on his remaining dagger. "I've a need, a man's need that can't be taken care of out here."

Rif relaxed. "Then we shall hurry, my friend. For you, of course." He chuckled to himself as he rolled his blanket tightly and stuffed it into his pack.

In no time at all, the group was loaded down with meat, ropes, gear, and weapons. Rif had fashioned a walking stick, a staff of which Varl could have been proud.

"Get you a staff, boy," Goranth stated. He scanned the nearby woods before raising his fist in the air to stop the others. He disappeared into the brush. A swish and thump later, he reemerged with two lengths of willow, each twice the thickness of his thumb. He handed one to Jaeg and kept the other for himself.

He started the procession anew to the foothills, on his way to the landslide down which he had scrambled what seemed a lifetime ago. It may have only been four days. He wasn't sure.

As Goranth had desired, with the sun's first rays peeking between the mountain tops, they were already halfway up the slope of the cave-pocked cliff face. In the daylight, Goranth increased his speed until he found the youth struggling to keep up, then called for a break.

They ate in silence and refreshed themselves with sips of water, although the real work was ahead. They had not yet begun to sweat.

The short break served them well. They stepped off with new vigor, especially Jaeg. Goranth stopped worrying about those behind him and focused his attention on what lay before: a rough climb that would expose them to the skies, within which a great dragon hunted.

He zigzagged across the face, finding the easiest route but always moving upward. The last stretch required a climb from ledge to ledge. Goranth didn't remember it.

He had failed to retrace his steps from his descent.

Goranth cursed all dragons and added Rif's name to his invectives for good measure. He leapt and grabbed the ledge above, then pulled himself up.

"Toss me the ropes," he called down. He lay on his belly, head and shoulders over to give the boy a target. Rif took the bag before Jaeg could throw it and stretched upward to hand the bag to Goranth.

"I have no desire to chase the bag down the hill, and you have little strength left to do it yourself," Rif told the young man. Jaeg nodded and tossed his staff for Goranth to catch. Rif cupped his hands for Jaeg to step into and hoisted him to Goranth's waiting hand. The Northman pulled him over the top and reached back for Rif.

"Hold my legs, boy. I don't want Rif to drag me down with him." Jaeg sat on Goranth's legs, nearly getting tossed in the air when the Northman caught Rif and pulled his hands to the ledge. "You are living an easy life, Barber. Any more feasts at your palace, and I wouldn't be able to pull you up."

The Barber scrambled over the ledge, breathing harder than he should have been. "Muscle weighs more than fat, my friend. This is king's-grade beef," he declared.

"Only ten more ledges to go. Are you going to make it?" Goranth wondered, waving away the answer. There was no choice if they wanted a dragonette. They repeated the process for the next climb, but after that, each was able to navigate the ascent on their own. If they managed to snare the dragonette, the Northman wondered how they would lead it back down.

Goranth carried the backpack in his hand, despite Jaeg's protests. The lad carried the staff, and at times they each clung to it in one way or another to steady themselves as they pressed upward. Finally there was only one short climb left, and erosion made that as simple as walking to the end of a crevasse. Goranth stepped onto the plateau first and crouched to keep a low profile until he could be certain the area was clear.

Carrion birds circled not far from where they stood.

"Come," he called over his shoulder and stalked toward the kill. When he arrived, his spirits sagged, and he bit his tongue lest he say something to crush his own soul.

"Is that…" Jaeg wondered.

Rif nodded. "Aye, lad. That's the dragon we almost had. It tells me that if we had captured it, it would still be alive. See these tracks? An adult dragon killed it."

"But didn't eat it," Jaeg noted.

"They aren't cannibals, but they are apparently unforgiving of their own kind, no matter how young," Goranth said.

Jaeg started to circle, looking for a clue or anything to bring them back to their mission. "More dragon tracks."

"The little guy put up a fight," Rif observed. Goranth looked at where Jaeg was pointing.

"Nicely done," Goranth said. "Looks like at least three different tracks, maybe four. Dragons of all sizes, one of them thankfully small."

"We're standing in the middle of their hunting ground." Jaeg looked at the older men.

"And that is the wisest thing you've said since we left Barbertown," Goranth replied. He gestured with his head and loped away. Rif ran after him, and Jaeg followed after grabbing the pack.

Goranth pointed at the mountains, where a shadow detached itself and glided downward.

Jaeg fell behind as the others sped up on their way to an outcropping that promised the only cover close enough.

Goranth reached it and threw his pack under an overhang. He drew his swords to find the lad well back. Rif dodged beneath the rocks, looking for a better place to hide.

"Get in here, boy!" Goranth roared.

"No!" he yelled, shrugging off the pack of ropes and twirling his staff. The dragon caught an updraft and rose to hover.

Goranth bolted into the open. "Fool boy. The ropes," he shouted. The dragon's head swiveled back and forth as if the men were baiting her into a trap. Goranth seized the bag and the delay. "This is a waste. You can't hope to fight that dragon. Too big. Come. NOW!"

The boy's sudden bravado gave way to a calmer head, and he ran after Goranth. The dragon saw its prey running.

It tucked its wings and dove. That added fire to Goranth's steps, and the lad, free from the burden of his pack, accelerated past the Northman.

A low rumble vibrated their bodies and became a mighty roar that shook the land around them. Goranth dove under the overhang but turned back, expecting to see the dragon's maw, but she was winging into the sky. She barked an anguished cry.

Goranth relaxed and studied her as the ground started to shake a second time. The truth dawned on him. "Earth tremors!" The ground rolled slowly as the earth mother twisted beneath them, releasing the stress of her stone and dirt, reshaping the land with each new quake.

The rumbling trailed off.

"Come," Rif said from behind them. "The best place to be when she returns is *not* here."

He followed a split between the rocks, a natural walkway that led to the border of the plateau. They jogged, hauling their gear in their hands to make their escape before adjusting for comfort.

The cut led to a cave.

"That big dragon isn't going to come in there after us." Rif led the others inside, walking as far as the light shone. Cracks overhead suggested more than a cave, taking the edge off the darkness. They dropped their gear to take a seat. "We can contemplate our next move and how to find a small one."

"What were you thinking?" Goranth asked Jaeg.

"I couldn't outrun the beast, and I'm not going to die while running away. Better to face it and have a chance than die a coward."

"Don't die at all. Give yourself the best chance to live," Goranth advised. "Fight when you have to fight, and then you fight to win. You will never prevail against a dragon with only a staff. Running was the only choice and not a sign of cowardice. Knowing that difference is what makes a warrior great."

Jaeg started to nod when the walls shook with refreshed vigor. The rumble suggested the cave might not have been the safest place to hide.

The rocks cracked and gave way, and a section of the

roof came down. Goranth threw himself over the lad and tightened his muscles to ward off the bludgeoning.

But the rockfall never reached them. The tremors ceased. Goranth opened his eyes to find dust filling the air and bitter grit settling on his tongue. Darkness was the only thing they could see of the entrance. Pinpoints of light from above were their only connection to the outside world.

CHAPTER SIXTEEN

The ice cave has a terrible beauty—crystalline shards of diamond and soft edges of new snow. Beware the icefall. Stay clear! Fight the horrors within from without.
Mothers' tales from Goranth's Homeland

"Noooooooo!" Jaeg sputtered, choking on the dust. "We're trapped. We're going to—"

"—be fine," Rif cut in. "We just dig ourselves out." The Barber edged past the youth, his form an inky slash amid the shadows. "An easy task, this. Goranth and I will have us out in—"

Minutes, Goranth thought. Rif was going to say minutes, but the earth had another idea. The tremors they'd experienced before had just been a hint of what was to come. He felt a bump under his feet like something rising up. Like the earth was taking a deep breath beneath them. The exhale was a rumble that jittered through the stone hard enough to set his teeth knocking.

Jaeg gasped. Rif cursed. Then came a groan—not from either man but from the stone.

Goranth bent his legs and held his arms out to his sides to keep his balance. The rumble was soft at first, almost like a big cat purring. Comforting. Then it spun into a roar of rocks grating against each other and stone falling. The ground beneath them added its angry unsettling voice.

"Kalida!" Rif hollered, the shout a whisper that barely seeped through the din. "Stop this!"

Goranth knew that while the priestess was powerful, she hadn't done this. Wouldn't have done this.

"Kalida!" Rif persisted.

"We're going to die!" This from Jaeg.

The boy's quavering and high-pitched voice showed just how young he was, Goranth thought. Foolish to stand outside and try to face a dragon, then be frightened like a babe by this earth shake. Aye, they might die, and Rif should have never brought the youth along. They might all well join Varl in whatever awaited beyond this world.

The pinpoints of light from above vanished as the stone shifted, and everything was the blackest black. Rif continued hollering for Kalida, and Jaeg shouted something unintelligible. Goranth focused on keeping his feet and listening, feeling the shudders through the soles of his sandals.

Kalida, he thought. *Where are you?*

The vibrations intensified and the roar grew until he could no longer hear his companions' cries, the sound painful. Goranth dropped, unable to stay upright. His head slammed into the stone. Ear to it, a new sound intruded. It was like running water—a fast river, then a waterfall—but it was stone making that noise, bouncing and cracking and sliding down the mountain within which they found themselves trapped.

We might well die, Goranth thought. Unbidden, his mind called up images—the eye of the giant squid, the great cat that had been Varl's demise, the massive mother dragon, his visage reflected in her pupils. The images flashed fast and bright behind lids that were squeezed tight shut— Kalida's smooth face and captivating wink, Rif's wide grin, the old sailor raising a mug of ale, the pile of gold and gems Goranth wanted a share of. He thought he heard the strains of a favorite sea chanty, sung by a familiar blind man to accompany the workers toiling on deck. All of that was replaced by the convivial chatter in a tavern, then the whistling of the wind and the flapping of sails.

Madness! His mind was jostled by memories that twisted and played out, overlapping and making it impossible to concentrate on what was real. Faces of people long lost to him flitted around like ghosts.

"Kaliiiiiiida!" Rif hollered. The Barber cried out other things, but they were lost in the storm of an angry mountain venting its fury.

Then Goranth heard a sharp *crack!* He tried to stand and shake off his visions but was pelted by fist-sized rocks dropping on his back. He clenched his jaw and pushed up, fighting the tremors and ignoring the falling stones, battling his way to his feet and listening to rocks thud against other bodies—Rif's and Jaeg's.

"Kalida. Help," Goranth said. Rif continued to shout for her, but Goranth knew a whisper would be heard just as well—if she was listening.

"We're gonna die!" Jaeg gasped.

All men die, Goranth knew. Short years or long, happily embraced or pitifully endured, it all ended in a loss of blood and breath. But it wasn't going to be today, not for him. He'd not fully embraced all of Kalida's charms or returned to his homeland or stuffed satchels with some of that treasure beneath Rif's home. He'd not gone back to the sea, which was more a home to him than anything.

"Not today!"

No, not today. Kalida was in his head again. Perhaps the three words were meant to comfort him or bolster his resolve, but he sensed her nervousness. She was not confident he would live to see the next sunrise.

Winds blow strong, oceans seize, she said.

Goranth staggered toward what he thought had been the mouth of the crevice, where Rif and Jaeg had been. One step, two, three.

Nature is not to be predicted. Storms roil. The earth shakes, she continued. *Today, the earth shakes.*

"Stop it!" Rif hollered. "Kalida!"

The shaking is not my doing, nor can I quiet it, she said. *The earth mother is angry, maybe singing her power, maybe shedding her old skin, or—*

The shaking stopped, and for the passing of several heartbeats Goranth heard the faint sound of stone dust falling like light rain and Jaeg and Rif's heavy breathing. Goranth had been holding his breath, listening and looking—and seeing nothing beyond this black that was darker than a starless sky. He might as well have been blind.

Rif grunted, coughed, cursed, and spat.

Jaeg moaned.

Goranth pulled in a lungful of dust. He covered his mouth with a sleeve and breathed deeply again and again, trying to find good air and failing. He tasted stone and sweat and lumbered forward, hitting his head against a lower ceiling within the newly misshapen cave. He ached from the beating the quake had bestowed.

"Northman! North—"

"Rif?" Goranth risked.

"Here," came the reply. "Somewhere here."

The Barber sounded near, but the heaving gasps and rock shifting and dropping distorted his voice. Goranth crouched and held his right hand out, finding stone and using it to guide him. He shuffled, taking small steps and finding places where what had been a flat floor was now uneven and littered with stones seeking to trip him.

"Northman!"

"Hold, Barber. I'll find you. Are you hurt? And you, Jaeg?"

Kalida was with all of them, talking about the earth mother and forces of nature, an unpredictable world with grand and foul shocks.

Goranth continued fumbling in the blackness, and his foot caught in a crack and set him off-balance. He fell, and his right knee hit a rough stone hard. He cried out in surprise and pain, then cursed himself for the weakness.

Goranth, Kalida mind-whispered. *Goranth, are you—*

I am fine, he thought, not wanting Rif or Jaeg to hear him. But he wasn't fine. A dull pain throbbed through every inch of his muscular form, and his head ached like it was a drumskin being pounded during a wild Borezhyan dance. He couldn't see, and he breathed sullied air. He could well be in his tomb. Goranth managed to get to his feet and again bumped his head against the newly lowered ceiling. *By the Ice Dogs! I do not like your earth mother, Kalida. Facing the dragon would have been—*

—your death. Kalida finished. *Neither did the dragon cause this. Rif blames her*, Kalida said. *Or blames me for not being able to stop it. No dragon caused this. Just nature. Just chance.*

Not a game of chance I wish to play, woman.

"Northman!"

"Aye, Barber. I'll find you." Goranth shuffled forward once more with even greater caution. He smelled the stink of his companion and bent, feeling with outstretched fingers to find Rif sitting, legs splayed wide, head against the rock wall. The Barber was huffing, and Goranth's fingers came away slick with blood. Rif was injured.

"Help me up."

Goranth's fingers searched until he found Rif's hands, then grabbed them and pulled. It was like lifting a dead weight. He felt the Barber struggle to stand, appearing to favor one of his legs.

"Twisted it," Rif said. "My leg, ankle. Hurts like hell." He let go of Goranth's hands. "If I can find one of those walking staves, I should be good." A pause. "If we can get out of here."

"Stay low," Goranth warned. "The ceiling seeks to crush our skulls. Jaeg?"

"Jaeg!" Rif barked.

There was a muffled reply, and Goranth shuffled past Rif, nearly stumbled again, and came to an area that seemed wholly caved in. The muffled words came from there.

"By the Ice Dogs, boy, you are a bother." Goranth carefully knelt, gritting his teeth as sharp rocks bit into his calves and knees and added to his misery. Rif bumped into his back, grunted something that might have passed for an apology, and joined him.

Together, they moved rocks to the sides of the crevice with Kalida directing them.

He is hurt, she told them.

"We're all hurt," Rif returned. "Woman, you could have used your magic to—"

I did not do this.

"No. I realize you're not so powerful as to change the face of this mountain. But you damn well could have tried to slow it down, to stop it, to—"

I tried. Kalida's words were so filled with ire that they felt like daggers jabbing Goranth's mind. *Don't you think I tried to keep you safe? I gave everything to try to protect you, and maybe I played a role. Maybe I kept this chamber from collapsing and burying you. I'm exhausted, and I can barely reach your minds now. You can find your own damn way out.*

And just like that, she was gone from Goranth's mind.

Rif cursed louder.

Goranth worked faster and was rewarded when he heard Jaeg sputter and felt his fingers grab his arm. The youth clawed his way out, coughing. Goranth felt him shaking.

"I can't see anything," Jaeg said as Goranth and Rif freed the rest of him.

The Northman probed the gashes that crisscrossed the youth's chest and arms.

"My nose. It's broken," Jaeg continued. "Bleeding. I am—"

"—alive, boy," Rif growled. "Thank the gods, you are alive. We all are, and for that, thank your gods."

"But for how long?" Goranth mused. "Just how much rock are we buried under?"

"Kalida could tell us, Northman," Rif said. The three men moved around so they could stand without sharing each other's breaths. "But she's gone to sulk. Never had good luck with women."

Goranth thought about the four soldiers he'd killed in the woods, the ones who'd come to assassinate them. Rif didn't have good luck with people in general, he thought.

"Let's keep moving these rocks," Goranth suggested. "I think we're not far from where we came into this hole. Unless we got turned around in the quake."

"No one will come here looking for us," Jaeg said. "My dad will never know—"

"—that I was foolish to agree to take you on this venture," Rif finished. "Shut up, boy, and help us dig. Just shut up."

Everything had gone to shit since he'd landed in Barbertown in answer to Rif's call. He'd been boiled by a dragon, buried an old friend, teased by treasure, hunted by men and beasts, and was now the victim of an earthquake. He sweated as if he were hovering above coals, his head still pounded, and his back ached from where the rocks had pummeled him. Misery had dominated each step of this journey.

Except for meeting Kalida. He tried to shake off the thought, but the sparkle in her eyes and the curve of her hip wouldn't leave his mind, nor would the necklace he'd intended to give her with a pendant hanging between her ample breasts. Was she the prize he couldn't have? Or was she the siren calling him to wreck on hidden shoals?

He worked faster, and from the grunts and thumps, he knew Rif and Jaeg toiled hard with him.

"Wish I could see," Rif grumbled. "Wish I could tell how much rock we have to move."

Goranth wanted to see, too; it would indicate that they'd broken through enough for the sunlight to poke its way inside. It would hint at freedom. The darkness didn't bother him, though. He wasn't afraid of it and could damn well use his other senses to figure a way out.

You cannot get out that way, Kalida said. She'd come back, at least to Goranth. *Too much of the mountain blocks your path in that direction. You haven't the numbers or the tools to break out. Futile.*

"So, we're doomed?" Goranth asked aloud.

"What?" Rif cut in. "It's not like you, Northman, to give up."

Kalida, it seemed, was not in Rif's head.

Not doomed, Goranth. *I want you to come back to me. Go the other way. Find the other end of this crevice. I sense that the stone is weaker and thinner, and there is a gap. Come with me to find it, like when we traveled into the mountain and near the healing stones. Let your mind slip away with me. Come.*

Goranth let out a deep breath, relaxed his shoulders, and focused on Kalida. It was a difficult matter because he was consumed by the rocky grave that trapped him, as well as his aches, the sweat, and the foul air he continued to take in.

Come!

He spiraled, a slow and uneven plunge that took him out of his body and through the still-nervous stone. Kalida was with him, her presence soothing and cooling. The gritty taste in his mouth gave way and good clean air filled his lungs, but in the back of his mind, he knew it was all imaginary. He was physically with Rif and Jaeg. Kalida sang in an unfamiliar language that might have been no language, just pleasant sounds. Or perhaps it was an incantation that helped fuel her magic and carried them down and away, deeper into the mountain.

A wider spiral now, still downward, when he'd thought she would be driving them upward and out of the mountain. He sensed the stone shimmy, felt her tense and then become splintered as she sent her mystic vision ranging to all points of the compass. He likened the experience to a mirror shattering, each shard revealing a different and distorted reflection.

In one shard, Kalida searched into the depths of a familiar cavern, the one with the sheep and goat bones where she'd said hatchling dragons had once lived. At the same time, another shard reached into the walls where they'd found the healing stones, but she didn't tarry long enough for Goranth to enjoy the curative emanations. She went deeper and farther; he had the impression they traveled north through the range, and she passed into a series of twisting warrens where diminutive gray-skinned people scampered and unburied others of their kind.

The Undmen had also been devastated by the quake. Goranth wondered if those he'd met yesterday were among the trapped or dead. Another shard and the Undmen were gone. Half-glimpsed impressions danced in the margins of his vision: insects, snakes, lairing cats, and broken shells where dragons had been born.

Another tremor raced through the mountain and Kalida spiraled up and to the south, he thought, though he couldn't be sure. Goranth was disoriented and considered himself a leaf caught up in the tornado of her whims. Next she circled outward, and the Northman worried that there was no pattern or reason to her earth-jaunt.

Rif, he thought. *And Jaeg. We need to get out—*

I've found a way, Goranth. Come. Don't fight me. Don't make me drag you.

He wasn't aware that he fought her, though perhaps his hesitancy amounted to that. Moments later, his mind was back in his beaten body, and he was again pulling in great gasps of the dusty air. Rif was still cursing and telling Jaeg to be quiet.

"This way," Goranth told them. "There's a way out. Follow me."

Rif growled but fumbled around until a meaty fist grabbed Goranth's shoulder. "Kalida show you?"

"Aye."

"At least she talks to one of us."

"The pack!" Jaeg panted. "The bag of ropes and my pack. Help me find them."

Rif grumbled and dug his fingers into Goranth's shoulder. Goranth brushed him off and kicked at the rocks at his feet. "Hurry," he told Jaeg. "Find them quickly, else we'll leave it and—"

"Found my pack. Found it. Found it." Jaeg coughed and bumped into something. A moment later, he bumped into Goranth. Then something rustled, and the Northman guessing the youth was digging in his pack. "But the ropes, Goranth. All the—"

Buried, Kalida said. *Beneath too many rocks. Do you really need them after all of this? You haven't the tools, the time, the—*

"Forget the ropes," Goranth said. "Let's just—"

Light flared behind him and Goranth swung around, accidentally knocking Rif against the wall. He saw Jaeg holding a fat-soaked torch. The youth, a mass of scrapes and forming bruises, had retrieved it from his pack and lit it.

"I've three of these," he said. "Won't last all that long, but it's something. My father packed them for me." Goranth noted a jagged gash that ran from Jaeg's forehead down his clearly broken nose, across a cheek, and to his jaw. It would scar, marring what had been a smooth, angular face.

This way, Kalida said. *Get them to move, Goranth.*

Goranth turned back to face the shadows and took a few steps. The blackness was peeled back by Jaeg's torch as the youth came closer. The cave-in was a jumble of stone, but as Jaeg edged closer still, Goranth spied a slash that might well be an opening. A pile of fallen rocks blocked their way, and he bent to start moving the largest chunks. His back pained him with each move. Nothing but suffering and misery since he'd rejoined Rif.

By the time the torch burned out and Jaeg lit the second, they were well into the gap and pressing forward, the opening so thin in places that Goranth had to step sideways. The rocks scraped his skin as he slithered through, and the air was tight and fusty. Farther on, after ascending and then descending, the Northman breathed easier when the passage widened and he could walk without crouching and without his shoulders being shredded. He felt the heat of the torch on his back and realized Jaeg was walking between him and Rif.

Goranth, I hear the cries of the Undmen directly below us, far and deep and desperate. A wall has crumbled, and many are trapped. I will see if I can help them. It would be wide of the mark to do nothing. Ahead, your path splits. Take the one to your right and you'll climb out on top of the mountain. I will find you there later.

He felt her slip from his mind. Once more, he was both relieved that his thoughts were his own and troubled that she was elsewhere. Could he truly be happy sailing away with a woman who would not allow him his secrets? Who could, at an impulse, know all his thoughts?

The torch was sputtering by the time they reached the fork she'd mentioned. Goranth felt a slight play of fresh air across his face and could tell the right-hand passage ascended.

"Let's hurry," he said. He heard Rif huff in agreement. "I want to get above ground." They'd been walking for some time, and the Barber's breath was labored and his gait shuffling. The quake had taken a toll on all of them, but Rif seemed to have suffered the worst. A glance over his shoulder and around Jaeg revealed that the Barber leaned against the wall as they went.

"I'm all right," Rif said. "I want to be above ground, too." A pause. "Even if the damn big dragon's up there."

Goranth kept moving forward, stopping when the light grew fainter. He turned. Rif was several paces behind him, his face a mix of anger and puzzlement.

"Jaeg," Rif said. "He went the other way." He looked to his left. "Fool boy! Come back with us. Damn him!"

The light dimmed further as Jaeg obviously ventured farther; Goranth was in thick shadows now. "Damn him." He retreated back to Rif, gesturing at the passage Kalida had indicated. "Up. We have to go up."

"Jaeg!" Rif hollered. "What the hell do you think—"

Goranth could barely hear the youth, but he made out: "...have to see this." He plunged into the shadows of the left-hand passage and nearly tripped over a rocky ridge but was able to catch himself against the wall. He sped up, spying the torchlight ahead, and in the same instant, he saw etchings along the wall at shoulder-height—nothing he could read but recognizable as a level series of symbols. Rif followed him, heavily favoring a leg and pausing to note the etchings.

"A language, you think?"

Goranth shrugged. "A fool youth is what I think. You shouldn't have brought him, Barber. He'll be the death of us."

"Look at this!" Jaeg was at the bottom of the passage, gesturing to Goranth, excitement clear on his damaged face. "This is amazing."

"What would be amazing is getting out of here." Goranth trundled down, thinking he would either bodily carry Jaeg back the right way or take the torch and leave the boy to the darkness.

But he saw past him. The torchlight played forward into a worked chamber lined with stone columns that were cracked and crooked either because of age and the weight of the mountain on top of them or the recent quake.

In front of them were broken pieces of furniture, rotted rugs, and books. A lot of books, the worn covers damaged by mold, stacked high along one wall. Across from it were cubbyholes in the stone filled with rolled pieces of skin and parchment.

"Isn't this amazing?" Jaeg said as he reached for his third and final torch and lit it from the dying end of the second.

"I don't give a damn about books," Goranth growled. "I just want out. Hold on." He forced the youth to face him. Goranth gripped Jaeg's nose between his fingertips and pulled, straightening it.

Jaeg grunted but didn't cry out.

Rif limped past him, grabbed the torch from Jaeg, and waved it around to reveal more books in darkened corners. "There might be something of value here," the Barber said. "What a fine discovery!"

Goranth growled louder.

CHAPTER SEVENTEEN

"You're a canvas shy of a full sail, aren't you, mate?"
A Black Sail Brotherhood Saying

"You have a death wish, Rif, and you're taking every person you've ever known with you," Goranth rumbled.

"You fail to see the potential, my friend. Aye, we're battered but not broken. This is our moment of triumph! We have crawled through the dark of the shattered earth to find this, delivered to us by the earth mother as a reward for surviving."

"It's a fool's quest, like all the quests. Opportunity? Bah!" Goranth took a deeper look at the untouched chamber, wondering if there was hidden treasure. Still, a nagging feeling cast a dark cloud over his head. Why had something like this not been looted when it wasn't far from the surface? Or perhaps it had been, and only old books remained.

Jaeg dropped to a knee and mumbled a prayer to Vujo.

"Get up, boy. The gods care not for the affairs of men. We are as ants to them. Nothing more. Save your words for ideas of import and save your strength for doing what matters."

"It matters to me, Goranth. I seemed to be drawn down here. That's why I had to come."

"And you don't see the problem? Treasure never tells you where it is. You have to find it. Demons call from within your mind and lure you into traps." The makhaira sang as Goranth pulled it and wheeled, looking for something he knew had to be there.

There was nothing but the musty smell of an ancient library. "By the Ice Dogs..." he grumbled.

Rif took the book in the best condition off a shelf and laid it on a reading stand. With the greatest care, he opened the cover, using his dagger to flip the fragile pages. "Hold the light closer, boy, but not too close. We don't want to burn our prize."

Jaeg raised the torch, staying an arm's length away. The dancing flames revealed a language they had never seen before.

"Goranth, have you ever seen such writing in all your travels?"

Goranth tucked the makhaira into his belt and moved closer. He traced the lines of glyphs, symbols, and characters across the page.

"Never. The picture writing of the Gabigar and the wizard ravings of the Tsentar and not even the utilitarian writing of my own people—this looks like none of that."

"Maybe this is an odd volume," Rif suggested.

He pulled out book after book to find that they were all written the same way. He replaced them with the greatest care, as if handling dainty crystal.

"Maybe Kalida—" Rif started.

"We've bothered her enough, old friend. Let us look further to see what we haven't seen. Why is there no gold and gems in a cave within a mountain filled with them?" Goranth asked.

"Maybe the heathens didn't believe in such things, embracing knowledge instead. There are secrets on these pages, and men will pay for secrets." Rif pounded his fist into his palm while leaning heavily on one leg. They had not taken stock of their wounds to understand how badly they had been injured.

Goranth's knee felt immensely better; apparently, it had only been a strain that the walking had set right. His back still hurt from the bludgeoning he'd taken from the falling roof.

"Here." Jaeg pointed to a half-full oil lamp hiding under an old cloth that shredded at his touch.

Goranth reached past the lad and took the lamp to wave its wick through the torch. It came to life. Goranth extended the wick to make it brighter. "Put that torch out. We may need it later."

Jaeg rubbed it out on the cave floor.

Once the smoke from the torch cleared, the calm flame gave them a far better view of the hidden library.

A chair that had succumbed to the ages was broken in a corner. The stone before the reading stand had been worn smooth by the countless feet that had stood there.

"What people these who would gather such?" Goranth asked mysteriously.

"We need to ask Kalida," Rif pressed.

"We need to look for a hidden chamber or secret drawers. There is more here than books. There must be."

Goranth shoved three heavy volumes aside within a thick paneled shelf. The books split in half and tumbled to

193

the floor, coming apart when they hit and becoming little more than fodder for a campfire.

"By all that's holy! You are costing us with your barbarian ways. Books, Goranth. All the knowledge of the world is in books, and people will pay handsomely *if* they are intact. What did an ancient wizard spend a lifetime writing into those volumes? We'll never know, thanks to you."

"Or a priest who worshipped a demon god writing edicts for the masses. Dark rituals and those things that should not see the light of day. But maybe you're right, Rif. Maybe these are every bit as valuable as those dragons you want." The glint of hope shattered in the pain of reality. "No coin will grace our purses from these. This is another of your ill-fated ventures."

"Maybe, but maybe not. Kalida, Goranth. She thinks ill of me, so you must call her and ask for her help."

"She was exhausted when last we heard from her because of her fight with the mountain and the earth mother. A fight she lost, but she tried! I will grant her that. And we live when we shouldn't. There is no luck, Rif, only a will to live and those who help. Leave her be. We'll search this cavern, bandage our wounds, and eat, and when she's rested, I will talk with her."

"You favor the wench, Goranth. It has to be you because she has no feelings for me. We'll do as you wish and wait."

"She doesn't favor you because she's seen into your mind. It probably left a bad taste in her mouth, and I'm lucky she'll still talk to me while I'm near you."

"Why doesn't she talk with me?" Jaeg asked.

Rif waved at the boy. "That question answers itself."

Goranth finished searching the heavy wood shelf, tapping it while looking for gaps or indents that might suggest a secret compartment. But there was nothing; it was only a shelf. He sat on the floor. The effort made him feel old. He shortened the lamp's wick to save the oil, dimming the chamber.

The others followed his lead, having found nothing besides the obvious.

Goranth caught himself brooding. He chuckled lightly as he dug into his pack for smoked sheep and ripped off a great hunk with his teeth. He took his time gnawing on it.

The only pack they had lost was the one with the ropes. They would make do because they had survived to fight another day. The tunnel led to the outdoors. He had smelled it before getting pulled sideways to the hidden chamber. If there was going to be no dragon, then maybe the ancient texts weren't such a bad idea. It would be far easier to carry books than lead a reluctant dragonette without ropes.

He could still feel the sting of its hot breath on his back. Rif would have to do without his dragon.

If they found the Undmen, they could trade steel for gems and further enrich themselves. Payment for time and blood.

Until Goranth could get back to Rif's underground horde, where he would take what he was owed and nothing more.

He glared from under heavy brows at the Barber, who had reclined with his eyes closed. Slow and steady breathing suggested he was asleep. Same for the boy. The day's trials had been too much for them.

Goranth took a measured swig from his flask and capped it tightly. He wasn't sure when next they'd find water, so he had to shepherd his supply. He glanced around the chamber one last time before allowing himself to drift off.

His mind dreamed of a wild journey through the

mountain and into the forest. To the steppes of the Mabayans and the peaks of his homeland. He stopped to embrace the power of the uncut gemstones cradled within the earth mother's bosom. He pressed on to find himself in Kalida's small home, where she waited for him. He saw himself securing the latch on the door before dropping his arms. He strode to her, his fingers finding her bare skin and making her shiver with anticipation. He lifted her to carry her to bed.

Kalida's mind guided him in what to do. He stopped, recoiling at the thought. "Can we not go where the winds take us?" he heard himself ask.

"It is better this way," she replied.

"Not for me." He stepped away to find himself shackled to a wall. She tickled him with feathers before running the tip of a dagger over his body. He could feel the cold steel...

He shot awake. Rolling and in a single movement as quick as an eyeblink, he came to his feet, crouched and ready to fight, with swords in both hands.

The daintily flickering light of the small lamp showed the chamber exactly as he remembered it before he fell asleep. He rammed his long sword into its scabbard, startling both Jaeg and Rif. They grumbled and groaned before rolling over and closing their eyes again. Goranth picked up the lamp to carry it with him a short way up the tunnel to study the carvings on the wall and collect his wits.

The symbols and images had been chipped by tools of high quality that left clean lines in the stone. There was a mark here or there to show they'd been chiseled and not magicked into place.

A hermit's chamber, writing in a made-up language, Goranth thought. One sheet short of a full sail, just like Rif and his endless quest for more treasure when he had hoard enough to last several lifetimes.

I trust you slept well, Goranth, Kalida purred. *I dreamt of you.*

And I of you, woman, but it gave me no joy.

Mine did, Northman. I cannot wait until you are in my arms and my bed. Her voice took on sultry tones within his mind. He felt drawn to her but fought it.

Can you read this language?" he asked, attempting to distract her.

Relax, Northman. I won't shackle you to my wall. If you don't fight me, I'll be able to see through your eyes.

No one shackles Goranth the Mighty and lives to tell the tale.

Relax, Goranth.

Goranth's knuckles turned white and he gripped his makhaira as if it were a lifeline to his sanity. He struggled to put it into his belt, and once there, he found his muscles settling. He realized that once again, he'd been healed by the power of the stones within the earth mother. His bruises were gone, and the ache in his knee was nothing more than a twinge.

He extended the wick to shine more light on the wall.

Kalida filled his mind, not with her desires, but with her intense interest in the language on the wall.

Closer, she urged, and Goranth complied.

I have seen this language before. It hasn't been spoken in a thousand years—the language of those who worshipped Ollimor.

There are books, too, a complete library.

Her answer was two words tinged with excitement. He could feel her vibrancy within him as if she were caressing his body with hers. *Show me.*

Goranth returned to the library chamber and kicked Rif's foot. "Get up, you bilge rat. Kalida wants to see the books. You opened them before without damage. Do it again."

"You uncouth buffoon! If it weren't for that witch in your head, I'd have my sleep. Damn! I hurt all over." Rif sat up and scratched himself like an ape. Goranth offered an arm to help him up. The Barber teetered on a single leg and studied the bigger man. "Look at you, fresh as a seagull in the morning mist. Kalida does you right, Northman."

"Just open the book, you vile, blubberous windbag." Goranth heard his voice, but it wasn't he who had spoken.

Rif started to laugh. "You are getting better, my friend. Just when I thought you would brood yourself into a dark pit, you emerge with a new shine. Bravo, you oversized, under-brained priestess' plaything."

The Barber removed the book from the shelf, again with the greatest care and placed it on the reading stand. He opened it with the tip of his dagger to the first page and stepped aside.

Goranth moved in, and Kalida started reading. Her mood soured within the Northman's mind. His lips moved, and he heard himself speaking again.

"One's best life is found after death. From a single bone, one can be reborn. The master casts his favors upon those who ask in the right way for those who have fallen and are waiting for their rebirth."

"What does that mean, Goranth?"

The Northman shook his head, unable to say what he wanted to say.

"Turn the page," Kalida ordered using Goranth's voice. She read and gestured again and again. She directed Goranth to the shelves and looked at the titles of those books showing them. His finger lifted and pointed. "This one."

Rif closed the book on the reading table and replaced it

with the indicated volume. He leaned down to look at the pages and see where to poke his dagger to open it. The first third of the book was stuck together in a single lump. Between the blade and the hard cover, he moved that block to the side and focused on the pages that would turn.

Goranth edged in, gesturing for Rif's blade. He spun it around and handed it over.

Page after page.

"Damn your eyes, woman. What do you see?" Rif fluttered his hands in his impatience.

Goranth was powerless to answer, but Kalida's reply was better and far more eloquent. "I see your greed overwhelming any good sense you may have once had. You'll know when I determine the time is right to tell you. For now, be quiet. I must concentrate."

She returned to studying the text, stopping after a long ten pages. Goranth spun the dagger and handed it back.

"Dragons. The necromancer who lived in this cave brought back the dragons. And the necromancer revered Ollimor."

Rif deflated. "It's probably best not to sell these books then, is it?"

Goranth turned his head of his own volition and found that his voice was his once again. "Did you have to ask that, Barber? These are best left in here and probably as part of a bonfire."

Wait, Kalida said before Goranth could act on his threat.

"Wait yourself, woman!" Goranth cried. "This sorcery isn't to be in anyone's hands, no matter how much good you think you'll find within these demon-scrawled tomes."

"Kalida's right," Rif interjected, motioning for Jaeg to step back and taking the lamp and flame out of Goranth's reach. "We won't take them, but I'll mark this place. I will bring Kalida back here to study them in person. If there is value to be had, she alone will determine that. Do you trust her to do no evil?"

"Evil is a word with many meanings, but I do trust that she has no stomach to raise the dead, nor will she tolerate those who do. Aye, your plan is agreeable. If you try to sneak back here without her, I'll fire the cave. Mark my words, Barber."

Rif bowed his head. "You have a deal, Northman." He turned to the youngster. "And that deal includes you. You cannot tell a living soul about this place. Not a one, or I'll cut your tongue out of that scarred face of yours."

Jaeg winced at the mention and nodded tersely.

"I'm serious, boy," Rif continued in a low and dangerous voice.

"I know. I shouldn't even be here, but I am. And now I know of this place. Even if I wanted to come back here, do you think I could get here on my own?"

Goranth could not disagree with the lad's logic.

"Let us abandon this place. Light the torch. We'll leave everything as it was when we got here. If the necromancer watches over this place in his death, he'll look more kindly on those who aren't stealing from him. I want to know none of his secrets."

"What if he has the secret of alchemy, turning lead into gold?"

"You and your gold. Drag me not into your quicksand, Barber."

The torch flared to life and Goranth snuffed the lamp, making sure the wick was cool before putting it back where they had found it. He took the torch from the boy and strode briskly up the tunnel, waiting when he heard his two companions limping and struggling to keep up.

Goranth slowed his pace and took a left into the tunnel

leading to the outside. They climbed, continuing upward. Four more turns and a long ramp later, Goranth saw the blazing light blue of the morning sky and felt the crisp cool of dew-laden air.

He snuffed the torch and handed it to Jaeg for safekeeping. "Thank your father for me. Those torches saved our lives."

Jaeg smiled proudly as he put extra heft into helping Rif climb out of the tunnel and past brush onto a ledge with a narrow rim leading away from it. The forest far below looked unfamiliar.

"How far have we traveled?" Rif wondered.

Goranth craned his neck but couldn't see the mountains behind them. "I don't know. And it doesn't matter, does it? We're out." He turned his attention to the climb, looking for an easy way down when he spotted movement below.

Men with horses. Mabayans.

CHAPTER EIGHTEEN

Through the morning mist we sail
To clear water and a calm sea
To better hunting and lest we fail
Our fate is sealed for eternity.
"Sonnet of the Black Sail Brotherhood"

The forms were small, but Goranth could see enough: six riders pulling a dozen people behind them—Mabayan raiders and their captives. He growled from deep in his belly.

"I'm not a hero, Rif."

"None of us are, Northman. We'll wait here and let them pass. Don't draw attention. Then we can—"

"Not a hero, but I have a conscience. Stay here and keep down, else you'll be added to their slave cache." Goranth touched the pommel of his makhaira; it fairly hummed with anticipation. Bad odds, maybe impossible odds, but he'd get closer and then decide if he was going to do something about it or "let them pass." Most of the people the Mabayans pulled appeared to be Undmen by the cast of their skin and bald heads, maybe the ones Goranth met the other day. Each horse pulled a pair, with the captives' hands tied together and gags in their mouths.

"If we had those ropes," Rif posed, "we could link them together, and that would be enough to capture a small dragon."

"Just stay the hell down," Goranth said.

Like a spider, the Northman skittered away from Rif and down the slope, hands and feet finding purchase in the clefts. He paused behind an outcropping that shadowed him and pulled in deep breaths of fresh air tainted by his own stink. He truly wished to plunge into some stream so he could better tolerate himself. The play of air across his skin was welcome, and the sun felt pleasantly warm; he did not want to go delving in the underground ever again. Those books? They could damn well rot there. And Ollimor, who was mentioned in those ancient pages? If that was a deity, it was not one he'd heard of or needed to revere. Best to leave unknown gods alone.

Perhaps best to leave the Mabayans alone, too.

The Mabayans weren't looking up, but they'd stopped, and he was still too far away to tell why. He couldn't hear them. The men were not getting off the horses, but the one in the lead was twisting in the saddle, casting his gaze into the wooded grassland behind them. Looking for something? Waiting for something? Still not looking up.

Goranth crept down farther and faster, cringing when he heard the scrape of a boot behind him and felt the shower of small pebbles bouncing against his shins. A quick glance over his shoulder confirmed that Rif and Jaeg were climbing down but at a slower pace. Both of them were injured because of the quake and clumsy in their efforts, and he knew they'd be no help to him. They'd more likely be a hindrance.

No use quarreling with them and risking that his voice might carry. Goranth continued down the slope and hid behind a tall patch of saw grass at the bottom. The ground felt spongy and damp like it might have rained while they were trapped inside the mountain. He dug his fingers into the loam, finding the sensation soothing. Where was Kalida? What were the Mabayans waiting for?

Six *armed* Mabayans, bows and quivers on two of them, spears and swords with all of them. One had a vicious-looking morning star. The slaver in the lead wore a boiled leather cuirass, the others padded vests that left their arms bare. He could see that they were all heavily tattooed, but he was too far away to decipher any designs that might hint at their prowess or station.

Two-to-one odds if Jaeg and Rif were at full strength and with him. It wouldn't be that onerous, only mildly risky taking on the small force, Goranth thought, since surprise would be on their side. But the Barber couldn't walk without help, and they had no distance weapons. A close-in assault would be the only way. Goranth would be on his own.

One against six.

Common sense told him to hold and wait until the riders left; let them keep their unfortunate prizes. But if Goranth had listened to his common sense, he never would have answered Rif's call. He'd be far from Barbertown and these wilds. He crab-crawled from one patch of saw grass to the next and the next. Rif and Jaeg were still descending.

Closer, he heard the Mabayans arguing and he got a good look at the horses they rode.

Ahak-Teeks, he noted with appreciation. Probably

stolen from merchants or taken from the hold of some ship. He was certain the Mabayans had come by them dishonestly. The beautiful animals were not native to the island continent of Migoro and were prized for their rarity, endurance, and speed. Six Ahak-Teeks. Men unfamiliar with horses considered them too scrawny and narrow, not muscular enough and lacking the deep chests of working breeds. Those who knew better recognized their elegance, nature's work of art. They were tall and grand in stride, powerful despite a lithe appearance. Goranth had had the pleasure of riding one when he'd spent a few months in a port city far to the south. The name of the city escaped him since he'd spend many of those days and nights in his cups—Raven-something—but the horses that had been brought to market there were etched in his memory. He'd wanted one then, but he hadn't the coin for it. The expensive horses were a shimmering shade of brown that looked almost gold. These were fifteen to sixteen hands high, and all had hooded almond-shaped eyes and manes that looked like spun silk. Their heads were slender, their necks long. Exotic.

How had the Mabayans gotten these?

Goranth cursed himself for being more interested in the stunning horses than the hapless prisoners the Mabayans had lashed together.

He picked through the men's arguments and recognized some words.

Selomonga. It was the country to the south and east of the mountains, where he knew Mabayan villages dotted the coast.

Barbertown.

Mugunta, the river.

Livestock. He suspected that referred to their captives.

Tremors. Maybe the Mabayans had been caught in the quake, too.

Vujo and the *earth mother.* Did men such as these pray?

Dragons. That word was spoken several times. Had the Mabayans spotted dragons on this slave raid?

Sea Foam and *Wave Wrangler.* He knew those to be big merchant ships that had plied the waters around Migoro and the Hawk Islands for many years. Goranth wished he could understand more of the heated discussion so he could tell what the Mabayans were planning for the ships and where they'd acquired the horses, and if they'd seen dragons nearby. Goranth desperately wanted to avoid dragons right now.

The apparent leader barked a command for his fellows and the prisoners to fall in line and follow him. When the line of horses veered north and a little to the east along a wide game trail, Goranth discovered there were actually nine horses and eighteen captives.

Nine to one.

The odds were overwhelming, yet Goranth crept closer still, moving low and fast to keep pace with them. He kept his eyes on the entourage, not wanting to be distracted by looking for Rif and Jaeg somewhere behind him. The first four horses walked in pairs, the remaining five went single-file, and all spread out because they tugged captives between them.

Goranth made for the last in the line. *Not a hero,* he told himself. *I was a fool to have followed Rif, and more fool to be following the Mabayans. By the Ice Dogs! Utter madness!*

He drew the makhaira and felt its welcome heat against the palm of his hand. The warmth spread up his arm and was at the same time comforting and anxious. Did the blade have a presence? Was it his imagination?

Utter madness. His smile was dark and grim; his life had

been built on the madness of action. He could feel the strength in his body respond to the fire of the moment— the fury of madness with the speed of a cobra's strike.

Goranth kept to the undergrowth, moving from grass clumps to bushes to high ferns. He came even with the last horseman in line and held his breath. His leg muscles bunched and he leapt, leading with the makhaira and vaulting high and fast, and had his blade at the Mabayan's throat before the man could react. The small blade nearly decapitated the rider, and Goranth dropped, tugging the body with him, then grabbing the horse's reins. The magnificent, well-trained animal, eyes wide and nostrils flaring, barely wuffled. It did not attempt to bolt.

Goranth made soft noises to it and tugged it to the side of the trail and then into the brush, gritting his teeth at the sound of branches bending and snapping. The two captives, Undmen, had no choice but to follow. The Northman put a finger to his lips and met their stare. He couldn't say if they had been among the ones he'd met the other day since there was much sameness to them. Quickly, he cut the ropes that held their hands, and they removed their gags.

"Shhhh!" His voice was barely above a whisper. He motioned for them to stay down, and he hoped they understood. Then he tended to the horse, whipping the reins around a branch and hoping the animal would stay. He reached up to the saddle and pulled free a quiver stuffed with arrows and a bow, giving him a way to touch his enemies from afar. They improved his odds.

Eight to one, still improbable. Still madness.

A glance at the trail ahead confirmed that his act had been undetected. The Mabayans and their captives had kept moving, and he barely saw the one trailing. The gods had favored him so far. Perhaps they were angry with the

Mabayans and had aided him to punish them. More likely, he'd merely been lucky.

One of the freed Undmen spoke to him softly in a language he couldn't fathom, but he wasn't going to dally to try to find a shared tongue. Once more, Goranth motioned for them to be quiet and to stay down, then he glided through the brush that paralleled the trail, careful and catlike and avoiding wood that might snap. That it had rained helped, he thought, removing some of the brittle dryness that would otherwise be noisy. The woods smelled fresh and helped cut his stench.

He repeated his stealthy tactics on the next rider, again using the makhaira and not the bow. Goranth could use a bow well, but he was not as proficient with it as with a blade, and he did not want to risk a missed shot that would alert his quarry and bring the Mabayans at him.

Two more Undmen freed, another horse tied to a branch.

"Shhhhhhhh!"

Seven to one.

Goranth planned to take out the rest of the single-file riders this way. The three of them were still far enough apart that it might work. The remaining four, riding two abreast, would demand a different strategy. He'd deal with that when the time came. He knew he could still turn back. He'd freed four Undmen and saved the four souls from whatever the slavers intended to do with them. He'd done some good.

Seven to one.

By the Ice Dogs! Damn me.

And yet, he'd committed to this misadventure. Goranth scuttled forward and closed on the next rider, feeling the makhaira tingle against his palm and the warmth spread up his arm, gentling his tight muscles. He came even with the rider, noting that this man pulled an Undmen and a human woman of middle years. From the cut of her clothes, she was a merchant, not a tribesman from a forest village. She was not gagged, and she cried out in surprise when she saw him.

Damn and back again!

Everything seemed to happen at once. Goranth rose from concealment and charged toward the horse. The rider swung around in the saddle and shouted something in Mabayan while he pulled back on the reins with one hand and drew a long, curved blade from his waist with the other. The horse reared and nickered loudly. The foliage near Goranth rattled with activity, but he couldn't divide his attention. His feet slammed across the loam even as the Mabayan shouted again and leaned over to slash at him.

Echoed shouts came from ahead on the trail, and a horn sounded.

Goranth avoided the Mabayan's swing and delivered his own strike, driving the makhaira into the rider's thigh. The blade struck bone before he pulled back and stabbed a second time.

"Kill him!" This from the captive merchant woman. She hollered something else, but it was drowned out by more shouts from the Mabayans ahead, the whinnies of horses, and the crashing of the quartet of freed Undmen, who had not stayed hidden as Goranth had instructed. Two of the Undmen had swords, no doubt taken from the Mabayans the Northman had killed. He cursed that his element of surprise had been dashed, but he welcomed their sword arms and fervently hoped they knew how to use the blades.

The wounded rider slipped off his horse and landed in a crouch, favoring the leg that gushed so much blood Goranth thought it was likely a mortal wound. Still, the man in his final breaths remained dangerous; his blade clipped Goranth's arm, drawing a line of blood.

"By the Ice Dogs, you'll not have me!" Goranth darted close and low and rammed the makhaira into the man's abdomen even as he felt the air stir over his head from a near-miss sword blow. The Northman pushed the Mabayan into the side of the beautiful Ahak-Teek hard and the horse reared again, then bolted forward, pulling the captives behind it. Another stab and the Mabayan collapsed, then Goranth drew his sword, wheeled, and raced up the trail to meet the charge of the next slaver.

Six Mabayans remained.

The merchant woman howled as she lost her footing and landed on her stomach, the running horse still pulling her and the Undmen. Goranth didn't have time to help her since a pair of Mabayans rode hard at him. They'd dropped their captives' ropes, making them faster and able to better maneuver on the trail.

The Northman had no time to reach for the bow. They were on him in the passing of a heartbeat. One wore a boiled leather cuirass, the man Goranth counted as the leader. He sped past Goranth as he leaned low and swung with the morning star, the deadly metal catching the sun and sparkling. Though the Northman narrowly avoided the blow, he turned into the path of the second rider, who thrust with a long, thin blade that bit deep into Goranth's shoulder.

The swing had been so precise that it sent a crippling wave down the Northman's arm. The sword dropped from quivering fingers he couldn't control, leaving him with one good arm and the makhaira. Goranth shrugged the quiver and bow off his back since they were useless to him now, and he planted his feet and lashed out at the rider before the slaver could dart away and swing around for another pass.

He heard a sharp cry down the trail in the direction the leader had ridden. It was an Undman's voice, and likely meant the Mabayan was dealing with the uprising captives. Then he heard rustling in the brush on the opposite side of the trail and saw Jaeg sprint from the undergrowth and charge Goranth's foe. The youth wielded a short-bladed sword and caught the slaver unawares. The Mabayan had focused on the greater threat of Goranth, and that doomed him.

Five slavers were left. Goranth held the makhaira's blade between his teeth, grabbed the reins with his good hand, and heaved himself up into the vacated saddle of the newly dead slaver. *Thank the gods this horse hadn't run.*

"Can't let you have all the fun," Jaeg panted.

"This isn't fun, boy. It's death's business. Look there!" Goranth pointed up the trail, where four Mabayans rode toward them fast. The fifth, the leader, had swung around and was charging from the other direction. They would be caught between the forces. "Death comes, boy!"

Goranth intended to deal some of that death before he was taken down. He raced toward the quartet, his horse's gait smooth, muscles rippling, mane flying and whipping the Northman's face. He tried to flex the fingers in his left hand and found they were still uncooperative. Rivulets of blood ran down that arm. Answering Rif's call had yielded way too much pain and not enough reward. He drove his horse into the gap between the front two riders, forcing them apart. His knees banged against their legs, and he was nearly unseated for his efforts as he slashed to his right and clipped one of the Mabayans.

He registered a greater pain in his left arm and did not need to look to know that he'd been slashed by the rider on that side. Then he was driving his mount through the next two riders, slashing again and this time unhorsing the Mabayan on his right. The man pitched to the side of the trail, and his horse reared and then plunged into the foliage. Again Goranth felt the bite of steel, his remaining foe connecting with his thigh this time.

Goranth gritted his teeth and swallowed the cry of pain. He'd lived a good life, traveled far, risked much, and loved often. If it ended here on this trail, in—

You'll not die today. Kalida was inside his head. *I'll not allow it.*

He managed to turn his horse around. One of the Mabayans had done the same, a tall, broad-shouldered warrior who maneuvered the horse solely with his knees. Each hand held a long, thin blade, one dripping Goranth's blood.

Not today! Kalida's cry was shrill.

Goranth stared in disbelief as the trail surged up around the legs of his foe's horse, causing the beast to stumble and fall. It took the rider with it and trapped him beneath its weight. The Northman rode forward and leaned down and over as far as he could before swiping with the makhaira and ending the slaver.

Three remained.

The odds were in Goranth's favor now because Jaeg was still on his feet, but for how long? Two Mabayans were on the youth, and with the thick foliage and the pair of horses blocking his view, Goranth could not tell if the leader also faced the youth. He urged his mount closer and slipped out of the saddle as he neared, limp-running the rest of the way, leading with his blade.

Jaeg had managed to skewer one of his opponents, and the youth let out an excited whoop and inadvertently jumped into the path of a sword swing. Jaeg screamed and

Goranth closed, pushing the boy to safety off the trail and catching the descending blade of the Mabayan's sword with his own.

Two remaining, one the leader, who Goranth could not see. Where was the man in armor with the morning star?

His only concern now needed to be the mounted man in front of him. The slaver had the advantage of height and a longer sword, but Goranth had desperation and anger on his side and the help of Kalida. Once more the ground rose around the horse's hooves, tripping it. Goranth sidestepped the slaver's swing and listened to a string of Mabayan curses. He did not need to know the meaning to understand his foe's ire.

"The horses!" Goranth shouted to the slaver. "Where did you get them?"

Perhaps the Mabayan didn't understand Goranth, or maybe he was too caught up in trying to get off the trapped horse. The Northman barked the question again, and when no answer was forthcoming, he danced around the back of the Ahak-Teek and came up on the other side, then drove the makhaira up to its hilt into the man's side. The Mabayan jerked and froze before slowly toppling. Blood pulsed over Goranth's hand, and he had to squeeze the pommel to keep from dropping it.

One left: the leader.

He wasn't on the trail in either direction. Goranth retrieved Jaeg from the brush and shredded a Mabayan cloak to make a bandage, first taking care of the youth, then accepting help with his own wound. His left hand was still numb. He would ask Kalida to take him on a healing trip through the earth; he was not done with the underground after all.

The aftermath was filled with picking through the blood and the bodies.

Four Undmen had been slain, leaving eleven alive and grateful. None had been among the diminutive folk he'd met the other day. The three remaining freed captives were merchants who'd come into the woods to trade with the Undmen and been surprised by the swift Mabayans. The goods to be traded had been taken away in another direction by more of the slavers.

Jaeg left Goranth to deal with the horses. "Rif is in the woods." The youth gestured toward the mountainside. "I propped him against a tree. Somewhere. Over there, I think."

"Find him, boy. We'll set him on a horse, and then he'll be a burden to neither of us."

"Beautiful horses," Jaeg said.

"Aye, they are," Goranth agreed. "And they are mine."

CHAPTER NINETEEN

Fleet of foot, swift and sure
Horses of the Selomongan moor
Keep us rich and enemies poor
"Tales of the Mabayan Raiders"

"Ho, you there!" Goranth called to the former prisoners. "Do any of you speak Mabayan or maybe Common?" Goranth tried his question in three different languages.

A woman raised her hand, an Undmen but different. Her skin wasn't as gray and she was larger, more the size of an Okutan, although nowhere near as big as women from Goranth's homeland.

"I can speak for us," she said in the common language of the traders. She moved to the front of the group. The rest of the Undmen looked confused, unsure of what to do with their sudden freedom after resigning themselves to their fate as slaves. "I am called Sathr."

"I am Goranth. Tell these people they are free to return

to their homes. They are to stay out of the open and travel quickly. I doubt we have seen the last of the Mabayan slavers. Their leader escaped, probably to warn the others or bring a pack of raiders to punish us for standing up to them." Goranth spat on the ground as he held his useless arm with the other to staunch the bleeding.

Sathr ripped part of her clothing free to use as a bandage, revealing a hard and lithe body beneath. "Let go," she ordered. He released the pressure, and she studied the wound. "Put pressure on it again. Do you have thread?"

"Aye, the lad does. Jaeg!" The youth appeared from the brush, helping Rif, who panted and gasped with each tortured step.

The woman spoke quickly, giving direction to the Undmen while explaining their situation. Two Undmen relieved Jaeg of his burden so he could dig the needle and thread out of his pack. She pointed at another former prisoner. After speaking to him, he bolted into the nearby woods.

Goranth watched her confidence as she gave orders and maintained control over her fellows. None of them made a move to leave.

"Are you their leader?" Goranth asked as she threaded the proffered needle.

"I am Sathr," she replied. "Nothing more than a refugee the Undmen, as you call them, took in and made one of their own. You can see that I am one of them while not being one of them. My eyes are not as good as theirs in the dark, but they are better than yours. Some think me a half-breed, the product of an Undman slave and her owner. I exist; that is all that matters. I help our traders because I have a gift for languages, a gift that you yourself have. The daylight draws me, but my family calls me back. My brother was taken with me, and he needs to return to them." She pointed at a young man, and he nodded at the recognition.

Goranth shook his head, sending his untamed mane back and forth in raven-black waves. "I learn the words I need to survive. As for your brother, take him home. All of you."

She laughed lightly and easily, despite having been a prisoner and her hands being covered in Goranth's blood. "You jest with the poor slave girl." She bit her lip as she worked, focused on the stitching, working quickly to stem the tide. "Drink as much water as you have, and we will get you more. Water is life, Goranth."

"There is not much left. We found ourselves trapped underground and struggled for what seemed like days through the caves beneath these mountains to finally emerge not far from here."

She looked skeptical at his claim. "The maze of the underground is not easily defeated. Do you carry an orb of scrying?"

"We do not. We...were lucky."

She stared into his eyes. "I thank you for rescuing us. Your luck turned into our luck." She ran her fingers down Goranth's chest. "A greater warrior I have never seen."

"He is called Goranth the Mighty," Jaeg remarked. Goranth snapped his attention to the lad, shutting him down.

Rif saw the humor even though he struggled to remain upright. "Goranth is a Northman, gracing us lowlanders with his presence, but you are right. There is no greater warrior in all the land, but as you see from the scars on his body, even he cannot go unscathed in a fight of one against many."

Goranth dismissed Rif and Jaeg with a wave. "Do you know the Mabayan who escaped? Their leader, no doubt."

One of the captives ran for a horse, jumped astride the beast, and kicked it to a run—the merchant woman.

"Was she with them?"

"No. She was the trader we met. They took us all together."

Goranth scowled, staring at the point where the horse and its rider had disappeared into the woods. Maybe she had gone for help. Maybe she ran for her life. Then again, mayhap she was an insider working with the Mabayans. Goranth left it but vowed not to let her get close should he see her again.

Sathr finished sewing, the work efficient with tight stitches. Goranth still couldn't feel his fingers. "When this is better, I'll take that Mabayan to task and turn him inside-out with my steel," the Northman swore. No one took it as an idle boast. The Undman returned from his foray into the woods and handed a weed stalk to Sathr, who ripped off the leaves and chewed them.

"The Mabayan's leader is called Narlun," Sathr said through the wad in her mouth. "He is a warlord, merciless. He will be back because he cannot allow anyone to best him in battle. He battered one of his fellow Mabayans for mentioning a battle many days back on the plains leading to Barbertown."

Goranth's eyes sparkled with grim pleasure at the Mabayan's anger at losing that fight, too. "Twice now I have defeated his forces. When will he learn that his is not the way?"

"He will be back then, placing a great bounty on your head," Sathr declared.

Jaeg trolled the line of the dead to collect the Mabayans' slave ropes. He filled two saddlebags to bursting while keeping a tight grip on the fine stallion's reins. Between him and the Undmen, they held the horses Goranth had claimed, all but the one the merchant had taken. It was little compensation for the loss of her wares.

Sathr stuffed a spit-heavy green mass against the wound on Goranth's arm and another into the one on his leg. The pain subsided faster than a diving hawk could catch its prey. He flexed his leg and found he could walk without limping. "You know the magic of plants. Do you understand the healing powers of gems?"

"I have some knowledge," Sathr admitted. "And take it easy on that leg. Just because it doesn't hurt doesn't mean it's not injured. Keep the weight off. Get onto a horse and ride. You've earned it." Her big brown eyes sparkled in the daylight.

One of the Undmen approached and rested his hand on Goranth's good arm. He spoke in the language of his people, and Goranth waited for Sathr to interpret the words.

"Fanor says he met you before in the forest. You were kind then, and you are even more kind now. He thanks you."

"He can thank me by getting underground, away from the raiders. Don't fall victim to them again. Take the bows and learn to shoot. Take the swords." Goranth pointed at the wreckage up and down the stretch of trail where the battle had been fought.

"Where is the tunnel that leads below?" Sathr asked.

Goranth, Jaeg, and Rif pointed up the hill. "There, in a gap behind the bushes. A short way down the tunnel, you'll find a cave with strange characters carved into the wall and a library of books and scrolls." Rif squirmed uncomfortably at the mention of their find. "I ask you not to disturb that place. It is protected by powerful magicks. I would not want anyone else to get hurt. Go on, Sathr, take your people home."

Sathr spoke to her brother, and it turned into a back-and-forth with hastily shouted words and too many gestures for Goranth to follow. Finally, she and her brother bowed to each other, and the brother cast a wary glance at the Northman.

"What?" Goranth demanded.

"My brother will take the Undmen home. I will remain with you since you need someone who speaks the languages of this area, but he wants your assurance that you'll protect me."

"I fight for me, and that protects those with me."

"A mistruth, Northman? You had no fight with the Mabayans, yet you bared your steel and challenged them. All you had to do was wait. This fight was not yours, but you chose it. Why?"

"Because I hate slavers," Goranth growled.

"Will you protect me?" she asked again.

"Aye, lass. You are easy on the eyes and someone I wish no harm to befall. Stay behind me and you'll have my protection. Is that the assurance your brother is looking for?"

She nodded and spoke to her brother, then went to him and pressed her forehead against his. She did the same with each freed Undman in turn. Once she finished saying goodbye, the group hurried away. They moved quickly along the hillside until they chose to climb, then they scrambled up the slope like so many mountain goats, soon disappearing behind the brush and into the mountain.

Goranth helped Rif mount one of the Ahak-Teeks. Despite the lean lines and narrow girth of the animal, it wasn't bothered by Rif's mass. With an easy hand, he pranced the horse around the open area, letting it dip its head to eat the sweet grass.

"Tie those horses together, two each that we'll pull

behind us." There were seven horses, so they would ride three and pull four. The plan made sense until he thought of Sathr. "Do you ride?"

"Behind you since you have sworn to protect me, but not alone, no. I have never been on a horse before."

"Aye, lass, but in front of me. These saddles are not made for someone behind. If we're attacked, I can swing you to cover more easily if you're where I can reach you. Your first time on a horse, eh? This will be a treat. These are some of the finest horses known. They are not of Migoro, but from far to the east. Seeing them here is a joy, but seeing them in the hands of the Mabayans set fire to my soul."

Sathr laughed. "You didn't rescue us. You saved the horses from a life with the Mabayans."

"And they'll be better for it, too. No, lass. The horses came second. Death to the slavers came first."

"I thank you, Goranth." Her appreciation was clear in her eyes and the set of her body. He limped to one of the fallen and tore the cloak off the man, then tossed it to her.

"In case it gets cold," he said. He liked what he saw of her, maybe too much. What of Kalida? She had been there and helped them win the battle. She'd fought for him. Sathr had, too, more so than Rif. Even Jaeg had risen to the occasion. "We fight together, we win together."

"I could not agree more," Sathr replied, making Goranth realize he'd spoken out loud.

"Tell me more of Narlun," Goranth said, climbing into the saddle of a silky brown mare. Jaeg handed him a rope tied to two prideful snorting beasts. He lowered his arm and Sathr grabbed it, then vaulted easily into the saddle in front of Goranth. "Not facing me, woman! You would distract me to the point that I'd miss a dragon standing on my head."

221

She smiled and wrapped her arms around his neck. "I would?"

"Turn around, woman. 'Temptress' isn't the look you want. If you can conjure a good meal out of thin air, now that has value."

"You take yourself too seriously, Northman. We need to find water for you and the horses. They sound parched." She stood in the saddle, her groin pressed against Goranth's face before she balanced and turned around to slide her backside down his body and sit before him.

He wouldn't lie to himself; he liked the attention. He knew Kalida was aware of the man he was. When any day could be his last, saving himself for another made no sense. He fought to win, and this felt like winning.

Goranth raised his arm over his head and hatcheted it toward the woods. The fingers on his dead arm twitched, and the tingling lessened.

"Your potion heals, Sathr. I feel it working."

"Once we acquire amethyst and sapphire, we'll be able to advance the process more quickly. Until then, healing herbs and water will have to suffice."

"You speak like one wizened with age while rubbing against me like a Borezhyan dance girl. Why?"

"In the caves of the underworld, touch is used in nearly all things. Outside, your eyes miss much that your hands and body would not. I am teaching you our ways, Northman. I think you will be happy to learn them."

"I cannot complain about what I've felt thus far." Goranth listened and watched but found no sign of Mabayans pounding toward them.

"One should not complain at all," Sathr countered, leaning forward for a better view. "That way." She pointed. "I see the green of bushes that would grow beside a stream."

Goranth urged his mount to a trot, and soon the horses were lapping from a small and clear pool. A fount bubbled from a crack in the rocks nearby. Goranth stayed astride his beast while lowering the lithe woman to the ground. She refilled the flasks, watched Goranth drink one, and then filled it again. She did the same for Rif, but not Jaeg. The lad was clearly healthy enough to handle his own flask.

Rif glanced between Sathr and Goranth.

"You amaze me," he mumbled.

Goranth knew what he was talking about. "Your luck is bad because of the dark shadows on your soul. Leave the dragons, Rif!"

"No!" The Barber came to life. "We have ropes and Kalida to guide us. A dragonette is out there. I can feel it in my bones."

"That's old age, Barber."

"You seek a dragon?" Sathr scowled. "Had I known the quest you set upon yourselves, I would have been better off going with my brother."

"We need you," Rif shot back at the woman. "Dragons prefer maidens who sing to them. You can sing, can you not?"

CHAPTER TWENTY

A song of fire and stone
Breaking heads, breaking bone
Setting a riven world aflame
At your end, you will know our name.
"Tales of the Mabayan Raiders"

Narlun's ire was a palpable shield keeping his men at a distance. He paced in front of a small fire where a blackened iron pot simmered with nameless acrid-smelling globules. He clenched and relaxed his fists in a rhythm that matched the beat of D'gok's drum. In the distance, a great cat snarled. Closer, monkeys hooted, and a large blue parrot shrieked in an irritating voice.

"Twice!" he snarled. His voice silenced the monkeys, and the blue parrot launched into the sky. "Twice Rif and his lackeys have forced failure on me. Twice, but no more!" Narlun glared into the flames. The Mabayan leader had been shaken when Rif and his followers caught them southeast of Barbertown days past. How had the Barber known of their raid?

And earlier today?

What god had thrust the Barber's men into the Mabayans' path near the mountains? They'd killed his men and freed the slaves. Stole the valuable horses. Ruined more plans. Narlun had barely escaped. Twice he had nearly died because of Rif the Barber.

Was there someone among Narlun's own people who had relayed information to Rif? Shared plans and routes? A spy? A traitor? He stopped and met the gaze of each man. They returned his stare unblinking, frozen, but there was a suggestion of dread in their postures. It was right for his men to fear him. Fear kept people in line, obedient, careful, and respectful. Narlun succeeded through fear and reward.

Was one of these men working for the Barber? Was one not afraid enough?

Narlun had spies in Barbertown and had bribed a handful of Rif's soldiers. He'd made them loyal with pouches of coins and promises of future stations and holdings when he swooped in and claimed the city. Narlun had a network that stretched throughout the villages on the island continent of Migoro, connected like the filaments in a spider's web by his youthful sorcerer D'gok.

D'gok continued to beat the drum, and Narlun continued to clench and relax his fists in time with it. He had no doubt of D'gok's loyalty, but his other men? The ones here? The ones living in his coastal villages and on his ship?

Was there a quisling in front of him?

One dozen Mabayans stood in a semi-circle in the low foliage at the edge of the clearing, Ahak-Teeks and tethered slaves behind them. This dozen had been an hour behind the band Narlun had led, far back and oblivious when Rif's men attacked their brethren. Had the entire force been together, Narlun doubted Rif's men would have struck; the odds would have been overwhelming. If they had struck, the Mabayans would have prevailed.

He noted sweat beading upon the forehead of one warrior. He would deal with him later.

Narlun had few sorcerers among his people. The oldest, who lived in a cave at the easternmost point of the shoreline, could delve into minds and hearts and eschewed civilized comforts. He would visit her soon and direct her to find any Mabayans who were untrue to him. Punishment would be swift and permanent and would settle Narlun's churning soul. He would find the traitor and finish him.

The most powerful of his sorcerers was sitting cross-legged in front of the fire, beating a drum. D'gok had gathered things from the woods and put them in the pot, added powders and seeds from the tiny pouches tied to his waist, and set everything to simmering. The spirals of steam that rose changed color and the scents varied from one moment to the next but always remained unpleasant.

Narlun knew D'gok was wholly loyal.

Narlun squatted next to the sorcerer and placed a hand on his shoulder.

"It is ready," D'gok said. "Sit across from me, the fire between us."

Narlun complied, glancing again at his twelve men and looking more deeply into their eyes for hints of unfaithfulness. The Ahak-Teeks behind them nickered softly. The captives shifted restlessly. Twenty-four remaining captives, although eighteen had been lost to Rif's assault. Narlun vowed to capture more slaves to replace them.

"Show me," Narlun said.

D'gok set the drum aside and pulled a knife with his left hand, dipped the blade in the mixture in the kettle, and slowly stirred. The fire's light danced off the lad's face, free of sweat despite the heat from the flames.

The sorcerer had seen only ten summers and looked younger than that because of his diminutive frame. He'd displayed an inner spark while he still suckled. The magic had manifested when he could crawl, and it had intensified when he'd taken his first steps. Narlun took him from his parents and removed him to his household in the large Mabayan village, then raised him as his son, servant, and lately, advisor.

"The failed battle for Barbertown first," Narlun directed.

"As you require." The boy's voice was soft and feminine. D'gok removed the knife from the pot, raised his right arm, and slashed the fleshy part past the elbow where several scars were visible. He leaned forward and let the blood drip into the mixture. The spirals of steam turned red, then black, then faded to a fog-like gray and formed a cloud that hovered above the fire and expanded. In that mist, Narlun saw images, and he smelled the sweat of his warriors and the horses from days past as they spread across the field toward the river. Smelled the freshness of the water and the scent of wildflowers. He felt the sun on his face and the comfortable leather reins in his hands. He registered the speed of the beast beneath him and the wind that kept the hair out of his eyes.

The men were unmindful of Rif and his soldiers moving in from the tree line, but he saw the enemies' approach now, retold through D'gok's conjuring. Narlun shook with fury at having to relive his failure.

He sensed the anticipation in the ride toward Barbertown and the joy below the surface that awaited when the city fell to him. Again he pictured racing into the city, slashing right and left and demanding the commoners surrender lest they die to his men.

All of it was to be his.

The city and the dragon. However many dragons Rif had managed to catch.

Narlun would tame them, as he had the several praevo-pavors in his stable.

This city, perched so finely on the river, so prosperous, would be only the first to fall. He'd take the ships in the port and bend the people to his rule. Barbertown would become larger and mightier, a veritable fortress from which he would strike with his praevo-pavors and dragons.

But the enemies closing in the misty vision had postponed that dream.

The mist brightened, the fire popped, and a figure loomed larger than the others running from the woods—the hulking man Narlun knew as Goranth. He focused on this man, stomach and throat tightening as he watched him slay Mabayan after Mabayan, then gain a horse and ride into their midst, wielding a weapon taken from Narlun's champion.

The makhaira gleamed in the mist-vision and spilled the life of too many of his people. A stolen weapon, a dashed campaign, and death. Too many dead. Too many dead Mabayans.

He watched Rif work the edges of Narlun's force and noted that the man was slower than Goranth and lacked his fierceness and agility. He'd looked in on Rif long months and years in the past, and while the Barber's ambition grew, so too did his girth. He was not as intimidating as in those months and years earlier, and now his lackey, his champion, Goranth, was the one deserving deference.

"Show me more," Narlun said. "Of this man." He pointed at Goranth and D'gok revealed the battle once more, but this time from the perspective of the Northman. Narlun leaned forward and breathed deep, taking the mist and the acrid smell to the bottom of his lungs. He closed his eyes, and in that instant, he was looking through Goranth's eyes as the Northman's sandaled feet pounded over the grass, muscles bunching as he leapt and pulled a Mabayan from his horse. Narlun shared Goranth's strength and determination and felt the fire in his heart. Out of the corner of his mind's eye, he watched Rif defer to Goranth, follow his lead, and try to match his efforts—and fall short. True, the Barber was still dangerous, but he was no longer the one Narlun's efforts should be directed against.

"Today. Earlier." Narlun's voice cracked. His mouth was dry, throat parched from inhaling the mist. Still, he took it deep and held it, then released it, peered through the cloud, and saw the cherubic face of his sorcerer.

D'gok's eyes were wholly black.

"Show me the raid today. Earlier today," Narlun wheezed. "All of it. Through the big man's eyes."

It was cooler on the mountain, the air fresh, bringing the scent of pine from small trees that grew in pockets of earth in crevices. It also brought the sour smell of Goranth, who'd gone too long without washing. He listened, trying to snare pieces of conversation and hearing Rif's voice and another, then he was scrabbling down the rocks, stopping, and gazing at the land all around.

And down to see the Mabayans and their captives.

Narlun heard Goranth's breath catch. The Northman hadn't been looking for them; the sighting had been chance. Then why was he in the mountains with Rif and one other?

"Dragons," Narlun whispered. "They were looking for dragons and found us." The encounter this day had been chance, but it did not explain why the Mabayans had been intercepted on their Barbertown raid.

The Mabayan leader continued to watch the scene from Goranth's perspective as he clambered down the hill with the steadiness of a goat. A glance behind showed Rif and the other barely managing the slope.

Again, he was struck by the notion that the person to be wary of was the Northman. Goranth was the true power of Barbertown.

The scene played out in the mist, all of Narlun's men watching, some whispering but none loud enough that he could hear. Narlun focused on the mist-play and the sounds D'gok's spell brought him.

"He hesitates," Narlun pronounced. "The Northman is unsure if he will strike at us. He weighs the odds, I believe. He contemplates outcomes." The odds were not in Goranth's favor. A fool could have realized that, he thought. The risk was high. "He embraces risk."

"Yes," D'gok agreed. "The great man is happy to dare."

Let him be happy to die. Narlun snarled at the mist and gestured for D'gok to continue the vision. He watched Goranth scurry behind the last horse in line, past the wide-eyed captives, come even with the rider, and dispatch him with a swipe from the stolen weapon.

"He moves like a cat," Narlun said. "He is a predator, someone others admire." *And respect, perhaps fear. Someone nearly my equal. Near, but a lesser man.* "The Northman takes too many risks, D'gok. He is impetuous."

"Unpredictable," D'gok said. "Dangerous."

"Yes," Narlun replied. "He is dangerous. And must be removed."

"Goranth and the injured one—"

"Rif," Narlun supplied. "Goranth and Rif must be removed." He sat back from the fire and tipped his head up, replacing the acrid air with fresh. "I will have Barbertown, its people, and its dragons. I slay Goranth and Rif, and the city will be easy to take. Kill the heart, take the body."

Narlun stood and looked across the fire at D'gok. The child's eyes were closed, lips tight together. His small hands were on his knees, and blood dripped down his arm from where he'd cut himself. The child had a tattoo on his left breast, the image of an eye with lightning bolts erupting from it. D'gok had designed it, and one of the elders had rendered it on a festival night. It had been laid in blue and green, but in the firelight, it looked red. Narlun thought the child able to make it whatever color matched his whim at the moment. And sometimes, like now, the eye appeared to close in sleep.

"Rif and Goranth knew you were going to strike at Barbertown," D'gok said in his soft, feminine voice. "They have an earth-seer like me. She warned them. But she is not as powerful as me, and her heart is conflicted. I see her now."

"Where is she?" Narlun bent closer.

D'gok shrugged. "A room. A hut. In a village, I think. Maybe Barbertown. Maybe somewhere else. I cannot tell. She is strong. She warned them about the raid. I think she protects them, Rif and the big man. She saw you coming for Barbertown, but she did not see you today. Not with the slaves and the horses."

"How do you know this?"

Another shrug.

Narlun knew D'gok's magic was imprecise, perhaps

because of his few years. He never pushed the child hard out of affection and caution. He did encourage him.

"Learn about her, D'gok."

"Her mind is not with her body."

"She thinks through the earth like you," Narlun guessed.

"I cannot tell where her mind travels."

"Then find where Goranth travels," Narlun said. "And I will carefully plan how to end him and claim my city."

CHAPTER TWENTY-ONE

This is our time to claim our birthright, place the crown upon our head, and be bathed in gold and jewels. It is ours for the taking. The time is now.
"Tales of the Mabayan Raiders"

Goranth sniffed the air. The pungent odor of the Ahak-Teeks blocked other scents wafting on the breeze. "Damn horses," the Northman grumbled, but he didn't bother to slide out of the saddle. He liked riding a beast any king would be happy to have. It made him feel more powerful than he already was. The beast became an extension of his body.

He tapped Sathr's leg as she remained seated in front of him. "Do you sense anything from those trees ahead? They are too dark for my liking. I suggest we go 'round, then cut due west."

"Ho, there!" Rif shouted. He spurred his mount to close

with the Northman. "We follow the mountains north until we find a dragon."

"Are you still about this fool's quest? Barbertown could be burned to the ground by now, and your venture will have served you naught. Everything risked. Nothing gained. Get yourself under control, Rif. Leave it and let us go home."

"Your wenches!" Rif blurted, glaring at Goranth until Sathr caught his attention, forcing him to look away from her withering eyes. "The dragon, Goranth. We cannot let Varl's sacrifice be in vain!"

"Varl's sacrifice was in vain the second the great cat attacked. It's by sheer luck we still have the pelt and the necklace she wore when she parted ways with the living."

"We're here for one reason, no matter what else has happened," Rif pleaded. "We came for a dragon. We were close once but betrayed by clumsiness." He glanced at Jaeg. "Kalida is back, and she believes there is one even younger that we may reach."

"She's not talked with me about it." Goranth glowered, gritting his teeth until the muscles in his face bulged. Sathr pressed her body into Goranth's and put her hand on his arm, the dead one.

But he felt her touch! He looked down to confirm it was real and relaxed.

"It is *my* expedition, Northman. I hold no sway over you, and my argument is weak that you joined of your own accord because of the promise of gold and jewels. Your purse bulges now because of payment for our first capture. Another purse full and you'll have enough to live comfortably, away from Barbertown if you wish, but with us. If you'll stay, I'll make it worth your while to be the captain of the town guard."

Sathr ignored Rif. Her eyes sought Goranth's, twinkling

in the daylight, shining with the joy of freedom. "Have you gems? Amethyst, emerald, or sapphire?"

Goranth opened his purse and dug inside. He removed the jewels, cut but unpolished, and handed them one after another to Sathr.

"A pretty smile and you part with a king's ransom?" Rif chided, shaking his head and frowning at the woman.

She closed her eyes and touched her closed fist to Goranth's arm, then whispered in the language of the Undmen. He understood none of it, but that mattered not. Warmth flowed up his arm and into his body. He felt a surge of power coursing through his veins.

He let it happen. A warrior like Goranth would trade all the gems of a kingdom to be strong for the next fight. His natural desire was to go to ground until he healed and could fight unhindered. With the return of his health and strength, he found it easier to stay on the trail.

Good, Kalida purred into his mind.

Goranth reached out to rest his hand on Sathr's shoulder and ran it slowly down her back, appreciating the vibrant woman beneath.

I feel no jealousy, Northman. That's for civilized fools and weaklings. There is a dragon out there, very young. You can capture it with little grief. The woman can tame it and bring it back, Kalida suggested.

You have a personal vendetta against the dragon god, priestess.

It changes nothing about the nature of our existence.

It does not, Goranth agreed, but he didn't know what he was agreeing to besides not arguing philosophy with the enchantress. *Do I have you to thank for the healing power of the crystals?*

You have the earth mother to thank. I am merely a tunnel through which her power passes. And your companion. She understands the power within. Between us, you will be healed from your gallant effort to free the slaves and gain those magnificent horses. To win the dragon, you will have to leave the horses behind.

Goranth's eyes shot open as he surveyed his small herd. "Kalida said I have to give up the horses if we are to capture the dragon. I will not."

You will leave them behind, and I will guide them to a glade, where you will pick them up on your return to Barbertown. I promise they will be safe and waiting for you.

You've not gone back on your word to me. My arm is well. I'm not an ingrate. I appreciate your help. Thank you for what you did in the battle with the Mabayans. Thank you for looking after my horses. I will be sorry to walk once again when these fine beasts are available, but because they will be waiting, I'm willing to walk. "And I'm willing to help find the damn dragon."

"Then I will help you, too," Sathr replied, not having heard the rest of Goranth's conversation with Kalida.

"Thank the Ice Dogs," Rif added. "Kalida, guide us."

Sathr clearly remained unsure of who Kalida was but did not ask.

"I've no desire to be the captain of your guard. One more trip to the trove when we return, and then I'll be on my way. Until then, Rif, you have my sword."

"I pray that we don't need it, but you know we will."

Goranth grumbled into Sathr's hair as he kicked his mare into motion. The horse trotted ahead, dragging two horses with her. The others encouraged their Ahak-Teeks to follow when he reined around the wooded area before them.

"I don't have a good feeling about that place," he reiterated.

Sathr shook her head. "I sense nothing from the woods.

Here, take your gems back." She tried to press them into the hand around her waist, holding her tightly in the saddle before him.

"You keep them for the next time." Goranth pushed her arm down and kept his wrapped around her.

"With these horses and our wits, there shouldn't be a next time," she countered.

Goranth threw his head back and laughed. "Naïve woman! There will always be a next time. Some men are followed by rain, others by sunshine. I'm followed by sharpened steel."

She elbowed him in the ribs. "Maybe you haven't been with the right people."

Goranth looked at Rif and then over his other shoulder at Jaeg. Kalida laughed in the back of his mind. "Aye, Sathr, you have a sharp wit and keen eye. When you are good at something, people ask you to do more of it. The day will come when I meet my better. Until then, I wear the scars from every battle that came too close to seeing me planted in the ground. While I can still raise my sword, I need to find better people to surround myself with, and there's only one here who agrees that dragon hunting is for the feeble-minded, and that includes you, Kalida."

He pulled Sathr tight to him as the only person who hadn't asked him to put his body in harm's way for something she wanted. Rif and Kalida were at odds with each other except for one thing on which they both agreed: dragons. Goranth was the warrior they needed to fight the battles they wanted to win.

"Hold," Goranth growled. He leapt from the saddle, bared the makhaira, and ran into the nearby wood. A blue parrot screamed and took flight. Sathr tried to hold the horse steady, but she was unfamiliar with the beast. The mare started to prance, nearly dislodging her rider.

A great cat's snarl cut through the quiet. Goranth saw her twist her hands into the horse's mane and hold on as her eyes sought to penetrate the darkness of the woods.

Goranth backed into the open before turning to walk to the horse as if nothing had happened. He tucked the makhaira into his belt and remounted behind Sathr.

"A predator?"

"Aye, lass. He ran when faced with his death." Goranth tapped his sword. "Like I said, I am followed by things that seek my blood."

The group fell silent as they rode north, settling into an easy pace.

"Tell me of the Undmen," Goranth asked softly, putting his head beside hers to hear better.

"The deeper you go, the lighter it gets," she started mysteriously. "That is where you find the Undmen. They work as men outside do, as farmers, shepherds, miners, craftsmen, artists, and more. The Undmen are protected by the earth mother physically more than in the spiritual sense as you have with your Ice Dogs."

"Ha!" Goranth laughed. "The Ice Dogs prey on those who are unaware. They are not gods, but demons sent to smite the unworthy. They are a curse, not a blessing."

"But you have gods, no?"

"The Northmen have the god of life." Goranth patted the hilt of the sword at his side. "I will admit that in battle when the end is nigh, every god finds worshippers begging for forgiveness."

"And you say I'm the one with a keen wit." Sathr put her hand on Goranth's and gripped it tightly. "The Undmen. You asked about the Undmen," she continued. "They are skilled in the ways of stone and earth. They can tell what lies behind rock by how it looks. This is not something that can be taught to outsiders. I have never learned to see as they can. They know the tunnels as they know the backs of their own hands."

"You said it was light. How can that be?"

"The walls have a faint glow. It grows brighter and brighter after days pass. In between the surface and the caves of the Undmen lies the dark of ink, places no light has touched."

"Except that of a torch. Surely you have torches?"

"Undmen have little to burn and nowhere for the smoke to go. We cook, but only in a special cave with a crack and vent that takes the smoke away. In the cooking cave, there is light from the fires. Sometimes it is too bright and we'll wear cloths over our faces. But in the tunnels between the land of the Undmen and the outside, we do not use torches. We follow them by smell, touch, and memory."

"I would someday experience this, Sathr. A land of silence and dark."

"Only dark. Sound travels in the caves. We can always hear. We know who is coming by their tread alone. Strangers never reach the Undmen. Outsiders cannot get there, even with torches. It is a long journey, and outsiders would lose the will to continue."

"No one has ever reached the land of the Undmen?"

"The land...interesting word. Only Undmen and me. Not one of them but those taken there to become one."

"Do you have children?" Goranth asked.

She laughed. "I don't have a mate. I'm too busy to be tied down. I travel with our traders, and I thank your Ice Dogs that they put you in my path to save me from the Mabayans. They don't treat their female slaves very well."

"I suspected. I have never met a slaver who did. But many slavers say I don't treat them well, and they would be right." Goranth ground his teeth but only for a moment.

He was quick to anger and quick to cool. He felt strongly about how people should treat their fellows.

"A goat!" Rif called in a low voice. Goranth looked over his shoulder at where Rif pointed. It was to their right in the hills but not too high, grazing. "Look at the size of that goat! We have bows now. I see our dinner."

"Have you not paunch enough, Barber?"

Sathr waved her hands frantically. "No! You mustn't. Those creatures are good luck for the Undmen. When we come above ground, the great mountain goats show us that there is peace in the area. You mustn't kill it. I can catch it."

Rif climbed out of his saddle and limped toward the hillside, bow in hand with an arrow nocked.

Sathr twisted her body around, taking Goranth's face in her hands. "You mustn't let him kill it. If I capture it, we can drink of its milk and be at peace with the earth. The Undmen have need of the goats, a need they can't fill if that goat is dead."

"We all want peace," Goranth grumbled, torn between the lithe woman rubbing against him and Rif seeking a meal. He had greater concerns than a big goat perched on a mountainside.

CHAPTER TWENTY-TWO

Take your treasure and run
Fast and far as you can
But know that we will come
For your treasure and your land
"Tales of the Mabayan Raiders"

Goranth guessed the goat was about the size of a pony and weighed about as much. He crept up the slope toward it, rope over one shoulder, fingers digging into gaps between the stones, knees being abraded, sandals barely finding purchase, and taking more than one try to manage that.

If Sathr wasn't so smooth-skinned and comely, if her voice wasn't so pleasant, if she didn't stir his blood when she rubbed against him, he'd be happily astride his Ahak-Teek and in pursuit of Rif's little dragon. He wouldn't be shredding his knees and elbows on an ascent no sane man would attempt. This was practically straight up. How had the goat gotten up there?

They should have ignored the damned goat and ridden on their way, but Goranth had surrendered to the inevitability of it. Rif and Sathr were fixated on the animal. Jaeg had sided with Rif.

It would have been easier to just shoot the beast as Rif wanted. Pepper it with arrows. Kill it and watch it tumble down the slope, tenderizing its meat along the way. It would come to ground at the base, where they could skin and cook it and the Barber could fill his belly. Then they'd be back on their horses and headed toward a dragonette. But that would displease Sathr.

Rif could stand to lose some of his girth and so could skip the goat meal, and Goranth could stand to gain more favor with Sathr. Her pale gray skin, the shade of morning fog on a river, made her an exotic beauty he'd not seen the likes of before. The goat was for her.

Again, Goranth marveled at how the goat was able to perch on an outcropping no bigger than his fist, a seeming impossibility. He recalled a port stop years past where a town boasted a flock of little white goats that would climb trees and leap from branches that bent under their weight. They were as agile as monkeys and drew crowds. He and his fellows had taken their tankards out of the tavern one afternoon to watch the animals cluster, looking like white flowers amid the green leaves. He'd seen nothing like it since—until now, with the mountain goat standing where it should not be able to.

This goat was a patchwork of cream and black with fur that hung long on its front legs and neck like an impressive beard and was short on the rest of its body. Its head was slender, and its wheat-colored horns curved up and back. Goranth thought it an ugly beast that should seem ungainly for its bulk.

Yet it stood on a near-vertical slab of stone.

"By the Ice Dogs! What am I doing?"

"The right thing," Sathr said. "A good thing." She clung to the slope below him, a coil of rope over her shoulder and her fingers and toes finding places to grasp more easily than him. Her skin blended with the rock face.

The wind gusted, sending his hair lashing into his eyes and bringing with it grit and pain. It settled in his mouth, and he worked up some saliva to spit it out. The goat looked down, watching him.

Goranth had thought he'd lost himself, caving to Rif's wild plans of dragons and power. But he was out here past Barbertown in pursuit of a second dragonette, not because of Rif, though the Barber thought that the case. And not wholly because of the treasure that gleamed beneath Rif's home in Barbertown; he pictured the coins and jewels now. He was on the dragon hunt because Kalida had coaxed him into it with honeyed words whispered in his head and the promise of her affections. He'd let a woman overcome his common sense.

He was toiling at the whims of others, and now he was clawing his way up the rock at the request of the mysterious gray-skinned woman who should have followed her brother underground. If he was thinking right, he'd climb back down and get on his horse and leave, but he hadn't been thinking right since he came to the island continent.

Right now, he was thinking about Sathr and her scent when he dipped his face close to her neck and inhaled. Women held the true power in this world, he mused. Not men like Rif who built cities and set themselves up as rulers, raised armies, and amassed wealth. Not Narlun and his Mabayans who slaved and raided and dealt death. It was women, or *some* women; he was weak in their presence.

Rif wanted a dragon. Sathr wanted a goat. He wasn't sure what Kalida wanted.

Goranth wanted Sathr.

And Kalida.

"I can still shoot it, Northman!" Rif called up from the base of the slope. "You'll fall and—"

"—kill yourself!" Jaeg finished.

"Come down!" the Barber bellowed.

The goat let out a bleat that echoed off the stone and scrabbled up farther. Goranth followed, cursing and spitting, trying to get the last of the grit out of his mouth. He wanted to look down and see how Sathr was faring, but he didn't dare take his eyes off the course ahead. They were higher now. Rif had better stay silent and not spook the goat again.

Where was Kalida? The enchantress hadn't slipped inside his mind for hours, and while he was pleased not to share his thoughts, which swirled around Sathr, right now, he would have liked her presence to assure him on this climb. She could be using her earth magic to fashion better hand and footholds for him or to snare the goat so it wouldn't climb out of reach. Perhaps she was busy with concerns in Barbertown or was mind-delving in the earth with the Undmen.

Perhaps she watched Narlun to see what the Mabayans were up to. Or maybe, he considered, she was hiding in the back of his mind, watching but unwilling to offer aid because another woman was occupying him.

"Keep going!" That was Sathr, and he could tell she was close. "Not much farther."

Not much farther to my doom.

"You'll get no milk from that goat," he said. "The beast has horns. Male goats don't—"

"That is a doe, not a buck," Sathr returned. "You can tell by the curve of the horns."

Travel Migoro and learn that female goats have horns, dragons breathe steam to boil the skin from your bones, and I'm an easy target. My life for a woman's affections. I've grown soft.

Goranth didn't want to know how far he'd already climbed. The muscles in his legs and arms had started to burn, a not-unpleasant feeling. He spat out more grit the wind brought his way and smiled; he was closing on the goat, which was looking up at a pair of eagles circling lazily. Moments later he was even with it, rope over his left shoulder, standing on a ledge half the width of his feet, the fingers of his right hand curled into a crack in the stone. He was angled so the wind took his hair away from his face and stole the sweat from his skin.

By the Ice Dogs, what do I do now? He thought this climb the most foolish action in a string of foolish actions. Through the years, captains had questioned his intelligence, calling him impetuous and rash. Aye, he was that. *I'm up here. Now what? I catch this creature, and how do I get it down without killing us both?*

Sathr scaled the rock on the other side of the goat; she looked as graceful as an Ermat veil dancer, no sweat showing on her perfect skin and her knees and elbows unmarred from the ascent. She held onto the rock with one hand and slipped the rope off her other shoulder. She had fashioned a lasso on one end, something he hadn't thought to do. Rash, he'd been. Impetuous. *The goat milk had better be damn delicious.* He'd worked up a thirst.

He shrugged the rope off his shoulder, catching it with his free hand and trying to manipulate it to form a loop. Goranth was almost successful when the goat sprang forward, head lowered, and butted him in the stomach.

The impact made him lose his grip and knocked him off his perch.

Goranth slid down the stone, hands and feet flailing for something to grab, heart hammering, throat tightening, rope snagging and catching an outthrust rock and nearly yanking his arm out of the socket as he held on. He dangled like a fish on a line, hearing the wind, the goat bleat in triumph, Sathr calling to him, and Rif and Jaeg hollering from below.

The Northman tried to shut out the racket and focus on the fingers of his free hand, which was feeling the rock for a hold while his other hand clutched the swaying rope. He was certain Kalida would have helped had she been hovering in his head, but there was still no trace of her.

Goranth managed to find a handhold and he hung flat against the rock, looking straight up and seeing nothing but stone and clear blue sky. The eagles were still circling. Maybe they were vultures waiting for their meal.

"Not today," he growled as he pulled himself higher, having found something to lodge his foot in. Higher again, letting Sathr's worried voice intrude but keeping Rif's shouts at bay.

Higher, searching and finding more handholds. He'd not considered climbing down since it held as much risk. He had Sathr to consider and he was not willing to leave her alone, poised on a ledge higher than the tallest building in Barbertown.

"Almost," she said. "You're almost there."

His fingers felt numb, and the easy burn in his arms and legs had become a painful fire.

Once more, he was on the ledge facing the goat. The beast had blue eyes that nearly matched the color of the sky, and its face appeared expressive like it was either mildly amused at the Northman or mildly disappointed it hadn't been able to kill him. There was a rope around its neck, and Sathr was holding the other end.

"I told you I could catch her! See? We should lead her up and over the top of the ridge," she said. "We can find an easier way down from there."

"How do you suggest we lead this beast up higher?"

"This way." Sathr made a clucking sound and scaled the stone using her free hand and feet as she tugged on the rope. *Clk-clk-clk-clk-clk.* He saw her give the rope a strong pull and the goat responded, nimbly ascending with her.

By the Ice Dogs! She hadn't needed his help, but then she hadn't asked for it. He'd insisted he go up the rock face first. *Twice* she'd told him she could catch it. Being bested by a woman did not bother the Northman; women held the power in his eyes. But being outdone by someone as small as her at a task that had seemed onerous that she made look easy? He continued to growl as he summoned all his strength and pulled himself up hand over aching hand until he reached the top of the ridge, where she stood facing the damnable goat.

Clk-clk-clk-clk to the goat. To Goranth, "Over here, I think, is a path we can take. Isn't she beautiful? Look at her size!"

Indeed, the goat was the size of a pony, twelve hands high. He still thought it ugly.

"This is one of the first things the Undmen taught me— how to work with the great goats. They're docile, really, if you don't frighten them. Easy to handle." Her eyes sparkled. Goranth thought her even more beautiful when she smiled.

"You must teach me how to climb as you do and how to tame the mountain beasts." Women drew him, but knowledge drew him more. "I seek to understand for next time two goats require capture."

She looked away from him demurely, clearly swayed by his appreciation of her skill.

Despite following what Sathr claimed was a path, it was demanding to descend. Goranth's muscles burned more. Rif had put away his bow and looked genuinely concerned for the Northman.

"You're hurt," the Barber said.

"I'm always hurt when I'm in your company," Goranth shot back. He made no effort to mask his irritation.

Sathr fashioned a lead and harness for the goat and lashed the end of the rope to the one that tethered the Ahak-Teeks behind Goranth's horse. The goat seemed not to care about her situation; she was as docile as Sathr'd claimed.

"While on the ridge, I saw a pond." Sathr gestured. "Not far. The goat and horses can drink, and then I'll treat you all to some fresh goat's milk. My people, the Undmen, use these goats in much the same way Rif wants to use the dragons...for labor, and sometimes for protection. We treat them well, respect them. But let's go to the pond. I could use a bath."

Rif and Jaeg leaned against the trunk of a black oak. They were drinking goat's milk and engrossed in conversation.

After their flasks were filled, the pond became a bath.

Goranth, who'd had more than enough of his own stench, doffed his shredded clothes and waded into the pond. The center was deep enough that the water came to his chest. He should've taken clothes from the fallen Mabayans, despite his misgivings, when he realized just how filthy and ragged his trousers had become. He would need to wash the rags, too, else bathing himself would not make him smell any better.

He held his breath and sat, letting the water swirl around him while he rubbed his skin to remove the scabs and dirt. His muscles ached a little less, and the burn was a memory. He started when arms wrapped around his waist and tugged him up. Sathr was behind him, leaning against his back, face turned and pressed against him.

"Water heals," she whispered, moving her arms higher and holding his shoulders, pulling herself up to be buoyed by the water. She nuzzled his ear and proved him right—women held the true power in the world.

He turned so she faced him, and she wrapped her naked legs around his waist. Going after the goat had proven to be a wise decision after all, he realized. Her hair, plastered against the sides of her head, gleamed in the rays of the late afternoon sun, and her skin looked like polished pewter. His breath caught, and she gave a half-smile.

"I've not been with a man before, Goranth. I'd had no reason—or desire. The Undmen who fancied me in the chambers below were interested only in a physical bout. But you...this...this is much more."

Goranth considered this a physical bout, no commitments, no mention of love. Lust and the rush of release it gave his body and spirit was all he needed. He should extricate himself, tell her this was not the "much more" she looked for. It would be the right thing to do, but being proper and decent were far from his thoughts. Instead, he let her take the lead and think what she wanted about this blissful interval. He drank in her heat and shut everything else out, if only for a short and passionate while.

When they stepped out of the pond, Rif was watching them with a sly expression on his face.

"While you two were busy," he began, "I did some thinking. Aye, I want a dragonette, and that will happen. But I also want those books and scrolls, as many as we can haul out of the belly of that peak. Sathr said they use the goats for labor. We'll use this one for labor, too. We can lash a good haul onto it or let it drag a litter. And these horses...they could carry books too."

"Every time you think, I get more scars. The books...those things should be left to rot there, Barber."

"I think not, Northman. Abandoning treasure is something I can't stomach. Not when we've the means to take it. We'll sleep here the night and go back to that peak at first light. You might want to wear something for the journey."

CHAPTER TWENTY-THREE

When the sky turns dark and the children cower in fear,
Look for us appearing from the heart of the storm.
As the thunder rolls and lightning strikes, you'll know we're near
And your world will change forevermore.
"Tales of the Mabayan Raiders"

Goranth slept in the nude with an equally naked and vibrant Sathr next to him. They had stayed away from the fire and out of sight of their companions, their shared warmth keeping them comfortable. A single blanket covered them both.

A mist swirled and drew Goranth in. He waved his arms and wailed until a gentle breeze caught him and buoyed him.

Kalida.

She swept him through the cave wall and down into the earth. They stopped at gem lodes, and his body reveled in the healing warmth that consumed him. He watched with interest, never completely trusting, wanting to be sure he wasn't tossed into a river of molten rock.

Never completely trusting, but giving of yourself as if you do, Kalida said, her words caressing him like a lover's touch. *You are a strange creature, Goranth. When you made love to Sathr, I was her.*

Goranth bolted upright, shocking Sathr awake. He felt for the scratches and bruises on his knees, but they were gone.

"Fever dreams, my Goranth?" She sat and hugged herself to him. He liked the company of a fine woman. Too long he'd been with the likes of the Barber. Too long, he'd gone without. He rubbed the stubble on his face over the top of her head.

"The earth mother took me by surprise, but the enchantress healed me. I need to relieve myself. Stay here. Stay warm."

He guided her back to the ground and covered her. He traced a line down her face with one finger, dipping his head to kiss her fiercely. It had been far too long since he'd had such company.

Goranth threw his sword belt above his naked hips and stalked into the wood. He stepped lightly, making no sound as he found a spot away from the others, away from runoff that might pollute the pond, refreshed overnight by the spring that fed it.

There was movement in the branches above, a familiar shape. Goranth finished and returned to the camp, where he helped himself to the Mabayan bow Jaeg had appropriated.

Goranth returned to the forest, entering slowly, taking one silent step after the other and freezing between each. The shape remained. The Northman took aim and pulled until the bow creaked and the string complained. He aimed slightly over the top of the shadow. If the arrow dropped a little, he'd hit the creature in the head. If it dropped a lot, it would be a gut shot. Aim for the best miss; that was the warrior's way. Always injure your enemy. Trying for a kill shot every time was dangerous.

He had a second arrow, but the creature would be long gone if the first missed. He exhaled and loosed the arrow on its journey through a gap in the foliage. By the time the arrow struck home, he had the second arrow nocked, only waiting for an aiming point. The creature gagged on a scream of pain.

A throat shot.

As it tumbled, he led it and loosed the second arrow, throwing the bow and arrows aside on his way to intercept the praevo-pavor with the makhaira's cold steel.

"Northman!" Rif shouted from the camp. Goranth ignored him and pounded ahead, focused on his enemy. He raised his blade and swung with the power of a lumberjack to meet the creature before it hit the ground, cleaving the flying terror's body in half. He watched for a moment to make sure it was dead. Neither arrow survived the fall, so he didn't bother to recover them. Let the creature remain as it died as a warning to others.

He recovered the bow and arrows on his way back to camp. "A flying terror," he called. "It was watching us. We need to go and now."

The others were already up and Sathr was dressed, unlike Goranth. She held out his clothes. "Thanks, lass," he told her while the others readied the horses. They packed their gear and swept the site for anything they didn't want to leave behind.

"South," Rif said softly. "The last place they'll look for us is where they last saw us."

And close to the cave with the ancient texts and scrolls,

Goranth thought. But hiding where the Mabayans had no need to look made sense. Sathr added the mountain goat to the beasts pulled behind Goranth's mare.

Rif heeled his mount and started the journey south, sticking to hard ground where hooves would leave no trace of their passing. The moon had set, and light crept up the horizon. They had slept their fill and would get no more that day. And Goranth would not get the chance to explore more of Sathr's tender mercies, at least not right away.

With a determination borne of flight, they covered the ground in half a day that they spent more than a day traversing the first time. The battlefield was as they'd left it. Since Goranth and Sathr had talked, she was ready to deliver that which he lacked—unshredded clothing. She slipped out of the saddle and scavenged, finding what she needed from the already-decaying dead.

"These need to be washed, but we will find a stream, and then you will not have to look like a trader's tent after a vicious storm." She hung the buckskin breeches, rough cloth shirt, and leather vest over the saddlebags to let them air while they prepared a goat-pulled litter for its dark-magic prize.

"With the vile texts behind it, will the goat turn into a demon spawn?"

Sathr laughed and play-pushed Goranth. "Why would you ask that? She is a magnificent creature, not to succumb to the corruptions of the likes of Rif."

"The likes of the tomes that Rif seeks. There is no treasure within that mountain, only darkness and pain."

"Sounds like everyday life for the Undmen, but there is also pleasure. Would you forego the potential for joy?"

"Joy is fleeting, woman," Goranth replied in his deep voice. "Enjoy each day but know that darkness will fall, bringing the heinous creatures, slavering under a gibbous moon. Would that the darkness not hide the enemies of humankind, then I would embrace it as a friend."

"The flying terror bothered you that much?" Sathr clicked her tongue to the goat while she added its harness and snugged the knots.

"From man to flying terrors to dragons, the worst of Migoro follows me like flies follow a caravan. That is the lot you have leashed yourself to."

"A worthy challenge for a warrior woman like me." She tipped her chin back, daring Goranth to defy her claim.

"Aye. I'll teach you, but be ready for bruises and cuts. Learning to fight is not an easy road to follow. But first, I will follow you up that hillside to those bushes where the cave mouth lies. Show me how to climb like your goat."

She handed him the goat's lead and smiled. "Follow me."

Sathr scrambled up the remnants of a rockslide consisting of gravel and bad footing. Goranth followed, surging through the stone like he was climbing a hill of sand in the Kuiper Desert. Even the goat struggled through the loose rock.

Sathr reached the stone face above and pointed at the hand and footholds before she used them. Goranth studied each one, seeing how they differed from holds that looked better. The goat hesitated and nearly jerked him off his tenuous perch. He turned to growl at the beast to find it eating a small bush, unperturbed by the Northman's glare. It finished and followed.

Goranth looked up to appreciate the view of the woman ahead of him. He stared too long and nearly missed a handhold, grumbling at his loss of focus.

It has indeed been too long, he thought.

He climbed on, bending his knees as Sathr did, pulling

as she pulled. His bulk didn't get past outcroppings as she was able to wind sinuously around. By the time they reached the ledge beside the cave mouth, Goranth bled from a dozen scratches and was covered in dust. Sathr was clean and not even sweating. She took a drink from her flask and handed it to Goranth. He slaked his thirst.

Rif and Jaeg were barely halfway up the hill when Sathr gestured for Goranth to follow her inside. Once in the dark and with eyes unaccustomed to it, she jumped on him, drinking in his passion with a fierce display that he embraced and gave his all to while the goat bumped him from behind. He ignored the creature for the short time the fire burned between him and Sathr.

"I see how you look at me, and it pleases me greatly," she said in the respite afterward. They collected their wits and pressed on down the tunnel. Sathr guided him through the darkness by holding his hand.

"Let us wait for the others. I do not wish to enter the library in the dark."

"Then let us sit. Our goat has come a long way and needs to rest more than we do." Goranth dropped to the floor and leaned against the cave wall. Sathr straddled him and slowly kissed her way around his neck.

"Have you no limits?" Goranth whispered in the darkness.

"A question I hope you keep asking in our time together."

Goranth cradled her butt, squeezing in rhythm with her even breathing.

He pushed her to her feet when the light from Jaeg's torch appeared. When Rif and Jaeg appeared, Goranth and Sathr were standing, holding the goat with the litter tied behind it. The creature watched them with big eyes but no fear.

The light separated in two as they got closer, for each carried a torch.

"Don't waste them. It's all the light we have," Goranth warned.

"Jaeg readied four extras from the Mabayan refuse. We shouldn't be here long, Northman. Heave ho and let's fill that litter!" Rif clapped the lad on the back, sending him staggering forward. Jaeg handed Goranth two torches.

"I thank you, but I'll wait to light mine." Goranth threw them on the litter.

Goranth and Sathr led the way to the Y intersection that took them to the library. As they passed, the carvings on the walls, Goranth shivered. Sathr lost her good humor and walked without the bounce in her step she'd had since the pond.

Goranth handed Rif the goat's lead. "I'll go no further and be a party to robbing a necromancer. *You* can be cursed, but I choose not to."

He looked at Sathr. She threw her shoulders back. "Where Goranth goes, I will follow."

"Leave the happy couple be," Rif told Jaeg. "I see the look on your face, Northman. You need not worry. You'll still get your share. Let us load up the books that will most likely survive the journey. This shouldn't take too long."

"We'll meet you in the main tunnel," Goranth replied. He lit his torch, holding it in one hand and the makhaira in the other as he stalked up the tunnel. Sathr walked behind, well out of the sword's reach.

"Tell me what unsettles you," Sathr pleaded while pulling her knife and carrying it before her. Goranth didn't answer. At the tunnel, he turned right to head deeper underground. "Do you wish me to take you to the Undmen?"

"Nay, lass. I only wish to know what is around us. Establish a perimeter within which we might be safe."

Not far down the tunnel, he saw a man-sized shadow and jumped toward the opposite wall. "Ho there!" he cried.

Sathr grabbed his arm. "There is no one there, Goranth. It is only the shadow from a side tunnel."

"We saw it not coming from the other direction." Goranth walked past it and held up the torch. The concealed entrance's shadow was not visible, looking like a blank wall. "It was hidden and cast no shadow as we worked our way from the rockfall."

He walked around the outcropping and thrust the torch inside, then stepped past it. It was a carved tunnel. "How did this tunnel come to be?"

Sathr shook her head. "It is unnatural and makes my skin crawl, but I must know what is inside."

"Me, too, when I know I should be running away as fast as my legs will carry me." He took a reluctant step forward. "Kalida!"

Yes, lover? she cooed. Goranth's stomach twisted into a knot. Had she fashioned this opening? Did she want Goranth to go inside?

"She's in my head, too," Sathr discovered. "It's like talking to someone in the dark, nothing more. Let us see what lies ahead. The enchantress' magics will protect us."

Goranth hung his head, but his sword flashed out to stop Sathr from continuing forward. "I will go first into this place." He looked past his torch. "Kalida, tell us what lies ahead."

There is a chamber carved using the magic that cut this tunnel from the living stone. A private chamber. I sense it was the home of a sorcerer of great power. Tell me what you see, Northman. My vision is strong, but it does not reveal everything.

Perhaps Kalida led me here because of her curiosity. He

eased forward, the torch's flickering orange and yellow light reflecting off the bared steel of his blade.

The end of the tunnel opened to a chamber with chairs, tables, and a bed, all created of stone but neither carved nor chipped. "Magic has done this," Goranth pronounced.

A shelf of stone blended into the wall. Scrolls curled undisturbed and undusted in cubbyholes designed for them.

Open one for me. I wish to read it, Kalida ordered.

"Off with you, temptress!" Goranth blurted.

Sathr rested her hand on his forearm. "Then do it for me." Her voice had a tinkle like an angel's bells.

"I don't like this, Kalida, but I'll do it. Leave Sathr be. Leave her be, or I'll torch this place."

Sathr's grip tightened before she let go. She shook her head.

Goranth pulled her close, holding the torch away, and kissed her softly and deeply.

Time is wasting, Kalida chided.

"You'll have your scrolls, but in my time, woman." Goranth released Sathr and pulled the first scroll from its resting place. He unrolled it.

You must let me take over your mind.

Goranth gritted his teeth before closing his eyes and letting her in. His eyes shot open with Kalida's drive to see what the scrolls had to say. Goranth watched himself hand the torch to Sathr and wink at her, then unroll the parchment.

Kalida studied it for a few moments as if memorizing it before it started to crumble. Goranth watched, powerless to affect anything. He unrolled a second scroll, but it shredded under the Northman's less-than-gentle touch.

Using Goranth's voice, she complained about her failure. A third scroll suffered the same fate, crumbling before giving up its secret. The fourth scroll remained stalwart, being made of hide that looked like it was tanned yesterday. Kalida found what she wanted.

She read aloud in Goranth's voice but in a language he didn't understand.

"Miag Millend," he read over and over in the short treatise.

Sathr winced at the name, recoiling from the strange language Goranth spoke.

"Miag Millend was a powerful sorceress who created a city from stone. She was the one who carved most of these caves after she fled from her city because those who lived there rebelled. To punish them, she brought the dragons back but left the beasts to their own devices after they destroyed her once-proud creation."

Kalida continued, "Those who lived above deserved their fate. They deserved to suffer at the hands of the reborn old ones, according to Miag Millend. Wait."

Goranth watched his fingers unroll the last of the scroll and lean close to read the finely written words. His voice spoke again. "Miag Millend found a way to live forever. She is the black heart of the dragon god."

Sathr stood with her mouth agape, looking from the scroll to Goranth and back to the scroll with the tightly shaped letters.

Kalida had seen what she needed to. She fled Goranth's mind with the parting words. *I must find her. I search.*

Goranth re-rolled the scroll and tied it closed. He took one last look at the chamber and gestured for Sathr to lead the way out.

She walked quickly, and Goranth kept pace. They reached the main tunnel and continued without pause. The scrape of the litter dragging sounded loud before them.

"Goranth," Rif said, holding his arms wide to take in the litter filled with books and scrolls.

"Add this to your prizes, Barber. A hide scroll."

"Nothing more, Northman?" The Barber studied Goranth as if he were hiding something.

"Fear not, Rif, you greedy bastard. I'm not stealing from you. I'll take what's mine when next we are in Barbertown. For now, let us leave this place."

Rif nodded, and they began their journey toward the cave mouth.

A dragonette is near, Kalida told them all. Her earth-search had been fruitful, but she didn't find Miag. *A small one, the likes of which you seek.*

"Damn woman," Goranth growled.

Rif turned to him and his eyes sparkled under the torchlight, almost maniacal in showing the whites. He cheered in triumph, pumping his fist in the air.

"All this treasure and a dragon. A good day, Northman."

"You've no concern about the Mabayans?"

"I believe we lost them by this sojourn into the caves. Time well spent avoiding an enemy while winning a treasure, my friend. Maybe they will have given up looking for us. And now we'll collect a dragon."

"Aye, Rif. I'll help you catch this one and take it back to Barbertown, but then we will part ways. The time has come."

"That is all I can ask of my old friend. Let us catch a dragon, shall we?"

CHAPTER TWENTY-FOUR

There is nothing more powerful than a good friend. Except treasure.
The Black Sail Brotherhood

You are still leaving after this one? There are other dragons in the woods and the mountains. Not many, but there are—

"Yes," Goranth replied to Kalida, who'd been hovering in his head since her failed attempt to find the undying Miag Millend. Heart of the dragon god? Ha! Nothing lived forever in this world, the Northman knew. No one could gain immortality, perhaps not even the gods in their golden halls. Still, he wished the sorceress was continuing her pursuit of her Miag myth. It would keep her busy and out of his head. He didn't want to share his thoughts this morning.

Then I am still leaving with you, my love, Kalida purred. *I have spent enough years in Barbertown. There is more of the world to see. With you. Together, we will explore all the realms.*

Goranth tried not to think about Sathr, which was difficult with her settled against him on the horse. Her delicate scent made him dizzy, and her soft skin pressed to his chest brought a welcome heat. Kalida did not need to know the extent to which the gray-skinned woman distracted him.

They rode along the base of the mountain in the shadow of the peaks, picking carefully across a stretch of stony debris that cut into the forest to the west. It was no doubt a displaced section of the rock face toppled by the quake. Sathr tipped her head back onto his shoulder and shared his breath. He focused on the dragon and the way ahead, centering on how difficult it had been to catch the first dragon when Varl was alive and could sing to it and how badly Esh had been injured. A shiver raced down his back when he remembered the boiling release of the angered mother dragon that had blistered his skin and threatened to cook him alive. She was huge, eyes massive mirrors that pierced his soul. Was she nearby? Kalida had not mentioned her.

"How much farther?" Sathr's voice was musical.

Tell her not far, Kalida said to Goranth. *Before the sun is directly above, you should find the dragonette. Be careful and quiet as you near lest you spook the creature and send it skyward and beyond your reach. Right now, she lies in darkness. I want you back in Barbertown soon, not traipsing through the woods for more days and days and days with a woman that belongs underground with her tribe. You belong with me.*

But you want dragons captured, Goranth thought. How fickle were women's desires? *In that, your goal aligns with Rif's. I can't be with you and after dragons too. You want—*

—you. I want you, she returned. *Rif can go after his dragons without us.*

Indeed, women were fickle. Was Sathr?

A while later, at Kalida's urging, he pulled on the reins and slipped off the horse's back. The Northman patted Sathr's leg, his fingers lingering. Then he looked at Rif and Jaeg as he took a coil of rope from his saddle. One rope would not be enough for a dragon, but it might come in handy in case he needed it to climb or descend into a tunnel to reach it. Kalida had mentioned the dragon was in darkness.

"Kalida says there is a place of new growth straight to the north, shadowed by an overhang of rock. She cautions us not to spook the dragonette. Stay here while I go ahead and take a look. If fate is kind this day, we will go together to catch it. I'll be back."

Rif clambered off the horse, holding its neck for support. Though he'd regained most of his strength, Goranth noted he still heavily favored his injured leg. Kalida had not taken Rif's senses through the earth to heal him. Jaeg had mended on his own, but the scars on his face would remain as evidence of his time in the Barber's company.

Rif regarded Goranth and then glanced north. "While you're gone, Jaeg and I will find wood to serve as clubs. Something to beat it into submission." He grinned broadly, glancing at the goat pulling the litter and the line of horses. "Ah, the haul we bring back to Barbertown. It will be grand, Goranth. Worthy of a crowd and a parade." His expression turned serious. "Be careful."

"Aye," Goranth replied. "And I will be quiet. Without the rest of you making a racket behind me, I'll be quiet."

He glided forward, losing sight of the trio but still able to hear the nickering of the Ahak-Teeks.

Goranth didn't like wearing a dead man's clothes, especially a Mabayan's, but they fit him well enough, though the seams strained across his broad shoulders. It was better than what had been left of his own clothes, which he'd buried. He would buy more when he returned to Barbertown; have some made to fit of fine and rugged fabrics, enough to fill a large pack, with a second pack to carry his wealth away from the cursed place. Would he be leaving alone? Did he want to? He had more offers than he could accept, which would create a minor dilemma, but later. Now it was no problem. He expected it to resolve itself before he had to make a decision.

Goranth studied the ground, stepping so he did not snap fallen branches or unsettle the stones beneath his feet. Despite his size, he had a grace that made him stealthy; it had served him well and hopefully would let him sneak up on the young dragon. If it was too large, he'd return and tell Rif there was no sign of the beast. He did not want to lose another companion to this foolish endeavor.

He wondered if the scrolls Kalida had read were true, that someone had brought the creatures back from oblivion. For decades upon decades there'd been no reports of dragons, and like the great three-toed black bears of the far north, they had been considered gone from the world. That Rif was hunting dragons was the first word Goranth had heard that they still lived. He'd never bothered to ask the Barber how he'd learned about the dragons. It didn't matter, Goranth decided. It only mattered that he find the one ahead, size it up, and if it was not too large, return to the others and plan a way to catch it. Rif would have clubs for cowing the thing. Maybe Sathr could sing to it.

The rock wall to his right became straight, like what he'd scaled to catch the damn goat. He spied an overhang ahead that rose and curved away from the crest like a wave captured in stone. It was a feature that could afford good protection from the wind and storms for those beneath it, he thought, a fitting lair for a dragon. If there was a cave under it, that could be the darkness Kalida saw the dragon in.

But how large a dragon? He inhaled deeply, taking in the scents of the ridge and detecting something musky like an animal.

I leave you to the dragon, Kalida said. *Something draws my attention elsewhere.*

What could be more pressing than this? Goranth briefly wondered. She'd led him here, only to disappear. She was inconsistent and erratic, yet he was drawn to her. Two women in his thoughts? The Northman shook his head and crept forward, shoulder to the rock face, finding shadows there.

Listening.

There was no breeze, and sounds carried down the slope. A stone dropped, though he couldn't see if an animal had been responsible. A hawk cried, and he caught a glimpse of it before it winged out of sight. Birds called from the woods, there was a scolding sound from a monkey hidden in the leaves, and he heard something like a snort or the wuffle a horse would make but different. It wasn't loud, and he hoped that meant the dragon—he was certain it was making the noise—was small like the snort-wuffle implied.

He took another deep breath, concentrating on the musk. Another step forward and another. Closer, the sound was no louder, but the musky smell became more intense. He put his hand on the hilt of the makhaira and registered its eager warmth. He drew it and came even with the edge of the rock just before the overhang. It was dark beneath, like a cave.

Kalida? Goranth searched his thoughts. She was absent

still, attending to whatever other matter had drawn her attention. Was she again in pursuit of Miag Millend?

He looked around the edge into the darkness, eyes adjusting and picking through the shadows—to find a young dragon looking directly at him. Goranth froze and put the blade back in its sheath.

Kalida had said it was a small dragon, or dragonette as she called the young ones. This was far smaller than he'd expected. It was smaller than the goat Sathr had captured on the ridge yesterday, the size of a sheep. The shadows from the overhang muted the colors, but he could tell it was more silver than gray and had scales the size of his fingernails. A diminutive spiky spine ran from the top of its horse-shaped head to the tip of its short, slender tail. The eyes locked onto him were wide-set and unblinking, and thin wisps of steam curled from its nostrils.

Goranth stepped closer, sharing the shadows. He debated turning around, returning to Rif, and telling him there was no dragon. That it had been spooked and had flown above the forest and out of sight. Part of him thought the creature should be free to grow up on the mountain, feasting on sheep and goats and the occasional fool who came looking to catch it. Rif didn't need a hatchling.

The dragon snort-wuffled, then made a mewling sound not unlike a cat's or a baby's. It *was* a baby, Goranth realized when he saw fragments of shell lying around it. There were more fragments nearby as if others had hatched and left the lair. The beast's wings were tiny and tucked close to its sides; they certainly weren't capable of lifting it. It was too young and small to fly, so it should not be difficult to catch. But should he?

Rif didn't need a hatchling, he thought again.

And yet he took a step closer, and another until he was

only two man-lengths away and the musky scent of this place was so strong it lodged unpleasantly on his tongue and made his eyes water. The dragon continued to watch him, making no move other than to raise its head higher by extending its neck. It gave another snort-wuffle and started mewling again, then it cocked its head and blinked.

"By the Ice Dogs," Goranth growled.

The dragon mewled a little louder and cocked its head to the other side, a gesture of curiosity. Its tail flicked and then drew close to its haunch.

"Kalida?"

No response. He wondered what so occupied her.

"Kalida!"

Goranth could leave and let the dragon be, but this was the step that would deliver freedom to him. He padded forward, stopping within arm's length of it. Sathr had slipped a loop around the head of that big goat. It had been docile and let her lead it down the mountain. Could he do the same with the dragon?

The Barber was gathering wood that could serve as clubs to beat it into submission. Goranth didn't want to take the chance that Rif would beat this creature. Nothing should strike something so young and vulnerable. It was almost beautiful. It was all angles and planes, shiny in its newness; he imagined it would sparkle under direct sunlight. The great mother dragon was ash-gray, as had been the dragonette they'd caught long days past. Perhaps the shine wore off with age, like men collecting white strands in their beards as they aged.

"What to do with you?" he asked. "I cannot—will not —sing."

The dragon lowered its head to the stone floor, continuing to keep its eyes on Goranth.

Maybe it was hurt. Maybe that was why it was staying

put. A dark thought flickered and made him inhale sharply. Newly hatched, maybe the creature waited for its mother to return. A glance into the deepest shadows revealed more broken eggs...and two intact ones. Maybe the massive mother dragon would come back. Did dragons sit on eggs the way birds did? Goranth knew very little about these creatures that had been gone so long from the world.

Another step closer. He reached out, bent, and touched its side. The dragon didn't move, just gave him a snort-wuffle-mewl. Its side felt like chainmail links with a tight weave, metallic and smooth. He continued to explore it with his fingers, keeping an eye on its head as he walked around it.

"What to do with you?" he repeated. "Whatever I'm going to do, I need to do it quickly." Leave and lie to Rif that there was no dragon, or catch the thing himself so the Barber couldn't beat it. "I need to do something before your mother returns."

Goranth stood directly in front of it, and it raised its head slightly. "You're injured." He couldn't see an injury, but it was the best explanation for why the creature just laid there. He took a step back and fashioned a harness from the length of rope similar to what Sathr had crafted for the big ugly goat. When he knelt and worked it around the dragon's head, he was rewarded with a scalding burst of steam that struck his chest and blistered the exposed skin.

"By the Ice Dogs!" Not so vulnerable and not injured, he realized in that instant. The dragon rose and made a noise like a growl, then opened its maw, and Goranth tightened the harness and whipped the other end of the rope around its snout like a muzzle to keep it from scalding him a second time.

The dragon thrashed. Goranth kept hold of the rope

with his right hand, spun to its side, and laid across it, heedless of the spikes that gouged him as his weight forced it down. It continued to thrash, striking him with its tail and trying to claw him. A few blows landed, but nothing as painful as the Northman's other bouts.

"Stay still, you!" Goranth hissed. The dragon writhed and dislodged him, but Goranth sprang right back on top of it and took it down again. The musty scent of the lair was stirred up and became so intense the Northman gagged. Dust swirled and found his open mouth and eyes. He held on tighter. "I don't want to hurt you, but I'll not—"

A loop of rope dropped around its head and Sathr appeared, pressing herself across its neck and adding her weight to help keep it in place.

"So small," she remarked. "So small, and it fights like a maddened cat."

"Aye," Goranth returned. "It fights, and I'm trying not to harm it."

They continued to wrestle the small dragon until it finally tired and gave up, exhausted. Goranth withdrew and sat back to regard it, watched its side rise and fall regularly, steam still spiraling from its nostrils.

"I don't think you hurt it," Sathr said. She stroked its neck as its eyes closed. "What a beautiful creature. Why does Rif want it?"

"Rif wants a lot of things," Goranth shot back. He reached for his waterskin, uncorked it, poured water in his eyes, and then took a deep drink before passing it to Sathr.

"I'm fine," she said, declining.

"Rif wants dragons for his city, I think to use as you do the goats in the Undmen warrens. But he has plans beyond that." He paused. "Maybe also for defense. Who would raid a city that has dragons? Maybe for war. Who could defy men who can tame dragons? Rif has a warrior's soul, though no longer a stout warrior's body."

"A weak man with a dragon would appear strong. Unconquerable," Sathr stated.

"Perhaps."

"I wonder if such as this can be tamed, or should be." She continued to stroke its neck. The dragon opened its eyes and looked at her. "What if we just let it go?"

Goranth stood and rolled his shoulders and neck. "That might be the best option," he admitted. "But lately, I've not followed the wisest choice. No, I'm taking it back to the Barber. Did he stay where I left my horse?"

She nodded. "With Jaeg. I told them I could be quiet, follow you."

Goranth removed the rope she'd brought and undid the loop. It wasn't needed for the little dragon any longer. He started working the length and putting sailing knots in it.

"What are you doing?"

"Making a net bag. We're taking the dragon *and* those eggs. Maybe they'll hatch. If not, they'll provide a fine breakfast." It took him several minutes to fashion something suitable for carrying the eggs. He hung the woven pouch over his shoulders and put the eggs inside. They were heavy but not too unwieldy. "Hand me that rope, Sathr. I'll tug our prize back to—"

"I can manage that, Goranth." Sathr coaxed the dragon to its feet. It wobbled and tried to fight the harness, but she yanked and it quieted. "No different than leading a goat. Though this is much smaller." She touched a spot between its eyes. "And so beautiful." She turned her head to him and smiled. "Life has been an amazing adventure since you saved me."

Goranth didn't know what to say to that, so he stepped

out from under the overhang and headed south. "Let's be free of this place before the mother dragon comes back."

"If she is going to come back," Sathr mused, following him. The dragon made a snort-wuffle-mew. "If she hasn't abandoned that lair and left the younglings on their own."

"I am happy to abandon the place," Goranth announced.

The sun was high overhead and baking his shoulders by the time they rejoined Jaeg and Rif, who had a dozen lengths of thick wood in a pile. Rif stared at the dragon, mouth dropping open.

"So small," he said. "So very, very small."

"Sorry it wasn't bigger," Goranth replied. "This will have to do."

"Wonderful!" Rif made a move to slap Goranth on the arm and stopped himself. "And eggs. Even more wonderful, Northman. This small, the dragon, I can train it. Like a dog, I can train it. Eggs, they'll hatch—"

"Maybe they'll hatch," Sathr said. She added the dragon to the horses and goat tied to Goranth's Ahak-Teek.

"Just wonderful. We can—"

"Take all of this back to Barbertown now," Goranth said. He mounted his horse and extended a hand to help Sathr up. She rubbed against him as she settled, then tipped her head back and brushed her lips across his stubbled chin. "If this babe's mother is in the area, I want to be well away. We cannot again survive the wrath of a mother dragon."

"To Barbertown, then!" Rif announced, awkwardly climbing into his saddle and taking the lead. "To home!"

"*Your* home," Goranth said too softly for the Barber to hear. "It will never be mine."

CHAPTER TWENTY-FIVE

Stand tall. Walk slow. Own the night.
Strike hard. Strike fast. Win the fight.
Crush their bodies, crush their souls
Easy come, easy go
"Tales of the Mabayan Raiders"

An Ahak-Teek whinnied at the fine grass on a small field. "Let them eat," Goranth ordered. He lifted Sathr to the ground before dismounting and throwing the horse's reins on the ground in front of it to let it graze. Three horses, a goat, and a dragon had been running with them. All were tired. The dragon lumbered to a stop while the horses strained to put distance between them and the musky-smelling creature.

Goranth untied the dragon and led it toward the woods, where he secured it to a tree. "Your bow, boy. I need to hunt for the dragon's meal before she gains too keen an eye for our mountain goat."

"I can do it. I'll kill a feast for the beast," Jaeg declared. Goranth had no patience for the lad's newfound bravado. Goranth held out his hand and pointed at the bow. The lad grumbled but handed it over.

Goranth tossed the quiver over his shoulder and nocked an arrow as he stalked toward the woods. Sathr intercepted him, and they exchanged looks. Goranth had no desire to argue. She had proven herself with the dragon and fought when freed from the slavers. He handed her his knife. She checked the edge and then measured how it balanced in her hand. After a few heartbeats, she faced the woods, ready to walk by Goranth's side.

"We'll be back with fresh meat for you, little girl. Be patient, and your gullet will be stuffed," he told the dragon as they passed. He stepped over the threshold between the sun and the forest's shadow, changing his stride to soft steps on the balls of his feet. Listening. Watching.

They ranged far from the small pasture until the chittering of the forest creatures became normal, accepting the interlopers as their own. A monkey the size of a small child watched Goranth from a branch nearby. He held its gaze, moving his bow with glacial speed to avoid spooking the animal. Sathr produced no sound because she had gone out of Goranth's sight. He thought she might rile the forest with her movements, so he increased his speed.

The monkey changed to a crouch from sitting, looking like it was ready to flee. In a single motion, Goranth brought the bow up the last few inches and loosed the arrow as the target appeared within his sights.

The arrow launched and covered the short space between, then dug deep into the monkey's heart. It was dead before it fell. Goranth hurried forward with the makhaira bared to deal a death blow should the monkey find resurrection, but there would be no second life for the creature. Its future was confirmed as a meal for the baby dragon.

"Sathr," Goranth called softly.

"Here," came her reply from nearby. She rustled through a bush and appeared, carrying a fat groundhog. "I thought we might want to eat, too."

"Aye, lass. That we do. The meat on those is greasy if you've not had one before. Cooking it on a spit will boil off most of the fat, leaving a fine meal."

"I've not had much of what is common in the overworld. What about that?" She pointed with Goranth's knife.

"Monkey? No. Never eat a monkey. They have a foul taste, and they remember. The next time they see us, they will throw their dung at us. Or rocks. They will chitter and drive off any creature we seek to hunt. They are humanlike in how they treat others they don't like." He laughed. "I paint a terrible picture of men, but I've traveled far and wide. The truth is not pretty."

Sathr studied him as if she struggled to learn his philosophy. "Never kill a monkey to avoid their ire, yet you stand there with one that you just killed."

At the camp, the dragon hunched catlike with its limbs tucked underneath its body. Goranth threw the monkey on the ground in front of it. "Eat up. Grow big and strong so you can escape this circus you've joined."

With one short mewling snort, the dragon sniffed its meal. Hunger was a strong condiment, and no matter how bad the monkey tasted, according to Goranth, the dragon wolfed it down, surprising considering it wasn't much bigger than the meal it inhaled.

Sathr started cleaning the groundhog while Goranth wandered the small grassy area on which the goat and horses grazed. He ran his hands over the Ahak-Teeks' flanks and along their necks, nuzzling each before moving to the next.

Even the goat received his attentions. He knelt, keeping his hand in front of him in case the she-goat wanted to butt him as it had on the mountain. But no. Thanks to Sathr, the two had come to an understanding. The horses drifted around the field to find their way to Goranth, surrounding him as a congregation would their priest. He stood in their company, and for a single moment, he felt the joy of being with those who wanted nothing from him except his friendship.

He was happy to oblige. And he did, until they swirled from his sight, even though he still stood among them.

Kalida.

A king's treasure you carry with you. Well done, Goranth.

It's a king's death to bring all this back to Barbertown. None of this should see the light of day. We'd be better off turning the dragonette loose and torching those books.

But you won't do that because treasure drives you. The prizes you bring will earn you gold and gems and status. You desire admiration, Northman.

Goranth's lip curled and he snarled. He had gold and jewels in his purse. He had a lithe and beautiful woman in his bed. He had horses enough to carry him the rest of his days. *I will have the treasure because Rif owes it to me.*

Even though you would give it away. You are a strange man, enticing. I will have you upon your return. Bring your wench. She might enjoy watching.

The more you speak, the less enticing you become. Once, I dreamt of you. I owe you a necklace, but not the one that graced Varl's chest. That goes to Esh. A new one from Rif's horde and that will pay the debt I feel I owe to you. Horses' muzzles pressed against Goranth, and he blindly stroked them.

Kalida laughed, for what reason, Goranth didn't bother to fathom a guess. Her mirth ended as abruptly as it started. *Something hunts you, Northman. Hunts you and all of Rif's party.*

What, woman? Don't make me wonder. His hands froze, no longer tending to the horses. They felt his angst and whinnied, nickered, and started to prance. The goat worked in close to him and nudged his hand with her horns.

It's dark, something of the old magic. But there's more. The Mabayans...

They are looking for us, I presume, Goranth guessed.

Yes, but no. They will try to kill you if they find you, but they won't find you out here in the woods. They are on their way to Barbertown. I fear you are too far away to stop their approach this time. And there are too many of them.

Goranth's eyes narrowed in ire. *They will get there before us. We can't allow that. We must take flight and move like the wind. Leave me be.*

I will show you.

Goranth wanted to free himself, but the images came fast. Narlun, the leader of the Mabayans, astride his Ahak-Teek while a lad rode beside him, a youngster who glowed with the energy of magic. Goranth gasped and would have fallen to his knees had it not been for the steadfastness of the goat that leaned against him.

Narlun's spinner of magic looked directly at Goranth, and his lips started to move as a glowing ball formed before him. Goranth stumbled back, blinking rapidly to end the mind quest Kalida had taken him on.

"Get us out of here!" he shouted in the real world

within the confines of the small pasture where his body labored without his mind.

It changed nothing. Kalida held him there until the blue ball of magical energy flew his way, growing larger as it closed until it swept over him. He staggered and fell, and there was a cry in the distance. It was Sathr, and she was running toward him.

Kalida laughed again. Goranth looked at the sky, freed from the unnatural world of magic and visions. The priestess spoke to him. *I wouldn't let a boy harm you. Even though he has much power, it is still raw. Over time, he will become a great threat to you and the rest, even the Mabayans. No one will be able to contain him, but for now, he can be managed. If you stay here, you will stay safe.*

Goranth did not consider that an option. The people of Barbertown did not deserve whatever fate the Mabayans would hand them. He wasn't a hero, but he couldn't let others fall to the slavers if it was within his ability to prevent it.

I can tell your mind is made up, and you will choose danger. In that event, you must hurry, Goranth. Get back to Barbertown with the dragon and the books as fast as you can. I will delay the Mabayans, but I don't know for how long. They are closing.

We will be on our way in less time than it takes to drain a flask, Goranth promised.

Kalida cried out in mental anguish.

The boy-sorcerer assaults you! I will kill that boy when I see him, Goranth vowed.

It is not him who pains me now, Kalida gasped from within his mind. *It is not the boy, not yet. I've kept him at bay. Something different. Something ancient and evil. I think Miag Millend has found me. My scrying awakened her. I see the land being covered in darkness as she rises, becomes aware. Hurry,*

Goranth. A fight is coming. A battle to end all battles. A fight that will determine the fate of all of us. Hurry!

Sathr helped Goranth to his feet, concern marring her features. "What is wrong?" she begged.

"We need to go. Now." Goranth took the leads of their mounts and hurried out of the field. The other horses followed as they'd been trained to do, and Sathr rushed behind with the goat in tow.

Rif roused from the cooking fire, where the groundhog had barely begun to sear.

"Leave it!" Goranth shouted. The Barber dutifully kicked dirt over the fire before shambling toward his horse, grumbling all the way. "Your girth will thank you for missing a meal, old friend."

"May the demons take your black soul and rip it from you while you watch." Rif directed Jaeg to tie three horses to his saddle. Goranth added the dragon to the herd behind him.

Goranth would have laughed had their plight not been so dire. Jaeg and Rif mounted while Goranth pulled Sathr into the saddle before him. No one had questioned his reasons for having to leave, but he owed them an explanation.

"The Mabayans are on their way to Barbertown to get there before us. They will destroy the city while they wait for us to arrive with the dragon. We have to get there first or die trying because it'll be our heads if we don't. Like the wind, we ride!"

Goranth heeled the ribs of his mare and she responded with a jerk and a hard pull, dragging the three horses, goat, and dragon along until they realized what she wanted. When they started to run, she ran harder until the group galloped. The litter bounced high, twisting behind a goat unused to fleeing for its life.

Rif and Jaeg watched it carefully, ready to stop should any of their ill-gotten gains fly out, but the blanket tied across the top remained secure despite the abuse the litter suffered at the hind end of a running goat.

"I pray the volumes make it intact. We need to earn the most coin from merchants seeking tomes of the lore of the wizards of Tsentar and beyond!"

"It's lore I would leave behind, Barber. It can only bring bad luck and misfortune."

Rif shouted to be heard over the horses' hoofbeats. "Mayhap the Mabayans already have been repulsed by my soldiers. By the Ice Dogs! There may be no need for concern."

Still, Goranth detected the worry in the Barber's voice.

The Northman forged ahead, guided by his unerring sense of direction. One hour turned to three turned to six, galloping interspersed with periods of trotting, but never walking, and stopping for no longer than it took to water the horses. He pushed them to their limits and beyond.

At one such stop, the dragon began to struggle. Goranth growled at it but felt sorry for the beast. It was nothing more than a babe. "We should put it in the litter. Torch those scrolls and carry the dragon."

"No! I'll carry the dragon on my horse, or maybe Jaeg can. Let the beast ride for a bit. It's no bigger than you or me. It can ride."

It mewled pathetically as if knowing they talked about it.

"Let us try to comfort the beast and get back on the trail. Barbertown must not fall," Goranth stated.

"For once, there is something we agree on," Rif replied. "It must not."

"My father is in Barbertown. We must hurry!" Jaeg made to spur his horse onward, but Rif grabbed the reins.

"What do you think we've been doing? Calm your legs, lad." Rif pointed at the dragon. "You'll soon be riding with your best friend. Make sure it doesn't fall off."

Goranth untied the baby dragon and lifted it up. Although it was denser than livestock its size, it was lighter than Rif.

"Barbertown lies open!" Narlun cried in triumph. The raiders spread out as they raced toward the city, but archers rose from the field in between and loosed arrows at the Mabayans. Narlun pulled up as an arrow thudded into his harness and resisted his efforts to pull it free. He yanked his horse's head around and raced out of the archers' range.

The others swiped at the bowmen as they passed and looped back to Narlun. They rallied around him and D'gok.

"They knew we were coming!" a raider cried.

"Same as last time. The enchantress told them of our plans, but with the leaders of the city gone, they can mount only a tepid defense. We shall worry them down, and when they are unable to continue fighting, we will ride in and destroy the city, take the dragon, and leave."

D'gok's eyes rolled back.

"What do you see? Where do you see?" Narlun demanded.

The boy mumbled and bobbed his head. "I commune on the plane that only sorcerers travel. I see truth and lies, fantasies and reality. I pick through the puzzle to reveal what rests beneath." He swayed, and his fingers wove invisible patterns in the air. After a few minutes, he shuddered and opened his eyes.

"There and there." D'gok pointed. "Small pockets of men, no more than a handful each. They've been in place for hours. By nightfall, their energies will fail them. You will take them one by one. By morning, no defenders will remain."

Narlun's dark smile radiated no joy. He swirled his arm in the air and rode to the tree line, where he set up two-man rotations to ride to the edge of arrow range and harry the defenders once every thirty minutes until dark. After that, they would sneak in on foot and begin the purge, clearing the field of the soldiers from Barbertown.

"Rest now, for this night will bring death to our enemies. Prepare yourselves for the Mabayan victory cry. It sounds like the lamentations of our enemy's women."

He dismounted, tied his Ahak-Teek to a tree, and joined D'gok. "What else did you see?"

The young lad looked around, and when he spoke, he did so in hushed tones. "An old magic lurks, but it doesn't look for us. It seeks the woman in the city. Let her deal with it while you address the mundane, those matters the gods cannot be bothered with."

The insight did nothing to calm Narlun's thoughts. He relaxed, but sleep remained elusive.

During the rest of the day, the raiders harassed the defenders. While no blood was spilled on either side, the Mabayans were wearing them down. When night fell, Narlun knew he held the upper hand. He and his men followed the tree line to the closest point to the city, then they ran crouched to where D'gok pointed.

The end of the defensive line. The flank.

They came in fast, and with barely a clink of cold steel on iron rings, the first defender died. The Mabayans swept inward to roll up the flank, attacking the soldiers of Barbertown from the side and rear. They had no chance.

The raiders silently cheered their success. They continued around the city until no defenders were left.

Barely half the night was gone.

"D'gok, wake up the city for us."

The boy thrust his fingers into the earth and a pale green glow, faint at first, then brightening and turning a sickly shade, flowed toward Narlun's prize. The Mabayan warlord watched as the base of Barbertown's wall picked up the color. Narlun saw D'gok's forehead bead with sweat and the tattooed eye on the boy's chest close as if in concentration.

Then he felt a tickle through the soles of his sandals as the ground vibrated softly. There was a faint *crackle*, and another and another, then a sharp crack. The stones fissured and chunks pulled away, and D'gok nodded as if in approval.

When the wizard pursed his lips and blew, the earth rose like an ocean wave and rolled toward the city, crashing into the weakening wall. A second wave was sent, and then a third.

The wall swayed under the onslaught and failed. One stone came down from the battlement, pulling more with it until the wall collapsed, raining destruction on everything and everyone who stood near it.

People. Animals. Buildings.

The city wall had been thoroughly breached. The cries of terror from within were sweet music to Narlun.

"Burn it," he ordered his raiders. "Burn anything that can catch fire. And find that dragon."

CHAPTER TWENTY-SIX

When the wind dies down and the fires crackle,
The darkness comes and energy rises
To mount the horses, ride and attack all
Who stand in our way, those who defy us
"Tales of the Mabayan Raiders"

I do not fear for myself, Northman. Always I can flee. Always I will find safety. The Mabayan sorcerer is not my equal. The Mabayan warlord is no threat to me. But to the people here—

Her words inside his head were loud enough to be heard over Rif's shouts and the pounding of the horses' hooves. There was an intensity to them he'd not felt before. Terror? Was Kalida not as invincible as she claimed? She *was* afraid for herself and not able to admit it. No matter; he was afraid for her.

The people of Barbertown, Northman. Some of them are friends. The people here will suffer horribly.

Goranth knew what the Mabayans were capable of.

The ones he'd served with at sea were not like those Narlun commanded. The warlord-slaver's blood ran cruel, and his aspirations appeared to be loftier than Rif's. Narlun's men seemed loyal enough to fight to the death for him.

The Ahak-Teek strained beneath Goranth, having been ridden too hard for too long. A glance behind him showed the other horses were ragged, too, mouths flecked with foam, eyes wide, nostrils flaring. He pulled up, and the mount gratefully stopped.

"Goranth, why do we—" He barely heard Sathr.

"What are you doing?" Rif screamed at him. But the Barber had stopped, too.

Goranth slipped off the horse and pulled Sathr down with him.

"I'm going to ride faster to the city," he told Sathr.

Kalida shouted at him too, her words sharp daggers that birthed a painful headache. He tried to push her out as he stumbled toward Jaeg, who had stopped a few yards behind them. Goranth furiously rubbed his temples, but the gesture eased nothing.

"The goat, the horses, your treasure, Barber. And the dragon. Aye, we free them all. Only take what we ride. We've no choice. Bringing back all of this was madness. We've lost time."

"Barbertown first," Rif agreed. Then he shook his head. "But we'll not abandon our prizes. We risked too much to gain them. They are too valuable to dismiss." He pointed at Jaeg. "Boy, you stay with them."

"Rif!" Goranth met the Barber's glare.

"He's young," Rif shot back. "Foolish. He'll not help us; he'll cause more hurt than help." He faced Jaeg: "The horses, boy, the dragon, the books. You stay with them and keep it all safe. Your charges. Guard it all with your life. We'll come back for you when this is done. And then—"

"*If* we can come back," Goranth cut in. He held Sathr's shoulders. "You stay here, too. Help Jaeg." He grudgingly accepted that the Barber was right. The youth was too impetuous and would be safer here. Sathr, too; she was not equipped to—

"I'm coming with you, Goranth."

"The horse is already taxed beyond—"

"You do not own me." She spun away from him and worked feverishly to release the horses and the goat tethered to Goranth's mount. Then she selected one of the freed horses and clumsily climbed atop it. She kicked her heels into its sides, and it shot forward.

"By the Ice Dogs, fool woman!" Goranth bellowed. Had she known how to ride all this time and merely professed an inability so she could rub her body against his? She had a knife at her side, but nothing that would make a difference against the Mabayans he knew she hated.

Rif grunted, untethered the horses he'd been leading, and went after her.

"Hurry, Northman," Rif shouted over his shoulder.

Goranth took a last look at Jaeg, who sat open-mouthed atop his horse, the dragon comfortably wedged in front of him. Goranth selected an Ahak-Teek that didn't appear as winded as the one he'd been riding and rode fast after the Barber. The breeze caught his hair, and the long unruly strands lashed at his eyes. Dirt found his mouth and lungs, and he coughed to clear it as Kalida suddenly reached up, grabbed his senses, and pulled them through the earth.

The world twirled and he plummeted.

He'd been drunk many times in many taverns after successful raids on ships, after failed raids to drown his sorrow, when he was happy in Varlten's company, and when he drank to forget her after she'd left. The overflowing tankards smoothed the edges of his life and flattened the turmoil to give him calm seas temporarily. It was like that now—the rush of strong ale, heady and muddy, numb and unfocused, his mind splintering like glass shards spinning in candlelight. Part of him knew he was on the back of an Ahak-Teek, riding aggressively for Barbertown. That part tried to force him straight, fingers tight on the reins, knees clamped to keep from falling off. The greater part registered a mass of swirling browns and greens. It felt like he swam through the sludge of a swamp, the ooze soothing his aches and cooling the sweat from his skin.

"Ride!" he heard. "Ride and attack! Burn the city!"

It was Narlun's hated voice, and it rumbled through the earth like a tremor preceding a quake. Goranth couldn't tell how far away the Mabayan warlord was or how many rode with him. He suspected it was an army greater than the one he'd brought before as the ground jittered from the hooves of horses that thundered across it.

He felt Kalida's fear and Narlun's anticipation, a mix of joy and sorrow that threatened to drown him. Goranth was a prisoner of the sorcerer's magic, but if she was trying to show him something, he couldn't see it. There were only the greens and browns of nature, the comforting sludge of the swamp, the healing aura of buried gems, and the sensation of losing himself. He drifted, spun, and dove.

His head continued to pound and deliver him to blackness.

"Burn it all," Narlun shouted. "Burn everything! Get me the dragon."

Dragon.

Dragon.

Dragon.

I've warned the soldiers, Kalida said. *Warned the shopkeepers, those nearest me. Not everyone believes the danger is real. And some of the soldiers...not all of them are loyal to Rif. Some of them take my words as true, though. Some of them are leaving.*

She recounted a battle in the woods. Sentries Rif had ordered to watch there had been slaughtered, caught by surprise and ended by a superior force.

Dragon.

Dragon.

Dragon.

Why does Narlun hate so? What does he want with Barbertown? The dragon? Is it all for a dragon?

Dragon.

Dragon.

Dragon.

Goranth didn't answer her. Kalida could see through the earth but not through some men's souls. Narlun was one side of a coin, the Barber the other. They both wanted power and recognition, and they both wanted dragons to further their ambitions. Better the dragons had stayed lost to time. If there were sides of the coin to pick, the Northman took Rif's. At least the Barber cared for the people under his authority and wanted them fed and sheltered and prosperous. He wanted to protect them...and protect his dragon, LeReon, and the treasure amassed beneath his home. Losing Barbertown would mean losing everything.

Goranth tried to feel the horse beneath him and touch the leather of the reins, but Kalida still held his senses. Was he riding to Barbertown? Following Rif and Sathr? Where was he above the earth?

"Kalida! Let me go!" Did he think the words, or did he

bellow them from his dust-choked mouth? Was the pounding in his head the sound of his horse's hooves or the thundering of Narlun's army? "Kalidaaaaaaaaaaa!"

She didn't answer or release him. Goranth continued to rush through the earth, and he swore he felt the bite of buried rocks and was snagged by tree roots, his skin burned by the heat of something he couldn't see.

"Kalidaaaaaaaaaa!"

She laughed, the sound racing through him in waves of hot and cold.

It wasn't her laugh, not her sound. This was eerie and lower-pitched, knifing and oppressive. It was louder than the pounding hooves and the wind.

Dragons.

Dragons.

Dragons.

My children.

Miag Millend. Kalida's voice was a whisper Goranth strained to hear. *The dragon god. She has—*

Laughter washed away the rest of Kalida's words, and Goranth struggled to free himself. Mired as he was in darkness, he shot up like a swimmer caught at the bottom of the sea. An eye loomed, but not the great squid that had taken his companions and nearly his life many years past. Not the mother dragon either. Something else. An eye of solid black, mirror-shiny and huge like a starless night sky. He kicked, swimming furiously upward, holding his breath and then gasping, tasting dirt and sweat, feeling hair batter his eyes.

His hands held leather reins that dug into his palms, he'd been holding them so tight. How long had he been caught by Kalida's earth vision? Minutes? Hours? The colors swirled like new paint smearing in the rain. The horse labored under him, but he urged it on.

Was he following Rif?

Was he still headed to Barbertown?

The colors sharpened. His breath steadied, and he blinked furiously. The breeze still tossed his long hair into his eyes. He'd shave his head, he vowed, if he lived beyond this day. He'd leave this island continent with or without treasure. He'd leave. He'd—

As the world came into focus and the walls of Barbertown revealed themselves in the distance, a shadow crossed in front of him. Talons raked across his chest before grabbing his shoulder and tossing him off the Ahak-Teek. The horse stumbled on until a shadow detached itself from the trees, dropped on the horse, and tore into it.

A praevo-pavor. One of the creatures had lifted Goranth off his horse. Another darted low and let out an unnerving cry that sliced through the thunder dancing in the Northman's head.

Goranth jumped to his feet and drew his sword and the makhaira in the same motion. The pommel of the makhaira trembled as if in excitement. The flying terror rose, circled, spread its leathery-feathered wings, and climbed higher. He saw its talons dripping blood and realized the damnable thing had wounded him. Thick lines of blood ran down Goranth's chest where the terror had clawed through his shirt. Dead man's clothes, the Northman wore. Would he, too, be a dead man?

"Not today. Not by you!" Goranth shouted. He kept his eyes on the flying terror as it drew its wings in tight and darted at him.

Talons outstretched, beak pointed at him like a deadly arrow, the praevo-pavor dropped. At the last moment, Goranth sidestepped it, pivoted, and swung with both blades, connecting with the sword and drawing a cry of anger and pain from the flying terror. It rose once more, flying straight up, and in that moment, Goranth took a quick look around.

His Ahak-Teek was dead, torturously gutted.

The figure ahead was too small for him to make out, either Rif or Sathr fighting another flying terror. He squinted...Rif since the figure was too thick to be the gray woman. No sign of the horse.

A cry brought his attention back to the sky and the closing praevo-pavor.

"Not today!" Goranth's leg muscles bunched as he crouched, then he sprang, leading with the makhaira while swinging madly with the sword. Both blades connected and sheared the terror's head off. The beast fell on him and knocked him to the ground, its ichor splattered him. A second flying terror cried before diving. The Northman barely had time to extricate himself from the headless beast to meet the other's charge.

There were more circling overhead; he counted a dozen. He knew they were here at Narlun's direction. How had the warlord tamed such as these? What could the slaver manage with a tame dragon? That notion made Goranth redouble his efforts, slashing with the sword and jabbing with the makhaira, which fairly hummed against his palm. He missed the beast's first pass, and as it rose, he raced toward Rif. He stopped and turned when the praevo-pavor cried out.

"You announce yourself, beast!" Perhaps that was something Narlun could not train out of the terrors. Fortunately for the Northman, it gave him a heartbeat to react. This time he dispatched it quickly and rushed to catch up to Rif. He felt the burn from the exertion in his legs and his chest and felt the blood running from the gashes in his chest. He wondered how Kalida fared but did not search for her in his mind, fearing she might drag his senses into the earth or that Miag Millend, whom she'd caught the notice of, might drown him.

Where was Sathr? Where—

He saw her beyond Rif, stabbing her knife at a praevo-pavor larger than those he'd fought. He churned past Rif, who was struggling with his own beast. The Barber had slowed over the years, but he was still formidable. Sathr had not faced such as these. A second dropped on the gray woman.

"Fool woman!" She should have remained with Jaeg.

Another shrill cry and he spun to see two flying terrors diving at him.

"By the Ice Dogs!" Goranth swung wildly, not with great skill but with boiling fury. "I'm done with things trying to kill me!" He slashed and stabbed and parried the beak of the smaller creature, then pivoted and brought the makhaira up, slicing its breast. It fell, wings beating helplessly against the ground, and he stood on it, able to maintain his balance while he lashed out at his other target. Two more swings and it was dead. Then he plunged his sword into the head of the one struggling beneath him and noticed a strip of studded leather around its neck.

A pet! Narlun marked his creatures like a man would mark a dog.

Rif pounded up behind him and they reached a bloodied Sathr. She had managed to slay one of the flying terrors, but not without gaining jagged wounds on her arms and legs. Goranth dispatched the other one that threatened her.

"You need—"

"—to go with you into Barbertown," Sathr finished, panting, eyes narrowed in anger. "There are worse monsters than these in that city. Ones with two legs."

"Aye," Rif agreed. "Narlun is the true monster." He

pointed at a spiral of smoke that rose. "He set these flying terrors upon us to keep us from entering my city."

"Or to keep the people from leaving," Goranth said. The Northman raced toward the city, ignoring every sensible thought that told him to go the other way.

CHAPTER TWENTY-SEVEN

Fury that the storm has brought
Wisp of war and cries caught
The clash of swords crossed
Treasure won and lives lost
"Tales of the Mabayan Raiders"

"Bind those wounds, woman. You'll be no good to us if you bleed out," Goranth growled, stopping his mad dash and whipping off his pack to get bandages. He added softly, "I wish you to live." He'd realized how wounded Sathr was.

"We've no time!" Rif screamed and took off running.

Sathr tried to pull away, but Goranth held her back.

"There will be plenty of fight left when we get there. Hold still." Goranth threaded a needle quickly and sewed like he was fixing a canvas during a storm, big threads and few, enough to hold it together.

She slapped salve on before he tied the bandages. She left enough to treat his wounds and threw the empty jar to the ground when she was done. He pulled her to her feet, and they took off after Rif. The Barber pounded toward what used to be the city's main gate. The walls next to it and around a great section of the city had fallen.

"What could do such a thing?" Goranth wondered, speaking between heaving great lungfuls of air.

"Earth magic," Sathr panted. "Stay wary."

"Aye, lass. This is not a normal fight."

In the distance, Goranth saw that Rif had entered the city and been set upon by raiders. Steel flashed as the once-mighty Rif the Barber sought to reclaim his former battle glory. His club spun and swung, deflecting cold steel and braining an attacker. Rif drove the other way far enough for him to recover the Mabayan's fallen sword. He faced the renewed attack with a blade, fresh vigor, and a war cry that brought chills.

Goranth and Sathr closed as Rif thrust up and into a Mabayan. The Barber pushed the body away, bracing his foot against the bloody corpse to get his new sword free.

Rif pointed in one direction before running in the other. Sathr sheathed her knife and followed Rif's example, picking up the second Mabayan's fallen sword.

Goranth snarled, eyes wild as he sought enemies in the direction Rif had pointed. It was opposite where Kalida lived, but a whisper in the back of his mind told him she was alive and battling at a level he hadn't known her to be capable of. She did not need him to protect her at the moment.

The ancient evil was here.

The Mabayans were here.

When he heard a woman's shrill scream, Goranth took off like an arrow from a bow. Sathr struggled to keep up. Ahead, a raider ripped at a barmaid's garments.

"Ha!" Goranth shouted, pulling the man's attention

away to give the woman a moment to free herself and clear the space through which Goranth's sword whistled.

The Northman didn't slow. He kept running toward the sounds of the fight—the clang of swords, the cries of the injured, the crackle of flames, and plumes of smoke.

Goranth gestured for Sathr to go wide while he waded into the middle of the fray. Executing lightning-fast strikes on unsuspecting raiders, he dispatched one after another. Sathr attacked them from outside the melee. Goranth carved a Northman-sized path through the enemy, turning the numbers against the raiders.

From the far side, opposite where Sathr's deadly blows struck and where Goranth was headed, the staunch defenders of the city broke, and those who could ran. The ones who held their positions were mowed down by Mabayans. Momentum changed from Barbertown to the raiders in a matter of heartbeats. Goranth cut his way to Sathr and turned back, but the numbers working their way toward him were too great.

"With me if you want to live!" He pulled the citizens out of the battle one by one while he swung his sword in a vicious and blurred arc to hold the surging Mabayans at bay. With a fake lunge, he put them on their heels and raced toward Sathr and the others. They ran down a narrow alley.

Goranth tapped the walls at his side, one with his sword and one with the makhaira. No man could pass as long as the Northman stood.

The first two came at him, one high, one low, but they couldn't match Goranth's speed. Like the striking tongues of two cobras, his blades licked out and released the blood of his enemies. Two men fell into their pooling blood, their deaths serving as warnings to the others.

The Mabayans had no stomach for a fair fight.

"Wenches!" someone yelled from out on the street, and the raiders in front drifted away. The last ran for their lives when Goranth came at them, but he had no desire to run after cowards.

Sathr returned to stand at his side. Her blade dripped Mabayan blood, and her face was covered in sweat and soot from the fires.

"You are true to your word," he told her. "You said you'd fight by my side, and you have."

She nodded tightly. "What next, Goranth? I believe this fight is lost. The numbers are overwhelming."

"It's lost only when we stop fighting," he argued. "It's time we find Rif and Kalida."

At the mention of her name, the ground heaved upward. A maniacal cackle accompanied the tearing of the earth's skin.

"Kalida's doing?" Sathr wondered.

"No. Run!" Goranth and Sathr pounded out of the alley and past Mabayans carrying looted goods, cups from the tavern, and fabrics from the clothier. Goranth zigzagged to catch the unwary with the tip of his blade, maintaining a steady pace to discourage the raiders from following while keeping himself from getting embroiled in a battle he had no time to fight.

No time or desire. He knew Sathr was right. When the raiders finally left Barbertown—if they left—there would be nothing remaining. Any survivors would emerge from hiding broken, their lives shattered. Goranth had seen it before. The best thing to do was run and come back when they were gone. Racing into the city like this had been foolhardy.

"Save yourselves! Run for the coast," he shouted at frightened faces peering through windows and from behind walls. "Run!"

Sathr raced with him, but her breathing had become labored. Goranth veered off the main thoroughfare and into another side alley as they approached the great central square, then pulled up to let Sathr catch her breath. Mabayans were everywhere, but not in great numbers. Pockets of defenders fought back fruitlessly. The raiders swooped in, rallying to the cry before drifting away to loot and pillage.

It had devolved into every man for himself. Goranth looked at the hard woman next to him, bloodied and fierce, fighting without question.

The ground heaved again and the Mabayans cheered.

"D'gok aids us!" one of them cried.

Goranth knew it wasn't the Mabayan sorcerer; it was the dark force Kalida had awakened. There was a war on two fronts in Barbertown.

A raider strayed into Goranth's alley and loosened his trousers to relieve himself. Goranth wrapped a heavily muscled arm around the man's neck and pulled, and the neck snapped like a twig. The Northman left him where he fell.

Then he pointed across the open square at one of the many roads that left it. "There," he whispered to Sathr. "That road leads to Rif's palace. We need to get over there."

"A palace? I thought he was little better than an average merchant."

"It's a small palace, and he isn't even as good as your average merchant, but he was once. That was the man I vowed to help. After today's fight is over, I will owe him no more."

Fierce determination chiseled her once-soft features. She clearly had not been raised to war like Goranth, but in his eyes, she acted as if she had been.

For the moment, the square was clear of raiders seeking their fortunes.

"We go." Goranth ran, not bothering to watch out for Sathr. He knew in his heart that she would be there when he needed her. They'd almost cleared the square when a Mabayan on an Ahak-Teek appeared with soldiers at arms surrounding him. A second horse followed carrying a young lad, blocking Goranth's path.

Narlun and D'gok. The boy sorcerer looked tired and had dark circles under his eyes, with a malevolent aura surrounding him.

"I want the girl," Narlun told the soldiers. "But kill him. Through cuts and stabs, through the blows of clubs and his throat ground under your heels. Kill him as ugly as you can." Narlun leaned back to watch as if gladiators were preparing to battle within a Kustarian arena.

Goranth tried to push Sathr behind him but she danced out of his reach, holding her sword before her and daring the men to try to take her alive.

The makhaira and the broadsword hung at Goranth's sides. He would conserve his strength and raise them when he had to. Raise them to drink the blood of his enemies.

A dozen men faced off against Goranth and Sathr. They spread out in a circle around the two. Goranth looked at the ground to allow his peripheral vision a better range.

Waiting to get killed held no allure to the Northman. He dodged sideways and engaged the closest soldier. The sword caught the raider's steel while the makhaira slashed through the man's forearms. A quick flick of the tip sliced the man's throat.

Goranth jumped backward. Sathr instinctively knew to fight back to back to limit the direction from which the enemies could come at them. She crossed blades with a raider as she covered her side of the circle.

Narlun snapped at his men. "Hurry!"

Four attacked at once, two at Goranth and two at Sathr. The Northman's blades spun and twisted as they met the assault, each seeking an opening to deliver pain and death. The raiders stepped back before lunging a second time, and Goranth took a tree-felling blow on his sword. The other hit the makhaira to drive it out of the way, but the blade sang its deadly song, slicing through the air and into the raider's arm, then across his face, cleaving his skull nearly in half. The man clapped his hand to his ruined face.

It was his last act in life.

The sword parried a lesser blow. Goranth lunged when the man leaned back to put more power into his next attack, and the makhaira carved a trench through the man's guts that nearly reached his backbone. He staggered away, a lost soul in the remaining moments of life.

Goranth jumped back again, finding nothing behind him. He dove to the side, slashing and rolling, and came up at the feet of another Mabayan. Two flashes of the blade later, the Mabayan stumbled and fell, hands failing to hold in his spilling entrails.

Seven raiders remained, two of whom held Sathr as she struggled to free herself, eyes flashing with anger at having been caught after having killed only one of their mutual enemies. Goranth ran at the next raider in the collapsing circle, dodged under his blade, and stabbed him through the heart. He let his sword go as he failed to free it from the man's chest on his way to the Mabayan leader.

The makhaira called for his blood. The Ahak-Teek pranced as Narlun sought to put the beast between him and the Northman.

"Kill her!" Narlun called.

Goranth caught the reins. "Then you have no one to hide behind," he growled.

Narlun pulled his sword free of its scabbard but made no move to dismount. He held up one hand to forestall Sathr's execution. Goranth looked into the reflection in the horse's eyes to see what was behind him. No one moved.

"Face me like a man." Goranth gestured with the makhaira for Narlun to climb down. With another glance in the horse's eye, he saw movement.

Goranth waited, shifting the makhaira to his right hand before dropping the reins. He ducked, slashed, and killed, then spun and pulled his dagger, propelling it with all the strength in his body.

The blade buried itself to its hilt in the eye of the raider who was leveling a death-blow at Sathr. He dropped, and with one hand now free, Sathr struck. She turned at the waist, building power and keeping her elbow close, driving upward with the heel of her hand to catch the other raider that held her on his chin. His teeth drove through his tongue, shredding the tip. The man let go and Sathr ran toward Goranth, plucking a sword out of the blood on the ground to arm herself.

The ground heaved as the earth sorcerers dueled.

"With me!" Narlun roared. The Ahak-Teek reared and spun on its back hooves before hitting the cobblestones and charging toward Rif's place.

And toward Kalida's hut.

The raiders found solace near each other as they backed away from the Northman. In that instant the ground rose, shielding the Mabayans. They turned on their heels and sprinted away.

"By the Ice Dogs!" Goranth pulled Sathr away from the wall building before them. "Run, woman!" He brandished his makhaira.

They fled the carnage in the square, the only testament

to the battle being waged. Once they reached the river, Goranth looked for a boat, any boat.

"You can't leave without your treasure," Sathr said, glancing from shadow to shadow and building to building, searching for enemies. "You can't leave while these people are threatened."

"Dead men can spend no treasure, and this is a battle the likes of which no one has seen for a thousand years."

Sathr didn't ask how he knew. The rumble of tortured earth swept back and forth across the city. The screams of the injured and the cries of the aggrieved punctuated the fight.

"Kalida is strong," Sathr claimed. "She will beat the child sorcerer."

Goranth stopped his frantic search. "The child. The times I saw him work his magic, the glow was obvious, his machinations clear, the unclean words tumbling from his mouth. But now? He was doing none of that. He appears nearly spent. This magic isn't his. It is the work of Miag Millend, and Kalida is fighting her. So aye, lass. Kalida is strong, far more powerful than I considered, but is she powerful enough?"

Across the river, the stockade in which the dragon was held rippled and buckled as if it were under tremendous pressure. Goranth watched the ground rise and fall until the walls exploded. A terrible cry sounded as the dragon LeReon tried to fly, but it had been pierced by the massive splinters of the destroyed palisade. It looked a pincushion and left a trail of its dark blood before it fell to the ground, staggered, and collapsed.

The earth cried out in agony, and unmistakable words pounded into their heads: *My child!*

"We have to get to Kalida. If anyone is going to fight this monster, it is her. We have to keep her safe, else this fight isn't just lost; the earth will deny that we ever existed."

Sathr gripped her sword tight and headed for the mound of debris that had been the town square. Goranth ran after her, his limbs aching from a fight that had just begun.

CHAPTER TWENTY-EIGHT

Feel the power of the blade
Vows taken and promises made
Leave the life of peasants behind
Taking blood oaths for the ties that bind
"Tales of the Mabayan Raiders"

Goranth didn't know enough of the Mabayan tongue to understand what they shouted. Some were hollering from rooftops, others called from side streets or ravaged buildings. The screams of the Barbertown residents were easy to understand—pain, fear, and desperation. The cacophony battered him from every alley and erupted out of businesses and upstairs windows. Glass broke, wood shattered, fires burned, and steel rang.

He couldn't be everywhere or save everyone. His goal was reaching Kalida. The sorceress might not need his help, but he and the city needed hers.

A raider rushed out the door of a tavern, dragging a

limp young woman by the hair and snarling when he caught sight of the Northman. The man howled at Goranth and shook the woman in defiance. The woman was naked from the waist up, barely moving and spattered with blood. Goranth was on the raider in a half-dozen steps, vaulting over a raised wood-plank sidewalk and extending his right leg. His heel slammed into the Mabayan's chest and sent the raider backward, but he caught himself. He released the woman, who fell and didn't move, and drunkenly swung a makhaira at Goranth.

It wasn't as fine a blade as the Northman's makhaira, but the Mabayan's was crusted with blood, evidence it had drunk deep of Barbertown's soul.

Mabayans were busy drinking and looting inside the tavern and paid Goranth no attention. Sathr jockeyed behind him but couldn't get clear to lend her sword arm to his.

The raider slung a string of curses at Goranth and thrust at him. The Northman ducked, then swept with his leg, catching the man off-balance, and rammed his blade up to the hilt between the raider's neck and shoulder. A rough tug pulled it free as Goranth took the raider's sword in his free hand and cut the raider across his stomach, sending his guts spilling into the road.

Goranth bent to the woman, whose breathing was shallow, eyes fixed, neck at an odd angle, dying. Nothing he could do to help. Goranth ended her suffering with a quick but gentle twist. He didn't have time to think twice about it. He would waste no time on those leaving this world. He sped on.

A child's high-pitched wail sliced through the wall of sound and he whirled. Sathr was racing ahead and he wanted to follow, but the child wailed again, and he darted toward its origin—the open door of what had been a bakery.

The goods had been looted, shelves smashed, crockery in pieces. Four women—one in a long apron who was likely the proprietress—lay dead, two from sword wounds, two from having their heads bashed in, the wounds fresh and the blood gleaming. The child, no more than four or five years old, continued to wail as it crouched beneath a counter, holding a red-faced baby who cried softly but so hard it shook.

"I can't help you," Goranth said. "Stay here. Hide." Were they older, he would have told them to run. Perhaps a better man would have scooped them up and tried to get them to safety outside the city somewhere, but he was hell-bent on reaching Kalida, helping her fight whatever force she'd woken up, and driving back the Mabayans. Perhaps a smarter man would simply run away from all of this and try to find his own safe place, the whole of Barbertown be damned.

But Sathr...

Narlun wanted the city, clearly for its position on the island continent. The warlord cared nothing for the streets and buildings Rif had sculpted, only the land and a dragon that was now dead. The warlord cared nothing for the people. The Northman swept a last glance from the wailing children to the slaughtered women.

"Quiet!" Goranth barked, and the older child howled louder, filthy cheeks stained with tears. The warrior darted onto the street and saw no sign of Sathr, so he churned over the hard-packed earth away from the wails in the direction she'd been running.

He searched his thoughts for Kalida but could not find her. No doubt she was too occupied. Narlun had waited until he and Rif were far away from Barbertown to attack and the city was unprepared, its limited number of soldiers unfocused and the gatekeepers unwary. Had Rif done something to Narlun in months and years past to stoke the warlord's ire? Was it all about the now-dead dragon?

Dragon.

Dragon.

Dragon.

My child.

That spearing, anguished voice in his head was not Kalida's. Whatever she'd awakened—a dragon god, she'd claimed—had also wisely chosen a time to go against Barbertown. He and Rif could not stand against two forces, but perhaps with Kalida's help, they could buy enough time for more people to escape. Goranth knew Kalida's tormentor Miag Millend was powerful, but he doubted she was a god.

The gods were too detached to meddle in the affairs of men and women. He believed their role was to sort through the souls of those passing from this world and decide the fates that awaited those on the other side.

He hurried past buildings that displayed symbols of the god Vujo, so revered on a recent holy day. Was Vujo watching? Was this hellish spectacle entertainment or beneath the god's notice?

Goranth's side ached from running, and the burn in his chest had grown uncomfortable. He'd pushed himself to limits he hadn't hit in many years. If the exertion tortured him, what was it doing to Rif? The Barber was in no shape for an epic battle like this. Was Rif, too, headed toward Kalida's? Did the Barber still live? And where, by the Ice Dogs, had Sathr gone?

He ignored the cries and screams coming from buildings. To act would be to try to put out embers while a fire raged elsewhere. Then, out of the corner of his eye, he saw a trio of Mabayans in an alley, weapons menacing a line of women and children.

Don't act, he told himself. *Ignore them.*

I can't help you, Goranth thought, so he went on, then abruptly pivoted, cursed, and ran toward the three men. Since they were slavers, these Mabayans were going to take whoever they didn't kill. As he pounded toward them, he noted that the hands of the women and children were tied in front of them and balls of cloth had been stuffed in their mouths.

He killed the closest of the three Mabayans before the slavers could act. The sounds of nearby destruction reached him, muted by the buildings' walls and the thrumming of his heart. He gulped air as he raised both of his weapons in an X before the charging duo. They shouted at him in their ugly tongue. Goranth didn't care what they said; they were part of an illness spreading through the once-thriving city, and he was going to slice it out.

The shorter of the Mabayans had a spear, and she managed to get past Goranth's guard and jab him in the side. He hardly registered the pain, so incensed was he. She pulled the spear free and jabbed again, but this time he sidestepped her and slashed down so hard that he sliced through the forearm of the taller slaver, leaving him screaming in agony. He crouched as she jabbed a third time, the sharp spearpoint cutting his shoulder even as he rose and stepped close before he rammed the makhaira into her stomach and twisted the blade. He kicked at her to free the weapon and watched her fall. Some of the bound women rushed forward to step on her and kick her while he finished the Mabayan who'd dropped to his knees, gripping his blood-pulsing arm.

Goranth caught the Mabayan word for mercy but he

offered the man none, just sliced through his chest once, twice, and watched him fall. He turned his attention to the women, cut the ropes from two of their wrists, and pointed at the downed slavers' weapons.

"Free yourselves," he said. "Then run. Somewhere. Just run." His words were tired, with no power behind them.

He left them and returned to the main street, vowing not to stop to help any more of Barbertown's lost souls. His hands were bloody, so he squeezed his weapons' hilts to keep them from slipping out of his grasp. Ahead, smoke roiled from a familiar shop—the healer's where he'd been mended and taken Esh. There were three charred bodies outside, and he didn't pause to identify them. He hoped Esh had survived, or that he'd died quickly and had found Varlten on the other side. Perhaps he would join them before this day was finished. Perhaps they would all find an ephemeral tavern and drown their bad memories in fine, thick ale.

Kalida's home was close now, only a block away. He couldn't see it since smoke was thick in the air and his eyes were watering from the acrid scents and the dust. The odor of burnt flesh and charred wood added to the misery, and the burn in his chest had become an inferno. He sucked in great lungfuls of the horrid air.

He heard his name, a whisper, and not inside his head. Not Kalida or the so-called dragon god. Sathr? Was she calling him? Again his name came, strangled and in a deeper voice—Rif's. Goranth whirled and looked through the smoke, seeing shapes on a narrow side street that cut to the north. Men on horses with a giant of a man in front of them. Rif.

He thundered toward his old friend. When he got closer and his vision cleared, he saw Narlun towering on the back of an Ahak-Teek that bled from cuts on its legs and neck. At his side was the child sorcerer on a smaller horse, hunched forward in his saddle as if asleep. Behind them were a dozen raiders on foot, most of them sooty and wounded and all of them attentive to Narlun.

In front of the deadly entourage stood Rif, legs spread wide and a sword in each hand. The Barber bled from shredded flesh—too many cuts and no one to sew them closed—but he remained defiant.

"*My* city, Narlun! *My* people!" He glanced over his shoulder at Goranth, who closed with him. "We end this, eh, Northman? All the treasure's yours if we end this now!" Rif's voice was coarse, his barrel chest was heaving, and he heavily favored the leg he'd hurt in the mountains days past. The Northman suspected Narlun had been toying with the Barber and could have finished him before now. He was drawing out his death like a cat playing with a captured rodent.

"I just want my share!" Goranth said as he came to stand at Rif's left shoulder. "My share, then I'm done with this. Should have been done with this days past." Close up, he could see a deep, ugly gash on the Barber's cheek and part of his lip hanging loose. Rif's left ear was missing, and a mass of blood was running down the side of his neck.

"We might both be well done with this," the Barber said, his voice losing its command and its vigor.

The street was so narrow that Goranth and Rif filled its width. That might be the one thing that offered salvation, Goranth thought.

"D'gok," Narlun said to the child. "I am tired of this game." To Rif, he said, "You stole from me, Barber, and then you managed to catch a dragon. I want what is mine and what you claim is yours. I want this land and your river, but first, I'll have your life. First, I'll—"

Goranth had no stomach for the drivel of tyrants. He

lunged, leading with his sword and putting all his strength into the blow. At that moment, Narlun pulled on the reins of the Ahak-Teek and the horse reared, its chest shielding the warlord from what could have been a fatal blow. Goranth's sword bit deep into the animal and it screamed and came down, hooves narrowly missing the Northman, whose sword remained lodged. Down to the makhaira, Goranth jumped back as the horse fell to its front knees and then toppled, still screaming. Narlun managed to leap out of the saddle and avoid being pinned.

There was movement to his right, and Goranth risked a quick glance to see D'gok raise his head. The tattooed eye on the boy's chest opened wide. As if in response, the ground rumbled, the vibrations racing up through Goranth's sandaled feet and setting his teeth clacking.

"No more games!" Narlun screamed. "End them!"

The vibrations intensified, and the stone building closest to Rif groaned as if in pain. Cracks danced through it in dizzying patterns like an enraged spider web. The child grinned evilly and gestured as he drove his horse forward, knocking the Barber over and riding past him. Narlun pressed against the opposite building, and the fractured wall came down in a thunderous rush.

Chunks of stone pelted Goranth and drove him down, half-buried him and trapping his legs. Rif was covered, only a hand with a sword clutched in it visible. Half the Mabayans beyond them had been crushed, and the remainder were picking themselves free and running as if the Ice Dogs were on their heels. One moaned and cursed the name of some dark god Goranth had only heard in whispers.

Goranth struggled to look behind him in the direction where the child had ridden, but he couldn't twist that far. To his left, Narlun was still pressed against the standing building, keeping his balance as tremors continued to skitter through the earth. The Northman bunched his muscles and managed to force himself out of the rockfall, knocking chunks of stone aside to regain his feet. He stood unevenly, barely stable on the remnants of the broken building, and turned to face Narlun, who was a man's length away.

The Northman had managed to keep hold of the makhaira. The pommel was warm against his hand, somehow revitalizing him and pushing the fatigue away but not able to drive out the hopelessness he felt at the endless death and senseless destruction.

Narlun gripped his sword, but it was down at his side, and his gaze darted from one end of the street to the other and back to land on the Northman. His lip rose, and Goranth noted scars on the man's face and neck, old ones from battles won or escaped from.

"Your boy," Goranth hissed. "He deserts you."

Narlun growled and raised his sword. Sweat poured down the warlord's face, and his chest rose and fell irregularly.

"That boy brought down a wall and killed some of your men. He could have killed you." Goranth breathed heavily, the stone dust finding its way inside and festering. "Maybe he wanted to kill you," the Northman risked. "Maybe he wants the city for himself, as well as your position and your power. The boy is your undoing. Maybe he's not such a—"

Goranth didn't get a chance to finish. Narlun leapt at him, hatred deepening the scars on his face and spittle flying. The Northman feinted, vaulted forward, and whirled in time to see the warlord trip over Rif's hand. The blade fell from the Barber's grasp and his fingers twitched. Narlun recovered and charged Goranth.

"Death to you! To all of this!" Narlun's sword cleaved Goranth's side, and the Northman gasped and jumped back to keep the blade from biting deeper. Blood ran down; he felt the wet heat seeping through the Mabayan clothes he was wearing.

Goranth growled and steeled himself. "My death is not yours to decide."

The makhaira glowed faintly blue, and runes appeared on the blade. Goranth tried not to look at them, but their appearance startled him. Why now? He thought he heard the weapon whisper to him in a language he couldn't understand but instantly dismissed it. Not possible; he was caught in some fever dream, dizzy from losing blood. In a heartbeat, the runes disappeared and the glow faded.

He slammed his teeth together and darted to his right. Narlun's blade grazed him. The ground continued to shake, and it set him off-balance. The warlord stumbled, too, and the instant Narlun reached out to steady himself, Goranth pressed forward. He slashed right and left with the makhaira, then drove it in straight. The tip of the blade found its way between the seams of the warlord's boiled leather cuirass, and with a shove and then another, Goranth knocked Narlun back.

Both men fell over a mound of broken stone. Goranth landed on top and drove the makhaira all the way in. Blood poured over Goranth's hand, and the hilt was so slickened he couldn't feel it. The Northman burned with anger.

He'd wanted nothing to do with any of this: cities or dragons or warring factions. He'd only come at the request of a friend and had found himself plunged into this hellish nightmare.

Blood ran from Narlun's open mouth and his lips worked, but no sound escaped. The warlord thrashed violently for a moment, then his lips quivered. Goranth hurriedly wiped the blood from his hand on his shirt, regained the grip on his weapon, and wrenched the hilt to the side, widening the wound. Narlun's eyes fixed open, staring at everything and nothing as his chest stilled.

Goranth pushed himself up and tugged until the makhaira came free and sent its warmth up his arm and into his chest. He sheathed the weapon and used both hands to dig away the stones that had buried Rif, glancing up now and then to look up and down the street for Mabayans. Who would command them now, the child? He shook the image of the boy's evil grin from his mind and redoubled his efforts to free the Barber.

His fingers bloody, he finally unearthed him. Goranth stepped back and stared.

Rif was broken, every limb, every part of him pummeled by the fallen building, the life crushed out of him. His head was twisted to the side, and half of his face was shattered; nothing remaining to hint at the powerful, proud man he'd been. "My town! My people!" he had screamed at Narlun. In the end, the Barber hadn't been about the treasure or his schemes, he'd been out to protect this place.

This crumbling, burning, wretched spot on the river.

Goranth stumbled out of the side street and back onto the main road. More buildings were on fire. The screams and the victory whoops continued and the earth still rumbled, the noise a dissonant miasma that cocooned Barbertown and pummeled his senses.

"Sathr," he called, but she was lost like every woman before. Like every warrior who'd dared to venture alongside him. He was alone and covered in the blood of his enemies—and too much of his own.

Smoke drifted across the city. Like the fog rising from a river on a chill morning, it obscured the forms of people running. Goranth couldn't tell if they were citizens, slavers, or a mix of both. He stumbled down the street, realizing the wound on his side had stopped bleeding. He briefly wondered why.

"Kalida." He concentrated. "*Kalida!*" Then he called for Sathr. Was the gray woman alive? Was Kalida still—

Rif. Kalida was in his mind again. *I felt him fall.*

"Aye, the Barber died trying to save his city. We all might die here."

I don't want you to die, Kalida said. Once, she'd told him she wouldn't allow it. *Hurry, Northman. By all you revere, hurry.*

"Esh," Goranth muttered as he plodded onward, seeing people dead and dying on the street, catching a glimpse of others huddling in doorways. A horse whinnied shrilly nearby. A horn sounded twice. The ground trembled more strongly. "Is Esh alive?" And Sathr? Did she live, too?

I do not know. Goranth, hurry. By all you hold—

There was a *crack*, then another and another. He felt a jarring sensation, and Goranth didn't have to look to know a building had toppled. Jagged lines appeared in the street and widened, one into a chasm that swallowed the bodies of those unfortunate enough to be in its path. Goranth increased his pace, and Kalida's home came into view.

The roof of it burned, green-black smoke trailing up to mix with the choking air.

"Kalida! Kal—"

"Here!" Kalida stood shoulder to shoulder with Sathr. The gray woman had gained a second sword and was holding one in each hand, keeping a thickset Mabayan at bay. Chaos reigned around them, Mabayans fighting Barbertown soldiers who had held their posts. Only one figure sat astride a horse—the child who knitted his fingers in the air and caused the ground to seize and buckle.

Goranth charged toward the women, leaping over a rising wave of dirt and jumping onto a raised wooden-plank sidewalk that rippled from the force of the growing earth-tremor.

"That boy!" Kalida gestured. "He is powerful, but not as—"

"—powerful as you," Goranth finished. "I'm not so certain of that."

The eye tattoo, difficult to see through the smoke, was wide open and rimmed with red.

"I think he was always the force to fear," Goranth spat. "Not Narlun. I think the warlord was the puppet, the child the master. He has to die."

"He's a child," Sathr said. She lunged as a raider darted in, her blades parrying his. She dropped below his next swing, then rose and gutted him—a warrior woman. Goranth thought she was perhaps his equal, or nearly so. "You can't kill a child."

"I can kill a monster," Goranth returned. He hurled himself off the plank walk, spinning and slashing at a Mabayan who'd darted too close. He killed him instantly and moved on, taking out two more before he reached the horse D'gok sat astride.

The child's eyes were narrow, his lips pursed. With skin so smooth and a frame so small, he had an innocence about him.

But also a malevolence.

"Stop this!" Goranth screamed. It was the Northman's offer to spare the child's life.

D'gok grinned and made a fist. In response, a chunk of the street flew up and struck Goranth, knocking him to his back. A section of the street surged up like a wave and threatened to drown him, but Goranth was fast, and the makhaira warmed against his palm.

The Northman jumped to his feet and rushed the horse, then leapt up and landed astride it behind D'gok. The Ahak-Teek bucked, but Goranth clamped his legs tight and hung on. The world shivered in a prelude to a quake D'gok called.

Goranth offered the child no second chance. His left arm wrapped around the boy's waist as his right hand drove the makhaira into his side again and again. D'gok screamed, a high-pitched feminine wail that tore through the Northman's senses and nearly made him lose his perch. Again he stabbed, blood rushing over his hand and onto his leg. The boy slumped forward and Goranth jabbed him once more, then tossed him to the ground. It shook even harder, and cracks spread. The Northman urged his mount forward as a rent swallowed the boy's corpse and many others, Mabayans and Rif's soldiers alike.

He slid off the horse and watched it race down the street, lost in the smoky fog, whinnying in terror. Then he was at Kalida's side, helping the women keep their balance while the ground trembled as if in fear.

Kalida's fingers traced patterns in the air, directing the ground to trap the enemy and hold their legs and feet fast while the remaining Barbertown soldiers dispatched them.

"I did not think we could win the day," Sathr said. She kept her swords at the ready, but there was no one close enough to fight. "I thought we would all die."

"Everyone dies someday," Goranth said.

"Not today," Kalida cried out. "Not this day!"

Everyone dies this day. The voice was angry and loud, cutting through the crackling of the fires and the rumbling of the ground and rising above the screams. It was inside his head, and it was everywhere.

"Everyone dies this day!"

"Miag Millend!" Kalida gasped. "She is here."

317

The buildings across the street toppled first, shards of glass flying like arrows and striking Goranth, Kalida, and Sathr. The buildings behind them fell as the ground roared and jumped and birthed fissures that swallowed horses and corpses and soldiers who were unable to get out of the way. They threatened to claim all that had been Barbertown.

Everyone dies.

Everything falls.

My children.

My beautiful children.

The dragon god Kalida had woken was enacting her vengeance, and Goranth prayed for the first time in his memory.

The ground reached up, a massive hand forming, fingers spread wide, then a second hand, both reaching. One grabbed Goranth and wrapped him tight, and the other took Kalida and Sathr.

Miag Millend pulled them under.

The Northman took one last breath, then the world went blackest black.

CHAPTER TWENTY-NINE

When the blood of his enemies mixed with his own, it made him
stronger.
When gods raged against him, he raged back.
When treasure came to him, it slipped through his fingers.
When women claimed him, they soon disappeared from his life.
"The Legend of Goranth the Mighty"

In the darkness, the chaos roared itself to silence. Goranth was held as tightly as a newborn babe wrapped in a blanket, his limbs encased in unmoving stone-laden silt. He could draw no breaths.

A sound came to him—whispers.

He wanted to roar his defiance at Miag Millend, but he choked on the dust. The darkness was broken by flashes, but that wasn't light. In the ocean all those years ago, when he went under and didn't come up for too long, he saw those same sparks. They were the fireworks celebrating the end of one's life.

It was coming, and Goranth could do nothing about it.

His limbs trembled in the tight grip of the earth mother as those of dying men do, spasming in a last act of defiance —a futile attempt to reject the crossing.

The whispers continued, and the trembling became violent shakes—more than Goranth's body refusing to submit. He was heaved upward by a force he was powerless against. He rode the surge until the dark became light and the silt slid away from his face. He drew a strangled breath, coughing to drive out the dirt in his mouth and lungs.

He fell over, half of him above the earth, half still underground. Beside him, Sathr gagged and puked. Her first breath wheezed in and out.

Kalida rose out of the earth, still chanting. Hers had been the whispers Goranth heard. Hers was the power driving Miag Millend back. Kalida settled on the ground, her wide stance holding her steady while she commanded the earth mother to end Miag's onslaught.

Goranth dug into the ground with his precious makhaira, using it as a pry bar to once again save his life. He dug enough to free himself and climbed out before helping pull Sathr free.

Sathr slumped against the Northman. The rigors of the day had taken their toll, draining her to exhaustion, but while they were underground, they had received the tender ministrations of the earth. Sathr's cuts had closed, as had his, as well as the spear wound in his side where Narlun's sword had carved a chunk from him. Only bloody mud remained.

"By the Ice Dogs!" Goranth swore as he embraced Sathr.

From the ground that had once been the road in front of Kalida's, a bulge appeared, and from it, a figure rose—a golem of dirt and stone. A rocky arm brushed at the thing's head as if sweeping her hair back. Her mouth worked, but without lungs, no sound came forth, only the silent scream of evil being born.

"Miag Millend!" Goranth blurted while settling Sathr on the ground. He raised his makhaira, which gleamed and was unscathed despite the blood it had drunk and the earth into which it had dug. The glow returned, and an urge to battle the creature.

Kalida leveled the ground between the Northman and Miag Millend. He rushed across it and launched a blow that would have felled a mature oak. He flinched at the impending clang of steel on stone.

Miag threw her head back and laughed, if that was what the soundless move meant. Stone fists pressed into hips as the golem appeared to welcome Goranth's attack.

Who was he to disappoint the self-proclaimed dragon god?

His steel crunched into the creature's stone chest, chipping away a chunk that flew high and behind him. He raised his arm for another blow, but Miag backed up, stone face shocked at the pain she shouldn't have felt.

Goranth chose speed over strength and rained quick blows upon the creature as she stumbled back, each blow chipping away at the body. Miag's mouth worked on her contorted stone face, this time in a silent roar of anger. She crouched and swept a massive arm toward the Northman but he dodged, barely escaping the crushing blow. He hacked at the passing arm, slicing a piece off the elbow. Miag swung with the other arm, but he was ready.

He dove underneath, striking her knee, then rolling to the side and hitting it from behind before Miag could turn her cumbersome body to face him. He dodged and stayed behind her, slashing back and forth across the knee to try to cripple the creature.

Miag charged across the open ground toward Kalida, but she was ready. The earth surged upward, blocking the dragon god. Goranth took the gleaming blue makhaira in both hands and lunged, then swung it over his head into the golem's rock skull to deliver an earth-shattering blow.

The rock head cracked, and the makhaira wedged into it. He tried to pull it free, but Miag started to turn, swinging her great stone arms. The injured elbow kept her from reaching him, and she staggered with a limp from the nearly hewn-through knee. Goranth danced away, powerless to hurt her more.

"Sathr, your blade!" he shouted.

She roused enough to lift the sword and threw it most of the way to him. Miag saw it on the ground and strode toward it, then raised her leg to stomp on it. Goranth dove and grabbed it, but he was too late; the foot came down and broke the blade at the hilt.

Goranth rolled away. The golem took one more step before she hunched over. Miag Millend attempted to reach behind her to remove the sword that dug into her head, working itself back and forth. She flailed while the makhaira glowed brighter and brighter. Miag tried to run, but the damaged knee buckled and she went down, plowing a rut in the dirt with her stone body. Goranth charged and leapt. He landed on Miag's back and seized the makhaira, adding his strength to the sword's to open the crack. The blade still gleamed; not a single scratch marred its surface.

The sinews in his arms strained, and the muscles in his back bulged with the effort to break stone with the thin-bladed weapon. It glowed brighter. He grunted. Miag Millend struggled to rise.

With a mighty crack, the stone skull shattered. A real brain fell to the ground and splattered as blood dripped from the golem's broken head. Goranth pushed free with the makhaira in one hand, looking plain but pure as if it had fought no battle that day.

The ground instantly settled, and the earth mother's heaving throes calmed. Silence returned but for the cries of the injured.

Goranth found himself holding an unconscious Sathr in his arms.

Kalida continued to spin her spells. Throughout the remnants of Barbertown, Mabayans found themselves swallowed by the earth. Unlike Goranth, they had no champion to free them. Smoke drifted skyward from myriad fires. Dust choked the air as the wind died.

A shadow appeared beneath the sun in the clearing sky and flew toward them, a mighty beast of old.

"The dragon!" Goranth had no energy left to fight her, and there was nowhere to run. He carried Sathr into a nook in a fallen house. At least she would have shelter. He returned for Kalida as she finished her spellcasting and collapsed into his arms. Her vibrant body surged with power briefly before she cooled. Her breathing steadied as she disappeared into a sorcerer's sleep, from which nothing would wake her until she recovered from her machinations.

Goranth carried her across the road and placed her next to Sathr. Both women wanted him. Both had fought for him, one beside him, spilling her blood for him. One had lied to him and played him while at the same time healing him.

He caressed Sathr's gentle face, then turned to Kalida and traced a line down her chest to the point between her breasts where the necklace would have hung. It still would.

The dragon soared above the town, head scanning. It let out a terrible cry when it saw what it was looking for.

The dragonette.

It swooped in and seized the pincushioned body in its great claws before beating its wings to take them both into the sky until it was barely a dot, then it flew eastward toward the mountains.

Goranth let out the breath he'd been holding. He found a blanket and hung it over the opening of the nook. He slid a great section of stonework over to hide the blanket and the opening and the women within. With his makhaira in hand, he had one task remaining.

The treasure.

He stalked to Rif's palace, to find the building had collapsed. Access to the narrow stair was buried beneath more rubble than Goranth could move, but he knew of a second entrance through the well where Rif had dumped the bodies of his enemies.

Goranth searched the area for an intact lamp but found none. Miag's destruction of Barbertown had been nearly complete, but an axe handle and cloth with lamp oil would suffice. He made two torches to take down with him and tucked two heavy sacks, one that had been intended for flour and one for potatoes, into his belt.

The well had collapsed, but the shaft continued downward as far as he could see. With his back pressed against one side and his sandals on the wall opposite, he started the slow process of easing himself down. He angled around bulging rocks where the shaft had twisted under the throes of the violent battle fought within the earth.

Goranth reached the bottom of the well shaft, and with a spark from his flint, he lit the torch. He leaned as far as he could to the side to drop it to the cavern floor below, where it got caught in the skeletons and carcasses of those who had crossed.

The Northman judged the drop and pushed off, twisting catlike to land with bent knees on the hard stone floor. He recovered his torch, headed into the corridor, and stalked forward with a cool blade in one hand and the burning torch in the other. He turned in the direction of Rif's palace. The formerly level passage now rolled like ocean waves that had turned to stone. The peaks forced Goranth to crouch. Sections had pulled free of the stone walls and were littered with dirt. At the treasure room, the doorway had collapsed.

Goranth refused to give up. He pulled away the stones on the top first, eventually clearing a space which revealed that the area beyond had been spared the wrath of the earth enchantresses.

He cleared more rubble until he could pull himself through. Inside, Rif's hoard lay undisturbed, the same as the last time he'd been there. He found a necklace for Kalida and a second one that he wanted to give Sathr, plainer and more what a warrior would wear. It wouldn't break in an enemy's hands around her throat before she gutted him with her dagger.

He put gold and gems into each bag, enough to fill the bottoms but not so many that the sacks would risk bursting.

Treasure was inordinately heavy; Goranth knew that from past experience. It wasn't that he let treasure slip through his fingers as he was oft accused of, but that he only took enough to carry without issue so he could fight with it filling his purse and not worry if it was lost.

Rif's hoard had brought the Barber no joy.

Goranth found all the pleasure he needed in gutting D'gok and Narlun with the lithe Sathr fighting by his side, to be taken to his bed when the day was done. She wished it, too, a willing partner in the pain of battle and the pleasure of coupling.

That was a life worth fighting for. She deserved what the gold and gems could buy until the next time he fought and escaped with barely the clothes on his back.

There would always be a next time. With a last look at the remaining treasure, Goranth left the room and worked his way back to the shaft, where he piled enough fallen stone so he could climb into the shaft and return to the surface.

Once outside, he carried both bags in one hand and the makhaira in the other. He was not yet convinced the battle was over. When he reached Kalida's house, he crossed the road, pushed the stonework out of the way, and raised the blanket to find the women still asleep.

He left the treasure with them so he could scavenge. One couldn't eat treasure, and in the aftermath of such a fight, there would be no food gold could buy.

Not far away, he had killed the Mabayan boy-sorcerer. The horse had gone under a falling building, so he searched and found the animal. With his dagger, he made short work of gaining a haunch. He built a fire not far from where the women slept, yet another pyre added to others throughout the rubble of the once-thriving town. Nothing to bring scavengers to him. He wondered briefly about the children that had been left in the bakery but whisked it from his mind. More children were out there. They would be saved by the survivors, who would band together.

He set the meat across two stones heated by the flames. Goranth stoked the fire to keep it burning and cooked the horse meat for a meal to satisfy the starving.

After it was ready, Goranth wrapped pieces of meat for

Kalida and Sathr and ate the rest. He sat, leaned against the stone next to them, and fell asleep. The blanket covered him and the small entrance to the nook that gave them shelter.

Goranth came to when Sathr woke. Her hand sought his while she ate with the other.

"And water?" she asked.

He produced what was left in his flask. She took two sips and saved the rest for Kalida.

The priestess woke not much later.

"Eat," Goranth told Kalida, torn about what to do with two women. He was usually hard-pressed with just one.

Kalida looked at the meat and handed it to Goranth. "I cannot," she said. "I must be nourished by the fruit of the earth."

"Have it your way." It was becoming clear that he needed to leave one of them behind, and he knew which one.

"You slew the golem of Miag Millend." Kalida blinked slowly, eyes gleaming behind long lashes.

"Yes, I slew her. The creature had a human brain that spilled into the road. I killed your dragon god."

"I'm not sure. She was far more powerful than me but straightforward, counting on her strength to carry the fight. I used tricks and subterfuge to get past her defenses and challenge her to come to the surface."

"Aye, she came to the surface with a vengeance. And I killed her."

"Your sword is special, Goranth. No other blade could have touched her, but I doubt it was enough to actually kill her."

"Flesh and blood was inside the thing. No, woman. The creature is dead."

"An aspect of her is dead," Kalida argued. "Miag Millend

seeks to be worshipped. I think we will see her again. Maybe not in our lifetime, but gods have patience mankind will never know."

"And for me, that is good enough. I wish not the trials of gods and earth." He dug into the flour sack, pulled out the two necklaces, and handed the gem-encrusted one to Kalida. "To fulfill my promise to decorate the perfect skin of your chest. And for you, Sathr, a warrior's decoration. It's sturdy, and it won't get in the way during a fight."

Kalida held the Northman's gaze. Sathr remained stoic, unsure about the gift.

"Stay," the enchantress said. "I am going to stay. I know I said I would leave with you, but things have changed with Rif gone. Stay with me."

"You know I cannot. You also know we cannot be together. Your way is not my way."

"It doesn't have to be, Northman. Separate lives lived together. Know that I can raise the buildings to their former glory. All of them, one at a time. It will take long months, but we appear to have plenty of time, thanks to you. Barbertown needs you."

"Do as you wish. For those who survived, rebuilding the town will be good. Give them hope for a better future. A leader will rise from the ashes; count on that person, be they man or woman, but it will not be me."

The click of hooves and the scratch of a goat-drawn litter came from the roadway.

Goranth stood and waved. "Here, boy."

Jaeg coaxed the Ahak-Teek to them. Three other fine mounts followed, with the goat pulling the litter filled with books from the sorcerer's library.

"The baby dragon...its mother came, and I released it to join her. The other horses bolted when she flew past. I could save little but the tomes and scrolls."

"You did well," Goranth told him. "Rif is dead, and we have no need of a dragon. There's already been enough death here without unleashing the wrath of the ancient beasts."

Kalida jumped up and ran over with unusual energy for one half-starved. She untied the cover and ran her hands over the books. "I shall take these."

"But they are to sell," Jaeg countered.

Goranth untied the Ahak-Teeks and the goat. "No good can come from them, Jaeg. Let the priestess have them."

Kalida took a knee and clasped her hands together. The all-too-familiar rumble began, forcing the Northman to fight with the horses to hold them steady against their fear.

But there was no threat, only noise and magic as Kalida's hut put itself back together, restoring the thatch of the roof and unburning the wood. "Bring them inside," she commanded. Jaeg guided the goat over the boardwalk and through the front door. He shortly reemerged with just the goat.

Goranth laughed. "I'm not sure that's what she meant, but I like it. Touching those tomes stains your soul. Why don't you head out to find your family?"

The youth nodded. The Northman offered his hand, and they gripped forearms. "Next time I need someone to fight by my side, make sure you're ready. Learn to use that Mabayan sword. And here is the treasure you were promised." Goranth handed him one of the bags.

Jaeg took it, clearly finding it much heavier than he'd expected. He threw it across the saddle, mounted his Ahak-Teek, and spurred the horse through what was left of Barbertown.

"We will leave you to it." Goranth helped Sathr into the saddle of one of the three remaining horses and tossed the burlap bag with the other half of the claimed treasure into her lap.

"Take care of the goat or turn it loose," Sathr said, puffing out her chest in a challenge to Kalida.

"Its milk will save the lives of those left behind." Kalida put her hand on Sathr's leg. "I envy you." She glanced at Goranth. "Next time, Northman."

She took the goat around the side of her house.

Goranth tied the last horse to his saddle and mounted. "Where to, woman?"

"Someplace with a bath, a stone hearth, a cave-bear rug, and as much as we want to eat," she replied, blinking at him.

"Sounds like a swim across the river with our horses and whatever we can forage in the lowlands to the north," Goranth replied.

"Or that."

His laugh sounded incongruent in the ruins of Barbertown, but he cared not. The day had waned, and he still drew breath. It had been a good day. He clicked his tongue and walked his horses toward the town square and then north.

Still mounted, they waded the Ahak-Teeks, who were excellent swimmers, into the slow-moving Mugunta River. Goranth splashed water over himself as the horse dog-paddled toward the other side. Sathr followed suit.

"Your bath, my lady," Goranth quipped. Sathr laughed, which lifted Goranth's spirits. They continued past what remained of the ill-conceived dragon stockade and rode away from Barbertown.

Goranth felt better with each step he put between him and the city, almost as if no danger awaited him. But he knew better. Like a moth to the flame, it would find him.

The End of The Black Heart of the Dragon God.

If you like this book, please leave a review. We love reviews since they tell other readers that this book is worth their time and money. We hope you feel that way now that you've finished the first, but surely not the last cooperative effort between Jean and Craig. Please drop us a line and let us know you like Goranth's adventures and want them to continue.

Don't stop now! Keep turning the pages as Craig and Jean discuss this project in their *Author Notes*, with thoughts about this book and the good stuff that could happen on the road ahead.

Goranth's adventures have just begun.

AUTHOR NOTES - JEAN RABE

Written December 28, 2020

Dragons!

The outline had called for dinosaurs, catching and taming them.

Craig suggested they be dragons instead. It took no persuading. I love dragons. Big, dangerous dragons. I learned to love them when I wrote many Dragonlance novels, first for TSR, Inc., and then for Wizards of the Coast. Malys the Red and Khellendros the Blue—the Storm over Krynn were my favorites; I caused a lot of destruction and angst with those dragonlords.

I've been writing mysteries for the past several years, and Craig asking to co-author a book with me turned my gaze back to fantasy and Sword and Sorcery. I'd been away too long. I missed letting characters swing swords, so thank you to Craig for making this happen. I had the best time, a bright spot in a not-so-bright year.

Consider signing up for my monthly newsletter at my website: jeanrabe.com. Friend or follow me on Facebook and Twitter. I try to answer all the emails I receive.

Amazon – https://www.amazon.com/Jean-Rabe
Bookbub - https://www.bookbub.com/
authors/jean-rabe
Facebook – https://www.
facebook.com/jeanrabeauthor/
Twitter – https://twitter.com/jeanerabe
My webpage – https://jeanrabe.com/

BOOKS BY JEAN RABE PUBLISHED BY BOONE STREET PRESS

The Dead of Winter: A Piper Blackwell Mystery

The Dead of Night: A Piper Blackwell Mystery

The Dead of Summer: A Piper Blackwell Mystery

The Dead of Jerusalem Ridge: A Piper Blackwell Mystery

The Bone Shroud

Fenzig's Fortune

The Finest Creation

The Finest Choice

The Finest Challenge

Re-releasing in 2020 from Boone Street Press

The Cauldron

Pockets of Darkness

AUTHOR NOTES - CRAIG MARTELLE

Written December 28, 2020

You are still reading! Thank you for staying on board until now. It doesn't get much better than that.

Jean and I were in a couple different short story anthologies together. I liked her style because I thought it looked like mine, but better. I wore her down by pleading and begging to co-write a book. She produced an outline that she had submitted to a legacy publishing house that they didn't consider since they were going out of business. The story-to-be sat on a digital shelf, collecting dust.

Jean asked me to take a look and see what I thought. I loved the potential. During the past three months, we made that outline come to life. I wrote one chapter, then Jean edited my chapter and wrote the next. I edited hers and wrote the next for twenty-nine chapters' worth. Then we both went through the whole thing and reviewed it once more, then turned it over to an editor, then to my insider team for their review, and then we found ourselves at publication day.

I have to give a shout-out to Alex Bates, who hooked

me up with Didier Normand, who did the original artwork for the cover—painted in oil. Very Frazetta since that's the flavor we were going for. We gave that original artwork to Ryan Schwarz, The Cover Designer, to add the typography. He does exceptional work, as you can see from the fine cover gracing this volume.

We hope you like this story. It flowed well between Jean and me, neither arguing over a point. It worked, and I think the story works as part of a traditional Sword and Sorcery tale of high adventure. The ring of steel on steel, the tingle on the back of your neck of dark magics being worked. And dragons.

One must die for another to live. Sometimes that's the only way.

The first tale of Goranth the Mighty was a bright spot in 2020. It helped take us away from a dark year, and we hope that whenever you read this, it takes you away to a different place where you can live inside your mind, fighting demons and those damn Mabayans.

Nothing like a bath in a river while riding a swimming horse to wash away the ills of the day.

That's our story. We're looking at the next tale of Goranth to take place on the steppes of Gabigar bordering the Kuiper Desert, butted up against mysterious Tsentar, where wizards ply their wiles.

So many tales to tell. We better get back to it.

Peace, fellow humans.

Please join my Newsletter (craigmartelle.com – please, please, please sign up!), or you can follow me on Facebook since you'll get the same opportunity to pick up the books for only 99 cents on that first day they are published.

If you liked this story, you might like some of my other books. You can join my mailing list by dropping by my website www.craigmartelle.com or if you have any comments, shoot me a note at craig@craigmartelle.com. I am always happy to hear from people who've read my work. I try to answer every email I receive.

If you liked the story, please write a short review for me on Amazon. I greatly appreciate any kind words; even one or two sentences go a long way. The number of reviews an eBook receives greatly improves how well an eBook does on Amazon.

Amazon – www.amazon.com/author/craigmartelle
BookBub – https://www.bookbub.com/authors/
craig-martelle
Facebook – www.
facebook.com/authorcraigmartelle
My webpage – https://craigmartelle.com

CRAIG MARTELLE'S OTHER BOOKS (LISTED BY SERIES)

- AVAILABLE IN AUDIO, TOO

Terry Henry Walton Chronicles (#) (co-written with Michael Anderle) – a post-apocalyptic paranormal adventure

Gateway to the Universe (#) (co-written with Justin Sloan & Michael Anderle) – this book transitions the characters from the Terry Henry Walton Chronicles to The Bad Company

The Bad Company (#) (co-written with Michael Anderle) – a military science fiction space opera

Judge, Jury, & Executioner (#) – a space opera adventure legal thriller

Shadow Vanguard – a Tom Dublin space adventure series

Superdreadnought (#) – an AI military space opera

Metal Legion (#) – a military space opera

The Free Trader (#) – a young adult science fiction action-adventure

Cygnus Space Opera (#) – a young adult space opera (set in the Free Trader universe)

Darklanding (#) (co-written with Scott Moon) – a space western

Mystically Engineered (co-written with Valerie Emerson) – mystics, dragons, & spaceships

Metamorphosis Alpha – stories from the world's first science fiction RPG

The Expanding Universe – science fiction anthologies

Krimson Empire (co-written with Julia Huni) – a galactic race for justice

Zenophobia (#) – a space archaeological adventure

End Times Alaska (#) – a Permuted Press publication – a post-apocalyptic survivalist adventure

Nightwalker (a Frank Roderus series) – A post-apocalyptic western adventure

End Days (#) (co-written with E.E. Isherwood) – a post-apocalyptic adventure

Successful Indie Author (#) – a non-fiction series to help self-published authors

Monster Case Files (co-written with Kathryn Hearst) – A Warner twins mystery adventure

Rick Banik (#) – Spy & terrorism action adventure

Ian Bragg Thrillers – a man with a conscience who kills bad guys for money

Published exclusively by Craig Martelle, Inc

The Dragon's Call by Angelique Anderson & Craig A. Price, Jr. – an epic fantasy quest

A Couples Travel – a non-fiction travel series

For a complete list of Craig's books, stop by his website – https://craigmartelle.com

Made in the USA
Middletown, DE
21 July 2022